Journey to the Isles of Atlantis
and Other Fanciful Excursions

IN THE SAME SERIES

Journey to the Isles of Atlantis
and Other Fanciful Excursions

Translated, annotated and introduced by
Brian Stableford

A Black Coat Press Book

Visit our website at www.blackcoatpress.com

ISBN 978-1-61227-794-3. First Printing. September 2018. Published by Black Coat Press, an imprint of Hollywood Comics.com, LLC, P.O. Box 17270, Encino, CA 91416. All rights reserved.
Printed in the United States of America.

TABLE OF CONTENTS

Introduction

This is the sixteenth volume in a series of Black Coat press anthologies translating antique items of *roman scientifique* that are too short to warrant publication as separate volumes; like most of the other volumes it includes stories ranging in length from brief vignettes to long novellas, and spans much of the history of the genre, to the extent that the history in question has now fallen into the public domain and is thus available for translation without inconvenience.

The first item in the present collection, "Paris en 5839 (Songe)," translated as "Paris in 5839: A Dream," originally appeared in the 17 August 1822 issue of the political newspaper *Le Miroir*. Together with another satirical article in the 28 August issue, entitled "Spectacles ambulans" [traveling shows], which targeted religion, it was cited as an offense against the King (Louis XVIII) in a criminal prosecution of the proprietor of the *Miroir*, François-Toussaint Michelot, who was assumed to be the author of both articles. Michelot was fined a thousand francs and sentenced to three months in prison. Protests issued against the unreasonably punitive sentence claimed that Michelot was not, in fact, the author of the articles. The excellent Jean-Luc Buard, who rediscovered the item and researched contemporary reports of the prosecution with the utmost care, suggests—very plausibly—that the actual author of the piece was probably the liberal journalist Félix Bodin (1795-1837), who was associated with the *Miroir* and who went on to wrote a historically significant work advocating the inauguration of a new literary *Le Roman de l'Avenir* (1834; tr. as *The Novel of the Future*).[1]

Buard's scrupulously detailed and very convincing argument is given in full in the booklet *Anonyme [Félix Bodin]:*

---

[1] Black Coat Press, ISBN 978-1-934543-44-3.

Paris en 5839 (Songe) ou la Science-fiction condamnée par un tribunal en 1822, published by Fabrice Mundzik's *Les Cahiers archéobibliographiques* in 2016. Further details of Félix Bodin's colorful literary and political career, and his crucial contribution to the prospectus for the development of futuristic fiction can be found in the introduction to the Black Coat press edition of *The Novel of the Future*.

Bodin was personally acquainted with several other writers associated with the Romantic Movement who made pioneering attempts to write futuristic fiction, including Charles Nodier and X. B. Saintine, whose significant endeavors in that cause have also been published in translation by Black Coat Press. The specific theme of the article—absurdly mistaken conclusions drawn by archeologists excavating the ruins of Paris in the far future—was taken up by the Romantic writer Joseph Méry in "Les Ruines de Paris" (1844; tr, as "The Ruins of Paris"[2])—and subsequently became the theme of a rich subgenre. The prosecution of the *Miroir* article, and the grounds on which it as pursued, illustrate the extent to which futuristic speculation was a dangerous activity at the time, as it had been in France for many years, both before and after the Revolution.

The second item in the anthology, "L'Horloger de Nuremberg," translated as "The Clockmaker of Nuremberg," was originally published in Julie Lavergne's collection of *contes*, *Les Jours de cristal* (1882). Julie Lavergne (1823-1886) produced several collections of such tales, many of them based in the folklore and legends of Normandy, from which her family hailed, although she spent most of her life in Paris. Her published correspondence is a significant document of her era, remarkable for her stoical refusal to rebel against the social conventions that imprisoned her, even though she suffered considerably from their restriction; she not only refrained from espousing feminist ideas, but remained a staunch Catholic and

---

[2] Included in *The Tower of Destiny*, Black Coat Press, ISBN 978-1-61227-101-9.

monarchist in a era when such support was swimming against the literal and political tide. Her fiction provides little propaganda for those causes, however, and its tacit rhetoric often seems to weigh in the opposite direction, giving her work a curious flavor of tragic stoicism. Her other collections include *Contes français* (1848), *Fleurs de France* (1880) and *Légendes de Fontainebleau* (1880).

"L'Horloger de Nuremberg" is one of numerous items of antique *roman scientifique* considering the possibility of technologically-acquired human flight, following in the footsteps of Nicolas Restif de la Bretonne's *La Découverte australe par un homme-volant, ou Le Dédale français* (1781; tr. as *The Discovery of the Austral Continent by a Flying Man*).[3] Many such stories belong to Bodin's hypothetical genre of futuristic fiction, as is only appropriate in an era when it seemed that such a technological conquest might, indeed, be imminent, but Lavergne's is set in the legendary past, that being the locus of all her fantastic fiction. It features a clockmaker, those being the artisans who take the lead in many nineteenth-century accounts of innovative mechanisms, the métier in question seeming to many observers to be the acme of mechanical ingenuity and delicacy; such fanciful tales form an interesting subgenre in their own right.

Lavergne's story is interesting in its refusal to construe the story it tells as a parable or apologue, narrating it is a straightforward tragedy, with a hint of irony but no explicit moral. That temptation was rarely avoided by many of the contributors to the subgenre in question, many of whom were attracted to it precisely because of the opportunity to formulate such a parable or apologue. That is very obviously true of the third item in the collection, Gaston Derys's "L'Inventeur" (tr. as "The Inventor"), which first appeared in the November 1902 issue of the *Revue hebdomadaire*. That timing is particularly interesting in retrospect, because it was on the very eve of the realization of the invention in question, the age of avia-

---

[3] Black Coat Press, ISBN 978-1-61227-512-3.

9

tion beginning and making very rapid progress during the following decade.

We are now in a position to make an accurate assessment of the extent to which the story's anticipations have been endorsed and falsified by the era in question, which adds an extra dimension of ironic interest to the gloomy prophecies that it summarizes so succinctly and flamboyantly. Its author, Gaston Derys (1875-1945), then at the beginning of his literary career, lived long enough to see how his anticipations worked out, although his exact death date is unrecorded, so we can only guess as to whether he heard the news of the atom bomb dropped by airplane over Hiroshima, and whether it reminded him of his own brief prophecy of the destructive consequences of the conquest of the air. His other literary works, most of which are downmarket romances, include the offbeat detective stories *Ressuscitée* [Resuscitated] (1926, in collaboration with Jeanne Landre) and *L'Ombre jalouse* [The Jealous Shade] (1926), both of which feature fake revenants.

The fourth item in the collection, *Le Roi Béta, conte de fées et d'enchanteurs où il n'y a ni enchanteurs ni fées*, (tr. as "King Beta," the subtitle translates as " a tale of fays and enchanters, in which there are neither enchanters nor fays") by Louis Lemercier de Neuville, which was published as an illustrated book by Combet et Cie in 1905, only three years later than "L'Inventeur," is very obviously a product of the era of rapid technological invention in which the age of aviation was launched. It names its archetypal inventor Vatenlair [i.e. Goes through the Air], although it equips him with an imperfectly dirigible airship, in order that he can go astray in flight and end up in the fictitious kingdom ruled by the eponymous monarch, where modern science is unknown and people still believe in the power of enchanters. The story, an inspirational text aimed at younger readers, is one of many trumpeting the triumphs of modern science and technological progress, and their vast superiority over ancient superstition, although it is not without a certain uneasy ambivalence, reflected in its conclusion.

Louis Lemercier de Neuville (1830-1918) was much older than Gaston Derys and was famous before the latter was even born. Initially a prolific journalist, who founded several periodicals, beginning with the sarcastically-titled *La Muselière, journal de la décadence intellectuelle* [The Muzzle, the Newspaper of Intellectual Decadence] in 1855—a provocative move at a time when Napoléon III's censors were even busier and more repressive than Louis XVIII's—he reached the peak of his fame after he founded a mobile puppet theater in 1860, in which he staged satirical plays, mostly caricaturing the celebrities of the day. It proved extremely popular throughout the subsequent half-century, and the bulk of his enormously prolific publication considered of scripts that he wrote for production therein and short comedies written to be performed by human actors. *Le Roi Béta*, a rare excursion into consecutive prose, was by no means his swan song, being followed by numerous pamphlets, but it was his most substantial work, and provided his endeavors with a capstone of sorts.

The conquest of the air and the social change consequent to that technological development also plays a large part in *Ce que seront les hommes de l'an 3000* by Gustave Guitton (1859-1918), here translated as "Humans in the Year 3000," which was first published by Jules Tallandier in 1907 (the date of 1921 cited in some bibliographies is incorrect). The volume in question carried a dedication "To the English novelist H. G. Wells, a pessimistic prophet." The purpose of the text, very obviously, is to oppose the supposed pessimism of the writer in question, and the pessimism of writers like Gaston Derys, by means of an optimistic account of the human future. The story's fundamental philosophy has a good deal in common with that of *Le roi Béta*, although it is far more ambitious in its imaginative reach, in which is resembles an earlier utopian fantasy written with young readers in mind, *Dans mille ans* by Émile Calvet (tr. as *In a Thousand Years*),[4] serialized in the *Musée des Familles* in 1883 and reprinted in book form the

---

[4] Black Coat Press, ISBN 978-1-61227-192-7.

following year. It also borrows extensively from a series of images of life in the twentieth century produced by the humorist Albert Robida, most significantly *La Vie électrique* (1892; tr. as *Electric Life*),[5] which similarly pays great attention to the possible social transformations that air travel might permit, especially its impact on the architecture of the future.

Like Émile Calvet's novel, *Ce que seront les hommes de l'an 3000* was certainly written with teenage readers in mind, but it was not published by Tallandier as a children's book, and does not seem to have reached its intended audience, or, indeed, any substantial audience at all, reflecting the perennial difficulties experienced by the author in trying to establish himself as a significant writer of *roman scientifique*. The preliminary pages of the Tallandier volume announce *L'Homme qui fait de l'or* [The Man Who Made Gold] as "*en préparation*," but it never appeared. Guitton had previously written three romances in the genre in collaboration with Gustave Le Rouge, *Le Conspiration des milliardaires* (3 vols., 1899-1900; tr. in four volumes as *The Dominion of the World*, Black Coat Press, 2012),[6] *La Princesse des airs* [The Princess of the Skies] (1902) and *Le Sous-marin "Jules Verne"* [The Submarine Jules Verne] (1902), but the present story appears to have been his only other venture therein to reach print. It was followed in 1908 by the third item in a planned tetralogy, *Les Quatre ages de la femme* [The Four Ages of Woman], but that series was never completed, and Guitton does not appear to have published anything new during the last ten years of his life, although his bibliography is complicated by retitled versions of his earlier works. Many of the author's publications appear to have been fugitive; the list of previous publications in *Ce que seront les hommes de l'an 3000* includes four titles that are not in the Bibliothèque Nationale, of which no trace can be found elsewhere, and which probably do not exist.

---

[5] Black Coat Press, ISBN 978-1-61227-182-8.
[6] ISBNs 978-1-61227-095-1, -096-8, -097-5 & -098-2.

The ideas developed by Albert Robida regarding the possible architectural consequences of the future vulgarization of air travel, modestly developed by Guitton, are taken to a remarkable extreme in "La Découverte de la Terre en 2009" (tr. as "The Discovery of the Earth in 2009" by Pierre Grasset, which appeared in the 15 December 1909 issue of *La Nouvelle Revue*—the "Christmas issue," in which it had become traditional for Parisian periodicals to publish stories of a more fanciful stripe than those providing their standard fare. In the previous year, Robida had contributed a brief account of "L'Aviation en 1950" (tr. as Aviation in 1950")[7] to the Christmas issue of *Les Annales politiques et littéraires*, and that might have prompted Grasset to produce his far more extravagant account, which extends, with a succinct elegance, to surreal allegory, demonstrating the extent to which such fantasies had been gripped by melodramatic inflation in the few years that had elapsed since the production of Gaston Derys's apologue.

Voyage aux îles Atlantides (tr. as "Journey to the Isles of Atlantis") belongs to an interesting series of French novels featuring Plato's fictitious island of Atlantis, many of which employ that vanished civilization as a satirical reflection of contemporary France, especially Paris. It does not have the vaulting imaginative ambition of Hippolyte Mettais' *Paris avant the déluge* (1866; tr. as *Paris Before the Deluge*),[8] or Han Ryner's *Les Pacifiques* (1914; tr, as "The Pacifists"),[9] which followed it into print a few months later, although obviously written some years before. The engagingly light humor of the first part of the Bilaume/Hégine novel makes it seem a far more frivolous work than most other Atlantidean satires, although it is not without a definite sarcastic bite. That first

---

[7] Included in *In 1965*, Black Coat Press, ISBN 978-1-61227-728-8.

[8] Black Coat Press, ISBN 978-1-61227-328-0.

[9] Included in *The Human Ant*, Black Coat Press, ISBN 978-1-61227-323-5.

part is so buoyantly entertaining, in fact, that it makes one regret deeply that the second part fails to live up to it. There are hardly any traceable references to either of the two names to whom the text is attributes, except in connection with the present volume, but certain peculiarities in the text—explained at the relevant points in the footnotes—suggest that the author of the first part might have died suddenly, at a young age, leaving the unfinished work to be patched up for publication by a friend, perhaps some years after its composition. If so, that task was surely worth doing in order to rescue the incomplete text, and the added text, although inferior, is not without interest, especially in its more fantastic embellishments.

The translation of "Paris en 5839 (Songe)" was made from the versions contained in the 2016 booklet cited, published by *Les Cahiers archéobibliographiques*. The translation of "L'Horloger de Nuremberg" was made from the version reproduced on the Bibliem website at *biblisem.net*. The translations of "L'Inventeur," *Le Roi Béta* and *Voyage aux îles Atlantides* were made from the versions reproduced on the Bibliothèque Nationale's *gallica* website, the first in the relevant issue of the *Revue hebdomadaire*. The translation of *Ce que seront les hommes de l'an 3000* was made from a copy of the Tallandier edition.

Brian Stableford

Anonymous: *Paris In 5839 (A Dream)*
(perhaps by Félix Bodin)
(1822)

I was reading a book by a celebrated archeologist; I med-
itated on those ancient ruins so well described, I calculated the
epochs, annotated the dates and admired the vast and useful
erudition of which every page of my book bore the imprint; I
took pleasure in the savant dissertations and the doubts whose
chimerical reality seemed to me to be so forcefully demonstrated; I savored all the suppositions, provided that they had
something seductive or specious; I was absorbed by a host of
confused ideas...

I fell asleep.

Suddenly I found myself on a ship manned by men of
North America who, driven by a love of science and a good
north-westerly wind, were heading for the coast of Europe. It
was 5839. For a long time, that part of the world, once the
most civilized, the richest in population and industry, had been
covered in debris, sad witnesses of its past grandeur. America,
by contrast, had inherited European splendor, and civilization
had taken refuge in a land fortunate in commerce, agriculture
and liberty.

How had Europe ended? That is what I do not know.
Was it because of luxury or despotism, ignorance or laxity,
superstition or incredulity? None of my traveling companions
was able to tell me. At any rate, Europe had ceased to be. A
great revolution had destroyed it; it only subsisted any longer
in the memories of a few learned men; and what were those
memories? Faded images and deceptive traditions! Time had
leveled everything, the centuries were equal in renown, the
ruins were mute. Europe was a desert, and a horrible desert;
only, the scattered tents of a few nomad hordes broke the mo-

notony of that frightful solitude and attested to the impotence of the soil as well as the absence of any sociability. There was no longer anything anywhere but an organized chaos.

It was toward the coasts of France that the pilot directed the ship that was carrying us. We arrived near the ancient cape whose sinuous indentations had formed the superb bay of the finest military port the French had ever had. Only the name of Brest had survived the ages; it was still inscribed in sufficiently legible characters on a large stone, a last vestige of the fine warehouse constructed under King Louis XIV, who had been called the Great, as if that were veritable grandeur.

I learned that we were bound for the ruins of Paris, which were the destination of our voyage.

From the frontiers of Armorica to the sterile banks of the Seine we found nothing on our route but arid mountains, impenetrable forests and valleys bristling with wild vegetation. We passed over without perceiving it the ancient city of Rennes, so celebrated in the eighteenth century for its public prosecutors. We camped on the hill where the city of courtiers had stood; nothing any longer remained of Versailles but the memory, conserved by a scholar in our caravan, of the famous "bull's eye," the gymnasium of the "red heels."[10]

We went up the sinuous course of the Seine, and when we arrived near the double branching of that river, with a descriptive map of the location in hand, the most learned archeologist in our little company enabled us to travel that immense terrain, disfigured by a long succession of years, where a few heaps of stones lay, devoid of form and proportion, the last monuments of the flourishing city that had rivaled the glory of ancient Rome and merited being named the Athens of modern times.

There, our scholar began to give us a profound dissertation regarding each location.

---

[10] *Les talons rouges de Versailles* [the red heels of Versailles] was a conventional way of signifying the noblemen of the court.

"This," he said to us, "is the site of a sumptuous edifice known by the name of the Palais Royal because it was the usual residence of the monarch. Alongside it, in a north-south direction is a street named Richelieu, or "the place where the rich live."

"The rich," he added, "had chosen that abode as the closest to the king's palace. Follow me in this direction; there is what was called the Louvre. The origin of that designation is unknown, but by analogy, I am led to affirm that Louvre is merely a translation of the Latin word *luparia: louverie*, the abode of she-wolves and wolves. The Louvre, therefore, was the dwelling of wild beasts that the kings kept enclosed in large iron prisons in order to give the people a spectacle on certain days. Those ferocious beasts were nourished on raw flesh, as demonstrated by this passage from Lafontaine, a French author of the seventeenth century:

> *Into his Louvre he invited them;*
> *What a Louvre! A true charnel-house,*
> etc.[11]

"And as it is a lion who is speaking in the passage I am citing, I draw two consequences from my citation: firstly that lions, inhabitants of the Louvre, were indeed nourished on raw flesh; and secondly, that the Louvre was obviously nothing other than the dwelling of ferocious animals.

"The area that you see in that direction was called the Carrousel. I do not know what it destination was, no vestige being able to enlighten us on that subject; the only reasonable etymology I can find for Carrousel is the ancient French word *carreau*, which designated a kind of brick made from baked earth, and what gives some appearance of verity to that belief

---

[11] The quotation is from Lafontaine's fable "La Cour du lion" (tr. as "The Lion's Court"), where "louvre" is used as if it were a common noun referring to the court in question by analogy with the Louvre palace.

17

is the proximity of that area with a large tile factory called the Tuileries. Tuileries were Parisian ceramics. On the Carrousel we perceive the trace of a monument of small proportions, which scholars assure us was a triumphal arch, but that assertion is evidently absurd; it is known that in the epoch in which the monument was supposed to have existed. Triumphal arches were not erected; it was about the time of the reinstallation in France of the pupils of Escobar.[12]

"Let us advance in this direction. The wood we are in was the field of rest—the cemetery—of the city. In was called the Champs-Élysées and this section, consecrated to certain sacrifices instituted by widows in honor of their husbands, was designated by the name of the Allée des Veuves. In that direction we find the pedestal of a bronze column. No positive tradition is attached to that debris; historians of the early nineteenth century claim that the monument was erected to the glory of the heroes who triumphed in endeavors in Europe. That is an evident error; the French had no triumphs in Europe. The writers of 1816-1830 formally deny the fact advanced by the contemporaries of a man who was doubtless a poor genius, since knowledgeable historians, like likes of Bonald, Salgues and Châteaubriant, say so on every page of their sublime writings.[13]

---

[12] The Jesuit ethical philosopher Antonio Escobar y Mendoza (1589-1669), whose apologetic arguments caused Blaise Pascal and Jean de La Fontaine to reply, in their different fashions, that good intentions cannot excuse evil deeds.

[13] The counter-revolutionary philosopher Louis de Bonald (1754-1840) was appointed Minister of State and President of the Censorship Commission in 1822. In 1822 René de Châteaubriand (1768-1848), now celebrated as the founder of French Romanticism, was a prominent ultra-royalist supporter of the future Charles X, a pillar of that party's principal organ of propaganda, *Le Conservateur*. Jacques-Barthelemy Salgues (1760-1830) was a writer on religious and political topics best

18

"Let us now go down to the right, and we will find a long scarcely-visibly line. These were the boulevards, or ramparts, which tells us that Paris was heavily fortified. The line of defense runs all around the city.

"Further away, the Place des Victoires doubtless thus named because of some great advantage won by the French over some other European people. The neighborhood of the boulevards/ramparts renders that supposition very plausible. There, going back up the Seine is, is the site where the Jardin du Roi was located.[14] That garden was the one adjacent to a house situated in the first Paris, inhabited by a king named Charles. Near the king's garden are the apparent foundations of a building known as the menagerie. Menagerie is a word derived from the Gothic *ménage*, which means "savings". The menagerie was the realm's savings, the State treasury. That building received the money from taxes, and served as the residence of the magistrate charged with administering finance. That man, who was necessarily a *ménager*, a saver, and an honest man, had the title of Minister of Finance..."

At this point a loud noise is heard in the street where I live; I wake up with a start. The Paris of 5839 disappears and the Paris of 1821 strikes my gaze. I remember my dream; I compare; my archeological good faith totters; I throw away a deceptive book and I cry: "Is there any truth, then, in that deceptive science? Everything we know about Athens and Rome might be as false as what was known about Paris in my dream! Who will clarify this disenchanting doubt...?

---

known for an account of popular errors and prejudices, first published in 1810.

[14] Le Jardin du roi was the original name of the Jardin des Plantes, the botanical gardens of Paris; in 1792 the Royal Menagerie as moved there from Versailles.

Julie Lavergne: *The Clockmaker of Nuremberg* (1882)

I. Nuremberg in 1595

I would like, beyond the mountains and the clouds,
To launch myself like an eagle in audacious flight,
To plunge into the ether, to dominate storms,
And disdaining the earth, arrive in the heavens.
H. de L.

It was the day of the fair. A noisy and well-dressed crowd filled the streets of Nuremberg. The main square was covered with flag-decked shops in which the richest merchandise of Bavaria and foreign lands was displayed. The sun had shone all day and its last rays were still illuminating the summit of the three hundred and sixty-five towers of the fortified enclosure of the town, its great red roofs, its numerous bell-towers, the rival steeples of the churches of Saint Sebaldus and Saint Lorenz, and the crenellated walls of the old castle of the Burgraves.

In the narrow and sinuous streets darkness had already fallen; the lamps were lit and hearths, vigorously stimulated by housewives preparing supper, were sending their reliant and mobile glow over the ceilings and windows. The appointed hour for the shops of the fair to close would soon sound, and the merchants, while still making a few sales, were hastening to tidy up and close their wooden huts.

One of them, an old clockmaker reputed to be something of a sorcerer, who was celebrated in Nuremberg for having constricted the beautiful clock of Saint Lorenz, was getting ready to lock the cases in which he had already placed his watches when a very young man, tall and handsome, who had gone back and forth past the shop ten times during the day, stopped in front of him and, with an embarrassed expression, said to him:

"Master Hyrcanus, I'd like to buy a watch from you."

"You've decided a little late, Herr Ritter von Ittenbach," said the clockmaker. "In ten minutes, the shop has to close, and I've already put some of my merchandise away. To oblige you, however, I'll open one of my boxes again. Is it a beautiful watch that you want?" As he spoke, the wily merchant made an inventory of the purchaser's costume from the corner of his eye. The young man's garments certainly did not indicate wealth: a doublet and mantle of slightly threadbare green cloth, long boots of Cordovan leather, a trimmed ruff that was very white but in rather coarse fabric, a sword with a steel hilt and a felt hat ornamented with a eagle feather formed his full equipment; but his benevolent face, his curly brown hair, and an extreme grace and vivacity, combined with the finest figure in the world, gave him the air of a true gentleman.

He was a gentleman, in fact; but, as the younger son of a house that had fallen a long way, Lorenz von Ittenbach had a purse even lighter than his head, although the latter was light enough. His older brother had tried to put him in the church, to place him as a page with the Duke of Bavaria and to send him to study at the University of Wurtzburg: wasted effort; Lorenz only liked hunting, while waiting for an opportunity to go to war. He lived in the fraternal castle, spending his small income on petty follies, coming to Nuremberg to amuse himself on days of fairs or processions. His good humor won him friends, and his good manners, as always happens, added to his other merits what varnish adds to a table.

So, while Lorenz von Ittenbach examined a few watches, Hyrcanus asked him, although he knew perfectly well, what the feather that ornamented his hat was.

"It's an eagle feather, Master Hyrcanus, and I can tell you how I earned it. I climbed the Westberg to find eaglets in the nest; I had already taken one when the mother, whom I had seen depart and believed to be far away, came back at speed and attacked me. I'd killed the male the day before; she knew that, for sure; I judged it by her fury. I was clinging to the rock with my left hand, with only a hunting-knife to defend myself. Saint Hubert protected me; I got away with a few pecks, which bloodied my hand and my forehead, but I cut off the eagle's head. The bird soared for a moment without a head, and then descended in a spiral into the precipice. I only went back to the castle after having found it, so I took back the eaglets, but they were dead. How much is this watch?"

"I'll tell you tomorrow morning, Herr von Ittenbach. The clock is chiming. Will you do me the honor of coming to see me at home, in Sebaldstrasse, at the sign of Time, tomorrow morning at eight o'clock. We'll strike our bargain glass in hand. Once the sun has set I no longer sell anything. That was the custom of my father. If Your Lordship has other engagements, we can meet here at midday. In the meantime, keep the watch to see how well it goes and how pretty it is."

Lorenz hesitated momentarily. Hyrcanus was reputed to be a magician, but Lorenz was brave to the point of temerity, as curious as an owl, and had a desire to acquire the watch, even though he did not have a quarter of its value in his pocket.

"I'll come to breakfast with you, Master Hyrcanus. Until tomorrow."

"I'll expect you," said Hyrcanus. "Here, Gnomo!"

A kind of monster, a man of Herculean strength but whose legs were so short that he seemed to be walking on his knees, emerged from beneath the counter, where he had been lying down like a dog. He was entirely clad in dark red Utrecht velvet, with a similar bonnet pulled down all the way to his black and bushy eyebrows.

"Let's go," said Hyrcanus, picking up his locked boxes and putting them on his knees. "Home, Gnomo!"

Gnomo then went behind the armchair in which his master was sitting, fitted his broad shoulders to a solid hook, lifted up the armchair, the clockmaker and his boxes, the first carrying the others, stood up straight, and took the road to Sebaldstrasse with a firm tread.

A few foreign students wandering in the square burst out laughing on seeing them pass by, and one of them said to a lace merchant who was bolting the shutters of her shop: "Who's the little old man with spectacles who has himself carried on someone's back like a sack of flour?"

"He's Master Hyrcanus, the most skillful clockmaker in Nuremberg," she said. "The poor man is paralyzed in the legs and can't walk. I can't see what there is to laugh at in that. Pray to God that nothing similar ever happens to you. Master Hyrcanus was a good dancer in his youth, so my late mother said."

"His porter looks more like a brute than a Christian," said another scatterbrain.

"Be careful. He'll come back to have supper and sleep in the shop. If he hears you mocking him, you'll receive more punches than you have ribbons in your shoes, my little sir."

"Ah! You're not very polite to strangers, my little lady. What does it matter to you if I speak my opinion of that wretched clodhopper?"

"Gnomo!" shouted the merchant. "Hurry up! There are clowns here who are talking about you."

Gnomo arrived at a heavy and urgent pace, uttered a dull growl, closed his fists and directed a bulldog glare at the students.

The latter, not deeming it appropriate to pick a quarrel with such a bear, hastened to decamp, and Gnomo, shutting himself in the hut, lit a lantern, stopped the thirty or forty clocks that were suspended around him, had supper and lay down on the straw, where he snored until daybreak.

II. The Dice

After having supped joyfully in one of the best inns in the town, Lorenz wanted to gamble for his share with a few scatterbrains of his stripe. He won two or three casts of the

23

dice, and his purse was soon so full that he found himself in a position to pay cash for the watch. It was ticking in the pocket of his doublet; the comrades wanted to play again, and Lorenz, too generous a player to refuse his adversaries their revenge, and reassured by his victory, played for so long and so hard that he lost not only what he had won but also his last florin.

The curfew had sounded and the landlord, worried by the noise that the gamblers were making, after having reminded them several times that the ordinances of His Highness Duke Maximilian Emanuel[15] prescribed the closing of taverns as soon as the curfew bell had rung, and seeing that no one was thinking of retiring, made the decision to extinguish the lamps. Without paying the slightest attention to the murmurs of the gamblers, he distributed little lanterns to them and had his waiters show them to their respective rooms.

Lorenz had some difficulty going to sleep, although he had only dined very soberly; he was annoyed by having lost his money, and thought with displeasure about the lecture that he would receive from his elder brother and his sister-in-law, very reasonable people, benevolent toward him, but who would nevertheless have a fine time telling him that if he was impoverished, it was his own fault.

He went to sleep, however, and dreamed that he had wings and was going to take eaglets from the nest. He did not find any in the aerial aerie at which he arrived in rapid flight, but he found golden eggs; he filled his pockets with them and stuffed them into his hose, his hat and his handkerchief.

Now I'm rich for life, he said to himself. *Let's hold on them tight.*

Alas, the malevolent dawn came to wake the cocks, and those pitiless singers, in shrill voices, caused the dreams to fly away. Lorenz woke up, and heard an unusual sound close by.

---

[15] This reference is mistaken; the Elector, or Duke, of Bavaria in 1595 was William IV; he was succeeded in 1597 by Maximilian I, also known as Maximilian the Great, but Maximilian Emanuel was Maximilian II, who became Elector in 1679.

It was the beautiful silver watch, inlaid with niello: the watch that he would be forced to return, for lack of money, alas, thanks to those accursed dice.

Lorenz got up, sighing, washed and dressed. While he was going back and forth in his room, he saw his face in a mirror and said to himself: *Come on, I'm crazy to torment myself like his, Master Hyrcanus isn't a Turk or a Jew. He'll give me credit, on my good appearance; in a few throws of the dice I'll win back what I've lost, ad after all, it'll soon be the end of the month. My brother will give me my pension, and anyway...*

And he started singing, to a tune of his own invention, an Italian proverb that a poor artiste had taught him: *Cent'anni di malinconia non pagano uno quattrino di debita.*[16]

He went down the stairs, letting his rapier bump into the steps; people who get up early have no greater pleasure than waking up those who are trying to sleep, and, with his hat tilted over his ear, in a joyful and confident manner, he headed for Sebaldstrasse

Hyrcanus' house, constructed in bricks and wooden panels, advanced two overhanging stories over the street, the small, irregular windows of which were ornamented with sculpted frames representing the most fantastic grimacing figures of humans and animals that one could ever see. The shop was not very well-illuminated, so the clockmaker did not work there, and his work-bench occupied a large room that opened over the garden. Above the door to the street, between the two first-floor windows, a master sculptor of the fourteenth century had represented Time. His huge scythe, his long beard and his furious expression terrified little children, but the neighborhood pigeons were not frightened of him and it was rare to pass along Sebaldstrasse without seeing one of them perched

---

[16] Presumably misquoted, as "pagano" [heathen] does seem to make sense in context; the intended meaning is presumably something like "A hundred years of melancholy does not stem from a quattrino [a coin of very low value] of debt."

tranquilly on the white-haired head, or the wings or the scythe of Time.

When Lorenz von Ittenbach went into Hyrcanus' home, an aged maidservant was at her stove, an apprentice was sweeping the shop, and Hyrcanus, seated in a wheelchair, was occupied in winding a clock. He greeted Lorenz with the greatest politeness, and, maneuvering himself, rolled his wheelchair into a small room where two places had been set at a table covered in the finest Flanders cloth. A simple but excellent breakfast was served on silver plate, and at dessert, Hyrcanus, dismissing the apprentice, offered Lorenz a glass of Xeres wine worthy of being presented to the Emperor of Germany. Until then, they had only talked about indifferent things. Lorenz wanted to broach the subject that preoccupied him, but Hyrcanus hastened to say that he would not conclude anything for a week.

"It's necessary to try the watch first," he said, "And besides, I have a favor to ask you. You're a gentleman, Meinherr, and I know that no von Ittenbach has ever failed to keep his word. Will you promise to keep the secret that I'm going to tell you?"

"Willingly," said Lorenz, from whom Hyrcanus' frank manner and hospitality had taken away all suspicion. "I give you my word. Here's my hand."

Hyrcanus clasped the fresh and vigorous hand of the young hunter in his thin and wiry fingers, and, lowering his voice slightly, said to him: "If you can give me the feathers of six large eagles, the watch will be yours and I'll remain very much obliged to you. But I absolutely must have six large eagles."

"You shall have them!" cried Lorenz, "even if I have to go all the way to the Donnersberg to kill them. But what are you going to do with six eagles, Master Hyrcanus?"

"That's my secret, Herr Lorenz. If you want to complete my satisfaction, bring me those wings—for I have no need of the bodies of the birds—in secret, hidden under your cloak, and as soon as the animals are taken, while they're still flexible. Don't mention our bargain to anyone, or it will be broken. In any case, I have your word; I'm tranquil. Adieu, then, and good hunting. It's now time for me to go to the square and practice my profession of merchant. Oh, Herr Lorenz, there's another that I love far more!"

"Making watches?" said Lorenz.

Hyrcanus shrugged his shoulders. "Watches!" he said. "Clocks! Thousands of men can do that. I want to make something unusual, unknown, impossible. But I need eagle feathers."

"You won't lack them. Oh, I forgot! Show me how to wind my watch."

Hyrcanus gave him a pretty key, a niello-inlaid silver chain, like the watch, and, smiling at his joy, happy himself in expectation, shook Lorenz's hand and sent the apprentice to tell Gnomo to come and carry his master to the main square.

III. At the Schloss von Ittenbach

The same day, Lorenz, having played dice again before dinner, won a small sum, which permitted him to pay the landlord. Determined not to risk the few florins he had left, he gave the order to saddle his horse, and, without listening to the pleas of his friends, who wanted to take him to see a cock fight, after which there would be dancing in the square, Lorenz departed, walking his horse rapidly as long as he was in the crowded town. He crossed the triple enclosure of the fortifications, completed in accordance with the plans of Albrecht Dürer, passing under the sonorous vaults and over the drawbridges, and, once he was in open country, urged his mount to a gallop.

Blum knew full well that he was returning home, so he ran like the wind across the fertile plain, where the hasty waves of the Peignitz caused numerous mills to turn. But the terrain rose up and the road became rocky, furrowed by little streams that flowed down the mountains; Blum was eventually obliged to slow down.

Then, letting the reins hang loose, and trusting in Blum's sagacity to avoid the obstacles he encountered, Lorenz gazed at the vast landscape while he rode. Cultivated fields became rarer at the sides of the road. Heather, increasingly numerous clumps of bushes, and widely-spaced thatched cottages offered a less cheerful aspect than the plans of Nuremberg, but the keen mountain air, the penetrating perfume of fir woods and the spreading horizon charmed the young hunter, and above the peaks, whose first slopes he was climbing, above the cascades falling like silver ribbons along somber walls of sheer rock, his piercing eye distinguished moving black dots circling in the azure of the sky. They were eagles, soaring on high, staring at the sun or watching out for prey: eagles in indefatigable flight.

Oh, Lorenz said to himself. *Why am I not on those peaks, with my bow in my hand? But I will be tomorrow.*

After having traveled for four hours he finally arrived at Schloss von Ittenbach, situated on a crag, which advanced like a promontory above a lake in a valley full of pastureland. Without paying any heed to the herds of cattle that were the pride of his brother, Baron Georg von Ittenbach. Lorenz went up to the schloss, led his horse to the stable himself, and, after having made sure that it was being well cared for, went into the main hall, were Baroness Adelaide von Ittenbach was occupied in making supper for her children. She had a great deal to do, as had her two maidservants, to content that turbulent and capricious band, the eldest of whom was not yet ten years old. There were eight of them, four boys and four girls, blonde-haired, pink, joyful, charming and absolutely insupportable. At the sight of their uncle they uttered cries of joy, launched themselves from their seats, overturning plates and goblets, and the smallest of all, attached to the arms of his high chair, unable to follow the general movement, screeched like a peacock.

"Have you bought me something from the Nuremberg Fair?"

"Give, give!"

"Me first!"

"No, me!"

Lorenz, putting on his authoritative voice, ordered them to sit down and shut up; otherwise, he said, he would not give them anything. Then, when the little troop was lined up again around the spoons, he took out of his pockets as many ginger-bread men and painted wooden toys as there were children, and distributed them all, beginning with the smallest girl, her sisters, and then the boys. He gave a ribbon to each of the maidservants and a little ivory box to his sister-in-law; those gifts, although very slight in value, caused veritable transports of joy.

An hour later, the children, having nibbled their ginger-bread, were asleep, the little girls with their dolls in their arms, the little boys beside the debris of their toys, already broken, and, Baron Georg having come home, the reasonable people were having a tranquil supper.

"I didn't expect you today, brother," said the Baroness. "The fair isn't over. Isn't it good this year?"

"As usual, my sister, it's quite brilliant, but having made my purchases I preferred returning home to exposing myself to the temptation of running up debts."

"What a marvel! You're becoming reasonable, brother. I congratulate you. But what's that pretty niello chain? I don't recognize it?"

"Look, my sister, isn't it beautiful? And, taking it from around his neck, he put it down, with the watch, on the Baroness's plate.

"A watch!" she exclaimed. "Oh, how pretty it is! I've never seen one so small. Georg's is twice the size."

"At least mine is good and solid," said Georg, frowning, "and furthermore, it's paid for. This is another one of your follies, Lorenz. That watch will cost you a year's allowance, and how will you replace your clothes? I'm not in a position to add anything to your pension this year, as you know."

"Don't worry, brother; my watch is paid for, or, at least, soon will be. I've struck a bargain to settle my account with the products of my hunting."

"That means that you're going to massacre our hinds and our hares."

"No, brother, I shan't kill a single one. It's with birds of prey alone that I'm due to pay for my watch."

"Kill them all, then, if you can, but don't break your neck. That's a singular bargain, though. If it weren't you who were saying it, I wouldn't believe it."

"Nothing is more true, brother. Tomorrow, I shall enter into campaign against the eagles."

"Oh, so much the better," said Baroness Adelaide. "Only yesterday they carried off a little white kid, one day old, and so pretty—so pretty that my little girls wept for it. I abandon the eagles to you, brother, with great heart. But how beautiful this watch is!"

After supper, the Baroness brought her servants together to say prayers, and the signal for bedtime dispersed the company.

IV. In flight

Lorenz scarcely slept. He only did so to dream that he was flying and pursuing eagles in the region of the clouds. His bedroom, large and vaulted, was illuminated at sunrise, and as soon as white light, rapidly pink-tinted, appeared on the horizon in the gap between two wooded mountains, he got up, put on his hunting costume and good gaiters, and picked up the iron-tipped staff that aided him to climb rocks, his best bow and his sharpest arrows. He went downstairs quietly to the servants' parlor, equipped himself with a few provisions, and, without waking anyone, went out through a postern to which he had a key.

His favorite dog, shut in the kennel, scented him passing and growled, his nose under the gate, but Lorenz said to him:

"Be quiet, Rapp. I'll take you when I go hunting fur, not feather."

He soon reached the forest of firs, whose somber depths were beginning to be penetrated by the sun's darts. He traversed it, reached the heather and the sterile rocks, lay in ambush in a fissure in a rock where he knew that eagles nested, and, silent and still, waited for them to pass.

Soon, a sound of wings resonated in the calm air, and an eagle passed rapidly overhead. Lorenz fired, but his arrow was lost in space, and the disdainful eagle continued its flight.

I'll wait for it to come back, Lorenz said to himself, and he waited for long hours. He did not get bored. When his eyes, fatigued by exploring the sky, were lowered toward the ground, he perceived on a slope of the mountain, perched proudly on its pedestal of rocks, Drakenberg Castle. At that distance, the fortress seemed to be the size of a hand, and it required the eye of a hunter to make out its sparse casements, but Lorenz counted them easily, and only looked at one of them: the one in the western tower, on the stone balcony of which, perched a hundred feet above the moat, Hilda von Nauemburg, the lady of his dreams, came to lean at an agreed hour every evening.

At the same hour, except for the days when he was playing dice, watching cock fights or bear baiting, supping in company or allowing himself to be drawn away by the pleasure of hunting. Lorenz gazed at the sunset and the evening star, and renewed in his heart the oath he had made never to love anyone but the beautiful Hilda.

Whether that charming individual was as inexact in her rendezvous with the stars as her young knight, I do not know, but she surely did not have as many good reasons for not thinking about it. A maid of honor of the aged Princess von Drakenberg, the most severe and most sedentary of women, Hilda had not crossed the enclosure of the castle for more than a year. Prince von Drakenberg, the son of the dowager princess, often absented herself, and when he was in the castle he did not bring any diversion with him. He had been the saddest

31

man in Franconia since he had lost his third wife and the heir to his name, the only child that remained to him of his three marriages. The Duke of Bavaria wanted Prince von Drakenberg to remarry, but stupid legends ran around on his account. It was said that he had killed his three wives, and throughout Franconia and beyond, not one noble damsel had consented to marry him, in spite of his wealth and his reputation for bravery and loyalty.

As for Hilda, a penniless orphan, she had been confided, when she emerged from the convent, to an old lady whose schloss was the rendezvous of all the nobility of the surrounding area, but, that noble and prudent lady having observed that Hilda liked amusing herself too much, and had chatted a great deal, while dancing, with the young Ritter von Ittenbach, who was also penniless and was reputed to be a crackbrain, had hastened to place Fraulein von Nauemburg with the venerable Princess von Drakenberg. There, Fraulein Hilda leaned to embroider in a hundred fashions, to hold herself upright and to keep quiet, to make reverences and cultivate patience, waiting for her proofs of nobility to be made in order to enter as a canoness into the Prague chapter.

What is she doing now? Lorenz wondered. *Oh, if I had the wings of an eagle, how I would fly to that balcony, how I would say to her: "Dear Hilda, don't go into a convent. At any moment, I hope, war might break out; I'd enlist, and perform prodigies of valor; the Duke of Bavaria would give me a choice of domains in the countries I had conquered. I would throw himself at his feet to say to him: 'My lord, I only want one very little grafschaft or markgrafschaft, but give me the white hand of Hilda von Nauemburg and deign to sign my marriage contract.'"*

Noon approached, and Lorenz perceived the eagle in the distance, in the aerial plains, returning back laden with booty. The hare that it was crying in its claws weighed down its flight. Lorenz took aim, the arrow departed, whistling, and the eagle, struck in the heart, released its bloody prey, spun, and came to fall, bleeding, a hundred feet away from the hunter, on a slope covered with heather.

Triumphantly, Lorenz went down, and admired the gigantic dimensions of the bird. He cut off its wings and abandoned the rest to the crows. He returned to Ittenbach and made his preparations to return to Nuremberg the following day.

V. Master Hyrcanus

In order to attract the least possible attention from the clockmaker's neighbors, Lorenz left his horse at the inn and, carrying the eagle's wings carefully wrapped in his cloak, he went to the main square. It was the last day of the fair, and Master Hyrcanus, surrounded by customers, seemed to be very busy. Nevertheless, he shivered with pleasure on hearing Lorenz's voice and seeing his joyful pink face appear above the crowded heads of his clients. Lorenz made him a sign of intelligence

"This evening, Meinherr," Hyrcanus said to him. "I can't go home before nightfall, but please, come to supper with me."

"Agreed," said Lorenz. "And my parcel?"

"Give, give, I beg you!"

And, extending his hand, he received the package, carefully wrapped in gray cloth and neatly tied up, which Lorenz handed him over the shoulders of two good burgers.

Hyrcanus stowed it preciously in his large drawer and a housewife cried: "What's in there that's so beautiful?"

"A deerskin that I'm going to have tanned in order to clean my clocks and watches," said Hyrcanus. And he continued selling his watches and his gold and silver chains.

In the meantime, Lorenz amused himself wandering around the fair. He recognized the Princess von Drakenberg's steward, who was buying colored fabrics, and, approaching him, tried to engage him in conversation.

"Has your princess quit mourning-dress, then?" he asked, saluting him.

"Yes, Meinherr," said the steward, removing his hat. "May it please God that it's for a long time!"

"Amen, with all my heart. Has the prince returned from the court?"

"He's expected soon, Meinherr." Addressing the merchant, he added: "Come on, hurry up and send all that to my inn, the Golden Sun. I still have other purchases to make. You can present the bill whenever you like."

He drew away, and Lorenz saw him buying lace, gold braid and a host of other objects, of which he had a list in his hand.

"Has Fraulein Hilda von Nauemburg given you commissions?" he asked the steward.

"Certainly, Meinherr, certainly."

"Ah! Would you care to give her a little packet that someone desires to send her?"

"Yes," said he steward, winking. "Gladly, but I warn Meinherr that, following the custom established at Drakenberg, the packet in question would pass through the hands of the Princess."

"Thank you," said Lorenz. "I'll go fetch it." And he drew away. But he did not come back, and wandered idly until the time for supper.

Master Hyrcanus treated his guest even better than the first time, and showed himself so content with the beautiful eagle plumes that Lorenz could not help saying: "But after all, Master Hyrcanus, what are you going to do with those feathers?"

"You'll soon see, Meinherr. Go hunting again as soon as possible, I beg you. The next time you me, I'll no longer have that accursed shop in the square to keep. I'll receive you in the morning, and you can see my workshop. Tell me, then, how you killed that eagle.

Like any hunter, Lorenz loved to narrate his exploits. As he spoke, Hyrcanus refilled his glass, and the attention he paid to the story excited the verve of the storyteller.

"Can you swim?" the clockmaker asked him, suddenly.

"Oh, yes," said Lorenz. "At swimming, as at running, I know of no one who can surpass me."

"And you like running, climbing the highest peaks and the tallest trees. Why?"

"Why? Well, for the pleasure of being able to see a long way, testing my strength and my skill, imagining that I can fly above the mountains, in the clouds in the sky. Almost every night, I dream that I have wings."

"Ah!" said Hyrcanus. "The dream of your nights is that of my entire life. Listen, Lorenz; since my childhood I've spend the entire year bent over a table fashioning gold, silver or precious stones, or next to a forge, always indoors. I've lived like that except for two years that I employed traveling around Germany in order to perfect my artistry, when long days were spent in journeys on foot. But in Sundays, as a child, I went up into the bell-tower and there, looking at the towns, the countryside and the immensity of the sky, I followed the flight of birds with an envious eye, and of all the riches that the earth offered to my eyes, and all the promises that religion makes us of heaven, I only desired one thing. Alas, I've desired and sought that treasure, and old age has arrived. I no longer even have legs to drag myself over the miserable earth, over the dust to which I shall soon return. But so long as my heart beats, so long as a glimmer of intelligence animates my brain, so long as my hand—the hand that is still the most skillful in Germany—can hold an implement, indicate a point and quiver on contact with an object, I shall pursue my goal, I shall strive, I shall seek..."

"What?" asked Lorenz, moved by the passionate expression that animated the old man's eyes.

"Wings," said Hyrcanus. "Wings."

VI. The Trial

Spring had ended, summer was advancing, and Lorenz, who had taken his sixth eagle to the old clockmaker a long time ago, no longer heard any mention of him. Whether he was afraid of having talked too much, or because he was not in a position to satisfy his young friend's curiosity, Hyrcanus had not kept his promise to show him his workshop.

"I'll show it to you later," he said, "when I've finished a certain mechanism that will interest you."

Lorenz began to forget the clockmaker. There was talk of war, and, avid for news, he traveled the country and often came to Nuremberg.

One day, when he had arranged to meet one if his friends, a recruiting captain, under the porch of Saint Lorenz, the friend did not arrive. A rainstorm followed, and Lorenz went into the church. It was very dark, because of the stained glass and the storm clouds, and a few frightened women were praying in the chapel of the Holy Virgin.

After a brief prayer, Lorenz glanced at the clock by the light of a lightning-flash. It was about to chime. He drew closer, as he had done in his childhood, in order to see the wooden figurines emerged at the moment when the hour sounded. It chimed, but Saint Michael slaying the infernal dragon did not appear, the angels equipped with trumpets remained mute and Saint Peter's cock did not crow. Only then did Lorenz perceive that inside the little perforated edifice that contained the clock, a light was shining, and the sound of a file could be heard.

He approached, put his eye to one of the holes in the wood and saw Hyrcanus sitting inside, working by the light of a little lamp. He greeted him, and Hyrcanus, recognizing his voice, uttered an exclamation of joy.

"Ah!" he said. "You've come at a good time, Meinherr Lorenz. I didn't know how to inform you, but I have great need of you. My Gnomo is in full revolt. I'll have to dismiss him soon, but I can't get rid of him until I've found a man capable of rendering me the same services as him. That isn't my greatest concern, however. Listen, it's absolutely necessary that you come to find me tomorrow in a litter, and that you take me, firstly, into open country outside the town, and then into a deserted wood. It's necessary that we're alone, absolutely alone, except for a groom who can lead the horses—a stupid man, if possible. It's also necessary that you buy a complete suit of armor of steel mail, the best and the lightest that you can find. It's necessary to keep the secret for me, and come to fetch me at my door tomorrow morning at eight o'clock. Is that agreed?"

"Damn, how you go on, Hyrcanus," said Lorenz, laughing. "A litter, mules and a stupid servant aren't difficult to procure, but I'll need some money. A suit of mail would please me, but that costs a great deal, and as for an excursion to the woods with you tomorrow, that would doubtless be very agreeable, but I've been invited to an archery tournament followed by a banquet, and I confess that I'd regret that competition."

"No, you'll never regret it, be certain of it. As for the gold, here it is. Do you want more? You can have it." And, extending his hand toward Lorenz, he gave him a purse full of gold florins.

"You have an excellent method of overcoming objections," said Lorenz. "Tomorrow morning at eight, I'll be at the rendezvous. Have you any further instructions?"

"No, no, go, quickly. Let me finish my work. Oh, what a torture to be constrained to focus my attention, to lose the most precious of my hours, on mechanical toil, when all my thought is elsewhere, when I'm so close to reaching the goal!"

He resumed filing an iron bar, furiously, and Lorenz ran to the armorer in order to make the purchase of the finest coat of steel mail that he could find.

The next day, at ten o'clock, the litter carrying Hyrcanus and a rather voluminous package arrived, escorted by Lorenz on horseback, near a wood situated a league from Nuremberg. It belonged to Baron von Ittenbach; it was surrounded by ditches full of water and closed by a grille, and Lorenz, who loved hunting, always carried the key on his person. Lorenz stopped near the grille, ordered the muleteer to wait for him. First he took the large package, carried it into the wood, and placed it carefully at the foot of an oak tree. Then he came back to fetch Master Hyrcanus. He loaded him on to his shoulders as he would have done a child, and carried him to the mysterious object. Then, retracing his steps, he made sure that the grille was locked and returned to Hyrcanus.

In the meantime, the little old man had not remained inactive. With an adroit hand, but trembling with emotion, he had opened the envelope that was sealed by lather traps, and unwrapped, before Lorenz's astonished eyes, a gigantic pair of wings attached to a sort of breastplate with complicated articulations. Lorenz recognized the plumes of his eagles, mounted with so much artistry that the artificial wings folded up like those of a living bird.

"Come closer," said Hyrcanus. "There! Put on this breastplate, but first, take off your clothes and put on the coat of mail. It's necessary."

Astonished, Lorenz obeyed. He equipped himself in a trice, and appeared to Hyrcanus like a Saint Michael, save for the sword. He was so handsome thus, with his great folded wings, that Hyrcanus exclaimed: "Truly, Lorenz, you seem more like a archangel than a human being. But listen: this the moment that will decide whether I'm an insensate or a man of genius. Come closer, bend down, and on your life, do what I tell you, nothing more and nothing less. I'm going to set up the mechanism, imprint the movement to your wings. As soon as you feel them quiver, raise your arms and bring our hands together, as if to swim, and launch yourself! If I've succeeded, you'll soar, and you'll be able to direct yourself like a swimmer in water. But don't go up high. Remain close to the ground, and when you want to stop or moderate the movement of your wings, press this spring."

Smiling, Lorenz said to himself: *The poor man is mad; if I launched myself from a high place...but to leave the ground with this heavy apparatus, this armor? What folly!*

However, he leaned over toward Hyrcanus, and the latter, having touched a few controls, said: "What do you feel?"

"A vibration over the breast," said Lorenz. "Something palpitating, like a heart of steel added to mine. Oh, my God! I can feel myself rising up, the wings extending, my feet leaving the ground!"

"Swim!" cried Hyrcanus, as pale as a specter.

"I'm flying!" said Lorenz. "Victory!"

And he started swimming through the air, twenty feet above the ground, turning, gliding, descending again at will, intoxicated by joy and surprise, and while he floated around the clearing, he saw another marvel: Hyrcanus walking, even running, following all his movements, his eyes on fire, his arms raised. Joy had cured and rejuvenated him; he was no longer the same man.

"Come down!" he shouted "I've only set up the mechanism for ten minutes. Your wings are about to close!"

Lorenz came back down, and as he set foot on the grass, his wings folded up gently, and the heart of steel ceased beating.

The inventor and his young friend embraced then, and Lorenz cried: "Truly, you ought to render great thanks to the good God, Master Hyrcanus. You're walking!"

"I didn't think of that—yes, in truth. I'm walking! Oh, Lorenz, it seems to me that it's the fire of Heaven that is circulating in my veins. I feel strong and agile, as I was at twenty years. I want to try my wings.

"Here they are, Master. Do you want the armor too?"

"No, the experiment is done. The armor will be necessary to make an aerial voyage, in order to brave arrows and bullets, but we aren't risking anything here."

He equipped himself, and soon, rising to the air, hovered above Lorenz's head—not with the same grace as him, assuredly, but just as easily.

At the moment when he descended to the grass again, Lorenz lowered his eyes toward the ground; he thought he saw in a bush a hideous head with large bright eyes under eyebrows full of greenish mud. Seizing his sword, he ran toward the apparition, but the creature he had glimpsed was already fleeing, and he heard it breaking branches in its passage and hurling itself into the water. When Lorenz arrived at the edge of the ditch, the water was still agitated, but he could not see anyone.

Not knowing whether it was a matter of a man or an animal, he returned to Hyrcanus, who was occupied in wrapping up his precious apparatus.

"Let's return to Nuremberg," said the inventor. "I'm in haste to get there in order to make a few improvements."

"Let me fly again a little," said Lorenz. "I'd like to rise up higher than the trees to see whether I can perceive Drakenberg."

"What business have you with Drakenberg? It's necessary not to risk being seen. The greatest secrecy is necessary to me. I want to leave for Vienna. I want you to try my wings before the Emperor. He alone can recompense me for my discovery."

"But what tells you that I want to play the acrobat before the Emperor?" said Lorenz. "I come from to good a family for that."

Hyrcanus shivered. "What!" he cried. "You're refusing me? Oh, Meinherr, that would be very cruel. Remember that I've counted on you. Where will I find united, as in your person, courage, agility and intelligence? What I fine spectacle it would be for the Imperial court to see you such as you were just now, floating in the air like a celestial messenger! Oh, Meinherr Lorenz, don't refuse me. Come with me to Vienna. I'll give you anything you wish; I'm rich, very rich, and ready to make any sacrifice in order to enjoy my glory, to become, thanks to my invention, the most famous man in the world."

"But you're no longer infirm," said Lorenz. "What prevents you from making use of your wings yourself?"

"Alas," said Hyrcanus, "I'm old, I'm ugly, and in any case, I sense that joy alone has rendered me strength; it's abandoning me already. I'm suffering, my limbs are stiffening. Oh, Lorenz, don't abandon me. I'll make you rich and famous. Think about it! You've dreamed of going to war. Think what services a winged soldier might render in sieges and battles!"

Lorenz felt his resolve shaken. That marvelous adventure and the promises of rapid fortune tempted him.

"Perhaps I'll decide," he said. "But let me try your wings again."

He tried them again, convinced himself of the excellence of Hyrcanus's invention, and only put one condition on his consent, which was that, the following night, he would make an aerial voyage to Drakenberg Castle. Delighted, Hyrcanus initiated him in all the details of the mechanism, making sure that he could control the apparatus perfectly; and, having returned to Nuremberg, the inventor and his aide awaited nightfall impatiently.

VII. Nocturnal Voyage

Night finally came, calm and serene, but moonless, and the stars, scintillating in a cloudless sky, were illuminating the bell-towers of Nuremberg softly when Hyrcanus, leaning on a staff, and Lorenz, carrying his wings, went to the bottom of the clockmaker's garden. The garden was situated near the ramparts. The curfew had sounded a long time ago, and everything was dormant. Hyrcanus opened a little door; it opened very near to a stairway leading up to the rampart. Lorenz equipped himself, shook the old man's hand, and climbed the stairway. Soon, Hyrcanus heard the sound of wings and saw a black form launch itself into the air. He listened carefully, The sentinel placed on a nearby tower had not heard anything. The hour sounded, and the distant voice of the watchman placed in the belfry cried: "All's well! Pray for the dead!"

Troubled, Hyrcanus wrapped himself in a fur-lined mantle and waited, unable to resolve to go back inside. He counted the hours with anxiety. Midnight, two o'clock and three o'clock resonated in the bell-towers. The stars were beginning to pale and anguish was already gripping Hyrcanus's heart when a flutter of wings caused him to raise his head, and Lorenz, pale and exhausted, alighted next to him. Hyrcanus made him drink a cordial and bombarded him with questions.

Lorenz recovered promptly, took off his intact wings, and, sustaining the inventor's steps, took him back to the house. They lit a fire and took some nourishment, but Lorenz remained somber and silent. He told Hyrcanus that he was obliged to return to Ittenbach and would not see him again for two days. Hyrcanus begged him not to stay any longer with his brother, and promised him that he would employ those two days in making the preparations for the journey to Vienna.

They separated at sunrise, and Lorenz did not take long to go through the gates of Nuremberg.

Soon, while riding through the fields where the reapers were already working, Lorenz, exhausted by fatigue, reviewed his nocturnal adventures mentally, and wondered whether he had not been dreaming.

To begin with, he had flown toward the mountains in a calm and rapid flight, and, by the gentle light of the stars, he had perceived the towers of Drakenberg, where the seigneurial banner floated. In spite of the advanced hour—it was after midnight—lights were burning in several casements. Only one, however, interested Lorenz; that was the little lamp illuminating Hilda's room at the summit of the western tower. In order not to be perceived by the watchman stationed on the tower, Lorenz flew lower and, skimming the walls, rose up silently and came to alight on Hilda's balcony. Her window was open. Not daring to enter, he called out softly and rapped on the window-panes. Profound silence. He advanced his head; the chamber was empty. A few scattered garments, an open casket from which a string of pearls emerged, and a bouquet of roses had been placed on the bed, which had not been disturbed. The chamber was in disorder, bit full of perfumes and a festival air.

A few distant chords of music reached Lorenz's ears. He went out again and, resuming his flight, passed over the western wall and came to hover over the courtyard of the castle. It was very large, and in the center, backed up against the tower, was the chapel. The entire castle appeared to be deserted, although illuminated, but the chapel was full of people and so well illuminated that the stained glass windows were resplendent. It was there that people were singing. The door was closed.

Lorenz hovered above the different buildings. He saw drunken servants sharing the debris of a feast and drinking to the health of the masters of the castle. He circled around the chapel, and, finally perceiving a window from which a fairly large section of the stained glass was missing, he was able to see what was happening inside.

The castle's chaplain was blessing a marriage. Prince von Drakenberg, clad in crimson brocade, drawn up to his full height, wearing with dignity his Golden Fleece necklace, his fifty years, his gray beard and his noble forehead white under the helmet, was leading a veiled woman of gracious height to the altar, whose long train of white and silver damask as being carried by two beautiful young women. Neither of them was Hilda, and Lorenz searched for her in vain in the audience with his eyes. But when the ceremony, which was nearing its end, was terminated, the bride returned to her prie-Dieu, and poor Lorenz recognized Hilda, beautiful, smiling and triumphant.

If he had not been clinging to the grilles that protected the window he would have fallen, forgetting his wings. He went pale and cold; then the blood returned violently to his face, his ears buzzed, anger chased away dolor and, rising into the air, he departed in swift flight....

Soon, however, he returned to Hilda's balcony, placed in her casket a ribbon, a glove and flowers that she had given him, tore up a beautiful lace, shredded the roses and would doubtless have committed other follies had he not heard a noise in the staircase. Then, taking flight again, he resumed the route to Nuremberg through the silent air.

Yes, it was like a dream, and yet it was true. Whether a man's breast is covered by warrior armor or a monk's habit, black or crimson, whether it is ornamented by regal diamonds or the stolen wings of eagles, the heart, alas, remains no less vulnerable, and all the wealth and inventions in the world can do nothing to appease its pain.

Lorenz was therefore riding sadly, without even looking at the mountains, which he was approaching, or the eagles soaring in the sky, when he heard trumpets resonating.

Blum pricked up his ears; Lorenz hoisted himself up on his saddle and looked in all directions. At a bend in the road he perceived a company of horsemen who were coming toward him, with banners deployed, plumes and cloaks in the wind. His brother was at the head of the troop, armed from head to toe. On seeing him he cried: "Come on, then, Lorenz, what were you doing in Nuremberg? A message from the Duke of Bavaria arrived last night. He's summoned us. War has been declared. One of us has to stay in Ittenbach to guard the schloss, and the other must depart at the head of my vassals. The Duke left the choice to me. Ittenbach is an important fortress that might be besieged."

"Stay here, I beg you, brother," said Lorenz. "Let me replace you in the army. It's my dearest desire, as you know. My friends, would you not be content to have me as your captain?"

"Long live Ritter Lorenz von Ittenbach!" cried the dozen men-at-arms. "Long live our captain!"

And Baron Georg, thinking of the happiness that his wife would experience on seeing him return, dismounted, exchanged his armor for his younger brother's clothes, gave him his purse, his rapier, his pistols and his fine charger, made him a thousand recommendations, embraced him, and, bestriding Blum, took the road to Ittenbach.

As he watched him draw away, one of the men-at-arms, passing his hand over his eyes and beard, said: "Will the rest of us ever return to our homes? More than one of us, alas, might not see the valley of Ittenbach again."

"Sound, trumpets!" cried Lorenz. "Saddle up, my friends! The rendezvous is in Nuremberg at sunset. Roll on the battle! Roll on the victory! Hurrah for the noble Duke! Hurrah for Bavaria!"

And they set forth at a rapid trot.

VIII. The Tempest

The affluence of troops into Nuremberg was so great that the city was unable to lodge them all; it was necessary to establish a camp in the meadows on the right bank of the Peignitz. Not daring to emerge from the town, the burgers and their wives went to gaze from the height of the ramparts at the banners and the movements of the various army cops. Hyrcanus had himself carried there by Gnomo. He had lost the use of his legs again. Anxious, desolate not to have seen Lorenz return, he bombarded Gnomo with questions and sent him to obtain information several times a day.

Gnomo, surlier and ruder than ever, ended up saying to him: "Even if you put me to the torture, I can only repeat to you what I've said a hundred times: Ritter von Ittenbach is in the camp; he's occupied from morning to dusk exercising his soldiers, and hasn't come into town once. I've had him told that you're asking for him, and he replied that he would come to see you after the war."

"After the war!" said Hyrcanus. "The fool! And what if he's killed?"

"If he's killed," said Gnomo, "there will be one coxcomb fewer, and your secret will be kept!"

"What secret?" said Hyrcanus, going pale. He was sitting on the escarp of the rampart. Gnomo, crouched beside him, had his back to the country and was gazing at the roof of his master's house."

"What secret?" Hyrcanus repeated.

"The secret of your wings, of course."

"I don't know what you mean."

"Yes, put on a show, lie, it's all the same to me. I was in the wood. I heard everything. Last Tuesday night I saw Lorenz take off from your garden and I saw him come back. I know everything. I have a key to your workshop. Blush, Hyrcanus, at having scorned the aid of a servant like me, in order to give your confidence to the first comer, a child, He's abandoning you; that's good. It's just the two of us now. I want half your glory, half your profits. I want to go to Vienna and use your wings in front of the Emperor."

Stupefied as he was, Hyrcanus could not help smiling at that idea.

"Spy!" he cried. "Traitor! Monster of impudence and curiosity, are you forgetting how you're made? Go look at yourself in a mirror and see whether a formless block like you would cut a fine figure with wings on his shoulders. The Emperor's entire court would die laughing."

"Don't laugh!" cried Gnomo, getting to his feet, furiously. "If I'm ugly, I'm also strong, you know that. Swear to me this instant to share everything with me, or I'll hurl you into the ditch. Look!"

He seized the frail old man, pushed him toward the gulf and forced him to look down. Then, replacing him on the grass, he said: "Swear! Or it's done!"

Trembling, Hyrcanus made all the oaths that Gnomo demanded, but promised himself to break them all as soon as he found a means of having his valet imprisoned. Gnomo, for his part, resolved not to quit him for an instant. Seeing a few strollers approaching, he loaded his master on to his shoulders and carried him to his house, without the terrified Hyrcanus daring to say a word.

Two days later, in the evening, a frightful storm burst over Franconia. Three bell-towers in Nuremberg were struck by lightning, and the turbulence of an impetuous wind overturned almost all the tents in the camp. The horses fled, frightened; the soldiers ran after them; all the bells in the town were ringing, clamors resounded everywhere and tumult reigned in the camp.

The leaders tried to reestablish a little order in the panicking multitude. Lorenz, perceiving a group of vivandiers, women and children who had taken refuge under large trees that the tempest was bending like reeds, ran toward them, shouting to them to move away, that they were about to be

46

crushed. Suddenly, a noisy mass passed over his head, crashed into the branches of an oak tree and agitated furiously, crying: "Help! Help!" in a strangled voice.

Lorenz leapt forward, and recognized Gnomo, clad in the flying apparatus, bloody and bruised. His wings were beating the air, breaking the branches to which he was clinging.

"Wretch!" he cried. "Press the stop mechanism."

"It's broken!" cried Gnomo. "Detach me! Help! Help!"

The tempest increased. Lorenz, moved by pity, seized a branch, hoisted himself up to the wretch, and, holding on to the shaking tree with one hand, his face lashed by hail, tried to detach Gnomo's breastplate. It was impossible. A furious gust of wind broke the top of the oak. He fell, breaking the branches. Gnomo let go, and his wings, agitating with a vertiginous force, carried him away into the air. Cries of despair were heard for a few seconds; then only the thunder resounded, and the opening clouds released the cataracts of the heavens.

An hour later, a rainbow was shining; the soldiers re-erected their battered tents; everyone was taking stock of the disasters and rejoicing in still being alive when horsemen of the watch, coming from the town arrived in camp and asked whether anyone had seen a winged man flying through the air.

"Yes, we saw him," said several vivandiers. "It wasn't a man, it was the Devil. He broke that oak over there in passing. Look there's the Ritter von Ittenbach over there; he spoke to him, at the risk of being carried away to Hell."

The cavaliers asked Lorenz if that was true.

"Yes," he said. "I saw Gnomo, Hyrcanus's valet. He was wounded, and flying with wings fabricated by his master. He must be dead now, poor fellow."

"It's the justice of God," said the cavalier, making the sign of the cross. "The wretch had just murdered his master. He counted on escaping before anyone discovered his crime, but, alerted by an old maidservant, we surrounded the house, in which he had barricaded himself. The storm broke. He went up on to the roof and suddenly, we saw him rise up into the air. I fired at him, and he disappeared in the direction of the camp. We broke down Hyrcanus's door a little while ago and found him with his throat cut. I hope to recover the murderer, dead or alive. His wings will be a good prize.

"Certainly," said Lorenz. "Inform me, Captain, as soon as you make that discovery. It's worth a king's ransom."

The horsemen of the watch searched the entire country in vain. They found no trace of Gnomo, and the war soon gave them many other concerns. For lack of heirs, the clockmaker's possessions were sold at auction for the benefit of the hospices, and the story of Hyrcanus's wings passed into the rank of legends.

Half a century later, Eric a young eagle-hunter found a skeleton girded by a rusty breastplate, of precious workmanship but broken in several places, in a cavern that was reputed to be inaccessible, at the top of an arid mountain. A few large eagle plumes were still attached to the articulated armatures fitted to the shoulders of the breastplate.

Surprised, the young hunter took possession of the metal debris and, leaving the bones where they lay, bound the iron fragments together with a strap and threw them to the bottom of the rock. Then, descending again with the agility of a squirrel, he picked up his find and took it home.

"Grandfather," he said, going into the vaulted hall of the Schloss von Ittelbach and addressing an old man with a long white beard who was sitting by the fireside in a armchair with a sculpted back, "look what I've found high up on the Altenberg, in a grotto into which only the eagles can go, according to the shepherds."

And he described what he had seen.

"Uncle Lorenz once told me a story about wings," said the old Baron, "A story that I've almost forgotten. Go fetch him, my little Eric. He'll be able to tell you who the poor fellow was who died up there. Look, here he comes."

Lorenz came in, a falcon on his wrist, still an upright and bold hunter in spite of his seventy years. He listened emotionally to his grand-nephew's story, and in the evening, after

dark, when the whole family was gathered around the old fire-
place, he told them the story that you have just read.

Gaston Derys: *The Inventor*
(1902)

Paul Vaudan was one of the thousand inventors who was seeking the dirigibility of airships, one of the audacious conquistadors of space pursuing the proud dream of freeing humankind from the laws imposed on them by nature, of subjugating to their will the gravity that the worlds obey, enchained in the sublime harmonies of their eternal choirs.

He professed that the aerostat, by the very fact that it is lighter than air, would always be at the mercy of the winds. What he wanted to establish was an apparatus of aviation imitative of the fight of birds, which, much denser than air, would be able to resist the violence of the wind like the birds themselves.

He assimilated everything that naturalists have written about aviation. He examined all the projects and scrutinized all the experiments of the men who had glimpsed the possibility of realizing the designs of presumptuous Icarus, from Roger Bacon and Leonardo da Vinci to contemporaries, from the flying dove of Archytas of Tarentum,[17] two thousand years old, to the mechanical bird of Gaston Tissandier.[18]

---

[17] The story that the Greek mathematician Archytas built a mechanical pigeon in the early fourth century B.C. comes from *Noctes Atticae* [Attic Nights] by the Roman author Aulus Gellius, written in the first century A.D. It is certainly fictitious.

[18] The famous balloonist Gaston Tissandier (1843-1870) did not invent a mechanical bird, but his 1886 book *La Navigation Aérienne* does include a description of a model ornithopter designed in 1876 by Victor Tatin (which could not fly).

After an entire year of dogged meditation, it appeared to him that a result might be attained by determining the kind of balanced equilibrium that reigns in the movements of a bird. It was a matter of combining the rowing action that impels a bird in the atmosphere as oars propel a boat, and the gliding flight that sustains the bird almost without any expenditure of energy.

He constructed an aviator equipped with large canvas wings extended upon an aluminum armature, and attempted to take off; he was able to glide for five minutes, but, for want of stability, the aviator crashed, and Paul Vaudan nearly broke his bones.

Without being discouraged, he reconstituted his apparatus, adding a few improvements to it. He maintained himself in the air for longer. The articulations of his machines were possessed of a greater suppleness. But the two elements that he wanted to amalgamate, gliding flight and rowing flight, were not sufficiently fused. He fell heavily on to a roof, and it was a miracle that he did not pay with his life for that second attempt.

He recommenced ten more times, offering himself to death, which spared him; she is a coquette who likes to spare her gallants. He persisted, superb in his stoical serenity, undefeated by those groping trials, but stimulated and exalted, understanding that he was getting closer and closer to the desired goal by means of patient ameliorations.

In the meantime, people mocked him and insulted him; but he smiled. All the insults and the disdain did not afflict him. Those people were ignorant; they would change their tone on the day of his triumph...for he nourished the indestructible certainty of emerging victoriously from the struggle that he had undertaken against the elements. The rhythm, the musical sequence of movements that caused the wings of his aviator to quiver with the very life of the wings of birds, science or hazard would be revealed to him, he was sure of it...

A powerful force shored up his faith in the final success: amour.

Under the shade of Chevreuse, in the hollow of an idyllic vale, there was a young woman waiting for him, his fiancée. That romance was unknown to the public: Paul had judged it unnecessary to offer his heart to be trampled. Once a week, he suspended his labor and fled to Chevreuse. Oh, how he execrated the slowness of the omnibus train and the rickety patache that carried him toward his friend. To traverse those thirty kilometers it required two mortal hours, during which he cursed the frequency of stations and the indolence of the coachman. When would the time come, then, when he would be in Chevreuse in a matter of minutes, borne by the vertiginous flight of his wings?

But also, after those two exasperating hours, what intimate and profound transports there were when his fiancée's small hands refreshed his fiery temples, when the tenderness of a soft voice singing like a spring, which alarmed his eyes shiny with fever and perils braved, poured pure balm into his entire being. What did the sarcasms of men matter, since a woman loved him, whose amour was as infinite as the ether he wished to conquer?

For her, he would collect the glory of transgressing the mysterious will of nature, and he drew fecund energy from the thought that he would offer her a wedding present more magnificent than those of which the most powerful potentates were able to dispose; for it would not merely be a province, or a state, or a continent, but the empire of Space itself. And he was so convinced of winning that empire that he deferred his marriage until the moment of the definitive victory.

And he found it!

The day came when he recreated the flight of birds, when he commanded the aluminum limbs of his machine like his own limbs, when the winged human cleaved through the clouds like lightning, and soared over crowds in the apotheosis of ovations.

And on that day, he suddenly abandoned the idolatrous clamors that rose toward him like a smoke of incense, and he flew all the way to Chevreuse like an arrow. And he threw himself into his fiancée's arms, with blissful tears...

"I knew that you would be victorious," she said. "I knew that you would fly to me like an archangel."

"Yes," he said, "I am victorious, victorious thanks to you, and for you..."

And he explained that he had almost perfected his machine. Something trivial was still lacking. The steering mechanism that regulated the flight of the aviator was too complicated. A keyboard with electric buttons would replace that helm...

And he set out in quest of the ideal perfection.

A hymn of praise burst forth all over the world. Every day he received letters of congratulation by the basketful. Sovereigns offered him mountains of gold in exchange for his secret. Reporters came into his house through the windows or climbed down the chimney. All the newspapers on the planet commented on his invention: it was distance suppressed; unknown lands and the poles would be explored without difficulty; all strategies would have to be remade, forts protecting frontiers having become ineffective and derisory; railways would be abandoned, as mail coaches had once been; roofs would be transformed into terraces; the pace of existence would be as radically modified as if humans had been suddenly transported to Mars or Neptune...

Enthusiasm! The limitless fields of the heavens were humans had placed their gods would be traveled in all directions! Would he not be accorded divine honors? Unanimous prayers of thanks would rise up toward him...

Enthusiasm! He traversed the clouds, he bounded like a meteor from one end of the provinces to the other, he was the master of the air and the master of masters; he mocked frontiers, and entered into the homes of kings as he pleased.

And three or four times a day he raced to the depths of France in order to go and kiss his fiancée...

After a week, however, it seemed to him that he no long-er experienced, on finding himself in the company of his friend, a happiness as intense and as complete as when he had gone to Chevreuse by train and patache and was subjected to their enervating slowness. He interrogated himself, and had to admit it: previously, he had suffered throughout a week of solitude, and those two hours of delicious torture, which fur-ther postponed his rapture, had prepared superhuman delights for him. Now, those fervors had become lukewarm, and he almost regretted the snail-like train and the tortoise-patache. Previously, in the middle of the distant forest, the little fiancée had appeared to him to be akin to a fay of legendary times, haloed by poetry. Now, when he fell upon Chevreuse like a bolide, that poetry had vanished...

And a dolorous anxiety insinuated itself into him; he was afraid of no longer loving as much, he was afraid of having expelled amour from his heart by stifling desire therein...

And his pride began to diminish.

He finished his new machine. It was the marvel of mar-vels. With the aid of a keyboard, with two fingers, one could steer wherever one wanted, at whatever speed one wanted...

He received the highest decorations of all the nations of the world, and he said to himself, as he gazed at them:

I am the most illustrious of the illustrious. I am the equal of Prometheus, the thief of celestial fire. I have conquered the heavens. I can acquire billions. I can toy with men and their laws. I am finally free. However, I'm not happy... Why? When my nights were consecrated to labor, when I exhausted myself in pursuit of my chimera, when I was struggling, I was happier than I am today. In my grim combats with that chimera, I tast-ed bitter joys. And now that it is tamed, I'm sad...sad and idle, I no longer desire anything. I'm bored. Only one thing could reconcile me with life, and that would be a return to the nature I've confronted, a return to the simple pleasures, the love of a woman I would love, a humble life in a remote location, while,

*little by little, the invisible and magnetic bonds that bind con-
fident couples together enveloped us invincibly...*

*But I almost no longer love my fiancée, who curses my
wings...*

Feeling melancholy, he climbed into his aviator and
soared over Paris.

Hosannas saluted him.

Those people who are shouting themselves hoarse, he
thought, are *mostly artisans and petty employees. They envy
my wings! That village where their parents are growing old,
those mountains, that sea which they adore and to which they
can only go once a year, they would like to be able to revisit
every Saturday evening...the insensates! That hope and that
desire, which comfort them and make them smile all year long,
they want to kill! They want to hate their old parents' village,
hate the sea, and hate the mountains, by virtue of seeing them
too frequently. When they have suppressed distance, the earth
will appear to them as a narrow prison; they will be everywhere at the same time, and satiety will reign over them, and
life will be bleaker and darker and emptier than death...*

And amorous young women blew him kisses.

Foolish women! he thought. *Because of me, amour will
desert the earth. Because of me, lovers will be able to see one
another at any time, because of me, the cause of the keenest
charm of amour, the obstacles and hindrances that irritate
desire, will melt away. I'm an executioner, and the most infa-
mous of all, the executioner of amour!*

Then he had a sinister vision: two clouds of fire, two armies of winged men pursuing one another...and soldiers falling in hundreds...

"Enough! Enough!" howled the frightened inventor.
"Am I going to increase the horrors of war, then?"

He fled toward open country at random, and was saluted
with joyful cries by the merchants of a small town, who had
not reflected that the unprecedented facility of communications would bring to their neighborhood inferior products at
minimal prices, annihilating their commerce and local indus-

try, and also by peasants who had conserved the costume and traditions of their forefathers, and had not realized that, when aviators multiplied journeys, the old customs, and even races, would be obliterated...

"I shall, therefore," he concluded, "spread desolation over the earth. I am not a benefactor, I'm an enemy..."

He returned home in despair, and in a magnificent fit of sincerity and philanthropy, he smashed his machines...

Then he thought about his little fiancée, who was still waiting for him in the middle of the forest. Oh, to nestle next to her, to forget himself next to her! He ran to the station and deplored the slowness of the lazy train and the creaking coach. His desire to see his faithful friend grew within him, filling his heart, impetuous and overflowing...

And he hugged her to his bosom with the same sobbing passion as before, and he took her far away, to a village where people would not be able to find them...the people who would now gladly have lynched him...

Louis Lemercier de Neuville: *King Beta*
(1905)

*I. In which the engineer Vatenlair arrives in a balloon
in a country that does not exist.*

Do not ask where that country is situated, the degrees of
its latitude and its longitude, the road it is necessary to take in
order to go there, whether it is an island or a continent, etc.,
etc. ; we do not know. What we can assure you, however, is
that it is not on the Moon.

Until now, we only have known five parts of the world,
which are, as you know, Europe, Asia, Africa, America and
Oceania; it appears that another exists, which is called
Alphabetia. That name was given to the country in question by
its first inhabitants, and this is why.

In an epoch so remote that it is beyond all tradition and
does not feature in any history, some Greek navigators got lost
at sea. Their primitive ship contained within its flanks twenty-
four men, all brothers, and their twenty-four wives. After having been tossed by the waves for a long time, it broke up on
rocks and the shipwreck victims, having lost all hope of ever
seeing their homeland again, settled in the country, which was
immense and unpopulated.

At first they lived communally, but after a number of
years the colony had acquired such a great development that
every family resolved to make the conquest of that new land
and each create a distinct kingdom. As there were twenty-four
families there were twenty-four kingdoms, and, in consequence, twenty-four sovereigns. Each of them took for a name
one of the twenty-four letters of the alphabet of their original
language, in order to be recognized in the future if, by chance,
other people arrived in the country, because they wanted to

remain united. Hence, the name of Alphabetia was given to that new country.

We have no intention of recounting the history of those twenty-four kingdoms; we shall only acquaint you with that of King Beta, in whose realm the events we are about to describe happened.[19]

Let us say right away that it bore no resemblance to any of those we know. It was still in the infancy that is the golden age of peoples. Civilization had not corrupted it; people there still believed in supernatural things, in enchanters, fays and sorcerers.

Yes, in the realm of King Beta, there were fays, enchanters and sorcerers, or, at least, all the misadventures that happened to you and could not be explained were attributed to those beings. Thus, for example, when someone did not succeed in an enterprise, or when a harvest was poor, it was said that a fay wanted to harm you or than an enchanter was your enemy.

King Beta, called thus because he had chosen for a name the second letter of the Greek alphabet, was not an imbecile; he maintained those ideas in the mind of his people in order to keep them under his thumb. Whatever the belief might be, when people have faith they are easy to direct; it is by their faith that they are led. Furthermore, by virtue of imposing them on his subjects, the king believed in those invisible beings and occult powers himself, and no one could have taken away from him the idea that a fay—a benevolent fay—had

---

[19] As well as being the second letter of the Greek alphabet, *Béta* [Beta] is also used in French, familiarly, to denote a stupid person, as if derived from the adjective *bête*; thus *Bétasse* would mean a stupid woman. King Béta, along with his wife Bétasse, his daughter Bétinette and an astrologer named Remplumé [fledged, or, more familiarly, perked up], had previously featured in *Le Mariage de Bétinette* (1896), a shadow-play written for Lemercier's puppet theater. That story ends with Bétinette's marriage to Prince Pathos.

presided over the birth of his daughter in giving her beauty, mildness, intelligence and grace: in a word, all the qualities that are generally the prerogative of princesses.

Queen Betasse further exaggerated the naïve beliefs of her royal spouse, but Princess Betinette, his daughter, was less superstitious. She had a positive mind that liked to take account of everything and for which, in consequence, fays and enchanters did not exist. That incredulity desolated the king, and, in order to oppose it he had often begged his great astrologer, Remplume, to work some magic, but the latter, who was nothing but an ass, to put it in three letters, had never been able to do it.

One day, as the royal family and the astrologer were strolling in the gardens of the palace, they perceived a black dot in the air, which was advancing slowly and visibly growing.

"What's that?" said the king, turning to Remplume.

"My word, Sire, I don't know. It's the first time I've seen such a phenomenon."

"Go fetch your telescope, and hurry."

Remplume drew away as rapidly as his aged legs would permit, and came back with his instrument, which he immediately aimed at the unknown object.

"Well," said the king.

"It's a star! A new star!"

"A star!" cried the princess, immediately, bursting into laughter. "A black star!"

"My word, it's not a star, it's a world," said Remplume.

The balloon—for, as you strongly suspected, it was a balloon—came down quite rapidly.

"Let me see," said Princess Betinette, taking the astrologer's telescope. "Yes, it's a world, a peculiar world that is approaching ours. It's very curious. And furthermore, it's inhabited—at least, I can see an animate being in a little basket suspended under the sphere, who gives the impression of conducting it."

King Beta, wonderstruck, took the telescope in his turn.

"Indeed, it is a world that is coming to meet ours. Well, Remplume, my friend, explain that to us."

"That's easy," said the astrologer. "The individual up there is an antisocial person who does a great deal of harm on the ground. He's probably an enchanter who has been condemned to live alone on a world expressly created for him, in order that he can't hurt anybody."

"But he's heading directly here," said the king, who had not quit the telescope. "In a few minutes he'll come down in the gardens. If, as you say, he's a malevolent individual, I don't want him to corrupt my people, and the first thing to do is to make sure of his person. Go inform my guards."

"Why do that, Father?" said Princess Betinette. "Isn't it better to practice generous hospitality? What Remplume has said to you about that world and its inhabitant is only a supposition. Moreover, that world is very small; might it not rather be a flying machine directed by a scholar? Before deciding anything, it would be wiser and more appropriate to give him a good welcome and question him."

"In fact," said the king, "my daughter is right. In any case, what do we have to fear? He's alone, and we'll be able to reckon with him quickly if he gives evidence of the slightest hostility."

During that brief conversation, the balloon completed its precise descent into the royal garden. It was then evident that the unknown world was only an empty sphere, which deflated when it touched the ground, and that the aeronaut did not have the malevolent appearance suggested by Remplume. On the contrary, he apologized right away for the slight damage that he had done and asked for permission to store in a safe place his instruments and his balloon, which he had just folded up carefully.

Reassured by his benevolent appearance, the king hastened to defer to his desire, and invited him to go into the palace with him, which the aeronaut accepted to do with alacrity.

*II. In which the engineer Vatenlair makes the acquaint-
ance of King Beta, and also Princess Betinette.*

The aeronaut was a man of about thirty, with an agreeable face that denoted intelligence. He was a distinguished engineer who, after ardent scientific studies, had devoted himself
specifically to the direction of balloons. Very audacious, he
had made several ascensions of long duration, and the latest
one had had for its objective the discovery of the pole, but
contrary currents had brought it to the realm of King Beta,
which was completely unknown to him. His name was
Vatenlair and he was an associate member of all the scientific
academies in the world.

As he took him to his palace, the king said to him: "I
hope that you won't refuse to be my guest for a few days, and
that you'll be good enough to recount your adventures to me.
We rarely have the opportunity to see strangers and we're glad
to give them a good welcome.

At that moment, Remplume pulled a face and whispered
to the king: "You're going too far, Sire; you don't know him."

"That's my concern," said the king. "Go up to your ob-
servatory and keep your reflections to yourself. Shouldn't you
have announced the advent of this stranger to me?"

Remplume was already going away, piteously, when the
king called him back. "At the same time, have the blue room
prepared, and give the order for all the traveler's baggage to
be installed there."

Having arrived on the threshold of the palace, the royal
family left the stranger to occupy himself with his installation
and withdrew to their apartments. For his part, the aeronaut,
preceded by a valet, went to the room that had been prepared
for him, put away all the instruments that his nacelle had contained, and put on a costume more appropriate than the one he
wore while traveling.

As he finished dressing, someone came to inform him
that the king would give him an audience.

The king! So he was in the home of the king of the country! He looked at his costume: his jacket was very casual, but after all, he had no other; he excused himself.

The throne room was situated on the first floor of the palace. It was an ordinary drawing room—very ordinary, in fact, for King Beta did not like ostentation. The furniture consisted of chairs and armchairs upholstered in tapestry, the work of Queen Betasse and Princess Betinette. As for the throne, it merits particular mention: it was a very large armchair, the back of which rose a long way into the air and supported a sort of awning, just like the pulpits of our churches. The seat was covered with drapes that fell all the way to the floor and hid a little cupboard in which the king put his crown—for King Beta only gave audiences with the crown on his head; he said that the ornament in question was the unique sign of royalty, that without a crown, a king was only a man like any other, and nothing distinguished him from his subjects. When he wanted to retain his incognito, he left his crown in the palace, and if anyone encountered him they had no need to salute him.

In fact, he had several crowns, which he changed in accordance with the ceremonies over which he was presiding and the importance of the people he was receiving. Firstly, there was the great crown ornamented with precious stones, for solemn audiences; then there was the half-crown, not as tall, for minor receptions; and finally, the ordinary crown, a simple gold circlet, for intimacy. Everyone in the realm knew that if you said that the king had received you in his gold circlet, you were considered to be his favorite. It was that one that the king put on his head to receive the aeronaut. Remplume, who was jealous by nature, tried to oppose it, under the pretext that a stranger did not merit that favor, but Princess Betinette, who had acquired a sudden sympathy for the stranger, had persuaded her father not to follow the astrologer's advice.

When the aeronaut was introduced into the audience hall he found King Beta on his throne, with his wife, Queen

Betasse, to his right and his daughter, Princess Betinette, to his left. Remplume was sitting in a corner on a stool.

"I permit you to sit down, for you must be tired," said the king. "What is your name, and who are you?"

"My name is Vatenlair, and I'm an engineer," said the aeronaut.

The brevity of that reply shocked Remplume, who combined the function of astrologer with that of Head of Protocol. He approached Vatenlair and said to him: "You are in the presence of King Beta, Queen Betasse and Princess Betinette; you ought to be more respectful; don't forget that."

"And don't you forget that I'm wearing my gold circlet," said the king, annoyed by Remplume's observation. The latter went back to his stool.

"And by what hazard do you find yourself in our country?" the king went on.

"Hazard is the word," replied Vatenlair, "for your country is unknown to me and I didn't expect to land here."

Remplume thought that he ought to intervene again. "When one speaks to a Majesty, one employs the third person," he said to Vatenlair.

King Beta frowned. He stood up, opened the little cupboard under his seat, deposited the gold circlet therein and sat down again.

"Now I've taken off the sign of power, Remplume, you no longer have anything to do here. Give me the pleasure of leaving us in peace."

Very vexed, Remplume withdrew, murmuring: "What a sovereign! No prestige! No prestige!"

"Now let's talk," said the king. "You know who I am, I know who you are, but I don't know your adventures yet. Who is the enchanter who led you to my Estates? Who is the fay who directed you toward us?"

The king's imagery made Vatenlair smile. "That fay is science," he said, "and the enchanter is the wind. We haven't yet entirely mastered the direction of balloons, and they carry you somewhat at adventure."

"Balloons?" said the king.

"Balloons?" said the queen.

"Balloons?" said the princess.

Vatenlair understood immediately that balloons were unknown in King Beta's realm, and started to explain the theory of the flying machine. That was not very easy, for the ignorance of his listeners was considerable. As the explanation went on, interruptions succeeded one another and the responses were not always understood, Vatenlair recommenced then, but without any more result. In order to put an end to it, King Beta proposed bringing Remplume back, but Princess Betinette opposed it.

"There's no point," she said. "He's even more ignorant than we are. But if you wish, Father, during his stay with us, Monsieur Vatenlair can give me a few notions of things we don't know. I'm intelligent, and when I've understood, I'll enable you to understand in my turn."

"I'm at your orders, Princess," said Vatenlair, "but I ought to warn you that you have a great deal to learn: mathematics, physics, chemistry, mechanics..."

"Who are all those fays?" interjected the king.

"They're fays, as you say, for they produce effects that seem supernatural; but will you permit me, Sire, to ask you a question?"

"Speak!"

"You've pronounced the words enchanter and fay several times: are those images, or do you really believe in the existence of those imaginary beings?"

"Imaginary?" said the king. ""But our land is full of them; nothing happens without their intermediation, and during the time that you stay here, it will be easy for you to perceive them."

"I confess that I'll be *enchanted*," said Vatenlair, emphasizing the word, "And if a little fay would like to attach herself to me, I'd be very grateful."

Princess Betinette blushed; perhaps she had understood what the aeronaut meant.

*III. In which Remplume begins to become jealous of the
engineer and the latter amazes the king with a box of
matches.*

Princess Betinette was a pretty young woman twenty
years of age, blonde, with beautiful dark eyes, a slender figure
and an intelligent physiognomy. Many a time she had been
remarked by the princes of neighboring States, who had asked
for her hand, but with her independent character, she only
wanted to marry a man that she loved, and thus far, no one had
been able to touch her heart. In vain the king had proposed one
of his numerous cousins to her: Prince Epsilon, Prince Lambda, and even Prince Omega, who was renowned for his beauty; she had always refused, alleging that each of them had not
been destined or her by the fays who had presided over her
birth. King Beta inclined before the will of the fays, and did
not ask Betinette how she came to know that will.

Every morning, Vatenlair gave her lessons of every kind,
which interested her greatly, and soon put her in a state to
comprehend the most complicated explanations of her professor. Queen Betasse attended these scientific lecturers; she generally went to sleep at the first words, but the master and the
pupil did not perceive that. King Beta was delighted with his
guest, and wanted absolutely to keep him close at hand; he had
even talked about giving him Remplume's functions, the latter
having become increasingly disagreeable, but Vatenlair did
not care for that servitude and preferred to keep his liberty.
However, he did not dissimulate that it was a means for him
not to quit his pupil, to whom he was becoming increasingly
attached; he discovered a more tender sentiment for her than
the one that a professor ought to have. He even sensed that the
young woman experienced something similar for him, without
being aware of it, but she was a princess, what hope could a
poor engineer like him have?

Thus far, he had not quit the king's palace. One day, after lunch, the latter proposed a little stroll around the city, for,

after all, he ought at least to see the capital of his sovereign and friend.

That city, which was named Betaville after its founder, was not opulent. There were no superb monuments to be seen there, no carefully maintained parks, remarkable edifices or exactly aligned highways. It was a town, but an immense town, neat and orderly, which denoted the ease of its inhabitants. Every house was surrounded by a garden, every garden by living hedges, almost always covered in flowers. Nature bore all the expense of that capital ornamentation. Vatenlair could have believed that he was in a Parisian suburb.

They strolled thus until nightfall; it was then that the engineer perceived that the city was only illuminated by oil-lamps. He made that observation to the king.

"But how do you expect it to be illuminated?" said the king. "We have no lighting here except oil. That's sufficiently bright indoors. I admit that in the streets it's a little dull, but what can one do? Oh, if our fays wished...but it's in vain that I've invoked them, none has wanted to respond to my desire."

"But it would be very easy."

"What are you saying?"

"I'm saying that if you give me the necessary money, in a short time, people in your capital will be able to see as clearly by night as by day."

"And you could do that?"

"Certainly."

"And you say that you're not an enchanter?"

"Only an engineer."

"Well, I'll take you at your word. You won't lack the money; go ahead."

"You're giving me *carte blanche?*"

"I'll give you anything you wish. but I want to know what you're going to do!"

"First, I'm going to construct a gas factory; then I'll channel it to all the streets—that will take time, but we'll begin with the principal arteries, especially your palace."

"What! My palace too!"

"Above all."

"And this gas is the same one that you told me was in your balloon?"

"The same one."

"I don't understand at all."

"What does it matter, if you profit from it?"

While chatting thus, they had returned to the palace, where Queen Betasse, troubled by their absence, received them with joy, because she believed that some misfortune had overtaken them.

Meanwhile, Remplume, seeing the increasing favor of Vatenlair, had acquired an aversion to him. Before the aeronaut's arrival, he had been incessantly in the company of the king, who had only seen through his eyes; he had given lessons in astronomy to Princess Betinette—who scarcely listened to them, it is true, but who had considered him to be the foremost scholar in the realm. He had told Queen Betasse's fortune; she believed in the power of cards and the virtue of coffee grounds. Now he was completely neglected, like an object that has ceased to please.

He therefore sought a means of getting rid of that dangerous rival. Vatenlair had already been in the palace or two months, and was not talking about departing. In any case, he thought, how could he leave? His flying machine no longer contained any gas, and there was no means of making any in the kingdom, so he was constrained to remain in perpetuity. What it was necessary to find was a means of putting him in disgrace. Far from the palace, he would no longer be inconvenient, and he, Remplume, would become indispensable again.

He was rolling those thoughts around his head every day without being able to find a solution when the king himself, unwittingly, furnished him with a means of exercising his knavery.

On the evening of the excursion in Betaville, King Beta summoned him. "Remplume," he said, "marvelous things are going to happen here; I regret that it won't be you who ac-

67

complishes them, but you're undoubtedly not as knowledgeable as the stranger to whom I'm giving hospitality. My entire capital is going to be illuminated by gas."

"By gas!"

"Yes, the same gas that the balloon contained."

Irreverently, Remplume burst out laughing. "Oh, Sire! How can you believe that pleasantry? First of all, we don't have any gas here."

"Well, we'll make some."

"You'll make gas? With what?"

"With charcoal."

Remplume was no longer laughing. He thought that the king had gone mad.

"That astonishes you? It's quite simple, though. Vatenlair has explained to me how it's done. One burns charcoal and one collects the gas that escapes from it, and then one directs it through subterranean pipes that end in orifices where one sets fire to it. It's no more difficult than that. We're going to be illuminated without oil and without wicks."

"My word, Sire, excuse my frankness, but I'll believe that when I see it."

"And that will be soon. I order you to put at Vatenlair's disposal all the money that he asks for. Then you'll give me the pleasure of hiring two or three hundred workmen that he needs, and you'll give the order in my name to surrender to him the uncultivated land at the far end of my park and confined in the outlying districts of my capital."

Remplume inclined sadly. "May you not by the victim of your credulity, Sire."

"My credulity!" cried the king. "What do you mean?"

"I mean, and I dare say it, out of affection for you, that the stranger wants to put one over on you. In fact, if he wants to make gas, assuming that he can, it's for no other motive than to reinflate his flying machine and quit you as rapidly as he arrived; but I don't believe that he'll achieve his objective. What is more serious is the personnel that you're putting at his orders: three hundred workmen constitute a small army, of which he'll be the leader. He's ambitious; he might make use of it, and you'll have introduced the enemy into the place."

That shrewd idea had an impact on the king, who was very jealous of his power; he became anxious and began to reflect.

During that conversation, night had fallen and they had not seen Vatenlair come into the room.

"Light the lamps," said the king. "I don't like to stay in the dark."

"I'll go fetch my flint, Sire."

"There's no need," said Vatenlair, coming forward. "This will replace it." And, taking a box of matches out of his pocket, he struck one, which immediately caught fire.

As soon as the lamps were lit, to the great satisfaction of the king and the astrologer, the latter said: "Is it still necessary to carry out Your Majesty's orders?"

"Do as I told you!" replied the king.

The instantaneous lighting of the match, as yet unknown in his realm, had made such an impression on the king that he had returned to his first opinion regarding Vatenlair, and, considering him from then on to be an enchanter, he was afraid of irritating him by not keeping the promises that he had made to him.

IV. In which we make the acquaintance of Prince Omega and the engineer fascinates Princess Betinette

The work on the gas factory progressed rapidly, thanks to the numerous workmen placed at Vatenlair's disposal. The king came to visit them from time to time, and his presence encouraged the workmen. Remplume also came occasionally to cast an envious eye over it, but he dared not make any observation on what he called squandering, although he desired that the factory be constructed promptly in order to see it functioning, for he still believed that the engineer would not obtain any result and that his defeat would be the signal for his disgrace.

In the meantime, King Beta was informed that his nephew Omega was on his way to pay him a visit. That news filled him with joy, for he had not despaired of persuading his daughter to marry him.

He's young and he's handsome, he said to himself. *When she's seen him, she won't be able to help loving him.*

He therefore announced that visit to Vatenlair, and begged him to hasten the work so that they would be concluded in a month, in time for his nephew's arrival.

Although the deadline was short, Vatenlair promised him that in a month, the royal palace, at the very least, would be completely illuminated by gas—which caused the sovereign to rejoice.

We have not described the palace, because it was not worth the trouble; it was a vast building devoid of architecture, flanked by two large square towers that were set back from the lawn of the gardens. Vatenlair was lodged in one, on the second floor, and Princess Betinette's apartments were in the other. Often, when he opened his window in the morning, he exchanged a salute with the princess, who always got up early herself, liking to respire the fresh air embalmed by the gardens. After that respectful salute, they had the custom of withdrawing discreetly, and he cursed fate for having caused him to be born in a humble condition that did not permit him to aspire to the hand of a princess. For her part, she said to herself that it was a great pity that a man she had remarked as much for his face as for his intelligence was not a prince, and, inconsequence, could not cast his eyes upon her, which was the greatest desire of her heart.

One day, however, as they were both at their windows, the engineer, delighted to see her, forgot to withdraw, and gazed at her fixedly. During that ecstasy, he took himself back to the day when, quitting his balloon, he had seen her for the first time, and he reminded himself that he had often visited that spot in the park, as if he might encounter her there, and that he would be glad if he could suggest to her that she go there.

Before that persistent gaze, the princess went pale and quit the window, but he soon saw her crossing the lawn and drawing away into the gardens. Vatenlair immediately had the idea that she had obeyed his suggestion; desirous of making sure of it, he went down in his turn and plunged into the park.

When he reached the place designated by his thought, he found the princess waiting for him.

"You wanted me to come here," she said. "Here I am."

Glad of the power that he had over her, Vatenlair did not think of abusing it; the experiment had succeeded, that was sufficient. Everything that he had wished and might say to her during her magnetic sleep would have been forgotten when she woke up, so there was no point in showing her the state of his heart. With a gesture, he obliged her to return to her apartment, and continued his walk, thinking about the discovery that he had just made and the results to which it might lead. That the princess loved him he had no doubt, but her quality as a medium had been revealed to him, and that might be a great help in that land of superstition.

When he saw the princess again at the morning lesson, she had her usual grace and amiability; she did not remember anything.

Meanwhile the factory was constructed; the work of canalization in the palace was concluded, and the trials were about to begin.

When the gas was lit for the first time, King Beta was stunned by admiration; he never ceased gazing at the flame, blue at first, then sparkling, and saying that Vatenlair was a genius. The genius of Fire!

Princess Betinette, for her part, while admiring the illumination that she had never seen before, seemed proud of the engineer's success. He had taught her his methods, and, although not doubting their success, she had seen their application with joy; so, in a spontaneous impulse, she forgot herself and squeezed both his hands, directly in front of Remplume, who murmured: "It's high time that Prince Omega arrived;

that little fool is capable of compromising herself, and perhaps the king might not recoil before such a misalliance."

Two days later, Prince Omega made his entrance into King Beta's capital. All morning, Princess Betinette had been in a bad mood, which caused chagrin to her father, and especially her mother, who wanted to have Prince Omega as a son-in-law.

Vatenlair, to whom the queen revealed her discontentment, reassured her. "It's a young woman's caprice," he said, "which won't last. You'll see that when she's seen the prince, she'll find him charming."

"Oh, as for that, no!" said Betinette, who had overheard the engineer's reply. "My cousin is an imbecile and a fop, and I'll never love such a man. So don't ask me to put on a good face..."

But, Vatenlair having employed his suggestive power on her, she added: "...unless he's changed a great deal and I discover qualities in him."

Prince Omega was a lady-killer, twenty-six years old. He was tall and strong; his regular face was insignificant, but he had a conceited and disdainful expression. His blond hair was curly, his long moustaches were turned up at the ends and waxed; he wore a monocle in his eye constantly, and swung his hips as he walked with a supreme impertinence.

He arrived on horseback, for he was a very good rider, followed by a group of squires clad in magnificent costumes. A guard of honor came next, and the cortege was terminated by numerous servants leading the gifts destined for King Beta, which were animals of all sorts: enchained lions, tigers, elephants, giraffes, monkeys, parrots, and even eagles and falcons in immense cages.

All that filed past the perron of the royal castle, where King Beta has had his throne set up between the seats of Queen Betasse and Princess Betinette.

After having made his horse prance, Prince Omega dismounted and bent his knee before the king, after which he kissed the hands of Queen Betasse and Princess Betinette. At that moment, as the princess frowned, Vatenlair suggested that she smile prettily at the prince, who dropped his monocle in satisfaction.

V. In which King Beta gives a grand ball and the engineer is the target of Remplume's malevolence

That evening, in order to honor his nephew and also to inaugurate the new lighting, King Beta gave a great ball. All the nobility of the country was invited; even the bourgeoisie was authorized to visit the gardens, which were, of course, illumined.

The dancing commenced at about ten o'clock in the evening. Prince Omega opened the ball with Princess Betinette. He was wearing a crimson velvet doublet with white satin slashes in the sleeves; on his blond hair, curlier than ever, stood a toque ornamented with ostrich plumes, retained by a clasp of diamonds and rubies; his stockings were pearl gray and his sharply pointed deerskin shoes were glittering with golden buckles studded with precious stones. A little dagger was attached to his belt, which was fine gold. He would have looked very good if he had not been wearing his inseparable monocle, which rendered him ridiculous.

Princes Betinette was no less richly clad. Her dress was made of woven silver thread and embroidered with scarabs; her hair was powdered with diamond dust, and a necklace of seven rows of the finest pearls was around her neck. She was ravishing thus.

The king's costume was all in gold. He was wearing his ceremonial crown, the diamonds and precious stones of which were sparkling, and, although it inconvenienced him greatly, he had not wanted to separate it from his solid gold scepter, which was very heavy. His royal mantle, of white satin lined with ermine, hung over his shoulders, under which he was stifling.

Queen Betasse was wearing a violet satin dress embroidered with all sorts of flowers; she too was wearing a golden crown, on which a bird of paradise was balanced.

Vatenlair, who had been obliged to adopt the costume of the land, had a doublet and footwear of black velvet, with a small toque in the same fabric and the same color, surmounted by a flame-colored plume. One might have thought: Mephistopheles.

Princess Betinette looked at him incessantly, and paid no attention to Prince Omega.

As for Remplume, he had put on the uniform of his employment, which is to say, a long black robe on which the constellations, the Moon and the Sun were embroidered, and coiffed in a pointed hat in the form of a long cone. He did not have his usual surly expression; on the contrary, his face seemed radiant, Vatenlair only remarked that he praised the illumination in an immoderate fashion. That enthusiasm seemed so suspect to him that he left the hall briefly in order to visit the meter and the switches of the canalization, but everything seemed to be in order and he hastened to return, for fear that the king might have had need of him during his absence.

In the ball, Princess Betinette won the admiration of everyone; her grace was well known, but her intelligence less so, for she did not like to talk much; so, when the great dignitaries were admitted to pay their respects to her and she replied to their compliments, they were delighted with her slightest remarks, with they found full of tact, good taste and even malice, for she was not embarrassed to make a few quips about Prince Omega and about Remplume, whom no one liked. On the other hand, she never ceased to heap praise on Vatenlair, whom she called a superior intelligence.

When she danced the minuet with Prince Omega, the latter tried to pay her a few insipid compliments.

"There is no fay comparable to you, beautiful princess," he said, "and I would be the most fortunate of mortals if I were able to touch your heart."

"I don't believe a word of it," she replied, "and I'm sure that you wouldn't make the slightest sacrifice for me."

"Speak, Princess! I'm in haste to know what you desire. Is it necessary to fight monsters? To lift mountains? Dry up seas? Say the words and I will…"

The princess interrupted him, laughing. "Oh, I don't ask so much. Merely remove your eyeglass!"

Prince Omega could see that she was making fun of him, but he allowed his monocle to slip from his eye. As he was genuinely myopic, however, when he bent his leg making reverences, he tripped over the princess's train and fell full length on the floor.

That unexpected fall put the princess in such a good humor that she was gripped by mad laughter, immediately imitated by all the courtiers eager to share the joy of the king's daughter.

Prince Omega was furious at his clumsiness; he excused himself as best he could and, after the dance, withdrew to one side. Remplume hastened to join him, and murmured to him: "Don't despair, Prince; that fall is a good augury for you; he who falls will rise again."

That little incident had no consequence. The dancing resumed, more ardently; refreshments circulated and the joy was at its peak.

Suddenly, at the very moment when midnight chimed on the great clock of the royal palace, the gas went out abruptly and the gardens and the ballroom were plunged into the profoundest obscurity.

Then there were cries of fright and an incredible confusion. Everyone wanted to get out the same time. Some people opened windows and, as the ballroom was on the ground floor, hoisted themselves up and jumped down into the gardens.

Princess Betinette had fainted, but Vatenlair, who had not lost sight of her, was able to reach her and lavish cares upon her. For his part, the king hastened to the queen, who had an attack of nerves, Prince Omega, who, on the advice of Remplume, had taken up a position near one of the exit doors a few minutes before, had run out first, without worrying about anyone else.

Only Remplume, calm, and smiling, strove to retain the guests, saying that he had ordered lamps and that there was no need to be afraid.

In fact, a host of servants was soon seen, carrying lamps, entering the ballroom and repairing the inconceivable accident as much as possible. The light immediately calmed the frightened crowd, the ladies adjusted their crumpled dresses, the cavaliers hastened around them, and the fête recommenced, but without enthusiasm.

On hearing Vatenlair's voice, Princess Betinette had immediately come round; they both profited from the obscurity to exchange a few words. Vatenlair explained to her that it was not an accident, but a criminal action committed by one of his enemies; the next day, he would visit the factory and discover what had occurred.

The king, having calmed the queen down, had her taken back to her apartments and, as befitted a sovereign, manifested the greatest self-control. He announced that the queen, slightly upset, had retired, but that he would remain in the midst of his faithful subjects and, in spite of his great age, would even dance a gavotte. At the same moment he went to take the hand of Duchess Potron-Minette, who almost died of joy at such an honor.

In the gardens, the bourgeois crowd was less surprised; its members thought that the illuminations had been due to finish at that moment, and returned tranquilly to Betaville, delighted by the evening.

But the king's efforts were in vain; the shock had been too great. The ball dragged on, but people no longer had any desire to amuse themselves, and when the time came for supper, many people had departed and those who remained were only nibbling.

When there was no one left, the king approached Vatenlair and said to him, in a severe tone: "Until tomorrow, Monsieur Engineer!"

VI. In which the engineer takes his revenge and puts Remplume in disgrace.

Vatenlair did not sleep all night. As soon as first light he went to the factory to take account of what might have happened. As in the palace, he found everything in order; there was no lack of charcoal, the fires had not gone out and the apparatus was intact. He had thought of leaks, of pipes blocked or intentionally cut, but that would have led to explosions, and there had not been any. It was necessary to look in another direction, and at was where he should have begun. He summoned the chief of the factory and interrogated him.

"At what time did you cut off the gas supply to the palace?"

"At midnight."

"Who gave you that order?"

"A servant from the palace, who came on behalf of the king."

"Very well. But the king only gives orders in writing or through the intermediary of a senior responsible functionary. You should only follow my instructions. Don't forget that in future."

Evidently, as he had suspected, the previous night's incident had been due to malevolence; it was the work of an enemy, but who was that enemy? He immediately thought of Remplume, whose hostility was visible, but he needed to be sure.

He returned to the palace, very preoccupied.

When he went into the room where he gave his lessons to the princess she was already there, and waiting for him impatiently

"Well," he said, "as I thought, I'm the victim of the operations of an unknown enemy. What happened last night resulted from an order given to my workmen without my knowledge; now it's a matter of discovering the guilty party."

"Distrust Remplume," said the princess.

"It's doubtless him," said Vatenlair, "who had the order given in the king's name, but he carefully refrained from giving it himself. How can I accuse him if I have no proof? Who is the servant he employed? If I interrogate them all, they'll deny it."

"That's true," said the princess, "but there's a means of discovering the truth. I'm your pupil, my dear professor; you've already taught me many things and you'll teach me many more; in my turn, I'll give you some advice. In bring all the marvels of science to this country, you've attributed all the merit thereto, as is only just; you've effaced yourself before it, and that's a mistake. We're too naïve and too ignorant here to understand and appreciate you as you deserve. Here, everything that is out of the ordinary belongs to the domain of the supernatural. At first you were thought to be an enchanter, and you rejected that appellation; then, in the eyes of everyone, you're only a man like any other, subject to error, impotent and, in the present case, you'll be taken for an impostor. It's necessary to avoid that. Don't hesitate any longer to satisfy the taste that people have for the marvelous; be audacious and tell my father loudly that you're an enchanter, sent to him by the superior powers to protect him and render him illustrious. Tell him that your mission is secret, and that's why you wanted to keep your incognito, that you know that you're the target of malevolence but that you let it take its course in order to confound your enemy and thus demonstrate your power. Above all, don't talk science; here, people don't understand it and don't believe in it."

"Yes, you're right, Princess, but all my science won't give me the means to confound Remplume."

"Think! Cunning will suffice. As for me, I'll go to interrogate all the palace servants adroitly, and I'll find out who took the order to the factory."

During that conversation, another was taking place in the king's cabinet.

Remplume said to him: "I told you so, Sire; that stranger has come to bring trouble into your kingdom with all his inventions, which signify nothing and are in any case incomplete."

"But you can't deny that the gas burned, at least until midnight."

"That's true; but the invention is impracticable, since it was extinguished at the moment when there was the greatest need for it. No, the scholar isn't a scholar; he isn't even an enchanter, as you seem to believe, for he would then have been able to repair the misadventure immediately—which I foresaw, for I had the lamps prepared in case of need. I tell you, Sire, this engineer, as he calls himself, is simply ingenious and all that he has found in a means to procure gas in order to reinflate his machine and depart as soon as possible. In your place I'd engage him to do so, and we'll be rid of him."

"Perhaps you're right," said the king, who almost always followed the last advice he was given. "I'll summon him and tell him to go away. Leave it to me."

Remplume went out, smiling, believing that this time, he had reckoned with the foreigner.

In his turn, Vatenlair went into the king's cabinet. He was still wearing his costume of the evening before, which gave him a fantastic appearance. He advanced proudly, and before the king was able to interrogate him, he said to him: "Before answering the questions that you're going to put to me, Sire, it's necessary that I reveal who I really am before I had the intention of doing so. As you have divined, I'm an enchanter, and if my experiment yesterday did not succeed completely, it's because I wanted it to fail, in order to have a pretext to show you the enemies who surround your throne."

"I don't know whether I have enemies," said the king, "But in any case, I doubt very much that you're an enchanter, because, strange as yesterday's illumination seemed to me, it's truly too incomplete to emanate from a superior power."

"Well, Sire, since you deny my power, I'll give you a further proof by telling you what my goal is in coming here."

"I wouldn't be sorry to know that, in fact."

"You are a great king; you render your people happy. One cannot say as much about all kings. You are, furthermore, one of the last believers in supernatural beings: fays, genii, giants, monsters, and I would even add enchanters if you hadn't cast doubt on my power just now. But that doubt won't last long. I have been charged by the king of the genii, to come to you in order to recompense you in a striking fashion for your faith in him. My mission is to prepare your daughter, Princess Betinette, to become a fay. The lessons I am giving her are gradually developing that faculty in her. Soon, knowing everything, she will be able to foresee everything and forestall everything. She will see the invisible and know the future. For the moment, she is only initiated in the knowledge of the past and the present."

"If what you're telling me is true," said the king, "I'll ask her right away what the cause of last night's event was. I'll send for her."

"There's no need, Sire; at this moment she is leaving her apartment and heading toward you."

As he spoke, Vatenlair extended his arm in the direction of the door, which immediately opened, and allowed Princess Betinette to enter.

She was walking in an automatic fashion, her eyes wide open and staring.

"Interrogate her," said Vatenlair.

The king, visibly troubled, asked the question: "Why did the gas go out by itself last night at midnight?"

"Because you gave the order."

"Me!" cried the king. "I didn't give any order."

"Send for the director of the factory," said Vatenlair. "You'll see that she's telling the truth."

"It is a palace servant," the princess continued, "who gave a verbal order on your behalf, but it was your astrologer who told him to act thus."

"Remplume? I'll interrogate him."

"He'll deny it," said Vatenlair.

"No!" said the princess. "You have only to say to him that Briquet has confessed everything."

"Briquet! The palfreyman?"

"The same."

"Oh! Well, if that's true, I'll give myself the pleasure of confounding him before you."

And the king had Remplume come back.

On seeing the princess and Vatenlair beside the king, Remplume grimaced. Had his ruse been discovered? *It's impossible*, he thought. He had not taken anyone into his confidence except Briquet, who believed that he was carrying an order from the king, and Briquet had promised to keep quiet.

"Well," said the king, who now had confidence in Vatenlair again, "it seems, my poor Remplume, that you're very zealous."

"I cannot do too much for Your Majesty."

"Perhaps you're wrong. Zeal isn't devotion. What gave you the idea that I wanted the gas extinguished at midnight?"

"But I didn't have that idea, Sire!"

"Really! Then what has Briquet told me?"

At that name, Remplume believed himself doomed. He threw himself at the king's knees, admitted everything, begged for mercy, and was as pitiful as sight as possible.

"Get up," said the king. "I'm dismissing you. You've deceived your master. I shall give you an exemplary punishment, but no rigor will equal the extent of your treason. Get out!"

The astrologer, bent double, withdrew.

"Now that justice is rendered," said Vatenlair, "it's necessary, Sire, to promise me silence with regard to the confidence that I've made you. No one must know that I'm an enchanter and that your daughter is going to be a fay, for the progress that I am bringing to your kingdom ought, in the eyes of everyone, to originate from your great intelligence. In a monarchy, everything belongs to the king. In a little while, you'll see many other marvels; they will be attributed to you.

It's necessary that your reign will be illustrious, and that your people, already happy thanks to you, will also be proud to have you for their king."

At that moment, Vatenlair, darting a glance at Princess Betinette, liberated her from the suggestion under the influence of which she was acting, and the king, moved, covered her with kisses and tears.

Vatenlair no longer had any fear of his enemies.

VII. In which Princess Betinette makes fun of Prince Omega and King Beta occupies himself with horticulture.

A few days later, the court was transported to the summer palace, which was situated in the middle of woods two leagues from the capital. Vatenlair, who had undertaken new works in his factory, asked the king for permission to remain in the winter palace in order to supervise them. He had, in fact, installed workshops of electricity and mechanics, in which new instruments would be manufactured, previously unknown in the country.

Princess Betinette was very annoyed by Vatenlair's resolution, and did not hide the fact.

"How do you think," she said to him, "that I can fulfill the role of fay that you have attributed to me, if you're not there? I know my father; he'll want to test my power, and I'll be incapable of satisfying him."

"It's the same for me, Princess; if I neglect the preparation of new surprises, the king will no longer believe in my power. But I won't leave you disarmed. This is a little apparatus that I brought with me in the balloon, and has the purpose of reproducing objects that are placed in front of it, in as great a quantity as one desires. I'll teach you to make use of it, and your prestige will remain intact with regard to your father. Within a week you'll be able to use it as well as I can."

"Your presence is more agreeable to me," said the princess.

"And to me. Believe me, princess, I'll suffer from your absence, all the more so because Prince Omega will be assiduous in your presence."

"Don't take umbrage! That ridiculous fop ought not to render you jealous. I've already told my father that I don't want to marry him, and that, in consequence, he shouldn't have authorized him to make his request, but my father is weak; he doesn't want to quarrel with his nephew and he daren't upset me. He'll temporize."

"Let's do the same, and all will end well. In any case, every week I'll come to spend a day at the summer palace and you can bring me up to date with what is happening there."

Life in the summer palace was rather monotonous. Queen Betasse, who was still ill, did not want to see anyone, and King Beta, who had a passion for flowers, spent all day in his gardens, grafting, producing buds and scolding his gardeners, whom he accused of doing nothing to his liking. Princess Betinette thus found herself in the company of Prince Omega, who paid very assiduous court to her and stunned her with his insipid chatter. He was, moreover, an utter blockhead; apart from horses and dogs, he knew nothing; he never read anything and hardly thought. Every morning he mounted his horses and asked the princess to do him the favor of accompanying him, but she always refused, under the pretext of continuing her studies. He therefore set forth alone, and did not come back again until the time of the midday meal. The princess immediately felt relieved of a presence that harassed her. She went out in her turn, on foot and, equipped with her apparatus, she went to capture the picturesque sites in the locale, taking care not to be followed in her artistic excursions.

After the meal, the queen went to take her habitual siesta, the king returned to his flowers and she went into the drawing room to run her fingers over her piano, for she was a good musician. Prince Omega followed her then, and, his monocle always in his eye, fell into admiration at every piece she played.

"What a talent you have, Princess. No artiste can compete with you!"

Those compliments, spoken in a pretentious fashion, wearied her, and she often put an end to them by closing the instrument and taking refuge in her room.

One day, however, she replied: "What about you, Prince? Since you can't play music, have you at least some pleasing talent?"

"I believe I ride a horse rather well," said the prince.

"That's not a talent."

"Well, Princess, in my youth I learned to draw, and even had a certain aptitude for it. I think that, if I went back to it, I could produce a water-color quite neatly."

"Really" said the princess. "If you wanted to be agreeable to me you'd make me one that I'd have pleasure in keeping. My father's château is rather picturesque; I'd be glad to have an image of it."

"Oh, Princess, you see me desolate at being unable to satisfy you, but I only do faces."

"Well, I consent to be your model. When is the first sitting?"

"Tomorrow, if you wish, Princess, after lunch."

"So be it. Tomorrow!"

To tell the truth, Prince Omega did not know a great deal about drawing; the ones he had made during his studies had always been retouched by his masters, but his vanity had enabled him to believe that they were entirely his. He thus found himself caught in a trap and forced to put on a brave face.

The princess had also fallen into the trap she had set; now she no long had a pretext for getting rid of her importunate suitor. She regretted her improvidence.

When the king learned that Prince Omega was going to paint a portrait of his daughter, he was delighted, and wanted her to pose costumed as a fay, in a white dress with a wand in her hand and a crown of stars on her head.

The sittings commenced. Straight away, the Princess perceived that the Prince was a complete novice in the art of drawing and that he would never succeed in reproducing her face; she rejoiced in that, for his failure would be one more weapon against him; King Beta would certainly not pardon him for his lack of success.

After ten sittings the prince had not yet sketched the face, and the king, who came from time to time to see how the portrait was coming along, was beginning to show signs of discontentment.

It was at that moment that Vatenlair, who had not come the previous week, made his first visit to the summer palace. The princess immediately brought him up to date with the situation.

"Well," said Vatenlair, "that's working our marvelously. Have a little more patience; Prince Omega will continue his daubing and your father will weary of it. Then it will be easy for you to cease your sittings and you'll be liberated from your suitor, who will be convicted of conceit and ineptitude. You can then make use of your apparatus to show your father that, without having been taught, you can be more skillful than the prince, and the king will be amazed, and attribute to your magic power an experiment that is purely in the domain of science. Next week, I'll come back to see what has happened. In the meantime, I've been working hard and I'm preparing, in particular, a curious application of photography that will be further proof of my magical power in everyone's eyes."

Prince Omega, invited by the king not to occupy himself with the portrait any longer, had been horribly vexed. He had resumed his early morning rides, momentarily interrupted, and continued them even after lunch, for he dared not find himself alone with the princess after the artistic check that he had suffered.

But those excursions had another objective.

When Remplume had been abruptly dismissed by the king, he had gone to relate his disgrace to Prince Omega, assuring him that it was unjust; that, but for Vatenlair, who decried him everywhere, the king would not have deprived himself thus of a devoted old servant; that his science was misunderstood; and that, finally, he had read in the stars that another prince, equally illustrious, would soon repair King Beta's injustice. Prince Omega, who was no astrologer, thought that he understood that the illustrious prince of whom Remplume was talking was himself. That supposition also flattered his vanity. But, in attaching to his person a servant whom his uncle no longer wanted, would he not displease him? That objection was quickly resolved by Remplume, who consented to fulfill his functions in secret during the prince's sojourn at King Beta's court. It was therefore agreed between them that Remplume would go every day to a designated spot, and that the prince would come to consult him there.

We have said that the princess spent her mornings taking pictures in the environs of the summer palace. One day, therefore, as she was about to aim her objective lens at a picturesque group of rocks, she perceived the prince descending from his horse and Remplume, hidden until then behind a bush, approaching him.

The motif appeared to her to be worth capturing; that was done in an instant, and neither of the two persons perceived her presence. Afterwards, she went back to the palace.

At lunch King Beta displayed an unusual gaiety, which greatly astonished Prince Omega, to whom he had shown a grim face since the adventure of the portrait. Princess Betinette made that observation.

"How cheerful you are today, Father! Has something fortunate occurred?"

"My word, yes," said the king, "I'll tell you, for now I'm on the point of succeeding, I have no more interest in hiding it. On arriving at the summer palace an idea occurred to me to carry out an experiment with seeds. I took a small pea, which I introduced into a haricot bean, and then I put the bean inside a potato, and hid the whole thing in a pot of earth that I put in my greenhouse. To tell the truth, I didn't expect very much from that mixture, and I'd even forgotten to visit it, when this morning, chancing to go past the place where I'd put it, I perceived a green leaf emerging from the soil. I had succeeded!

What will the mixture give me? I don't know yet. Will I have peas that taste like haricot beans and potatoes? Or beans that taste like peas and potatoes? Or, finally, a plant producing potatoes, beans and peas all at the same time? I'll know that in a few more weeks. For the moment, I'm rejoicing in seeing that my seed has germinated. I've created a new species!"

"It will be necessary to call it the royal potato," said Prince Omega.

"Well," said Princess Betinette, "It's necessary that the discovery doesn't remain under a bushel. We'll have it proclaimed throughout the kingdom; we'll have an explanatory notice made with an image of the new plant and a portrait of the king, its inventor." She added, maliciously: "Price Omega can make the portrait of the king!"

The prince grimaced.

"Oh, no," said the king. "If the prince were to draw me, the plant would have grown and withered before he'd begun."

"Well, then," said Betinette, "I'll do it. I only ask a week for that."

"Granted," said the king, "but I'm very busy and I can only give you one sitting."

"I won't need any more," she replied. "In a week, each of you will have a portrait of my father."

"When will it be necessary to pose?" asked the king.

"After the meal. I'll only ask you for a quarter of an hour."

The lunch concluded merrily. The king, who thought that his daughter was joking, teased her slightly by saying that he would be cross if she didn't succeeded, and Prince Omega assured her ironically that he was glad to know that she had a talent that she had hidden from him thus far.

When they had got up from the table, the table, the king said: "Well, daughter, I'm waiting."

"If you'd like to follow me to my apartment," said the princess, "I won't keep you long.

Prince Omega, who had not been invited to go with them, hastened to mount his horse in order to go and met

Remplume and ask him what the princess's boastfulness might signify.

VIII. In which we see a nautical fête in which Prince Omega and the engineer Vatenlair compete.

The place where Prince Omega met Remplume was one of the prettiest and most solitary in the forest. In the midst of green oaks and fire trees, rocks of all forms were heaped up, covered with ivy, moss and climbing plants, which overhung an immense lake, sometimes broad and sometimes so narrow that the crowns of the trees either bank overlapped. It was alimented by the river of Betaville, which, after a thousand detours, came to traverse it in its width and, before continuing its course through open country, activated the wheel of a mill. A few pleasure boats were moored at the foot of the rocks.

While waiting for the prince, Remplume had sat down in one of those skiffs, and was thinking melancholically about his lost position and the unexpected fortune of Vatenlair, for whom he was acquiring an ever-greater animosity. He told himself that he had been maladroit in being jealous, and thought that the engineer was only an ignoramus by comparison with him. He knew the king, he knew that he would never get back into grace and, on the other hand, Prince Omega, being too young, did not appear to him to be serious enough. It was, however, necessary to attach himself in that direction.

The sound of a galloping horse interrupted his reflections. It was the prince. He dismounted and came to find Remplume in the boat.

"Take the oars," said the prince. "I have a lot to tell you today."

"What is it?" Remplume asked.

"I've told you that in order to pay court to Princess Betinette I tried to paint her portrait."

"And you didn't succeed."

"That's true, I thought that it was easier, and the Princess scarcely lent herself to it, but, in sum, it was worth a few conversations with her, which unfortunately ceased because the king no longer wanted me to continue.

"Which is annoying."

"Undoubtedly; all the more so because the princess is avoiding me more and more. I believe that I'm not sympathetic to her."

"It's certain, according to what you tell me, that she doesn't love you yet, but it's necessary not to despair. In any case, the princess adores her father and will always obey him. It's him, above all, that it's necessary to seduce."

"I understand that, so I was profoundly afflicted to see that he no longer wanted the portrait; but there's something else: the princess has boasted that she can make one of the king."

"Does she know how to draw, then?"

"I don't know, but this morning, after lunch, she asked her father to come and pose in her apartment."

"It's a joke, to tease you!"

"No, she said that she'd only keep him for a quarter of an hour and that she'd show him his portrait in a week, and moreover, that she would give a copy to everyone in the court."

"Vatenlair must be behind it," Remplume thought aloud.

"It seems impossible to me," the prince went on. "Can you explain to me how she's going to do it?"

"It's necessary to wait. She might not succeed. I think it's a trick. A portrait of the king! That can be understood in different ways. Instead of drawing, she'll probably employ a stylus and it will be a written portrait, a eulogy of the king describing his physiognomy and simultaneously tracing his qualities."

"Yes, perhaps."

"The king, who loves the marvelous, has been deceived by the fashion in which the princess made him the proposal; that's why he lent himself to it right away, but he'll be disappointed when he sees the results. It will be necessary then to bring him back to you by showing him something extraordinary."

While they were talking thus, the boat had traversed the lake and was now near the mill, whose wheel was turning slowly under the action of the river.

"Something extraordinary!" repeated the prince. "That's easy to say, but what? It's up to you to find that for me. Since you've been in my service you've only given me a few items of advice, which haven't been any use to me."

"You won't make me that reproach any longer," replied Remplume, obstinately watching the mill-wheel. "Yes, it won't be said that Vatenlair has a monopoly on enchantments; we too are going to make the king marvel."

"What are you saying?"

"I'm saying, prince, that I've found it!"

"Found what!"

"You'll see. Tell me, how did I propel this boat to this spot?"

"With oars."

"And what if I found a way to propel a boat without oars?"

"That would be marvelous."

"Yes, it would be marvelous. And I'd eclipse Vatenlair!"

"You're forgetting that it's me who needs to eclipse Vatenlair."

"Pardon me! That's true. So, this invention will be attributed to you."

"But what are you going to do?"

"This. You see that mill? What sets it in motion? It's the wheel pushed by the water. Well, by doing the opposite, I'll arrive at the desired result."

"How's that?"

"We're going to construct a boat, and on its sides we're going to fit two small wheels like those of the mill; then we'll make them turn with the aid of a handle. The wheels, in driving back the water, will make the boat advance with more or less rapidity, depending on the effort one puts into it, and in order to change direction it will be sufficient to slow down the wheel on the right or the left depending on the direction in which one wants to steer. The wheel pushing the water instead of the water pushing the wheel, that's the whole system."

"Yes," said the prince, "That does, in fact, seem very ingenious. Well, let's set to work. Have the boat constructed as quickly as possible."

"It will be ready in time. In September, a few days before the return of the court to the city palace, it's the king's birthday. On that occasion there are regattas on the lake. You'll enter as a competitor and your success will be certain; you'll get back into the king's good graces."

Remplume and the king resumed the route to the rocks where they had embarked, and they separated, both delighted. Remplume, however, was annoyed, deep down, at not being able to attribute the invention to himself, which, he thought, would have put an end to his disgrace and put Vatenlair in the shade.

In the meantime, Vatenlair was entirely devoted to the organization of his workshops. The terrain that the king had given him was vast, and he had created a little industrial city there, in which all the métiers were represented; joiners, carpenters, smiths, founders, mechanics, electricians, etc. flowed into his vast workshops, where powerful motive forces activated machines of all sorts. He had had difficulty training that personnel, composed of at least twelve hundred people, but he had succeeded in it by dint of firmness and generosity. All his workers loved him and defended him with regard to a few malcontents that he had sacked spoke ill of him.

One day, one of them, a joiner named Rabotin[20] come to find him and said: "Monsieur Vatenlair, I have something to ask you."

"Speak, my lad."

---

[20] A rabotin is a plane used for smoothing wood.

"Well, if it's an effect of your generosity, I'd like to take a leave."

"A leave! You know that we have a great deal of work at this moment, but, after all, if it's necessary for you to absent yourself, I'll permit it."

"Thank you, Monsieur Vatenlair, but aren't you going to ask me why I'm absenting myself?"

"That's your business."

"It's just that I don't want you to be discontented with me, and I'll tell you everything. Someone came to bring me a commission; I don't want to accept it if it displeases you, and, on the other hand, in order to carry it out, it's necessary for me to ask you for a leave."

"You've done well not to accept it without talking to me. It's not customary to quit the work of one's employer in order to work for someone else, when there's no shortage of work. But I like your frankness. What is this commission?"

"A boat. In the month of September it's the king's birthday; then there are regattas on the lake of the summer palace, and someone has come to ask me to construct a special boat. Here's the plan."

"Well, well! A paddle-boat with handles. And who has ordered that?"

"Monsieur Remplume, for Prince Omega."

"Aha! He wants to compete, then, Prince Omega?"

"Probably."

"Well, I give you permission to absent yourself, and I'll even, in order to go more quickly, send a few companions with you, but it's necessary to hurry, for you're a little slow and I'll have need of you to construct a boat for me too, because I want to compete with the prince."

That idea had suddenly occurred to Vatenlair. Remplume's invention did not alarm him greatly; he counted on being able to offer a much more marvelous vessel.

A few days later, the greatest activity reigned in the workshop of the mechanics and electricians.

The month of September arrived; it was the eve of the king's birthday. The lake was surrounded by masts with pennants. A stand had been erected on the shore, at the foot of the rocks; there the members of the royal family were to be placed, as well as the principal dignitaries.

It s necessary to say here that what are called regattas in Betaville are not, as in our country, races of rowing or sailing boats, but rather a competition in which the prettiest and most ingenious vessels win the prizes. All kinds of them were presented, in accordance with the fortune and the imagination of their constructors, and the spectacle of all those boats of the most varied forms was truly curious to behold.

All the competitors had to put their names down, and present their vessels in the order of inscription. The inhabitants of Betaville had done that far in advance, so that Prince Omega was the penultimate and Vatenlair the last of all; but that was of no importance, as the king made notes on each competitor.

Prince Omega, who had taken delivery of his boat nearly a week before, had gone out every day to test it. The wheels rotated well and the boat glided over the water quite rapidly, but maneuvering it was rather tiring.

When the day came the king sat down on the platform between Princess Betinette and Queen Betasse. Behind them were Prince Omega, the engineer Vatenlair and all the courtiers. The people were arranged along the edges of the lake. Remplume could have been seen at a window of the mill, with his telescope, hidden behind a sack of flour.

The list of competitors having been given to King Beta, he scanned it slowly. When he arrived at the end he claimed "What, my nephew! You want to compete too?"

"With your permission, Uncle. And I hope that you'll appreciate my invention."

"Oh, you've invented something? That's astonishing!"

Princess Betinette started to smile; the prince bit his lip.

"Ah! But that's not all!" said the king. "The engineer Vatenlair has also entered the ranks."

93

"Sire," said the engineer, "I don't have the right to compete with your subjects. I ask to be classed outside the competition."

"You're too modest," said the king. "I demand that you be treated like everyone else. If you merit the prize, I shall be happy to award it to you."

Vatenlair bowed.

At that moment the time for the competition arrived. The boats began to maneuver and place themselves in order. They were arranged along the lake, and were so numerous that Prince Omega's and Vatenlair's were hardly visible in the distance. Departing from the right they were to pass in front of the stand and then arrange themselves to the left, in order to avoid hindering the competitors.

The first one that went past was an ordinary boat, decorated with flowers for the occasion; a single oarsman guided it rather awkwardly; the others succeeded it, rather slowly.

Although their motor was always the oar, they affected different forms; there was one that represented a swan; the oars were hidden under the wings and the slender neck moved up and down gracefully. Another had the appearance of a crocodile, whose forepaws served the function of oars. Another was a small raft surrounded by bladders; it was comical to behold, but it lacked stability and the person manning it had difficulty steering it. There was one made from a tree trunk still covered in moss. Another had the form of a fish. Another had that of a duck. One, which had a certain success, represented a swimming stag; it was manned by two men, one plying the oars while the other blew a hunting horn.

The entire court took great pleasure in watching those evolutions.

The king said to his daughter n a low voice: "I wonder what Prince Omega has been able to find superior to all that."

"If he invents as well as he draws," replied the princess, "I'm afraid that he won't win the prize."

"All the more so as Vatenlair is competing," replied the king. "He hasn't told you about his invention?"

"No, father, but I don't believe that he's invented anything, and that if he shows us something marvelous it will be due to his power as an enchanter."

Meanwhile, the parade continued.

One boat passed that had the form of an immense seashell; it was manned by a young and pretty girl clad in white and crowned with roses; six young men in silver leotards were directing it while swimming. Then a large closed yellow flower imitating that of a water lily floated by; when it passed in front of the king the flower opened and allowed the sight of a ten-year-old child guiding it with oars in the form of leaves.

We shall renounce describing all the forms that were given to the boats; those we have designated were the principal ones.

Everyone waited impatiently for Prince Omega's invention. When its turn came, and he was seen working frantically between its two wheels, he appeared so funny, moving his arms alternately, like a squirrel in a cage that there was universal laughter on the stand and along both banks. Meanwhile he advanced with difficulty and his fatigue was evident. Suddenly, as he passed the stand, the boat's wheels were snagged in the weed on the bed and refused to rotate. For a moment he exhausted his strength trying to free it, but could not succeed in doing so, and a boat had to be sent from the shore to go and fetch him.

He was very confused when he disembarked and dared not return to the stand, but the king, who sometimes held back his laughter, pretended to congratulate him.

"Your invention, my dear nephew, is very original. Until today, people had applied themselves to making boats move; you've found the means of immobilizing them. I offer you all my compliments."

Only one competitor remained: Vatenlair. His boat was so far away that no one had perceived it, so to speak; in any case, it did not look like much; it as a kind of long oval iron box, like a stout pipe tapering at both ends. One might have thought it an enormous dead fish with eyes in its flanks. Everyone sought the engineer with his gaze to see how he was going to mount the machine, but he was invisible.

Princess Betinette was very worried. She did not know what to think. Where was he? Had someone set a trap in order to prevent him competing? Why was the boat remaining still?

Suddenly, a great cry went up from both banks. The completely sealed boat moved on its own, sometimes slowly and sometimes rapidly, and no one seemed to be steering it. When it was in front of the stand, a small hatch placed on top opened, and Vatenlair was seen to emerge and salute the king. Then the enthusiasm reached its peak; people did not know how to express their admiration; the entire audience was carried away. After a few moments, Vatenlair bowed again and went back into his boat, sealing the opening again.

Suddenly, Princess Betinette uttered a loud scream. "Look! Look!" she cried. "The boat is sinking! Help! Save him!"

The boat was, in fact, sinking, and soon disappeared under the water,

All the boats hastened to go to the place of the disaster; divers began to sound the lake; for at least ten minutes there was a frightful agitation, anxiety and disorder.

Ever maladroit, Prince Omega had leaned toward the princess and said to her: "You see, Princess, I'm not the only one not to succeed."

The princess launched a thunderous glare at him, and then, turning her head, suddenly uttered anther scream, this time of joy. At the end of the lake she had just seen Vatenlair emerging from the water and heading rapidly toward the royal platform. In a matter of minutes he had made the journey, and this time, the engineer came out of the vessel and set foot on the shore.

The king, transported, could not contain himself; forgetting his royal majesty, the queen, the princess and the entire audience, he threw his arms around the engineer and embraced him. Princes Betinette, who was very emotional, blushed deeply, and if it had been possible to read her heart, it is probable that one would have seen that she would have liked to be in her father's place.

IX. In which King Beta holds a great review of his troops and Princess Betinette, having become a fay, demonstrates her power.

A few days after the regatta, the court returned to the city. There was much talk about the vacation. The portraits the Princess Betinette had made of the king were passed from hand to hand and caused great astonishment. Vatenlair's diving boat was also the subject of all conversations, so Prince Omega, furious at his defeat, began to take a dislike to Remplume, who was decidedly good for nothing.

In the autumn, after the grand maneuvers, King Beta had the custom of passing the army in review personally. That spectacle was very curious, for the king's army bore no resemblance to those of the sovereigns of the rest of the world, and we cannot dispense with its description.

We have said that King Beta's kingdom was very backward: sciences, arts and letters were all still in infancy; ideas were primitive and, until the arrival of Vatenlair, everyone had been content with that. But the progress that was lacking in that direction was in advance in the matter of warfare, for a means had been found of winning battles without losing a single man, and even of being defeated while conserving the personnel intact. To obtain such a result, the isolation of the United States of Alphabetia was necessary, or the consent of the other peoples of the earth, but as the latter had never even been asked to give it, it follows that the particular fashion of making war of which we speak was completely unknown to them—which is profoundly regrettable, as we shall see.

The principle of that manner of sorting out quarrels reposes on humanity. With good reason, those new peoples had judged that the death of combatants ruined the adversaries without procuring in any way whatsoever the justice of their

97

cause, and that it was more humane and more profitable to have all conflicts settled by animals.

The army was therefore composed of animals trained and directed by humans. To begin with, that had a great economic advantage, because it suppressed arms and munitions. Wars were nevertheless costly, for animals were expensive and difficult to replace.

In a great plain that extended not far from Betaville, a rich stand had been set up for the royal family and the court. Vatenlair had asked for the king's permission not to remain on the platform, in order to examine the strange ceremony in all its details. He had set out early in the morning with a special photographic apparatus and had not been seen again during the day. Princess Betinette, who had not been forewarned of his absence, appeared very nervous and gave the poorest of welcomes to Prince Omega, ever obsequious.

Soon the review commenced.

To begin with, a group of richly dressed valets was seen to advance, carrying immense cages filed with singing birds of all kinds: nightingales, starlings, blackbirds, orioles and parrots of every color. That represented the band; and it was, in fact, a slightly barbaric orchestra, but which made itself heard without interruption. It was installed at the foot of the stand.

Then filed past, in turn: the elephants, whose trunks were gilded, marching heavily, guided by mahouts sitting on their backs; the lions, enchained, which roared before the king as if they wanted to give him an ovation; the striped tigers, which crawled and bounded by turns like cats; the bears, black, brown and white, which showed their ivory teeth and stood up on their hind paws as they went past the stand; the hippopotamuses with rough hides, responsible for battles on rivers and lakes; the wild boars with redoubtable tusks, which battled in forests; and the giraffes, inoffensive, but whose long necks, visible from afar, served as telegraphic signals. Then finally, came the jackals and vultures, attached to perches, whose mission was to clean up the battlefield.

All those animals advanced in order, accompanied by numerous servants charged with their maintenance. That original, but also impressive, procession lasted for three hours, during which the music did not stop for an instant.

When the court had returned to the palace, the members of the royal family withdrew to their apartments, and Prince Omega went back to his room, where Remplume was waiting for him.

"Truly," said the prince, "my uncle has a very fine army. I defy Princes Betinette to reproduce it on paper, as she did the king's face.

"Why is that, Prince? Dos she not have a machine disposed for that?"

"For one thing, she didn't have it with her; for another, the king stood still when she made his portrait. It would be impossible for her to reproduce an animate scene."

"That's true," said Remplume. "But since she's so clever, suggest to the king that he ask her to make him an image of the review."

"She won't be able to do it."

"Undoubtedly! But the king will be discontented to see the princess's impotence and that will efface the bad effect that your failure produced—and then, it's a small vengeance."

"Which won't do me any good with her."

"How do you know? On seeing your finesse, she'll no longer be so disdainful and will hold you in better account."

Prince Omega's apartment was situated in a wing of the castle alongside the engineer's bedroom, which had originally been part of it. A door, which had been sealed, communicated with the prince's drawing room, and was so thin that the words spoken on one side could be heard distinctly on the other. Having returned home directly after the end of the review, Vatenlair heard the previous conversation in its entirety and he promised himself that he would profit from it. He had just spent all day taking pictures of the review, which permitted him to thwart the pernicious plans of Remplume. It only remained to warn the princess.

For her part, she was eager to see Vatenlair in order to discover where he was in his labors, for it was necessary, in his interest, not to allow the king's admiration to cool, by not showing him any more new enchantments. Lying on her chaise longue, she was thinking about ways to see him in secret, when she suddenly sensed a cloud pass over eyes and lost the notion of things. At the same time, she stood up and went down to the gardens, to which the engineer's suggestion had already taken her once before.

Having arrived there, she suddenly regained consciousness, and was astonished to find that she was no longer in her room. What had brought her there? With what objective? She did not know. After a moment, Vatenlair arrived and recounted the conversation he had overheard; at the same time, he explained to her the means of subverting the plot that had been made against her, and told her that in two days, he would have everything prepared to thwart her enemies.

Following Remplume's advice, Prince Omega had not delayed speaking to the king; to begin with he had offering him excessive compliments on his review; then, gradually, he had insinuated to him that such scenes merited being conserved in images, that memory was insufficient to retain an exact idea of them and that it was necessary to ask Princes Betinette to employ her talent to make a new masterpiece.

"That's a good idea," said the king. "Thank you for having suggested it to me; I'll talk to her about it this evening."

And indeed, that same evening, the king took his daughter to one side and expressed his desire to her. At first, the princess refused to attempt that proof.

"Are you not a fay, then?"

"Yes, but fays are not omnipotent! However, Father, since you ask, I will try, and in two days, if the enchanter Vatenlair will come to my aid, I shall pass your troops in review for you gain."

On the appointed day, Vatenlair had set up in the palace festival hall a small cabin made of black cloth, in which he installed his apparatus. On the opposite side, a large white sheet was applied to the wall. The armchairs reserved for the audience were facing the sheet. Vatenlair and the princess had made preliminary arrangements in order to give the session a fantastic character.

At ten o'clock in the evening, in the brightly lit hall, the king, the queen and the courtiers were installed on the seats that had been prepared for them. Soon, Princess Betinette, dressed as a fay, made her entrance and spoke in these terms:

"You have asked me, Father, to reproduce in images the magnificent review of your troops, which you passed the other day. I have obtained pleasure in obeying you. But I've done better; the scene that will demonstrate your power will be preceded by two others; one will represent the factory where your engineer is having your gas manufactured, the gas that is illuminating us at this moment; the other will show you the market of your capital. Those three scenes will be animated. You will see the animals file past as if they were alive; you will see the workers in the factory performing their different functions and men and women bringing to market and selling the various products of their cultivation and their industry. On that I put one condition, which is that the gas that is illuminating us, and which has already done you a bad turn by going out in the middle of the ball, will disappear forever. You have seen it this evening for the last time."

And before the king had time to respond, the hall was plunged into darkness.

At the same time, a large tableau appeared before the spectators.

Immediately, they saw designed on the tableau the gas factory with its ardent furnaces. Workmen, blackened by the smoke, were going back and forth, hurling charcoal into the braziers; others were opening valves; others were fabricating strange and unknown machines. There was a continual coming and going, of which the eye was never weary.

That tableau was succeeded by the sight of the Betaville market. The merchants were laying out their produce, buyers were stopping at the displays; carts were passing by; there were oxen under the yoke drawing carts full of grain; here there were pigs being led, there poultry agitating in baskets; elsewhere, cabbages and vegetables of all kinds were being piled on the ground; in sum, there was an extraordinary animation.

The court was greatly amused, and seemed wonderstruck, but waited impatiently for the final tableau: the review!

Finally, after a few minutes that seemed like hours, they saw fixed on the sheet the royal stand with all the people who had been there two days before. They were motionless. The effect was gripping. Suddenly, the people were animated; the birds forming the band were seen to arrive, stopping in front of the stand, and then, successively filing past, the elephants, lions, tigers, bears, hippopotamuses, wild boars, giraffes, jackals and vultures. All of them seemed to be alive.

The court was transported. The king was mad with joy, and murmured in a low voice: "My daughter is a fay! A true fay!"

But the gas was not reignited, and the hall remained plunged in obscurity, Vatenlair took advantage of that to make his little cabin and his apparatus disappear through a door at the back.

"Oh!" said the king. "Is it true what you said, my daughter, that the gas will not appear again?"

"It's true, Sire," said Vatenlair, who had come back into the room. "The gas having displeased you, I've dismissed it; but I've replaced it."

At the same moment the festival hall was illuminated instantaneously by electricity, which was a further surprise, inexplicable for all the members of the audience.

Prince Omega was enraged.

X. In which the engineer Vatenlair perceives that he has not finished with Remplume.

Prince Omega had already been a guest of King Beta for four months, and he had not mentioned leaving, which exasperated Princes Betinette to the point that one day she made the remark to her father.

"Don't you think, Father, that Prince Omega is treating us very casually?"

"Perhaps a little, my daughter, but I can explain that. He dare not..."

"Personally, I find that he dares too much!" Betinette interjected.

"You're interrupting me," said the king. Let me finish: he dare not ask me for your hand, because he perceives that you are scarcely amiable with him; so he's waiting patiently, and even impatiently, for you to look more kindly upon him, in order to risk his request."

"Well, Father, he'll wait for a long time, for I shall never encourage him. Furthermore, I'm glad that I'm now obliged to renounce him."

"Why is that?"

"Are you forgetting that I'm a fay and that I can't marry a mortal unless he's initiated in the science...of magic."

"That's true, you're a fay. I'd forgotten."

"Then again, fays choose their husbands themselves, and I don't love Prince Omega enough to cast eyes upon him. So, Father, I'd be very grateful if you would make him understand that he has nothing for which to hope in my regard and that you won't keep him any longer."

That delicate mission did not please the king very much. He did not want to displease his nephew, which would have displeased his brother. He was placid by nature, and rather soft, avoiding annoyances at all costs. He was known as Good King Beta. However, he promised his daughter to make the prince understand that any request would be futile, which would oblige him to cut short his sojourn.

"However," he added, "I would have liked to see you married; your mother and I are old; in accordance with the ordinary order of things, death might soon take us and you'll be left alone. You might be a fay now, but you might still find others more powerful than you, who are jealous of you; a husband is an adviser and a protector. I'd be more reassured if you had made your choice before my definitive departure for another world."

"You'll be obeyed, Father, and as soon as Prince Omega has gone, I'll name for you the one I've chosen."

"You already have someone in mind, then?"

The princess smiled. "Yes, Father, and he's worthy of me."

Satisfied to see that the princess was beginning to see things his way, the king did not ask any more and quit her in order to go to the summer palace, where his gardeners were waiting for him, in order to show him the plant obtained by his original seed.

The reader will certainly suspect that the husband on whom Princess Betinette had cast her eyes was the engineer Vatenlair, her professor. Although, thus far, no sentimental words had been exchanged between them, she had sensed an attraction toward him that she divined to be reciprocal. More than once, she had thought that he was about to declare himself, but he had doubtless understood the distance that separated them and had kept silent. For her part, she had not thought that she ought to encourage him until she had deflected the certain refusal of her father; now, thanks to the trickery she had employed in passing herself off as a fay in the credulous mind of the king, she was reassured. In fact, although a princess cannot marry an engineer, a fay is not lowering herself in having an enchanter for a husband.

The hour for her daily lesson having arrived, she went to see Vatenlair and made him party to the conversation she had just had with the king.

Vatenlair understood then that the moment had come to reveal the depths of his heart to the princess. His confession was welcomed, as it had to be, and from that day on their union was decided; but it was necessary to wait for the departure of Prince Omega before it could be consecrated. It was no longer anything but a matter of finding a means of making him leave as quickly as possible.

It was agreed that as soon as the prince went back to his apartment the engineer would go to his bedroom in order to listen to the words he was exchanging with Remplume. He had noticed that every day, at a fixed hour, the latter met with the prince; that espionage was very useful to him for thwarting the maneuvers that they discussed in order to harm him.

That day, in fact, the conversation was one of the most interesting. The prince complained about the coldness of the princess and the indifference of the king; Remplume advised him.

"Permit me to tell you that you're taking it badly. You're a prince, young and handsome, and as if you had no consciousness of your own value, you're making yourself the slave of a petty coquette who is mocking you because you're humiliating yourself before her. Pretend to neglect her and you'll see immediately that she'll seek you out. As for the king, you know him, as I do; he's weak, credulous, devoid of personal conviction, always listening to the last voice he hears. It's therefore good to flatter him, to approve of him, to advise him, to keep away as much as possible those who approach him, and to be with him constantly. Soon, he'll only see through your eyes. That's the way to go."

"Undoubtedly," replied the prince, "but what you're advising me to do isn't easy. The princess avoids me; she began by pleasing me, but her way of treating me didn't take long to weary me. She's a silly little goose whom I'd have let alone a long time ago if it weren't for the millions of her dowry, of which I have need. Her mother is a nullity and my uncle an imbecile; I know all that. In sum, I'll try again to make myself welcome, but can't you find a means of being more useful to me?"

"I think about nothing else! Do you know what I've been doing this morning? Making you indispensable to the king. Oh, my spells are natural; I don't employ gas or electricity; my observation and ingenuity replace everything. The king doesn't like to be annoyed, that's a fact; whereas he's full of benevolence for whoever causes his annoyance to cease. Well, those two facts observed by me have made me pose this problem: how does one remove the annoyance of a man who isn't annoyed? By annoying him."

"That's not very clear."

"Yes, you'll see. At the moment, King Beta is very happy. The brilliant review of his troops has out him in a good mood; everyone who approaches him feels its effect. This isn't the moment for you to go to him."

"What?"

"No. He'll be amiable with you, as with everyone else, but no more. Now, it's necessary that his satisfaction comes entirely from you, and in order to arrive at that result, this is what I've imagined. I've had all the bells that are connected to the king's apartment stuffed with cotton wool. When he needs something, it will be impossible for him obtain it, and he'll get angry; you'll arrive then and put yourself at his disposal. He'll be very grateful to you and you'll be able to obtain anything you want from him."

"That's ingenious enough," said the prince, "but not very practical. How will I know that the king has rung if you've muffled all the bells."

"I can see that you don't know His Majesty's habits. King Beta is methodical. Everything he does is regulated in advance. So, it's now quarter to ten; well, at ten o'clock precisely, he's going to ring to ask for his breakfast; that will be the moment to present yourself. You can even tell him that you anticipated the accident, which will give you the slight air of a magician, and earn you his consideration. You'll add that you can easily return the voice to the bells, which have proba-

106

bly been rendered mute by the engineer, whose metallic wires are cluttering the palace, and you'll thus combat his influence."

Vatenlair had not missed a word of that conversation; he had even collected it in a new little apparatus that he had placed next to the communicating door.

It was true, as Remplume had remarked, that the palace was furrowed with electric wires, which were intended to serve various usages: lighting, first of all, as we have seen; then he counted on employing them for the transmission of voices, and the moment had come to utilize them. The little plot that he had just overheard scarcely alarmed him, therefore; he would be able to thwart it.

At that moment, the palace clock chimed ten. He heard the prince leaving his apartment and heading toward the king's. A moment later he went out himself and closed his door carefully, in order to avoid Remplume's indiscretions.

XI. In which King Beta is injured while hunting and Prince Omega is separated from Remplume.

King Beta had just broken his bell-cord and, pale with anger, was agitating it and shouting: "My chocolate? Where's my chocolate?" when Prince Omega suddenly appeared, smiling.

That smile, as stupid and conceited as possible, exasperated the king, who said: "What are you doing here? I didn't summon you."

"I know," said the prince, "and it's to replace your servants, who weren't able to hear your appeal, that I'm presenting myself before you."

"But if you knew that, you should have warned me."

The prince did not know how to respond, for the king's reply seemed just to him. He became anxious, and stammered: "If Your Majesty will permit, I'll give orders to have him served."

At that moment, Vatenlair arrived on the threshold of the door, which was still open. Having perceived him, the king said to the prince: "You're my guest, nephew, and you have no orders to give in my house, be good enough to withdraw. You stay, Vatenlair."

The former went out, discomfited, promising himself to reprimand Remplume forcefully for having given him such poor advice. Contrary to the anticipations of the astrologer, the king's wrath had fallen upon the prince. Now he had calmed down again.

"You desire to speak to me?" he said to the engineer.

"Yes, Sire," said Vatenlair "I desire to make you party to a new means of communication with your servants, without needing to have them in your presence. In a word, you'll enable them to hear you at a distance and listen to their responses without leaving your apartments. I've been occupied with the innovation for some time; today, I can reveal it to you, for it's ready to function."

"I don't understand very well," said the king. "Or, rather, I dare not understand, for it would be too marvelous. So, I could speak to you and you could hear my in your apartment, and could respond to me without leaving your room?"

"Exactly, Sire. I've established communications with the Queen's apartment, Princess Betinette's, Prince Omega's, the first chamberlain's and mine, in order to ender to your orders. I've just sent those various individuals the instructions necessary to communicate with you and I'll give them to you myself vocally. Can you see that little panel fitted to your desk, next to which those two little cornets are hooked?

"Indeed. I hadn't noticed them…"

"Well, in front of that panel there are five buttons, on which you'll find the names of our interlocutors; by pressing one or another of them, you'll obtain communication with the person you've selected. Each of the buttons activates a bell that warns the other person that you want to speak to them. Then, by holding those two cornets over your ears in order to hear the replies, you speak in front of the panel, which will transmit your words.

"Truly, my dear Vatenlair, if I didn't know that you were an enchanter, I'd believe you were trying to trick me."

"Try, Sire, you'll see that I'm not lying."

Following the engineer's instructions, the king pressed a button and got ready to speak.

"I forgot to tell you, Sire," said Vatenlair, swiftly, "that's it's necessary to precede each conversation with a magic word that I'll reveal to you, which is: Hello!"

"Good!" said the king. "We'll see!" And, approaching the panel, he said: "Hello!"

"Hello!" replied the instrument.

The king recoiled, frightened. "It answered me," he said.

"It's not the panel, it's the Queen," said Vatenlair, who had seen which button the king had pressed.

"How was your night?" said the king, replacing himself before the panel.

"Very good," replied the queen. "I feel a little better this morning."

"That's incredible!" said the king. "Oh, my dear enchanter! How will I ever be able to thank you as you merit?"

All morning, the king, forgetting about his breakfast, conversed with his daughter, his chamberlain, the queen, and even Prince Omega, to whom he said: "No need to disturb yourself henceforth, nephew; I have no more need of bells to have myself served."

King Beta was not an egotist; when he experienced pleasure, he wanted everyone to share it, and as he did not intend to deliver his apparatus to all his courtiers, he expressed his satisfaction to them by organizing a great hunt for the following day.

For a long time, as he no longer had the full use of his legs, he had no longer devoted himself to cynegetic pleasures, so that decision was welcomed with delight. They were to hunt in the vicinity of the summer palace, where a splendid meal would be prepared; the queen, Princess Betinette and the ladies of the court would follow the hunt; the cortege would be splendid.

Indeed it was, and the inhabitants of Betaville who came out to watch it pass by had never seen such a spectacle.

Before departing, Prince Omega had had a conversation with Remplume, who said to him: "All the means I've indicated to you to obtain royal favor have failed; this is an opportunity that won't be presented again, it's necessary not to let it pass."

"What should I do?" said the prince.

"It's necessary to find a means of saving the king's life."

"But the king's life isn't in danger."

"Who knows?" said Remplume. "A hunt is always dangerous." And he insinuated: "A poorly aimed bullet might hit him; his horse might bolt and carry him away, I don't know. In any case, I engage you not to quit him, and, if some misfortune overtakes him, to find yourself there to help him."

Prince Omega quit him, pensively.

In such hunting parties, people avoided killing the animals that might serve in the army, but carried out a massacre of hares, rabbits, grouse and pheasants, which were inoffensive. Ordinarily, hunting was done on horseback, to the sound of the horn, but since the king had grown old, he deprived himself of that pleasure and contented himself with simply shooting as much game as possible in the coverts of the forest. The guests were disposed in a single line at a certain distance from one another, and beaters drove the game toward them.

The king, who could not stand up for long, hunted sitting in an armchair; the courtiers, in imitation of their master, did the same, except that they only had stools. Behind them, in open carriages, the queen, the princess and the maids of honor watched the cynegetic exploits.

Twenty paces away from the king to one side, Prince Omega was stationed, and on the other, Vatenlair; and the other hunters were spaced out at further intervals of twenty paces.

The spectacle was very original.

The king, of course, shot the first victim, which was a pheasant, after which the killing preceded without any order of precedence.

Prince Omega, who rode a horse very well, was, on the other hand, not a very brilliant hunter. His monocle inconvenienced him when taking aim, but he could not do without it. At a certain moment, as a rabbit passed in front of him and veered sideways, he pressed the trigger of his rifle so clumsily that the entire charge of shot, instead of hitting the rabbit, lodged in the side of the king, who uttered a cry of pain.

Frightened, the prince threw away his weapon and ran to the king, as all the other guests did.

The hunt was immediately interrupted. The queen lamented as if she had been shot herself. Princess Betinette was no less troubled; the courtiers, the squires and the other hunters were in the greatest agitation; only Vatenlair had not lost his head. He went straight to the physician who was in one of the carriages, and brought him to the king.

A few moments later, the king was installed on a bed in the summer palace, and the doctor, having undressed him, inspected all his wounds. The lead shot had formed a cluster, and the king's whole side was riddled with little projectiles. His life, however was not in danger; he only complained because the extraction of the lead pellets was causing him a great deal of pain.

Only the queen and the princess witnessed that operation, the king not having wanted to receive Prince Omega; he had also ordered that the hunt should continue without him, since his wounds were not serious.

That accident, however, had disconcerted everyone, and no one had any enthusiasm any longer, so the hunt did not go on for long. Then they returned to the city with the same pomp with which they had departed, and, in order to explain the king's absence, the rumor was spread that His Majesty wanted to repose for a few days in the summer palace.

After a fortnight, all his wounds having scarred over, the king returned to the city palace. His gaiety had returned; he had even given a good welcome to Prince Omega, who had come to meet him on horseback, inviting him to remain by the door of his carriage.

Unfortunately a new accident suddenly arrived to drive him to despair. Glad to see the welcome the king had given him, in his joy, the prince made his horse prance, which made an abrupt sidestep and collided with the horses of the carriage; the latter, frightened, took the bit between their teeth and bolted, smashing into a tree by the roadside. The carriage was immediately tipped over, and the king was pulled out covered in bruises.

This time, Prince Omega understood that it was all over. The only thing that remained for him to do was to renounce Princess Betinette and leave immediately.

"I'm going!" he said to Remplume, when he returned to his apartment. "Bad luck is pursuing me. My uncle will never forgive me; it's better to give up."

"Are we leaving right away?" Remplume asked.

"I am, yes; but I'm leaving you here. You've given me too much bad advice. Since I've been following it, nothing has succeeded for me."

"Bad advice! Me!" cried Remplume. "On the contrary, excellent advice, from which you haven't been able to profit. When I told you to suggest to the king that he ask the princess to reproduce the review, was that bad advice? Wasn't the king satisfied beyond all possible expectation?"

"Undoubtedly, but it didn't do me any good; and when, by an excess of zeal, you permitted yourself to render all the bells in the palace mute, in order to offer me a pretext to hasten to the king, you caused me to suffer an insult that I haven't forgotten."

"But my intentions were good!"

"Was it also a good intention to insinuate to me that the king might be wounded in the hunt?"

"I didn't tell you to wound him yourself!"

"That's true. It was clumsiness on my part, which I regret, but I understood your intention, so I didn't respond to it."

"What did you understand, Prince?"

"That if I had ordered you to direct the stray bullet, you wouldn't have hesitated."

"What! You were able to suppose...."

"I'm capable of anything, so I'm separating myself from you."

"What am I going to do now, if you abandon me?"

"Consult the stars, my friend, that's your métier. As for me, I have no more need of your services, and I can't do anything for you."

And Prince Omega dismissed him.

XII. In which the marriage of the princess is decided and the king heaps the engineer with favors.

The king's contusions were not very serious, but, in view of his advanced age, it was feared that the new accident might influence his morale.

"I shall never ride in a carriage again," he repeated. "That blockhead Prince Omega will be the death of me if he stays here."

On hearing those words, Princes Betinette judged that the moment had come to reveal his nephew's felony to him.

"You wanted to make me marry Prince Omega," she said to him, "You found him full of qualities and you didn't perceive his faults. I was more clear-sighted; I mistrusted him, and I was right."

"What have you seen, then?"

"First, Father, what has become of Remplume?"

"I don't know and I don't care. I've expelled him from the palace; he must have departed."

"That's what you think! What if I told you that he stayed here, or, at least, that he comes every day, and that he's not unaware of anything concerning your person?"

"That's not possible. I haven't seen him."

113

"He's in hiding."

"And what does he come here to do?"

"To take orders from Prince Omega, who has taken him into his service."

"That's not credible!"

"Look, Father, here's an image that I made during your sojourn at the summer palace. Do you recognize that individual?"

"Remplume! The Prince!"

"I caught them one morning when I was out walking with the instrument that served to make your portrait."

"That's certainly near the rocks in the forest, which I also recognize."

"But that's not all. Would you like to know now what they said to one another, there and elsewhere? You'll know the depths of their thought."

"What did they say?"

"If I repeated it to you, you wouldn't believe it; it's better for you to hear it for yourself. When they were speaking rather loudly in the Prince's apartment, Vatenlair collected their words in a marvelous instrument that will repeat them to you. Have the enchanter come here and you'll see what your dear nephew thinks of you and me."

"Hello!" shouted the king, speaking into his panel.

The acoustic cornets replied: "Hello!"

"Come and enable me to hear the conversations of Prince Omega with Remplume."

After a few moments, Vatenlair presented himself before the king and placed a small box on the table, which he opened. Wheels could be seen inside and a small scroll pricked with dots. The engineer set the mechanism in motion, and immediately, the voices of the prince and the astrologer could be heard distinctly. We have related that conversation previously, and you can imagine the effect that it produced in the king's mind. One hearing the words of the prince, calling him an imbecile, his wife a nullity and his daughter a silly goose, he could scarcely contain himself; Remplume's ruse of blocking all his bells made him jump.

"That's too much," said he king. "I'll wash my hands of my nephew and ask him to stay at home."

And, turning back to his panel, he called the prince; but Prince Omega who was fearful a final conversation with the king, did not reply; he had been in haste to leave without telling anyone—which brought the king's fury to a peak.

Princess Betinette hastened to calm him down, and, finding the moment opportune, she said to her father:

"Calm yourself, Father; the villainy is unmasked; that should suffice for you. You know now the man you had destined for me as a husband. There is another on whom I have cast my eyes and who has not ceased since we have known him to render you precious services and to show you his devotion. Do I need to name him?"

"Vatenlair," said the king.

"Yes, Vatenlair, the enchanter, whom I beg you to accept as a son-in-law. I have been able to appreciate his qualities; I believe that he will make me happy. He has made me a fay, whose power is not yet very great, but which he will be able to develop subsequently. In choosing him, I am not making a misalliance; on the contrary, I am elevating myself, for no prince is his equal." Kneeling before the king, she added: "Give us your consent and you will have secured your daughter's happiness."

Vatenlair had also thrown himself at the king's knees. "Sire," he said, "I beg you humbly to give me a favorable response. My power as an enchanter inclines before yours. I only want to take your daughter's hand by your will."

The king was deeply moved; he took the hands of the two young people and joined them together, and having searched in vain for a phrase that was both dignified and cordial, he simply said to them: "Be happy."

That decision was not taken without discontenting Queen Betasse, whose mind was very narrow and who thought there was nothing finer than a prince. For a week she had arguments with the king, who, in order to put an end to them, made the decision to give Vatenlair titles. He named him successively Baron de Feusansmeche, in memory of the installation of gas in the palace, and then Marquis de la Tablette, in recognition of the services rendered to him by the instrument that permitted him to speak and hear at a distance. The queen still raised opposition. Then the king decided to name him Comte de Lumière, in order to make allusion to the instantaneous illumination of the palace.

"Certainly," said the queen, "all these titles bring him nearer to us, but you wouldn't give our daughter to any of your subjects nearing those titles."

"Well, Madame, since you want absolutely for him to be a prince, and you consider that dignity to be above all the others and are forgetting that he's already an enchanter, I'll unite the two titles and appoint him Prince. He will, therefore, be Prince Enchanter! Now you have no further objections to make to me."

The queen gave in.

They immediately occupied themselves with preparations for the mirage, which was to be as brilliant as possible. First of all they invited the king's twenty-three brothers, all sovereigns of one of the provinces of Alphabetia; then they had the gardens decorated, and also Betaville, through which the cortege was to pass. For a month there was an extraordinary animation, which changed the aspect of that tranquil land completely.

For his part, Vatenlair, who wanted to make new surprises, did not waste his time. His mechanical factories were full of skillful workers whom he had trained since his arrival, and who, under his direction, constructed a host of machines each more ingenious than the last.

Since his carriage accident, the king no longer wanted to go abroad other than on foot. That irrevocable decision annoyed Princess Betinette, who thought that it detracted from the magnificence of the royal cortege. Vatenlair reassured her.

He promised to make horseless carriages, and also machines that would replace horses.

Everything was therefore going well and nothing else seemed likely to delay the ceremony when the king suddenly complained of sharp pains in his side, which obliged him to consult his physician.

The king's physician was also a surgeon; he examined the sovereign's scarred wounds again and declared that he could not understand the further suffering. All the lead pellets had been extracted, and, unless others still remained in the flesh, he could not see what could be causing the unusual pains. On the other hand, is any remained, how could they find them reliably? It would be dangerous to make further excavations at random.

Vatenlair, informed of the result of the physician's consultation, took charge of resolving the question. He had a mysterious box bought to the king's apartment, and then a white screen, and, having placed the king between the two objects, he said: "I'm going to make the invisible visible for you. On this white screen, as soon as I've activated my machine, the king's skeleton will be reproduced..."

At the word *skeleton*, the king, who already saw himself dead, cried: "No, no, Vatenlair! I don't want to be subjected to this operation!"

"It's not an operation, Sire," the engineer replied. "No one will touch you, and you won't suffer at all. You will, in fact, see your bones on this screen, as they are under your flesh, and if they contain a foreign body, it will show up in the same way. If, therefore, you still have lead pellets in any part of your body, the physician will know where they are."

In spite of those explanations, it was not easy to persuade the king to consent to the exploration of his body.

When the king's skeleton appeared on the screen. Queen Betasse had an attack of nerves that it was necessary to treat first; and it was quite an affair thereafter to explain to her that the king was not running any danger.

They recommenced the experiment, and they did, indeed perceive several lead pellets, represented by black stains, which were still lodged beneath the king's epidermis. The physician was then able to operate safely the extraction of those foreign bodies, and the king was immediately relieved.

"My dear enchanter," said the king to Vatenlair, "I have given you titles; I have given you my daughter; I'm still in your debt, and I won't ever be able to acquit myself. Since I've known you, you've shown me so many marvelous things that my poor head is lost therein."

"I'll enable you see others," said Vatenlair, "and gradually, all those marvels will seem natural to you."

"But can't I become an enchanter too?" said the king.

"That," said the engineer, "isn't in my power. For the moment, content yourself with being enchanted."

XIII. In which there is question of weddings, deaths and conspiracies, and in which Remplume is seen to reappear.

The day of the marriage of Princess Betinette and Prince Enchanter had arrived. In Betaville, ornamented with flowers, flags and streamers, the bells were ringing at full tilt. Songs of delight were heard on all sides; the people had put on their festival clothes and all faces were smiling.

The king's brothers had arrived, except for King Omega, who, discontented with the fashion in which his son had acted, had judged it appropriate to absent himself.

One saw, therefore, King Alpha, who presided over all congresses; Kings Gamma, Delta, Zeta, Eta and Theta; Kings Epsolin and Upsilon, who were twins; Kings Pi, Phi, Chi, Psi and Xi of southern Alphabetia; Kings Iota and Omicron, who were both small, and finally, Kings Kappa, Lambda, Mu, Nu, Rho, Sigma and Tau, magnificently clad. Each of those sovereigns had brought a numerous retinue, the multicolored costumes of which, gilded in all the seams, sparkled in the sunlight.

While they were chatting on the lawn of the royal palace, one of King Beta's chamberlains came to announce to them that his master begged them not to make use of their mounts, for his intention was not to ride on a horse. That unexpected decision, which prevented them from showing off all their advantages, could not fail to discontent them, but another chamberlain came in his turn to tell them that places were reserved for them in new vehicles that moved without horses, and were the invention of the bridegroom Prince.

Immediately, they saw two hundred chariots advancing, each conducted by a servant. They were all of different forms, but those reserved for the sovereigns resembled boats and had masts ornamented with pennants and supporting royal coats of arms. King Beta's, in which the queen took her place, had the form of a violet flower, which represented in large scale that of the potato. That was a flattery on the part of Vatenlair, to recall the product obtained by the king with the original seed that he had made in the summer palace.

The young spouses had a special means of locomotion, which had two wheels placed one in front of the other and linked by iron rods that supported a small saddle. The machine was caused to move with the aid of pedals, on which they placed their feet.

That innovation had an immense success. No cortege so luxurious, so brilliant and so original had ever been seen.

In the mobile flower sat King Beta, full of pride, his number one crown on his head and his scepter in his hand, while Princess Betinette and Prince Enchanter rode to either side of his chariot.

That evening, at the ball, there as a new marvel for the guests, in seeing the brilliant lighting in the drawing rooms, which was a novelty for them.

For an entire week there was nothing but fêtes and surprises of every kind, so that the sovereigns returned to their Estates delighted with the reception that they had been given, but also a little jealous.

Those excessive pleasures had wearied King Beta a great deal, however, and especially Queen Betasse, whose health left much to be desired. She took to her bed after the departure of the kings, languished for a few months, and eventually died, leaving the king inconsolable.

It was in vain that Prince Enchanter multiplied the most astonishing inventions in order to distract him, and Princess Betinette surrounded him with cares and covered him with filial caresses; the king did not want to be consoled, and a month after the queen, he followed her into the tomb.

Princess Betinette succeeded him on the throne, but she was not loved as her father had been; the people did not know her, for she rarely showed herself to them; then too, the choice she had made in preferring a stranger for a husband was contrary to all custom. Remplume maintained those pernicious ideas throughout the realm, and did not hesitate to calumniate Vatenlair by saying that he had passed himself off as a sorcerer with the king in order to marry the princess, but that he was only an impostor.

As soon as he had knowledge of these malevolent rumors, Vatenlair strongly suspected that Remplume was their instigator, but he wanted to make sure of it. Evidently, there must be a conspiracy, and therefore conspirators, but how could he discover the place of their meetings and introduce himself into it? That was the difficulty.

He summoned the prefect of police—for he had a prefect of police, who had been that of his father-in-law, King Beta. He was a little old man with a forbidding manner; his eyes, veiling by thick eyebrows, never looked anyone in the face; his toothless mouth was dissimulated by a unkempt beard, and his cranium, as bare and yellow as a duck's egg, was sheltered beneath a black skullcap that never quit him. His name was Ratatinus.[21]

Throughout King Beta's reign, Ratatinus had had nothing to do; his position had been a veritable sinecure. On the

---

[21] *Ratatiné* means shriveled or shrunken.

death of King Beta it had been necessary for him to emerge from his torpor somewhat; Remplume was agitating the country, and Vatenlair charge him every day with missions to which he was not accustomed, but as the inhabitants of Betaville were all his friends, he was reluctant to act against them, all the more so because he gladly accepted their interested little gifts.

Vatenlair, however, who did not joke, had threatened him with disgrace if he did not show more activity. He had therefore harassed a few petty merchants who had not been generous with him, a joiner, among others, who had worked several times for Vatenlair and complained of his exigencies.

Ratatinus therefore rendered to the engineer's orders.

"Monsieur Prefect of Police," said the engineer. "I know that there is much chatter on our account; I'm astonished that you have not yet old me anything about it."

"I can't prevent inconsequential gossip," said Ratatinus. "It existed in the time of the late king, who did not complain about it."

"The late king, who was too good, acted in his fashion. Queen Betinette, whose husband I am, does not want to be subjected to that species of opposition, and she has charged me with telling you to put a stop to it."

"By what means, Prince? What means? I can't stop people talking."

"You don't know your profession, then, Monsieur Ratatinus? Well, I'll teach you. On my arrival in your country I stirred up a great deal of jealousy; people forget the progress that I have brought about, but they profit from it nevertheless. My science is denied because no one can equal it, and in order to succeed in undermining me, they dare to attack the queen. You must know the man who is at the head of the conspiracy."

"You're mistaken, Prince. There is no conspiracy, merely a few malcontents..."

"All right, malcontents. You must know them."

"Oh, they're people of no importance."

"You speak very lightly. I want to know who they are."

"Well, I can cite one to you, a joiner, Rabotin, is one of your workers, a vulgar man. Those people don't always measure their words and go beyond their thoughts."

"And that's all? You don't know any others?"

"There are a few others, but their names don't come to mind."

"Isn't Remplume, the former astrologer of the late king, also one of them?"

"Remplume!"

"Yes, Remplume. You know him well."

"I know him, but I've never heard him say anything against the queen."

"Nor against me?"

"Oh, he wouldn't dare."

"You think so? So much the better for him. In any case, I want to interrogate the joiner Rabotin. Be kind enough to send him to me today. Then I intend, you understand, that all these rumors cease immediately. You have powers to make them cease, of which you're not making use: fines and prison. If you want to keep your place, you have what you need. Go, Monsieur!"

No one had ever talked to Ratatinus like that. He was exasperated. He quit the prince with ideas of revolt and vengeance, and promised himself to recount his conversation to Remplume, whom he congratulated himself quietly for not having denounced. Suspicions now weighing on Rabotin, he immediately sent him an order to present himself to the prince, and as the poor joiner was inoffensive, the thought that Vatenlair, reassured, would not take his investigation any further.

Rabotin was a joiner who had crossed his path. He was not a bad man; on the contrary, he liked work and as skillful, but he had the fault of being too slow and too meticulous. When he was pressed he lost his head and sent away all callers. It was then that he inveighed against Vatenlair, who was almost his only client, and who always demanded that his orders be carried out with rapidity. When he had vented his spleen, he resumed his work with a will and quickly forgot his ill humor. He was an orderly man who kept himself to himself and did not frequent his comrades; urged by Remplume, they had tried several times to make him share their ideas of revolt, but he had always refused their propositions and criticized their actions.

"Why," he said to them, "do you want me to be hostile to a man who gives us work? Without him, would I have been able to establish myself? And what were you doing before he came? Believe me, don't kill the chicken that gives us eggs!"

Before his inertia, the others had not persisted, but they had ceased their confidences.

When the prefect of police gave Rabotin the order to go to see the prince he carefully refrained from telling him why he had been summoned; the joiner thought, therefore, that he was going in search of a new commission, and it was with a light step that he went to the palace.

On entering the prince's cabinet, Rabotin saw immediately that it was not a matter of a new commission. Vatenlair seemed anxious.

"Approach," he said to the joiner. "It appears that you've been speaking ill of me?"

Rabotin went scarlet. "Me! Who told you that?"

"Ratatinus, the Prefect of Police."

Rabotin reflected momentarily, and then responded abruptly: "Well, yes, it's true."

Vatenlair seemed astonished

"Yes," the workman went on, "there are times, when you press me for the work, that I don't know where my head is any longer, and I say a heap of stupid things to relieve myself; but it's to myself that I say that and not to others, I'm not like..."

Suddenly, he stopped, sensing that he was about to go too far.

"Why are you stopping? You're afraid of denouncing someone? But my poor Rabotin, you're forgetting that I know everything, and don't need to be told anything. Do you think I don't know about Remplume's maneuvers?"

"What! You know?" said the naïve joiner

"But I scorn them, and when I want to stop them, I count on being able to find you, if I need you."

"I'm entirely devoted to you," said Rabotin.

"Are you sure? Just now you didn't want to name my enemy."

"There was no need, since your prefect of police had already designated him to you."

"That's where you're mistaken. It's you that Ratatinus had designated, in order to deflect suspicions and save Remplume."

"What! It's Ratatinus who denounced me! But he's a miserable calumniator."

"So I didn't believe him, and that's not why I sent for you."

"Speak, Sire; I'll obey you."

"Sire? No, no flatteries. I'm only the queen's husband, and for you, at the moment, the engineer, your employer. Now, this is what I'm asking of you: join the league of malcontents."

Rabotin started "Me! Ally myself with those wretches! Obey Remplume, who's the vilest of men! I'd rather..."

"Stop, Rabotin, for I've just asked you to join them."

"What! You want...?"

"Yes, I want you to be part of the conspiracy, because I need a friend within it."

"A friend?"

"Don't you want to be one?"

"Yes, oh, yes! What would I have to do, then?"

"Well, if there's a conspiracy..."

"What! Of course there's a conspiracy! You know that full well, since you've named its leader."

"Remplume—yes. But the conspirators meet somewhere."

"Oh, that's not a mystery; everyone in Betaville knows that the conspirators spend the night of Saturday and Sunday in the Leopard Tavern. At midnight, when all the drinkers have gone and the tavern is closed, they go back through a little door and are admitted by a password. The room where they meet is dimly lit, so they don't know one another; the only know the leader, Remplume."

"And what do they say."

"Oh, that I don't know yet, but since you want me to have myself admitted to their company, it'll be easy for me to tell you."

"Thank you! I don't want you to play the role of spy; I want to hear their conversation myself. For that, when you're initiated, it's necessary for you to find a means of getting me into a meeting unknown to them. Isn't there a bull's-eye at the back of the Leopard Tavern, in which a clock-face has been inserted?"

"Yes, that clock is on the first floor."

"Someone goes up to the first floor to wind it, then?"

"Yes."

"Well, it's necessary that on the night when I come, it's under repair and replaced by a partition of boards, made by you in accordance with my instructions."

"That can be done."

"Now leave me. You're going to find Remplume and complain to him about Ratatinus, who has denounced you as the leader of the conspiracy. You'll feign great anger and tell him that, since you're suspected now, you won't hesitate any longer to join them. They'll welcome you all the more because it's on you that all the weight of the conspiracy will fall henceforth, and, as he's a coward, he'll hasten to seize that opportunity to wriggle out of it in case of failure. Go, worthy fellow, I'm counting on you.

XIV. In which we witness a secret meeting of conspirators.

A week after that conversation with Rabotin, the joiner ran to the Palace at nightfall. It was only with difficulty that he was able to see the prince, for the latter was not expecting him and had not given orders to receive him. He was with the queen at that moment, who was lamenting with him the indifference of their subjects.

When Rabotin was introduced to Vatenlair's presence, the queen wanted to withdraw, but Vatenlair retained her. "Stay," he said. "This man will bring us up to date with what's happening in the city. Well, Rabotin, what do you have to say to me?"

"Prince, I've done everything you asked of me, but I fear that we'll arrive too late, for Remplume is in haste to overturn you; it's you above all at whom he's aiming."

"Aha! Tell me about it."

"As you ordered me, I enlisted in the league of malcontents. Remplume seemed very satisfied to know that all suspicions had been directed upon me. 'He's a clever man, Ratatinus,' he said, 'but that denunciation will oblige us to hasten the denouement.' This very evening, I attended a meeting at which it was decreed that you'd be sent a list of demands. It was discussed and drafted there and then, and, doubtless to test my devotion, it's me who was charged with delivering it to you. Here it is."

The prince scanned the letter.

"What are they demanding?" asked the queen.

"They speak in the name of the people and say that they don't recognize me as king, that only Princess Betinette has a right to the throne, and that, above all, she must repudiate her husband, who is only a foreigner and an adventurer."

Princess Betinette was indignant at that audacity, and wanted to punish the rebels immediately, but Vatenlair opposed any act of rigor.

"Since I'm the obstacle," he told her, "it's up to me to withdraw, but before then I want to show them that I'm worthy to govern them. This insulting petition they're sent us we ought to consider as not having arrived. It might even be appropriate to disdain it and not respond to it, but that fashion of acting would doubtless augment the number of malcontents. I want to see them and speak to them, and if they persist in their revolt, I'll employ further means to calm them."

"Do as you wish," said the princess, "but nothing can separate us."

As she said that, the princess rose to her feet and left Vatenlair alone with the workman.

Rabotin had sat down, and Vatenlair paced back and forth in his cabinet. He reflected on the advice of the princess, which he thought dangerous, because, not knowing exactly the magnitude of the conspiracy, he feared that threats or repressions might exasperate the conspirators. On the other hand, he thought that not responding to the petition might produce the same result. He was very perplexed. Finally, he told himself that the science that had served him so many times might come to his aid again, and, having made his decision, he stopped and sat down at his work table. The response was quickly drafted. It said that the following day he would receive the malcontents in a solemn audience, that he invited them to appoint delegates in order to explain their demands, and assured them that, if they were well-founded, the queen's desire was to rectify them.

When he had read his missive to Rabotin, to whom he handed it, after having sealed it, he added: "I know that this negotiation with the conspirators is absolutely lacking in dignity, but we're in exceptional circumstances, and in politics, besides, all means are good as long as they arrive at the goal. So you're going to deliver this letter to the conspirators this evening. Are they meting this evening?"

They now spend every night at the Leopard Tavern."

"Good. Tonight I'll be there too. Is the clock under repair?"

"Since yesterday."

"Have you replaced it with the panel for which I gave you the model?"

"Yes, Prince. I assume that's the place where you want to listen to the meeting. The staircase will be free; I'll let you onto the place myself."

"Good. But before then, take care to place behind the panel a box that I'm going to give you."

"It will be done. At midnight I'll be at the little door to the garden that's behind the tavern. No one goes past on that side at that hour."

"Go, then, my friend. I'll be very grateful for your devotion."

A few moments later, Rabotin, the bearer of the princely letter, carrying a maple-wood box on his back, emerged from the royal palace and disappeared into the darkness.

The twelfth stroke of midnight had just chimed in the belfry of Betaville, the streets were deserted, only illuminated by moonlight. The Leopard Tavern had been shut for an hour already, and one might have supposed that the inhabitants were already plunged in slumber if one had not seen, hiding in the shadows of houses, individuals in dark clothing with their hats pulled down over their faces, heading toward the meeting-place of the malcontents and crossing the threshold after having exchanged a password with an invisible person.

Remplume, who was a poor astronomer, had, on the other hand, a certain knowledge of humankind. As he had no money with which to purchase partisans, he had attached them to him initially by promises, which cost him nothing, and then by oaths, bonds that were more fragile, but which he surrounded by mystery that seemed to augment their value. All of them had sworn on the sword and the dagger to obey the orders voted by the assembly without being able to debate them; the nocturnal meetings had been held in almost complete darkness; the conspirators, only known to Remplume, were not known to one another; they had to arrive alone and leave in the same fashion; he had commanded them to denounce any weakness, to keep watch on those who seemed to them to be false brothers, and Remplume had carried out several fake executions in order to terrorize the affiliates.

The good bourgeois of Betaville were not cut out to be redoubtable conspirators; more than once they had asked themselves how they had got mixed up in that adventure and would have liked nothing better than to extract themselves from it, but Remplume did not lose sight of them; he kept them breathless, excited them incessantly and threatened them with the vengeance of their brothers, who, privately, were beginning to weary of these mysterious meetings that did not lead to any solution.

The room was long and rather narrow. A hundred people could gather therein easily. At the back was a table covered with a cloth, on which a shadowed lantern had been set. It was there that Remplume was installed. Opposite, behind the conspirators, was the bull's-eye that we have mentioned, blocked by the panel prepared by Rabotin.

There was no need to call for silence; the conspirators were mute.

Remplume spoke thus:

"Brothers, we have arrived at the end of our meetings; tonight is probably the last in which we will assemble. Yesterday, we sent the prince our conditions in the form in which we voted them. We demanded his divorce and his expulsion. He has replied to us immediately."

A frisson passed through the auditorium.

"The response is not what we wished; we expected that, but it gives us a certain satisfaction. He consents to discuss with us; the prince asks us to nominate delegates, whom he will receive today in solemn audience; he will listen to their demands and will answer them if they seem to him to be just. That tells us nothing, it's true; it is not a promise, but the interview will nevertheless have the advantage for us of being considered as a party and not as rebels; we will therefore have more authority to discuss our demands. Now, Brothers, we are going to choose our delegates.

At that moment, a member of the audience stood up and said: "In order to nominate delegates it is first necessary to know one another. We don't know one another, since we always deliberate in darkness."

"But I know you and me, and I can choose myself."

"No, no!" cried the conspirators, "light!"

"Well, yes," said Remplume. "In any case, the moment has come when we have no more need to hide; I'll have lamps brought."

At the same moment, a vibrant voice was heard at the back of the room, and these words were heard: "There is no need."

Immediately, the room was invaded by a dazzling light; everyone could see there as clearly as in broad daylight. The conspirators stood up and recognized one another with amazement. They called one another by their names, and, thinking that the spontaneous illumination was the work of Remplume, they jostled one another in order to get closer to him.

Remplume, however, standing at the table, was trying to take account of the phenomenon. Where was the light coming from? Was it another maneuver on the part of Vatenlair? To know who they were, doubtless. There were, therefore, false brothers in the assembly. Above all, it was necessary to reestablish silence. Climbing on to a chair, he shouted: "Shut up! You're making an infernal noise!"

At that word, the white light suddenly became red. The conspirators gave the impression of damned souls struggling in furnace, but the strangeness of that light had filled them with terror. They screamed as if they were really being roasted.

"Shut up, wretches!" cried Remplume. "Your cries will be heard outside. Let me speak! Let me say..."

But no one was listening. Suddenly, the silence that he could not obtain by persuasion fell abruptly. The red light had become green, and the members of the audience had the aspect of cadavers. Fear extinguished their howls; now they were trembling with fear.

Immediately, the green light disappeared and the room was plunged into darkness again.

Aided by Rabotin, Vatenlair hastened to replace the projection apparatus in the box, which the joiner immediately took away; they left the Leopard Tavern with it by the same route that they had come. Now he knew his enemies and would be better able to reckon with them because, save for Remplume and a few ambitious individuals, the rest had neither influence nor firmness; they were not very redoubtable devotees, simpletons ready to turn at the slightest wind.

With the obscurity, Remplume recovered his aplomb and his influence. Although he could not explain the electrical phenomena that had just been produced, he wanted to attribute them to himself, which gave him one strength more.

"Brothers," he said to them, "you see that I have no need of the aid of science in order to show you how far my power extends, and that is very little by comparison with what I can do. I have other surprises in reserve for you at more opportune moments. This evening I only wanted to prove to you that you can have confidence in me. In the meantime, let us not forget the object of our meeting. It's a matter of nominating delegates. You want to nominate them yourselves; you know one another now. Speak!"

The decision that it was necessary to make threw a certain disturbance into the minds of the conspirators; they were not habituated to struggle against royal power; it required all of Remplume's eloquence to convince a dozen malcontents to go to the palace, and then they would only consent to take that step on condition that the astrologer would accompany them and serve as spokesman.

Although Remplume was not enthusiastic to find himself in the presence of his former protectors, he consented to be part of the delegation, for he knew that no one else would dare to expose themselves to the anger of the king and queen by demanding their separation.

When they had returned to the palace, Vatenlair said to Rabotin: "That's not all, my lad; I still have need of your services. Go and get a little sleep, and come back early tomorrow with three or four companions. My intention is to prove to the delegates that I really am an enchanter capable of overturning my enemies and that, in marrying a princess, I am raising her to my level instead of being elevated by her."

At first light, Rabotin arrived with his workmen, and Vatenlair had them prepare his audience table in a special manner. Instead of armchairs, two long benches were disposed covered with shiny cloths that were linked to the throne by means of electric wires. Various other fitments were made, and then the Prince dismissed Rabotin and his fellows.

Toward the middle of the day, the delegation was introduced into the audience hall, where Vatenlair and Princess Betinette were already seated. In order to conceal his embarrassment, Remplume had assumed a rather impertinent attitude, which made Vatenlair smile. As for the other demonstrators, they lowered their heads and seemed ashamed of the step that they were taking.

As soon as they were seated, Vatenlair, who feared that Remplume, in accordance with appearances, might be impertinent, which would oblige him to end the session immediately without explanations, spoke first.

"You have informed, Messieurs, that you do not recognize me as your king; it is therefore to the queen that you are going to address your request. I see at your head a former intimate of the Palace in the times of the late King Beta; he knows the customs of the court because he was the chief of protocol; I can therefore hope that the discussion will be courteous, and that he will not forget the respect that he owes to Her Royal Majesty."

That appeal to the courtesy of a man totally devoid of it could not fail to embarrass Remplume, who had promised himself to be very violent, but he soon pulled himself together, stood up and, addressing the queen, he spoke thus:

"We have come to express to the queen our desire to see her reign alone. Until now, no foreigner has been established in our land, and we consider that it would be dangerous to its propriety to see it governed by a stranger who came among us without being invited and who, before the favors and titles with whim the late king heaped him, was of the most infimal condition."

Princess Betinette, who could scarcely contain herself, replied swiftly: "You're forgetting that my husband had no need of those titles. He is more than you and me, for he is an illustrious enchanter, and had proven it sufficiently."

"We have seen no magic, Madame; what you call thus are natural things that have not caused us any astonishment. They have been obtained by mechanical means, undoubtedly ingenious, but which do not emerge from magic. He has always required special apparatus to produce them, apparatus that any of us could construct. The engineer Vatenlair, whom you have made your husband, is therefore neither a magician nor an enchanter; perhaps he is a simple scholar, of whom there are many others, but he is certainly an ambitious upstart whose authority we do not want to recognize."

The princess had become pale with anger; she was about to give the order to arrest the delegates when Vatenlair intervened

"Since this concerns me," he said, "I can defend myself. You deny my power because, until today, it has only been employed to your benefit, but if I had exercised it against you, it would be a very different matter. When I have shown you that you can do nothing against me, you will doubtless change your opinion."

"Well," said Remplume, "since you claim to be an enchanter, prove it, here and now, without apparatus of any sort; if not, we, who are the delegates of the country, will use force in order oblige you to withdraw."

"A revolution?"

"It will be the first, but it will be to our advantage."

As he spoke, Remplume sat down; placed his hands on his knees and, raising his head insolently, looked at Vatenlair with a defiant expression.

"Very well," said Vatenlair, very calmly, "since it is me who inconveniences you, come and get me. I've given orders to my guards to go away; no one can defend me; there are ten of you and I'm alone. Act!"

As he spoke, the engineer sat down on his throne and folded his arms.

"With me, friends!" Remplume cried, immediately, trying to hurl himself on Vatenlair, but it was in vain that he tried to get up; an invisible force retained him on the bench, as well as the other delegates. In vain they tried to overcome that supernatural attraction; they remained in place, paralyzed, making the most comical efforts to free themselves.

"Well," said Vatenlair, "do you believe in my power now? Do I need apparatus to immobilize you?"

"No, no!" cried the delegates. "We can see that you're an enchanter. Let us go!"

"Get up, then," said Vatenlair. "And remember that it is necessary not to touch magic."

The delegates got up and prostrated themselves before the engineer, protesting their fidelity. They even accused Remplume of having deceived them, and went away, entirely convinced that Vatenlair was a magician.

XV. In which this story concludes to the satisfaction of everyone.

When they remained alone, Princess Betinette said to her husband:

"You've summoned science to your aid once again, but a time will come when it will be impotent. Remplume won't lay down his arms; it's him alone that it's necessary to attain, why prevent me from punishing him? His hostility will reveal itself in another form; we'll be living in continual anxiety. I'm not cut out to lead a wayward people who will be incessantly discontented. Under my father's reign there was never the slightest revolt; now that our subjects have commenced, they won't stop. Sovereign power scarcely tempts me; I'd rather live with you far from society, happy and tranquil. Nothing retains me in this country any longer; my mother and father are dead, you alone are everything to me. Believe me, let's leave these idiots to fight among themselves, with their leaders, and go away."

"But where can we go? The kings, your uncles, seemed to be jealous of your father's glory; they wouldn't welcome us."

"Well then, let's leave this land and go to yours. As long as I'm with you, I'll be happy. Yes, you can now inflate the balloon that brought you here. Don't hesitate—it's deliverance!"

"So be it. But we ought not to depart in secret as if we were being expelled. It's necessary that our departure take place in broad daylight before the assembled people. I'll make all the preparations for that. We'll announce a captive ascension, which will prevent anyone from supposing that we're thinking of fleeing, and once we're in the air, I'll cut the cable…unless they have the idea of cutting it themselves.

And, in fact, in spite of the failure of the Betaville delegation, Remplume, as Princess Betinette had foreseen, raised his head again. He had regained the confidence of the malcontents by telling them that he recognized that Vatenlair really was an enchanter, but an evil enchanter, as was proven by the means that he had used to demonstrate his power. He said that there was nothing more to discuss with him and that the only thing to do was to suppress him. But how? He sought a means.

A month after the visit of the conspirators to the king's palace, Prince Enchanter summoned Ratatinus, his prefect of police.

"Monsieur," he said to him, "The malevolent rumors are recommencing, Remplume is active again. You knew that, and didn't tell me."

"I swear to you, Prince, that the little plot that you stifled so skillfully no longer exists; I will even say that all the delegates to whom you granted an audience are now your most ardent defenders. As for Remplume, he no longer has the slightest influence."

"But he's still talking and recommencing his petty calumnies. I warn you that I'm not in a humor to tolerate them, and I beg you to tell him to remain quiet, or I'll do him a bad turn in my fashion that will close his mouth forever."

Ratatinus, who saw that the prince as beginning to get annoyed, warned Remplume, but the latter only laughed at the threat.

"You're wrong," said Ratatinus. "I assure you that the Prince seemed to me to be firmly determined to repress any kind of conspiracy. He knows full well—I don't know how, but not from me—that you're creating agitation, that you've reunited your partisans, and I believe that it would be dangerous to stand up to him."

"Bah! You don't know him. He's not a man of government; as long as people admire his inventions, he's satisfied. Believe me, he's a vulgar scholar who wants to impose on us and is turning the whole country upside down. The oil merchants are ruined because of the gas and electricity; the horse-dealers too, because of velocipedes and automobiles; painters no longer make a sou because of the vulgarization of photography; all the workers are furious at seeing themselves replaced by machines of every sort; in sum, everyone's complaining in low voices. But they're beginning to have had enough of all these improvements, which have completely changed the customs of the land, and soon, you'll see, they won't be embarrassed to tell him so to his face. But this time, in spite of all his magic, we won't stop half way, and we'll overturn the usurper."

Ratatinus, frightened by Remplume's determined attitude, made no reply, for he was very perplexed. If he did not carry out Vatenlair's orders, he would lose his position, and if he carried them out by denouncing the conspirators again, he would risk losing it if, by chance, Remplume succeeded

Finally, he said: "You understand, my dear fellow, that if I've warned you, it's in your interest."

"Oh, I know that. But be careful, Ratatinus of looking after both the goat and the cabbage."

"What do you mean? You know very well that I won't make any report on your actions."

"I don't know anything; in any case, if it's true, you're not making me any on Vatenlair's actions."

"You haven't asked me for any."

"That's true, but perhaps it would be good politics for you not to be so secretive."

Ratatinus took that as read.

A few days later he took Remplume aside. "I know something," he said. "The Prince has had his balloon removed from the attics of the palace and transported to the factory, where it's being repaired.

"Well, well," said Remplume. "What is he going to do, then?"

"I don't know. You can't say now that I haven't warned you."

Remplume racked his brains to divine Vatenlair's intentions, but he did not search for long. The day after Ratatinus' indiscretion, immense posters covered the walls of the city; they were conceived thus:

CITY OF BETAVILLE

In recognition of the devotion and fidelity of the inhabitants of Betaville, Prince Enchanter invites them to a fête that will be held on the first of the month in the palace gardens. As well as diversions of all sorts that will be offered to them, they will witness a spectacle new to the land in the elevation of a

CAPTIVE BALLOON

which is to say, a balloon tethered to the ground by a cable, in the nacelle of which one can rise up without danger, and which will rise to a height of four hundred meters. At the end of the day, Prince Enchanter and the Queen will rise up in their turn, to show the people that they do not disdain to partake of their pleasures.

Remplume read and reread the poster without being able to comprehend the objective that Vatenlair intended; in the end, he told himself that it was doubtless to render himself popular, and with an afterthought of vainglory, such as all inventors have. At the same time as he thought that, however, a less banal idea occurred to him. He imagined insinuating to the inhabitants that Vatenlair's proposal to go up in a balloon was a trap, and that, in consequence, he engaged them not to risk themselves thus in the air. Then, he whispered to his accomplices, suggesting the idea of getting rid of Vatenlair while he was in the balloon by cutting the rope that retained the aerostat.

The day of the fête finally arrived. In the palace gardens the balloon, inflated that morning, was swaying, retained by a cable wound around a windlass. An immense crowd surrounded the aerostat at a distance. A man who had been given instructions—the man in question was Rabotin—was standing next to the windlass with a crew of workmen. His apparent mission was to unwind the cable and wind it up when it had reached the extremity of its length. The nacelle was made of wicker. Underneath it but adhering to it and forming, so to speak, a lower story, a closed chamber had been established in which ballast and provisions for the voyage had been placed. Several cables hung own from the nacelle, including the guide rope and another one, rather long, terminated by rolled-up sheets and thinner cords.

The queen and the prince soon arrived, followed by the principal individuals of the court. At that moment, Ratatinus, at the prince's invitation, asked whether anyone wanted to make an ascension in the balloon, but no one volunteered. Remplume's advice had been followed.

The prince and the queen decided then to climb into the nacelle.

Until then, Remplume had not shown himself, but when he saw the balloon rise up slowly, he emerged from hiding, and, with an ax in his hand, ran to the cable in order to sever it abruptly. But he had not taken two paces before he was seized by the men posted by the prince and tied up tightly with one of the cords falling from the nacelle. At the same time, the prince shouted: "Release all!"

The balloon was seen to rise up swiftly, with Remplume underneath it, tied up like a sausage.

The entire population uttered an immense clamor. It was perceived then that nothing any longer retained the balloon to the ground. The prince had detached it. But another clamor was heard; the rope that retained Remplume to the balloon had just been cut in its turn. The unfortunate astrologer was about to be broken by his fall. Nothing of the sort happened, however. Above his head, a hemisphere of cloth suddenly deployed, which softened his fall, while the unballasted aerostat soon disappeared in the sky.

And since then, no more mention has ever been heard of engineer Vatenlair and Princess Betinette. They probably came down in another unknown world or, perhaps, have even been able to recommence their experiments in fantastic realities

There is, I think, no need to give our young readers explanations of the marvelous experiments that we have described. They are in the domain of modern science, which is making progress from day to day. They have all recognized, in passing, gas lighting, hypnotic suggestion, photography, cinematography, electricity, the phonograph, Röntgen rays, the submarine boat, automobilism, bicycles, projectors, the electromagnet[22] and, finally, the balloon and the parachute. Re-

---

[22] In spite of the author's optimism, it might not have been obvious to young readers in 1905 how Vatenlair was able to immobilize the delegates with the aid of an electromagnet. Nor will it be obvious to today's readers, who might well suspect the author of having made a mistake. They might also wonder exactly how Betinette developed her photographs and how Vatenlair manufactured the cathode ray tube necessary to produce X-rays at such short notice.

move those marvels from the domain of science, and they appear to emanate from magic. But in our day people no longer believe in fays or enchanters; even illusions no longer create illusion, and there no longer remains on earth a mortal as naïve as King Beta.

Gustave Guitton: *The Humans of the Year 3000* (1907)

I. On Vacation

The village of Montbarzy, in the Ardennes, situated in the heart of the forest, is five leagues from the nearest railways station. Letters and news only reach that lost hamlet slowly. Its inhabitants—woodcutters, charcoal burners and cultivators—still live the contemplative and laborious existence that their ancestors lived a hundred years ago. They have retained mores full of simplicity.

Montbarzy is one of the rare places in France where one can still live cheaply, on condition of being content with the local wine, milk, poultry and vegetables. Food and lodging cost three or four times less than in Paris.

That was the principal reason why, for several years, Monsieur Vernoy, a deputy curator in the National Archives, had chosen the village for his annual vacation. The calm beauty of the landscape, the vivifying atmosphere of the woods of oaks and firs, the unalterable tranquility and profound peace that one enjoyed at Montbarzy were also advantages much appreciated by the archivist, curbed all year over dusty parchments.

Monsieur Vernoy was accompanied by his wife and his only son, Marcel, who was about to reach his seventeenth year.

As they did every year, the Vernoys stayed in the home of the Maire of the little commune, Monsieur Blancheron, who rented them the entire first floor of his house, three large rooms, for the modest sum of fifty francs a month.

Monsieur le Maire, a woodcutter and shoemaker by profession, also kept one of those shops that one encounters in the depths of the country, filled with the most disparate goods: wooden clogs, *images d'Épinal*, throat pastilles, cotton thread, agricultural implements and salted herrings. Madame Blancheron, in spite of the occupation that the commerce in question provided, found the time to prepare simple but copious meals for the Vernoy family.

Confidence and esteem were reciprocal between the Vernoys and the Blancherons. Every year the latter awaited impatiently the arrival of "the Parisians," and only saw them depart with regret.

Monsieur Vernoy was only veritably happy in Montbarzy. Only there did he feel relieved, as if of a heavy burden, of his administrative preoccupations and the everyday cares that assail the head of a family devoid of fortune with a meager salary. He abandoned his frock coat for a twill jacket, and, in the company of his wife and Marcel, there were long and fortifying walks in the woods, excursions to the famous sites in the vicinity, harvests of mushrooms and wild flowers, and picnics on the grass: a whole series of innocent and healthy distractions. The weeks of the vacation passed like a dream.

Monsieur Vernoy, his tall stature slightly curbed, had an angular profile and prominent cheekbones. His slightly curly hair was going gray. His gestures were slightly jerky, and the gaze of his blue eyes revealed a resigned and pensive mildness. Sober in speech, morose and sullen when in Paris, he became exuberant and cheerful in the country. His good humor was even proverbial among the inhabitants of Montbarzy.

Everyone, but particularly Monsieur Blancheron, was surprised, that year, to see Monsieur Vernoy arrive with a melancholy expression that they had never seen before. They thought that he was ill. They asked him. He replied, with slight annoyance, that he was quite well, thus cutting off any further questions.

In fact, Monsieur Vernoy was under the impact of preoccupations caused by abrupt changes in the character and behavior of his son Marcel.

Previously, the young man had been cited as an example to his comrades. He was considered as a brilliant pupil. In the end of the year examinations and in compositions his fellows tried in vain to compete with him for first place. The teachers only talked about Marcel Vernoy, already crowned several times in general competitions, as an exceptional student, equally well endowed for the sciences and letters.

To the great surprise of everyone, the young man had been suddenly discouraged. Without yet being classed among the dunces, he did not do his homework and only learned enough of his lessons to avoid punishment. He seemed to be uninterested in the eventual success of his studies. His end of the year report was very poor. A long note in the head teacher's handwriting had informed Monsieur Vernoy of that deplorable state of affairs.

The parents had also remarked a complete change in their son's character. Ordinarily cheerful, Marcel had become somber, preoccupied, and even sly.

Previously, he had kept his father and mother up to date with his class work, his reading and the slightest incidents of his life as a schoolboy. Now he was reserved, scarcely responding to his father's affectionate questions, and as soon as meals were concluded he ran to shut himself in his bedroom, skimped his homework and spent hours reading novels, looking out into the street, and dreaming.

Madame Vernoy, as anxious as her husband, tried in vain to react. Ordinarily very affectionate with his mother, the young man only responded to her admonitions with surly retorts, affirming that nothing had changed in him; he had only been less happy than in previous years, that was all.

The mother was not duped by that lack of confidence. Without letting anything be seen of the chagrin she felt, she redoubled her persistence and her coaxing. It was futile; Marcel remained idle, morose and secretive.

Monsieur Vernoy, whose duty it was to give proof of authority, did not have the courage, so afflicted was he, struck in the heart in his paternal affection and in his dearest hopes. He did not address any reprimand to his son, convinced that the crisis of indolence would soon pass, but he tried in vain to dissimulate his sadness.

He had thought that the country air, the joy of the vacation and the pleasure of a change of scene might return all of Marcel's former frankness and laborious ardor. On the contrary, the sojourn in Montbarzy only augmented the schoolboy's melancholy discouragement.

One day, having arrived in Montbarzy a week before, the Vernoys were finishing the morning meal in the room with the old oak furniture smelling pleasantly of wax and lavender, which they had made into their dining room. It was midday. Without waiting for the coffee to be served, Marcel had already departed for one of his customary solitary walks. The father and mother remained silent.

Finally, Madame Vernoy exclaimed: "My God, what can be wrong with that poor child?"

"I don't know," replied Monsieur Vernoy, shaking his head in a discouraged manner. "At present, Marcel is going through a grave crisis. What makes me despair is that I can't help him, with my advice, to recover his mental equilibrium. For some time now, he no longer confides in me."

"Once," the mother murmured, sadly, "he didn't hide anything from me. Now he hides everything."

"It takes so little at his age, alas, to transform the best student into a slacker and the most obedient and submissive child into an unruly one."

"A bad book or a bad acquaintance can sometimes have the deadliest influence."

"If only he'd consent to explain the reasons for his discouragement to me," exclaimed Monsieur Vernoy, impatiently, "perhaps I could succeed in repairing the damage..."

The Vernoys' conversation was abruptly interrupted by Marcel's return. He had forgotten his knife—a solid knife equipped with a saw-blade, which he used to cut walking-sticks or fishing-rods in the woods.

Marcel was about to leave again when his father blocked his passage.

"You're in a hurry," he said.

"I'm going for a walk," the boy replied, sullenly.

"You can go in a little while. I need to talk to you seriously. Give me the pleasure of sitting down and listened to me attentively."

In spite of the annoyance he felt, the young man took a seat.

Monsieur Vernoy looked his son in the face, and in a voice pierced with contained emotion, he said: "Listen, my dear friend, you're no longer a child; you've reached an age at which one is responsible for one's actions, when one directs oneself in life. You're almost a man; it's as a man what I want to talk to you."

"I'm listening, Father," said Marcel, with more politeness than respect.

Monsieur Vernoy continued: "You know the care and solicitude with which your mother and I have surrounded your first steps and have occupied ourselves with your education. Why, for some months, have you completely changed in our regard? Not only don't you work any longer, but instead of making us party, as you once did, to your annoyances or pleasures, you enclose yourself egotistically within yourself. I don't want either to punish you or to reprimand you; I'm simply appealing to your frankness. What's wrong? What strange thing is happening in your young brain?

Marcel's embarrassment was visible. Blushing, confused and discountenanced, he lowered his eyes and agitated on his chair, searching for a response.

There were a few moments of painful silence. The affection he had for his parents and his self-esteem were engaged in a violent conflict in his heart.

Marcel had, as they say, a bad head but a good heart; his pride could not hold out against the sad and grave expressions of Monsieur and Madame Vernoy.

"Well, all right," he said, abruptly making a decision. "I'll tell you why I didn't win any prizes this year and why I'm so discouraged."

"You might be more fortunate next year," said Madame Vernoy, anxiously.

"I had as much chance this year as in the previous ones. If I haven't won any prizes, it's because I haven't tried."

"We've perceived that," sighed Madame Vernoy. "But why that idleness?"

"I haven't tried because it's futile. I could work myself to death, but I'll never succeed in realizing my ambitious desires."

Monsieur Vernoy suppressed a start of surprise. The trouble was more profound than he had imagined.

In a tone of sincere despair, Marcel continued: "Yes, study...hard work...are a sham. At school, I see nothing around me but the sons of millionaires, famous men or politicians. Whatever I do, I'll never be able to rank alongside them in life, so what's the point in wearing myself out? One way or another, the result will be the same: I'll obtain some modest employment like yours, Papa. You merit better yourself, but you're neither rich nor a schemer..."

"Marcel," Monsieur Vernoy replied, severely, "I'm sorry to discover in you a sentiment as base and despicable as jealousy. I've never inculcated such principles in you; I've never taught you to envy the good fortune of others, even when it's unmerited. Certainly, the struggle for existence is harsh, but that's why it's necessary to show more courage. Even if they're rich or the sons of illustrious fathers, the idle never obtain the first place in society."

"However, Father," the young man replied, bitterly, "your own example..."

"Precisely... Well, have you ever heard me complain? I'm quite happy as I am, and I don't envy anyone."

Marcel, troubled in his naïve ambitious egotism, listened to his father with astonishment.

"Does that surprise you?" said Monsieur Vernoy. "I'm happy, though, because I do my duty; and I'm more favored than many others, because I've chosen a task that pleases me, which is in conformity with my tastes and aptitudes. Know that we're not in this base world simply to satisfy our appetite for wealth and domination; we ought to work disinterestedly, as the generations that preceded us have worked."

Monsieur Vernoy was animated. The flame of a generous ardor was shining in his gaze.

"You don't seem to realize," he went on, "that the well-being and security that you enjoy, and the very brain that permits you to think, are the fruit of the effort and suffering of thousands of generations. Like all modern humans, you're the creditor of the past; you owe gratitude to all those who preceded you: to the prehistoric man who was the first to carve a flint ax and undertake the destruction of large predators; to the pioneer who began to clear the forests, the heathlands and the marshes that covered the globe; to the poet and the philosopher who opened the domain of thought to humankind thousands of years before you.

"It isn't only the teachers who have tried patiently to sculpt the still-primitive block of your intelligence to whom you owe a debt. The glass from which you drink, the book that you read and the house in which you live are the results of inventions, and long and difficult cumulative effort. Alone, naked and unarmed, what would you be without the powerful human solidarity that has surrounded you since birth with a benevolent atmosphere? It's that millenarian solidarity that permits you to live, but on condition that you render services in your turn, that you bring your stone to the common edifice—in brief, that you increase, for the Future, the heritage of the Past."

"I've never thought of that," admitted Marcel, pensively.

"The superiority that delivers a fortune, or the easy attainment of a sinecure, is illusory and deceptive. It doesn't procure veritable happiness."

"But in that case," said Marcel, increasingly attentive, "What is the veritable goal of life, and how can one be happy?"

"One can only be happy by means of one's own effort, by the satisfaction of one's own conscience. All the satisfactions of luxury and vanity aren't worth as much as the calm pleasure of duty accomplished. And that intimate serenity, that profound satisfaction, is only obtained by rendering oneself useful to others, in the measure of one's abilities. For me, there are several sorts of superiority, as there are several sorts of happiness. The artisan, who works manually, ought to be esteemed, and perhaps happy, in his humble condition. Above him is placed the man who, by virtue of his intelligence and his capacity for organization and work, procures wellbeing for a number of his peers. At a superior level is the man who, by means of an invention or an act of courage, adds to the grandeur and wealth of his homeland. But the man who surpasses them all is one who enables humankind entire to take a step forward on the path of progress.

"What you're telling me, Father, appears to me to be all very well in theory, but very vague and abstract. I'd understand it better with a few examples."

"You only have to look around you. Do you think that the likes of Bernard Palissy, Pascal, Denis Papin, Jacquart, Hugo or Pasteur didn't have, in the bitter struggle that they sustained against the prejudices of their times, higher and more beautiful enjoyments than the majority of men? The scientist and the artist, poor but passionate about their work, experience a thousand joys that the ignorant and idle rich will never know."

Marcel remained silent. Monsieur Vernoy added: "I don't have the pretention of changing your ideas at a stroke and modifying your egotistic prejudices instantaneously; I only implore you to reflect on what I've said, and I'm convinced that, with your intelligence and common sense, you won't take long to perceive that I'm right, that my theory is the only sound one."

Marcel scowled, nodded his head affirmatively, and withdrew, far more annoyed than convinced.

II. The Misadventure of an Angler

As a veritable Parisian, Monsieur Vernoy took a naïve pleasure in all rural activities. He delighted in seeing vegetables growing and fruits ripening, on the espaliers and beanpoles in Monsieur Blancheron's garden. Insects, flowers and minerals interested him equally. Far from the dusty paper of the Archives, he felt that he had the soul of a botanist, a geologist, or even a horticulturalist.

Sometimes, with a geologist's hammer at his waist and the green box of a naturalist slung over his shoulder, he launched himself into the woods and over the hills. Sometimes, he spent entire hours poring over an anthill or posted in the vicinity of a beehive. And he took pleasure in observing that animals, when they live in a society, are sometimes more prudent and better organized than human beings.

Madame Vernoy, although she did not understand her husband's theoretical and technical side, almost always accompanied him, amused by the innumerable anecdotes with which the archivist's memory was ornamented.

In addition, the two spouses had another source of distractions in the conversation of the peasants of Montbarzy, who showed a great deal of respect to "the Parisians" and consulted them in a host of special cases. Many a time, the logic of the archivist and the conciliatory mildness of Madame Vernoy had put an end to quarrels or prevented lawsuits. All the details of the lives of the people of Montbarzy interested them, and, as everyone has weaknesses, they often lent a complaisant ear to the gossip of the peasants.

There was one topic that returned incessantly to conversations: the person and the way of life of Monsieur Belzevor. The owner of the Château de Montbarzy served as a pretext for perpetual commentary in the village; he led an absolutely claustral existence. Devoted to scientific research, he never emerged from the enclosure of his park. People spoke with a respect mingled with an almost superstitious dread about the laboratory, the greenhouses and the luxurious and bizarre furniture of the Château de Montbarzy.

Because of his solitary existence and a few cures that he had operated in desperate cases, Monsieur Belzevor was not far from being considered as a sorcerer in the locale. Monsieur Vernoy, admiring the facility with which legends are created in simple souls, contented himself with smiling at those tales. He knew, in fact, that Monsieur Belzevor—an eccentric, original in his private life—was fundamentally a man of the highest science, universally appreciated for important discoveries in toxicology. He was a rich inventor, habituated to satisfying all his whims, but not a diabolical individual, as the majority of the inhabitants of Montbarzy imagined.

Monsieur and Madame Vernoy would have been perfectly happy if it were not for the chagrin that Marcel was causing them, whose ill humor and mutism persisted. Initially touched by the paternal reprimands, he had quickly forgotten them. He did not modify his way of life at all. He departed in the morning, whatever the weather, and only returned at meal times, sometimes soaked by rain, sometimes covered in mud, his clothing ripped and his hands covered in scratches.

Persuaded that his son was taking advantage of those solitary excursions in order to think seriously, Monsieur Vernoy did not address any remonstration to him. After a week, however, he did not take long to perceive that Marcel had not mended his ways at all. Still as somber, as sly and as economical in speech, the young man did not manifest any species of confidence toward his parents. He did not give any evidence of the frank repentance that makes everything forgivable.

In reality, Marcel, a precociously discouraged ambitious youth, was filling the void of his days with long walks through the rocks and clearings, but he soon wearied of those aimless excursions, and was attracted by fishing and hunting.

In a forested region like that of Montbarzy, everyone is something of a poacher. Perfidiously advised by an aged vil-

150

lage marauder, the schoolboy soon knew how one places a snare and how one extends a deep fishing line. Either by virtue of lack of skill or bad luck, Marcel was rarely fortunate in his expeditions, but so far as he was concerned, that was one more reason for obstinate persistence. He put into the project of becoming a skilled poacher the same determination that he had once put into obtaining to marks for a composition.

Thus far, Marcel had not taken the risk of trespassing on private property, but he succumbed to a temptation stronger than the rest. It was said that there were marvelous rabbit warrens and fish ponds in the grounds of the Château de Montbarzy, but since they belonged to Monsieur Belzevor, no fisherman or hunter had dared to penetrate them. Marcel's imagination was stimulated,

That Monsieur Belzevor, he thought, *is doubtless an old library and laboratory rat; he must have a profound scorn for sports. I'd swear that game and fish are pullulating on his land as in a veritable earthly paradise. And then, a person of that sort can't mount a very attentive surveillance of his property.*

Having convinced himself by that reasoning, whose indelicacy his parents would certainly have criticized, Marcel got up very early one morning. He was carrying in his wicker basket all the equipment of an angler.

The village was still asleep. Marcel only encountered a few woodcutters, who were setting off to work with their axes over their shoulders. They greeted the young man with a sympathetic *bonjour* and their heavy and regular step drew away. Secretly ashamed of what he was about to do, Marcel only breathed freely when he was in the heart of the forest.

Half an hour after leaving Monsieur Blancheron's house, he arrived at the foot of the high ivy-covered walls surrounding the park of the château. It was child's play for him to reach the crest of the wall, aiding himself with branches and fissures, and then to slide down on the other side, to the great detriment of his breeches and boots.

He crossed a ditch encumbered by brushwood and found himself in the park, with foliage beaded with dew, from which the matinal perfume of wild flowers was exhaled. His heart beating with emotion, he followed a path, and then another, perceived the white façade of the château in front of him and turned back abruptly.

The park seemed abandoned. The trees, where garlands of clematis and honeysuckle dangled, did not seem ever to have been pruned. Under the pressure of holly and ferns, the paths were effaced. Flocks of birds fled, chirping, in front of the indiscreet visitor.

Marcel was delighted with his escapade. "Oh," he murmured, "this is a veritable fairy tale château." He did not lose sight of the practical objective of his expedition, however. After a few minutes' research, he arrived at the edge of a pond bordered with reeds and arrowheads, encumbered by nenuphars with broad green leaves and silver and gold flowers.

A stream alimented the large expanse of water, and beneath the foliage of the aquatic plants the backs of fishes could be seen gleaming like flashes of steel.

Marcel Vernoy immediately set to work.

He chose his spot and unpacked his devices; and after carefully checking his hooks, he attached his line to a tree root, promising himself that he would come back in half an hour.

Meanwhile, Doctor Belzevor, having spent the night working in his laboratory, as was his custom, had decided to make a tour of the park before going to bed, in order to cool his brow, which was burning with a studious fever, in the breath of the pleasant morning breeze. The peace of the solitude was only troubled by birdsong, the murmur of insects awakened by the early sunlight, and the rustle of plants.

Monsieur Belzevor was savoring the calm beauty of that corner of nature religiously when the sound of trodden foliage and broken branches caused him to prick up his ears. *What!* the proprietor said to himself. *Has some poacher come to visit*

my rabbits? That would be rather astonishing, given the repu-
tation of a terrible sorcerer that the people of the region have
been kind enough to given me.

Dr. Belzevor set himself to lie in wait behind an oak tree.
He expected to see some vagabond covered in rags, or some
peasant in a blouse and clogs, so he was quite surprised to see
that the scoundrel who had not hesitated to cross the boundary
of the park was a young man coquettishly clad in a maroon
suit and coiffed with an elegant sportsman's hat. His collar
and cravat were irreproachable, his physiognomy full of mildness and intelligence.

Those blue eyes and that fine profile aren't those of a
professional malefactor, the doctor said to himself. *I'm cer-*
tainly dealing with some truant from college, to whom it might
perhaps be useful to give a good lesson.

Monsieur Belzevor waited until Marcel had finished setting his lines. Then, emerging abruptly from hiding, he advanced toward the young man.

Marcel almost uttered a cry of fright on seeing, two paces away from him, the strange person who appeared to have
surged forth, as if miraculously, from a dense thicket of aca-
cias and hawthorns.

Monsieur Belzevor, with his short stature and his clean-
shaven face, brightened by two dark eyes sparkling with vivacity, seemed imprecise in his antiquity. His complexion was
faded and his brow was furrowed by numerous wrinkles, but
his hair was still unusually black and his eyes, animated by a
juvenile gleam, disconcerted the observer. Was he thirty years
old or sixty? It was impossible to tell.

His attire was implacably correct. Coiffed in a soft silk-
lined hat, with varnished shoes and yellow gloves, Monsieur
Belzevor was clad in a black jacket with a slightly pretentious
cut, and pearl gray trousers with gaiters. A malicious smile
uncovered his exceedingly white teeth.

Marcel was so alarmed by that apparition that he did not
have the presence of mind to flee. Ashamed and blushing, he

remained in front of the doctor like a guilty man awaiting his sentence.

"I see," said Monsieur Belzevor, sarcastically, "that you're an early riser, young man. Unfortunately, so am I."

"Monsieur…," stammered Marcel, piteously, taking off his cap.

"I shall take account of your age, this time, and let you go without putting you in the hands of the gendarmes, but don't come back here again. What is your name?"

"Marcel Vernoy."

"You're doubtless at school?"

"Yes, Monsieur," the young man murmured, in a voice as faint as a breath.

"Well, you're not making your masters any compliment for the lessons in morality they've given you. Either their morality is deplorable or you haven't profited from their instruction. I incline toward the second hypothesis."

Marcel was plunged in confusion. Mechanically, he twisted his cap between his fingers. He would have liked, as the saying has it, to be a hundred feet underground, having disappeared through a trap-door, as he had seen done is fantasy plays at the Châtelet.

Dr. Belzevor took pity on his embarrassment. "That's all right," he said. "Go away."

Marcel had set forth, crestfallen, in the direction of the wall of the park, when the doctor called him back.

"You'll have too much difficulty getting out that way," he said. "Leave honestly through the gate. The domestics will think that I've had a slightly early and somewhat unexpected visit, that's all."

Discountenanced, Marcel followed his guide, without saying a word. They were approaching the majestic wrought iron gate that opened on to the main road when Dr. Belzevor changed his mind for a second time.

"By the way," he said, "now I think about it, what about your lines? I wouldn't like to confiscate your apparatus, like a simple gamekeeper."

To the great joy of the doctor, Marcel bit his fingernails in his shame, his rage and his wounded pride. He was obliged to submit to the torture of returning all the way to the pond. Then, under the shrewd gaze of the doctor, he lifted the five lines from the depths in which he had just extended them.

A superb pike was attached to the last of them. Pulled out of the water, it was still thrashing in the grass.

"Damn! A fine fish," said Monsieur Belzevor, in a complimentary tone.

Marcel picked up the fish, still quivering, and presented it to the doctor. "It belongs to you, Monsieur," he said.

"Not at all. You can eat it as penance...personally, I don't like that fish." And he added: "Now that you know the way, there's no need for me to guide you again."

Monsieur Belzevor had already disappeared behind a clump of bushes while Marcel, his cap in one hand and his lines and the pike in the other, was still in the same place, downcast and utterly nonplussed.

He hastened to leave the park and return to Montbarzy, where he arrived, contrary to his habit, well before the time for the morning meal.

Monsieur Vernoy, who was far from suspecting what had happened, congratulated his son on his fortunate fishing expedition. Marcel gave his father's compliments a very poor welcome. He was simultaneously repentant and vexed. So, when the fish had been confided to the skillful Madame Blancheron and the young man found himself alone with his parents, he could not help recounting his misadventure in an abrupt fit of frankness.

"That's very bad, what you did!" exclaimed Monsieur Vernoy. And he explained to his son at length that there is no small sin; that the person who steals the property of another, for the first time, for a trivial reason, will be disposed to recommence on a more important occasion.

"I believe," added Madame Vernoy, turning to her husband, "that it would be as well for you to go and present your apologies to Monsieur Belzevor with regard to Marcel's conduct."

"Perhaps you're right," he replied. "But me, a poor employee, a subaltern functionary, presenting myself at the home of that great scientist, that millionaire château owner…do you think so?"

"The step is entirely indicated, though," replied Madame Vernoy, softly. "If this Monsieur Belzevor had been malevolent, or simply severe, he could have caused Marcel and us serious problems. In such cases, thanks and apologies, are necessary."

After a few hesitations, Monsieur Vernoy followed his wife's advice. That same evening, ceremoniously clad in his newest bureaucratic frock coat, he went to ring the bell at the gate of the Château de Montbarzy.

It was six o'clock in the evening.

"Your timing is good," said the domestic to whom he addressed himself. "Monsieur has just got up. He'll doubtless be able to see you shortly."

After a quarter of an hour waiting in a magnificent drawing room in the modern style, with bright cedar paneling and pale green silk hangings, Monsieur Vernoy was introduced into the presence of Dr. Belzevor, in a study that surpassed in luxury anything that the honest archivist had been able to admire at official receptions.

Monsieur Vernoy was immediately sympathetic to Dr. Belzevor, who stopped him in the middle of his excuses. After five minutes, the archivist had lost his initial ceremonious stiffness, and they chatted about science, literature and erudition, touching one a thousand various subjects without any prior decision.

By the end of that first visit, Dr. Belzevor had taken Monsieur Vernoy in amity. He had even promised to confide to him certain research on a lost manuscript of Bombastus Paracelsus, which Monsieur Vernoy, by virtue of his official functions in the Archives, was in a position to complete.

Dr. Belzevor had imagination and science; Monsieur Vernoy possessed erudition. The two men complemented one another admirably.

In response to the invitation that had been extended to him, Monsieur Vernoy returned to the château on a daily basis, where he spent an hour or two, extremely agreeably, in discussion with his new friend.

Incidentally, he mentioned to him the anxieties that Marcel was causing him.

"You see everything in black," the doctor replied, cheerfully. "The young man—poaching apart—pleases me greatly. Why not bring him with you?"

"I dare not...and he professes a salutary terror in your regard himself."

"It's true that I made fun of him a little cruelly...but if he comes tomorrow evening, I'll study him. We'll see whether there isn't a means of curing him."

III. Belzevorine

The following day, Marcel Vernoy was introduced by his father to Monsieur Belzevor, and did not take long to become one of the friends of the château. The slightly fantastic personality of the doctor impressed the young man. He felt very small in confrontation with the ideas of manifest genius and the impeccable logic of the aged scientist.

The latter, who judged him to be very intelligent, was amused by his astonishment. He never wearied of making him admire his vast hothouses, where the gilded light of Edison lamps outlined the disquieting profiles of tropical orchids, creepers and nightshades.

What struck Marcel most of all was that Monsieur Belzevor did not possess any "luxury plants," so to speak. He only attached importance to vegetables whose active principle could have a powerful effect on the human organism. *Datura stramonium*, Saint Ignatius' beans, the lianas that produce curare and *Ouabaia strophantus* had pride of place in his collections.[23] Those poisonous planted were the ones that the doctor pampered the most, surrounding them with the most scrupulous care.

Another particularity that struck Marcel was the reverence that Dr. Belzevor professed for perfumes, and the magisterial science with which he dosed essences. Each of the rooms in the château was embalmed with a particular odor, from the rose and myrtle dear to antiquity to the most modern perfumes: ylang-ylang, chypre, patchouli and syringa.

The doctor cherished above all the ultra-modern odors that are, in the art of perfumery, what "modern style" is in furnishing: discreet and subtle odors like that of *Tilia*, the linden tree, the lily-of-the-valley and *Corylopsis*, or fragrant winter hazel. Whenever Monsieur Belzevor went into a room, there was a marvelous expansion of delectable fragrances.

Apart from his immoderate and slightly ridiculous liking for perfumes, Dr. Belzevor was also fervent about gems and precious stones of all kinds. His left hand was ornamented by five gold rings, exact similar in form, but whose bezels were each ornamented by a different stone. On the index finger there was a topaz, on the middle finger a ruby, on the ring finger a black diamond, and on the little finger a uvarovite.

Marcel never wearied of questioning the doctor about the most diverse subjects. The latter took advantage of that to study him surreptitiously, passing him through the sieve of his pitiless analysis.

---

[23] *Datura stramonium* is the hallucinogenic jimson weed. "Saint Ignatius' beans" are actually the seeds of fruits of a tree, *Strychnos ignatii*, which are rich in alkaloids, including strychnine. Curare alkaloids can be derived from numerous plants, but the liana that the author has in mind is presumably *Chondrodendron tormentosum*. *Strophantus* is a genus of plants that produce the African arrow poison *ouabain*, whose isolation by a French chemist in 1882 stimulated some interest in its potential medical and recreational potential.

"Your son," he said one day to Monsieur Vernoy, "is precociously ambitious. Like the majority of young men raised in Paris, he suffers from a considerable intellectual overload. Too much disparate knowledge has been stored in his brain. Like certain hothouse plants, he's been overheated. What is the result of that? It's that he possesses, with the soul of an adolescent, the ambition and cupidity of a mature man."

"You're frightening me," replied Monsieur Vernoy.

"It's necessary not to attach more importance to the observations I've made than they really have. Marcel is, like many others, the victim of a defective method of education, but he has pride, imagination and, which is the essential thing, a lot of good will and sincerity. With that, we'll save him."

"But how?"

"I'm convinced that if Marcel could contemplate, if only for a few hours, the marvelous progress that the future will accomplish, of which contemporary discoveries only give us a feeble idea, he would lose forever the jealousy and egotism that he owes to bad acquaintances or reading beyond his scope."

"How do you expect my son," interjected Monsieur Vernoy, discouraged, "to be able to take account of the marvelous progress to which you allude?"

"That might be less difficult than you think."

"You're joking, Doctor."

"Not at all."

Monsieur Belzevor and his guest were sitting in comfortable porcelain armchairs, warm in winter and cool in summer. It was already several years since the doctor had sent to Canton for those chairs, extremely practical, which have been in use in China and throughout the Far East for thousands of years.

The doctor got up and, pushing the armchair back with a gesture that caused it to glide on its rubber castors, he said to Monsieur Vernoy: "Follow me to my laboratory, I beg you..."

Dr. Belzevor's laboratory did not resemble those of the majority of scientists. One only saw there a gigantic dynamogenic apparatus, a few oak cupboards filled with books and enormous sandstone jars full of tropical flowers with heady perfumes.

The doctor approached a glass case and showed Monsieur Vernoy a flask at the back containing a white mud. "Do you know what that is?" he asked.

"It says *absolute alcohol* on the label."

"The deposit you can see in the bottom is copper sulfate, which becomes blue instead of white under the influence of water. If that alcohol ceases to be absolutely pure, the blue color of the copper sulfate will inform me of it."

"That's very ingenious," replied Monsieur Vernoy, who only had a rudimentary knowledge of chemistry, "But where are you trying to get to?"

"Patience. Listen to me carefully. Alcohol is one of the substances most fatal to the organism. In our epoch, as you know, alcoholism has become a veritable disease, a scourge in the face of which governments remained unarmed. But let's pass on. I simply want to tell you that inveterate alcoholics, drunkards afflicted with *delirium tremens*, always see identical objects and beings in their hallucinations."

"Yes, I've read that," relied Monsieur Vernoy, surprised by the turn that the conversation was taking. "They believe themselves to be tormented by rats, toads and serpents."

"Well," the doctor continued, excitedly, "exactly where I wanted to get to is that all alcoholics, whatever their age, sex and social condition, have exactly the same hallucinations. They never get away from rats, toads and reptiles."

"What does that prove?"

"The importance of that observation is enormous, from the scientific viewpoint. It proves that each stupefying agent acts on a distinct and well-defined part of the brain. Hashish initially leads to wordplay and gaiety, and in the second period of intoxication it inspires the mania of grandeur. The man who has taken hashish believes himself to be an emperor or a god. The effects of opium are even more characteristic. That maleficent drug, which is presently poisoning more than a hundred million human beings, has the effect of displacing notions of time and space in a strange fashion. In order to convince yourself, read the memoirs of the Englishman Thomas De Quincey, which are as remarkable for their literary form as they are from a scientific viewpoint.

"The eater or smoker of opium loses the notion of time and that of space. He perceives in his dreams, without any perspective, cities, seas, rivers, forests and immense countries, distinguishing the background as clearly as the foreground. His superhuman contemplations leave him with a weakened eyesight and brain. When he emerges from his orgies, he is almost an idiot and almost blind. With regard to time, the effect is similar. Thomas De Quincey relates that he experienced, in a few minutes, the sensation of living for several centuries, and that, in the midst of abominable suffering, he saw filing before him, in the same minute, Roman legions, the crusaders of Peter the Hermit and the Roundheads of the English Revolution. He emerged from those morbid hallucinations absolutely exhausted in body and soul."

"What you're telling me is strange. So there really are substances that act of certain mysterious regions of our brain and not on others?"

"More than that," the doctor continued, becoming animated. "Among the rocks and glacial mosses of the Antarctic Pole, a paltry variety of hemlock grows, the essential principles and juices of which contain, in a sense, the soul of prehistoric eras."

"I don't understand," said Monsieur Vernoy, looking at the doctor fearfully.

"I'll explain. The person who has taken a decoction of that mildly poisonous hemlock falls into a comatose state for twenty-four hours, and his dreams invariably retrace for him scenes and landscapes from the early ages of the globe. He sees—and I have seen myself—the plesiosaur agitating its serpentine neck, fifteen or twenty meters long, above a body as large as the hull of one of our transatlantic liners; he sees the mammoth, under the envelope of its long coarse hair, breaking with its giant tusks the horsetails and ferns blooming in the not damp vapor of the infancy of the earth. He sees—and I have seen—pterodactyls extend their large membranous wings above hundred-meter coconut palms, and catching monstrous insects in flight with their crocodilian mouths. He sees turtles with enormous and bulbous carapaces dragging themselves slowly through the mud of the first ages. Animality alone lived then, in all its grandeur and liberated brutality. Thought was still slumbering...."

"So substances exist capable of transporting us into the past, of enabling us to live the marvelous life of vanished eras?"

"They exist. I can affirm that to you on my honor as a scientist...as I can affirm to you that future things are no more hidden from our gaze than past things. I have discovered plants and substances that conceal within them the decors of the future. Is not the future in seed in the present, and is not the present itself born of the past? Divination and memory are, fundamentally, the unique manifestation of a similar law. The poet resuscitates disappeared eras and predicts future discoveries; the philosopher and the historian announce events that will not occur until long after their deaths... And I have discovered the elixir that can transport us into the future. I hold the key to future worlds. I can cause to appear, at will, civilizations and peoples that are not yet born."

Monsieur Vernoy put his hands together with a sort of religious fear. He was torn between admiration and stupor.

"So," he stammered, "I believe I understand that you want to transport my son into the future, in a dream, for a few hours...that you want to enable him to see what the future existence of humans will be."

"Precisely. You've divined correctly. That long preamble has only led to me asking you to attempt an experiment on your son, harmless in truth, after which Marcel will come back to you cured, enthusiastic and disinterested."

"He really wouldn't be running any danger?"

"That I can affirm to you. Marcel will go to sleep for a few hours, peacefully, and he'll wake up as healthy in body and mind as he was before.

Monsieur Vernoy remained silent momentarily.

"All right," he said, with an abrupt gesture. "I have absolute confidence in you, Doctor. I'll bring you Marcel."

"And take note, my dear Monsieur," Dr. Belzevor went on, with a decision that put an end to Monsieur Vernoy's last hesitations, "that this is not, in truth, a matter of an experiment, but of a cure. I'll answer for the success."

The following day, in fact, Monsieur Vernoy, who was not unaware of the doctor's eccentric habits, presented himself at the château at the usually hour when he got up, at six o'clock in the evening. He was accompanied by Marcel and Madame Vernoy.

In conformity with the doctor's instructions, Monsieur Vernoy had not warned his son about the little conspiracy fomented against him. Only Madame Vernoy was in on the secret.

In spite of the good reasons that her husband gave her, she could not help trembling for her dear Marcel. The good humor and enthusiasm of Dr. Belzevor reassured her.

As usual, after dinner, they took tea on the veranda, which overlooked the forest.

The gold and crimson of a splendid sunset were trailing over a horizon of infinite summits.

The conversation languished.

Dr. Belzevor had lit a Havana cigar, the perfume of which filled the whole room. Modestly, Monsieur Vernoy was holding his meerschaum pipe, and Marcel had obtained permission to light a cigarette of Oriental tobacco.

A domestic, as silent as a grave as a master of requests at the Council of State, brought liqueurs. Monsieur and Madame Vernoy accepted a few drops of the pink kirsch that is only found in the Vosges. Marcel was about to follow his parents' example when the doctor made a gesture.

"No, no," he said, in a tone that did not admit any reply. "Taste this one for me instead. It's a liqueur that I recommend to you, and of which you can give me news. It's Belzevorine. You'll search for it in vain in commerce."

The doctor took a Bohemian crystal carafe with topaz reflections and poured a few drops of glaucous liquid into the schoolboy's glass. After first tasting the unknown liqueur, Marcel drank it all.

"You elixir is delicious, Monsieur le Docteur," he said. "One might think it an extract of wild flowers."

"Yes," sniggered Monsieur Belzevor, "It's most agreeable to taste."

Very anxious, Monsieur and Madame Vernoy alternated their gazes between Marcel and the doctor.

Suddenly, the young man closed his eyes. His head slumped on to the table.

"He's asleep," exclaimed Dr. Belzevor, rapidly. And with his foot, he pressed the button of an electric bell hidden in the parquet. Two domestics appeared.

"Carry Monsieur Marcel Vernoy into the Blue Room," he ordered, "and lie him down on the bed..."

IV. In the Year 3000

Marcel Vernoy woke up to the sounds of an infinitely soft and harmonious music, which seemed to be whispering a thousand benevolent but confused thoughts in his ear.

Without opening his eyes, plunged in the torpor that follows sleep, he tried to divine what instruments were being played. He could not succeed in that.

The mysterious melody possessed simultaneously the heart-rending eloquence of violins, the angelic sweetness of harps, the imperious vibrations of brass instruments and the sonorous profundity of organs.

"It isn't an orchestra I can hear," he murmured. "It's music itself.

Vaguely, he thought that it was some artistic surprise of Doctor Belzevor. What confirmed him in that supposition was that perfumed breaths reached him in gusts, odors that were vaguely reminiscent of mimosa and wild lemons, but much more refined, much more delicate and much more ethereal.

Meanwhile, the music continued mutedly, decrescendo, as if the invisible orchestra were slowly drawing away.

Marcel rubbed his eyes and sat up abruptly. He almost uttered a cry of surprise, and his gaze wandered with alarm over the décor that surrounded him.

He found himself in the middle of a vast round room, the cupola of which was formed by thick glass bricks of very bright colors, which scintillated like precious stones in the first rays of the sun.

The walls, of a hue that was infinitely relaxing to the gaze, appeared to Marcel to be sandstone or porcelain. They offered sparkling glints of crimson, amethyst and saffron.

The bed on which the schoolboy was lying did not resemble any that it had been given to him to see thus far. It was a sort of conch of gracious form, but not presenting any spiral, angle or ornament. The bed was made of stone, like the walls of the room.

In spite of his astonishment, Marcel was not at all afraid, for the benevolent harmonies were still whispering in his ear in a fashion almost as clear as speech, holding him under its charm, without leaving any room in his mind for fear.

It seemed to him that he was having a pleasant dream, and he was apprehensive that it might end.

In order to convince himself of the reality of what he saw, he palpated the bedclothes by which he was enveloped.

"This soft and shiny fabric certainly isn't borrowed from the animal or vegetable realm," he said. "Only might think they were made of asbestos or glass fiber..."

Marcel got out of bed and got dressed; for he had perceived his garments, carefully folded, which an unknown hand had deposited on a broad tabletop close at hand.

At intervals, the walls were ornament with iridium plaques, violet with shifting reflections.

The young man was wondering what the utility of those metal plates might be when a curtain was abruptly drawn, allowing the columns of a circular gallery to be seen.

Adolescents draped in brilliant fabrics surrounded the surprised and nonplussed Marcel Vernoy. He had never been in the presence of beings so beautiful; he would never have imagined that their like existed.

His comrades at school with pale or excessively colored complexions, narrow chests and knock-knees, would have seemed monsters or invalids compared with this humanity, which had attained the optimum of physiological harmony. The gestures of the young people, all admirably proportioned, were full of ease and nobility. The pure lines of their profiles did not evoke any animal resemblance. There was no grimacing face among them, or any rendered ridiculous by the exaggerated development of one part of the physiognomy: a hooked nose, a jutting chin or an overly fleshy mouth. Their complexion, of the same very delicate pink, revealed the vigor of health. There was no chlorotic pallor or congested redness to be seen in any of them.

The expression of their faces was imprinted with such serenity that one divined that they neither laughed not wept in bursts. Only a smile was designed on their lips from time to time.

Their hands, very slender, were not charged with any jewelry. They were casually draped in brightly colored chlamydes, which a single precious stone retained on the right shoulder, in such a way as to leave the arms fee.

At the sight of Marcel, the young people, a dozen of whom had come in, manifested a great deal of astonishment. They had approached him, and palpated curiously the cloth of his jacket and the silk of his cravat.

At certain details of that costume, although it had emerged from the establishment of a good Parisian tailor, they smiled ironically—by which Marcel felt quite mortified.

They were speaking to one another in a language that appeared to the young man to be similar to Latin, of which he understood a few fragmentary phrases, without being able to grasp the integral meaning of any remark.

Nonplussed, Marcel had beaten a retreat to the back of the room. A certain anguish was mingled with the embarrassment that he felt.

The young men perceived his emotion. One of the tallest advanced toward Marcel, took him by the hand, and in a very pure French with musical intonations, he said: "You're wearing the costume of the twentieth century, I believe? Doubtless you know the old French of that distant epoch? Our professors' lessons permit us to speak it correctly enough."

"Where am I, then?" exclaimed Marcel, alarmed. "And who are you?"

His interlocutor appeared very astonished by that question.

"At this moment, you're in one of the sleeping rooms of the Lycée de Paris. It's eight o'clock in the morning, and we're in the month of July in the year 3000."

"Excuse me," replied Marcel, dazedly, putting his hand to his forehead. "I can't succeed in recalling the sequence of events by which I was brought here, and how, without being conscious of it, I've been able to traverse so many centuries."

"Our amazement equals yours. We've only seen individuals dressed like you in museums of retrospective anthropology and cinematographic albums dating back a thousand years."

On hearing those words, Marcel's emotion reached its peak. He did not think for a single instant of the perils that he might be running among the people of the year 3000. He felt the same profound and almost religious fervor that Christopher Columbus must have felt on setting foot for the first time on the soil of the New World.

Christopher Columbus had encountered savages and ferocious beasts; more fortunate than him, Marcel had fallen into the midst of an admirable civilization. He found himself in the presence of people who were welcoming him with sympathy and who were capable of speaking the same language as him.

He had a sort of vertigo; he believed for a moment that he had gone mad. Thoughts crowded so numerously in his brain that he remained silent for some time, reflecting on the fantastic implausibility of the situation in which he found himself. He was trembling with emotion.

One of the young men misunderstood, and thought that because he was shivering he was cold; he hastened to press a porcelain button.

Immediately, the oval plates of iridium embedded in the wall turned red. The temperature of the room increased by several degrees.

"What have you done?" Marcel asked.

"As you seemed cold, I made the atmosphere a little warmer."

"I confess that I don't understand how you achieved that result."

The adolescent raised his arms skywards with surprise.

"Oh, that's true!" he said, smiling. "I forgot, stupidly, that in your era barbaric and complicated apparatus was employed for heating, which exhaled poisonous gases like carbon monoxide, and into which it was necessary to throw tree trunks or lumps of coal continually."

"Truly," exclaimed another, turning toward Marcel, "you had scarcely made more progress than the African savages who, according to what I've read, were reduced to rubbing two sticks together in order to light a fire..."

"But in sum," said Marcel, wounded in his self-esteem of an anthropopithecus of the twentieth century, "all that doesn't explain to me how your heating apparatus works."

"In a very simple fashion," replied the one who had spoken first. "First of all, you should know that, thanks to certain meteorological apparatus that we can show you, we've been able to regulate the seasons, so to speak. Glacial cold and torrid heat have been banished from the climate of the year 3000.

The temperature, even outside, never surpasses a certain median range. In apartments, we obtain the precise degree of warmth we desire thanks to the simple apparatus you see here. It consists of thick plaques of iridium linked to powerful electrical machines. It's sufficient to turn the button of a commutator with a dial, as you've just seen, for the plaques to turn red, giving off the exact quantity of heat indicated by the figure at which the needle stops. I'll add that iridium heating has been used for some nine hundred years."

That explanation, which his interlocutor had furnished with perfect good grace, left Marcel torn, between stupor and admiration. What he had learned thus far about life and science was seething in his mind with everything that he could now see and hear. The past and the present were confused within him a sort of chaos from which he had difficulty emerging. He was extracted from his reflections by a question.

"What is your name?"

"Marcel Vernoy...and yours?"

"Blas." The young man added, introducing his comrades: "These are my friends and study companions: Lucius, Harry, Fritz, Serge, Alcantor... I hope that a perfect entente can be established between them and you. However, from the outset, you can count on the amity of Blas."

Blushing with pleasure and emotion, Marcel shook the hands that were extended toward him all round. He experienced an inexpressible happiness on observing that, in spite of the paltry views of pessimists, humanity had ended up being orientated toward mildness, fraternity and concord. And he felt, right away, very much at ease with these young men, of whom, in accordance with the normal laws of nature, he might be the historical ancestor. The anguish that he had experienced to begin with had disappeared entirely.

Henceforth, he no longer wanted to take the trouble to reflect. He gave himself entirely to the pleasure of conversing with his new friends. He was avid to learn everything, to know everything, about the mysterious world in which he had just landed.

"It seems to me," he said to Blas, that yours is a Spanish name. Among your friends, I noticed some that had an English, Russian or German appearance. How does that come about?"

"You're making a slight error," replied Blas. "My name isn't Spanish, it's neo-Latin."

"Neo-Latin?"

"Yes. At present, throughout the surface of the globe, only two languages are spoken, neo-Latin and neo-Saxon. Spanish, French, Italian, Portuguese, and the colonial dialects of each nation, by virtue of the force of things, thanks to the diffusion of ideas and the rapidity of communications, have melted into a single language, neo-Latin. That language is so clear simple and facile that you'll understand it very rapidly.

"And neo-Saxon?" Marcel asked.

"By virtue of an entirely natural evolution, neo-Saxon formed in the same way a neo-Latin. It's the resultant of German, English, Danish and Dutch.⁵"

"Since you've reached that point, why two languages instead of one?"

"Thus far, the unification of the human language, which will surely happen one day, hasn't yielded practical results, in spite of serious attempts. Volapük, Esperanto, and Bolak, the blue language, in spite of the good will of their inventors, failed pitifully. Neo-Latin and neo-Saxon subsist because, thanks to them, one can understand all the masterpieces of the human mind. One is literary, the other scientific. Between the two of them, they symbolize the word in its full essence."

"What about Arabic and Chinese? And the idioms of the Orient and the Far East?"

"They've passed to the ranks of scholarly languages. They're no longer spoken. The dialects employed by the negroes of Central Africa disappeared first. Our libraries conserve the lexicons of Malagasy and Dahomeyan piously. Then it was the turn of Arabic, Armenian, Persian and Chinese, as well as Japanese. The increasing complexity of ideas in the human brain, and the formidable power of the Latin and Saxon nations, caused the Oriental languages to fall into desuetude quite naturally."

"How can neo-Saxons and neo-Latins comprehend one another, then?"

"All the habitants of the globe speak both languages. Thanks to our simplified methods, there are even a few students who understand five or six dead languages, such as Sanskrit, Egyptian, French and English."

"I'll find myself very ignorant in your midst," sighed Marcel.

"Not at all!" exclaimed Blas, with a cordial smile. "Thanks to our logical methods and our multilingual phonographs, you'll soon have caught up with us, believe me."

"It's necessary, in any case," Harry put in, "to inform the director of the school, Monsieur Futural, of the arrival of our new comrade."

"But what will he say about my presence?" asked Marcel, with a certain anxiety. "I've arrived in such strange conditions..."

"Have no fear," replied Serge. "You'll be welcomed with open arms."

"However, the disconcerting fashion in which I find myself among you..."

"Don't worry about that," replied Blas. "Your presence here must be a phenomenon of a purely natural order. Our scientists will take charge of explaining it, Have no doubt about that—they've explained many others." Turning toward one of his comrades, Blas added: "Lucius, would you be kind enough to go and find Monsieur Futural?"

"With pleasure," the young man replied, and went away.

In spite of his neat attire, Marcel felt poorly dressed and unkempt by comparison with his new companions. He darted a glance at his hands, and blushed in confusion on perceiving that they were not irreproachably clean.

"Where can I wash my hands, if you please?" he asked, in a discreet tone.

"What?" replied Blas, in surprise. "You haven't made your electrical ablutions?"

"No," replied Marcel, confused.

Blas took pity on his new comrade's embarrassment, and, indicating a sandstone pedestal near the bed he said: "Climb on that. Don't be afraid."

Marcel obeyed, not without a secret apprehension. He feared that an unexpected showed might douse him, and contracted his muscles instinctively. He was very agreeably surprised, therefore, to feel himself traversed, from the soles of his feet to the roots of his hair, by beneficent electric effluvia. He experienced a sensation of wellbeing and lightness, which he had never felt after a bath.

His garments, including his shoes, were rid, as if by magic, of their traces of grease and dust, which fused into impalpable powder in the form of gray smoke. Not only did Marcel feel admirably refreshed and washed, but his cuffs and collar had recovered all their whiteness and brilliance.

Blas enjoyed his friend's astonishment. "However," he said, after a moment's reflection, "you ought not to be surprised by the fashion in which we operate our toilette. The electrical oscillation apparatus that you see is already more than a thousand years old. It's due to one of your contemporaries, the engineer Tesla, who statue you'll soon be able to admire."

V. Elixir and Jam

Marcel had just completed his toilette. He was still under the impact of the impression of wonderment caused by that rapid and complete fashion of proceeding with his ablutions when Monsieur and Madame Futural made their entrance.

The director of the school was tall. His green chlamys was draped in broad pleats over his shoulders, where it was retained by an emerald. His beard and his hair were going gray. His physiognomy, perfectly regular, respired a majestic mildness. His dark eyes were sparkling with intelligence.

He was accompanied by Madame Futural, clad in a long blue tunic. Marcel noticed, with surprise, that she was not wearing any jewelry, nor a frilly hat. Her abundant blonde hair was simply retained by a silver ribbon. His figure was not barbarically compressed by a corset with an armature of steel or whalebone. Hygiene and good taste had done justice to those instruments of torture, as they had also caused earrings, rings and bracelets to disappear.

Later, Marcel saw in a museum the jewels and trinkets of an elegant woman if the twentieth century. They were exhibited in a glass case, alongside the golden ornaments of a Gaulish chief, not far from the necklaces of seeds and seashells of the indigenes of Oceania and Central Africa.

Monsieur and Madame Futural gave Marcel the most sympathetic welcome. They had perceived his timidity, so, in order to reassure him, they heaped him with attentions. They assured him that he would be cordially received by his new comrades.

"Your arrival among us," said Monsieur Futural, "which seems extraordinary and disconcerting at first, will not be inexplicable for our scientists. In any case, that detail is of no importance. You're now one of ours; I'm delighted by that. Thanks to you, we shall be able to elucidate some obscure points of the history of the twentieth century."

Graciously, Madame Futural added: "We'll try to make sure that you won't have to repent having left your century for ours. You won't take long, I hope, to perceive that the year 3000 has a lot to recommend it."

"Evidently," said Monsieur Futural, smiling, "it will produce a great change in your habits. You certainly only have a faint idea of the state of simplification at which we've arrived in all things, principally regarding education."

"I'll try, Monsieur," Marcel replied, modestly, "to conform as exactly as I can to the discipline of the school into which you've been kind enough to welcome me."

Monsieur Futural smiled. "Our discipline is very mild," he explained. "The epoch in which adolescents were imprisoned in schools as if in jail and deprived of their liberty came to an end long ago. Cruel and grotesque punishments no longer exist here, and the deplorable habit of making the memory of pupils toil to the detriment of their other faculties has been abandoned once and for all.

"Here," Monsieur Futural emphasized, "you can work in the fashion that you please, and go anywhere you wish. You'll understand quickly that you'll have as much interest as pleasure in following the extremely simple and well-designed plan of study that will be submitted to you. You won't be bored for a minute, I can guarantee that."

Marcel lowered his head, stammering a few words of thanks. He was veritably confused by the warm welcome that he had received, and the simple and cordial generosity testified to him.

Henceforth, he felt, so to speak, entirely at home.

"I hope," Monsieur Futural added, "that everything will go as smoothly as possible. At any rate, I'll confide you to the care of young Blas, since you're already on the best of terms with him.

Monsieur and Madame Futural left. Almost immediately, the young schoolboys withdrew discreetly, not without having reassured their new fellow pupil of their good dispositions in his regard.

Marcel remained alone with Blas.

"What are we going to do now?" he asked him.

"I believe," Blas replied, after a moment's reflection, "that the most urgent thing is to rid you of the uncomfortable and complicated clothes in which you're wrapped, and which must hinder you considerably. I don't think I could live swathed like that."

Marcel followed his companion meekly out of the room. They found themselves in a vast vaulted gallery paved with shiny stones.

"One might think they were sapphires," Marcel remarked.

"They are, in fact, sapphires," replied Blas tranquilly. As Marcel manifested his astonishment, he went on: "There's nothing that should surprise you in that. Chemists have been manufacturing precious stones for centuries, of any size that they please, and nothing has become less rare. We make use of them in our buildings because of their inalterability and their splendor."

From the pavement of sapphires rose tall columns. Through arched bays, broadly open like those of a cloister, Marcel saw a grandiose landscape deployed at his feet. Porcelain towers of all covers sprang from clumps of verdure. One might have thought that the world had become an immense park strewn with fantastic architecture, the turrets, minarets and corbels of which surpassed everything that had been created of the most sumptuous and the most complicated of Gothic architecture and that of India.

Blas extracted Marcel from that contemplation, which had rendered him mute and dazed with wonderment.

"You can admire all that at your leisure and in detail. For the moment, it's a matter of changing your costume, and then having breakfast.

Marcel, who was increasingly convinced that he was moving through a dream of enchantment, followed his guide along arcades, lingering involuntarily before the magical horizon that, thanks to the circular form of the gallery, was renewed at every step.

Finally, having arrived at the extremity of a vaulted corridor. Blas drew a curtain and a spacious vestry appeared. Hanging in good order on platinum and burnished gold pegs, hundreds of shiny chlamydes were aligned.

At that moment, Marcel could not retain a cry of fright. He had just perceived a strange individual standing beside him. He was completely molded from head to toe in a gutta-percha garment; of the face, nothing could be seen. The head was completely surrounded by a helmet, furnished with two crystal lenses and a latticed opening for the mouth.

Marcel drew closer to Blas, fearfully. "What is that person?" he asked, in a low voice.

Bas suppressed a burst of laughter. "Have no fear," he said. "This individual is the most pacific in the world. I have the honor of introducing you to the honest Mastif. He's a trifle surly and abrasive, but he's an excellent fellow regardless."

"So much the better," exclaimed Marcel, with a sigh of relief. "I confess that I wasn't reassured. Why is he wearing that singular accoutrement?"

"It's necessary to tell you," Blas replied, "that almost no one works manually nowadays. The items of electrical apparatus of which we make use in the school require little care and scant surveillance. Mastif is in charge of their maintenance. That's why you see him dressed from head to toe in an insulating costume of gutta-percha. His work requires him to spend part of the day in the basements and the attics, in the midst of a redoubtable intersection of electrical currents. If he were dressed in any other way it wouldn't be long before he was electrocuted."

While this dialogue was taking place, Mastif had drawn away, muttering.

A few moments later, Marcel Vernoy, rid of his millenarian costume, for which he no longer had anything but a profound disdain, was dressed in the fashion of the year 3000, in a dazzling orange glass-fiber chlamys.

It was time for the morning meal.

Blas and Marcel soon arrived in the refectory, which groups of schoolboys were entering and leaving incessantly.

The room was decorated in white and gold stucco. The simplicity, richness and good taste of that decoration delighted the young man. He took his place at a small table of blue marble veined with gold, which he recognized as lapis lazuli

"You know," Blas explained, "that it costs our chemists no more effort to produce agates, onyx and rare marbles than precious stones, cheaply and in abundance."

"In my time," Marcel replied, with a comically piteous expression, "lapis lazuli wasn't so common. The proof is that we only made cravat pins and the stones of rings out of it."

"We make use of it to make tables and build walls."

While speaking, Blas lifted the lid of a large crystal urn placed in the center of the table, and with the aid of a small gold scoop, very simple in form, but practical, he served Marcel a few spoonfuls of a blue paste. Then, from a jug sculpted in the same substance as the urn, he poured an amber liquid into Marcel's cup.

At that moment the latter experienced a certain hesitation. He could not help saying to his guide: "I confess that I have no idea what the foodstuff and the beverage you're offering me might be."

"I'll bring you up to date briefly. In your time, people were obliged, in order to nourish themselves, to have recourse to substances directly prepared by nature. I've read that they devoured, barbarically, animals and plants, which contained a host of products useless or harmful to nutrition. We've simplified that, like everything else. The aliment you see is absolutely complete and perfectly assimilable. You'll observe, moreover, that it doesn't have a disagreeable taste."

"Indeed! It's exquisite," replied Marcel, who had already expedited the whole portion of blue jam that he had been served.

"What an appetite!" said Blas, astonished. "Empty your cup. You can tell me now what you think of our elixir of Bacchus."

Marcel set his cup down without having left a drop of the liquid therein. "Your elixir," he said, "is a marvel. It concentrates and synthesizes the different flavors of wine, cider, tea, beer and hydromel."

"You have delicate taste. The elixir of Bacchus does indeed contain the beneficent principles of all the liquids you've just named. Only alcohol is almost completely banished from it; there is only an infinitesimal dose therein."

"For what reason?"

"What! You can ask that, having lived in a epoch where the pitiful monsters with human faces called alcoholics still existed? The study of history, informing us of the wars, maladies and misery caused by that terrible scourge, has put us forever on guard against it. The disappearance of alcoholism has been the signal of an immense progress in humanity."

Meanwhile, Marcel had taken more of the marvelous azure jam. He had the sensation of never having eaten anything better. The most delicate fish, the finest game and the most succulent fruits seemed insipid and indigestible by comparison with that nutritious and perfumed essence. He was about to take a third helping when Blas dissuaded him gently.

"My dear friend," he said, "be careful. Your stomach isn't accustomed to such generous nourishment. You've seen that I've been content with a few spoonfuls. If you continue to feed yourself so copiously, you won't feel hungry for two or three days.

Marcel blushed at being caught *in flagrante delicto* in gluttony. The spatula that he was about to raise to his mouth stopped half way. He remained silent for some time, seemingly giving all his attention to the music that was being played by an invisible orchestra.

Monsieur and Madame Vernoy, who were fervent music lovers, had taken their son to the Opéra and great concert halls several times, but Marcel had never heard such harmony. The music was neither insipid not noisy. It poured forth torrents of delight, calm and serenity, without fatigue for the listener, and an impression of beauty, courage and fortunate strength emanated from it. Certain melodic phrases arrived as clearly at his understanding as the verses of a poet of genius or the cadenced sentences of beautiful prose.

"How admirable that music is," Marcel exclaimed.

"Yes. The melodies are already old. They were composed in 2700 by the master Arachnus, one of the masters of our modern music. The fragment you've just heard is taken from a symphonic poem entitled *The Delight of Living*. But

Arachnus is particularly and universally celebrated for his cantata *Redemptive Science*."

Marcel remained silent. The refectory was gradually emptying.

"We can leave now, if you wish," Blas proposed.

"One more question," said Marcel, whose attention had been attracted by the prismatic reflections of the cups, urns and plates. "Of what substance are these utensils made?"

"They're carved in large crystals of pure carbon, artificially manufactured. It is, if I'm not mistaken, what you once called diamond."

Marcel did not reply. He had decided not to be astonished by anything henceforth.

Following his guide, he went back into the circular gallery, to which the doors of the refectory opened, and which linked all the rooms of the school, from the bedrooms to the amphitheaters, the museums and the libraries.

The center of that ensemble of buildings, disposed in a sequence in the form of an ellipse, was occupied by a vast garden. It was filled with trees that Marcel did not recognize, refreshed by fountains and springs of fresh water, the crystalline waters of which flowed over a bed of metallic powders and gems. The perfumed calices of giant flowers swayed.

Marcel Vernoy did not ask any more questions. He had arrived at the point at which admiration can no longer find words to express itself, and he contented himself with following his guide, looking around and listening attentively.

He noticed for the first time that everything was admirably clean. Nowhere, on the floor, the ceiling or the walls, was any trace of dust to be seen, nor of the mildew that presently dishonors the interior of our most beautiful edifices. Everywhere, the sandstone, the porcelain and the stucco were shining, as if they were brand new. It would have been impossible to discover the smallest cobweb or the tiniest stain.

Once again, Marcel had recourse to his guide. "Howe do you keep everything here so clean and bright?" he asked.

"Notice," said Blas, "That as we have banished wood, calcareous stone and oxidizable metals from our houses nothing is easier to maintain. Their walls don't present any sharp angles or complicated moldings, veritable nests of dust and microbes. Everything is smooth or rounded. At night, artificial electrified rain washes the exterior of buildings; by day the interiors automatically receive the same kind of aquatic cleaning.

"But your clothes must get wet," Marcel objected.

"It doesn't matter. They're glass fiber. Water doesn't do them any harm."

"And how do you dry all that?"

"With the greatest ease, almost instantaneously. It's sufficient, thanks to our electrical heating apparatus, to raise the temperature momentarily. Everything is dry again and perfectly sterilized. That's one of the reasons why we're almost never ill.

While talking, Blas and Marcel had arrived outside the study room.

"This is where I'm taking you," said Blas. "Come in with me. You'll see how we work."

VI. Study

Blas had moved aside the curtain of polychromatic glass fiber that took the place of a door. The two young men went into a hall where about sixty pupils were gathered. The tables at which they were seated seemed to Marcel to be made of shiny and richly veined wood.

"I thought you had entirely banished wood and oxidizable metals from your constructions and furniture," he said to Blas.

"I beg your pardon," said Blas, "But this isn't, properly speaking, wood. It's a kind of artificially manufactured lignite, absolutely incorruptible, and as hard as granite."

Each work table was separated from its neighbor by a space of about a meter. All around the study room, high semi-circular bays allowed floods of oxygen and light to penetrate.

"A long time age," said Blas, "we renounced uncomfortable desks and long, narrow, uncomfortable tables, where schoolchildren were packed together. Dark, smoky and malodorous rooms have had their day. Here, everything is sacrificed to hygiene, and we do very well in consequence."

None of the pupils had raised their eyes when Marcel and his guide arrived.

Blas installed Marcel at a table next to his own, which was unoccupied, like many others, at the back of the room. Marcel sat down, slightly surprised not to see any pens, ink, books or paper on the petrified mahogany tabletop. In front of him, there were only three machines with ivory keyboards, reminiscent of miniature pianos.

Observing his friend's astonishment, Blas anticipated the questions that the other wanted to ask.

"The first apparatus, to the left," he said, "is a much-improved writing machine. It only requires ten minutes of application to master its manipulation perfectly. In any case, the machine is already beginning to fall into disuse. In many establishments it has been replaced advantageously by the logophone, a direct descendant of your ancient phonograph.

"I can imagine what the advantages of that machine's employment might be, but the other two intrigue me more—the one in the middle, for instance, which has six keys at its base and the upper part of which is entirely garnished with porcelain buttons bearing numbers. As for the third, it seems to me to be even more complicated.

Blas smiled. "They're both quite simple," he replied. "The first is a calculating machine, which saves the brains of the pupils the fatigue of absolutely mechanical operations By the year 2400 people were able, with a little habituation to multiply, divide or obtain a square root while thinking about something else. From reflex action to automatic movement there is only one step, which we cross easily. Now, pupils no longer consume long hours in mechanical mathematical exercises, whose effect is depressing for the intelligence and the imagination."

"That's marvelous."

"As for the last, it is, to tell the truth, a little more complicated than the others, with its numbers, its letters and it colored plaques. It's the Logical Reasoning Machine, for resolving inductions and deductions with no chance of error."

"That's frightening!"

"Less than you imagine. In order to construct the apparatus, old Aristotle's *Logic* was employed. The universitarian theories of the Middle Ages, with their syllogistic reasoning, had almost succeeded in rendering certain mechanisms of human reasoning automatic. The work of philosophers of the twenty-third and twenty-fifth centuries completed the task. The machine has two modes of operation, one for induction and the other for deduction. In deduction, as in induction, one composes, with the characters of the first set of keys, a phrase containing the general idea whose consequences one wishes to ascertain. A series of triggers operates and a phrase is soon inscribed on the porcelain tablet that you can see, giving an exact and mathematical solution to the question. If necessary, the machine furnishes two, three or even four consequences of the principle proposed. The most recent machines constructed can go as far as six or seven conclusions."

"But if your machine is asked questions or given proposals that are too abstract," Marcel objected, "what happens then?"

"In that case, the porcelain tablet remains blank; no triggering has taken place. I will add that the machine only has any utility when concrete problems of reasoning are submitted to it. It has rendered incalculable services in science."

There was an absolute silence beneath the cupola of the study room. Nothing could be heard but the slight sound of the machines and, from time to time, the faint whisper of a conversation in low voices. Marcel looked around in surprise.

"Where is the study master?" he asked. "Is he invisible? In my time, the pupils, even the most serious, threw paper pellets at one another, played tunes on the elastic of their boots, ate sweetmeats or read novels. Even the master wasn't safe from practical jokes; his chair was coated with shore-polish or glue, the rim of his top hat cut into saw-teeth or the back of his frock-coat ornamented with discourteous inscriptions."

Blas burst out laughing. "Study masters!" he exclaimed. "My God, that takes us back a long way. In fact, I've learned of the existence of those modest functionaries from treatises in pedagogical prehistory."

"In my time," Marcel replied, slightly vexed, "the situation of study masters had been considerably ameliorated. Almost all of them, grave, learned and irreproachably clad, were laborious scholars, future professors, preparing for their license, or even a degree...."

"As many forgotten titles and terms, like 'study master' itself. By the twenty-fifth century, study masters—pawns, as you used to call them—had disappeared. An attempt was made to replace them with nickel steel watchmen, which you can see in the automata section of the galleries of any museum, but it only had a paltry success. The schoolboys of that time, full of hereditary malice and stupidity, played a thousand tricks on their steel pawn. They altered the motivating electrical current surreptitiously at a fixed time, unscrewed the feet, the head or the arms.

"One pawn—the anecdote is historical—was completely dismantled by indelicate schoolboys and sold to a second-hand dealer, who expiated his lack of respect for the law by means of a severe sentence. The government—I'm still reporting memoirs of the period—was obliged to reform matters so scantly respected. The State budget that had been allocated to that perilous experiment experienced a deficit of several hundred millions.

"The automatic pawns, sold off cheap were acquired by horticulturalists desirous of keeping the birds away from their peas. They believed that they had reached the culmination of progress in transforming them into improved scarecrows. Unfortunately, the results were deplorable; the automatic pawns were rusted by the rain, brought down fruits that had scarcely begun to ripen with their jerky authoritarian gestures, demolished the glass panels of hothouses and cucumber frames, and trampled the flower-beds and seed-nurseries with a supreme carelessness."

"You're interesting me keenly," Marcel exclaimed, very amused.

"To complete the disaster," Blas continued, without departing from a humorous gravity, "those poor rejects from the university couldn't be utilized anywhere. Except for a few carefully preserved specimens that still figure in our galleries, they were all sold for scrap. The birds, informed by their instinct, learned in a matter of days how to distinguish the metal automata from veritable gardeners of flesh and bone. They perched on their shoulders in dozens. A few songbirds even had the impudence to nest inside their ears or mouth."

"And what was done after the failure of the automatic pawns?"

"There was a temporary return to old methods, but study masters soon became unnecessary. Pupils now take too much pleasure in studying, and are too well aware that it is in their interest to develop their intellectual faculties for them to need surveillance. You have only to look around you..."

Marcel could, in fact, see that all his knew schoolfellows were observing the most profound meditation. Only a few pupils were conversing quietly about their studies, taking a thousand precautions to avoid disturbing their neighbors.

In a matter of two hours Marcel Vernoy had seen and heard so many extraordinary things that his ideas were seething. He felt an intolerable headache. Blas perceived that, and led his friend to one of the exterior bays, from which a vast horizon was visible.

"You can't begin to study today," he said. "Content yourself with observing at leisure this landscape unfamiliar to you, and I'll try to answer the questions suggested to you by the spectacle."

Marcel leaned his elbows on a stout bar of burnished gold that served as the window sill, and gazed.

Azure-colored domes, elegant edifices with silver facades and gigantic columns, equipped at their summit with balconies and balustrades, sprang forth in the solar light with the most sparkling colors. Gigantic trees, their foliage dotted with green and blue flowers, loomed up, surging from the ground in all their vigor and splendor.

For some time, Marcel remained plunged in the contemplation of the landscape, from which perfumes emanated as powerful as they were subtle. His headache disappeared as if by magic under the influence of a fresh light breeze. He inhaled life and health by the lungful, so to speak.

Then his attention was directed toward the architectures whose brightest colors tinted the green and bronze background of the landscape. The tall towers equipped with balconies at their summits, reminiscent of great golden lilies, intrigued him especially.

"What use are those high columns," he asked, "which remind me of the factory chimneys of the past, albeit with less ugliness."

"Those monuments aren't there solely for decorative purposes. They're veritably useful to us. It's thanks to them that we can regulate the temperature, avoiding exaggerations of heat and cold, so harmful to hygiene."

"I'd like you to give me a summary idea of their function."

"Those high columns, which you can see, are very numerous, and whose summits almost reach the clouds, are aspirators of electricity. Thanks to them, we capture the stormy fluid and utilize it as a motive force. It no longer rains nowadays unless our meteorologists determine it. In certain cases, in the presence of a tornado, a cyclone or a typhoon, the powerful artillery pieces that you can see at the summits of the towers avert the cataclysm, pulverize it, and reduce its disastrous effects to negligibility. Now you ought to understand why the people of the thirtieth century enjoy a climate that is always even. Hundreds of years have passed since white frosts have been observed, or any cases of sunstroke have been produced."

Marcel noticed that the perspective he was contemplating was entirely composed of curved lines, oval or serpentine. The irritating straight line and brutal angles had disappeared from the world forever.

Blas had respected his friend's reverie religiously. He waited complaisantly for the latter to break the silence.

"This landscape is marvelously beautiful in its simplicity and elegance," Marcel said, finally, "but doubtless our view, here, is overlooking some exceptional park. The cities must be very different..."

"You're error is great! Cities, as you understood them a thousand years ago, no longer exist. The barbarically superimposed stories, the cloacas of stone devoid of verdure and air, were assassinated a long time ago. A city is no more now than a forest of rare trees in which edifices rose up here and there. Before anything else, humans need oxygen and space."

At that point, the conversation of Marcel and Blas was interrupted by the sound of muffled footsteps on the sandstone pavement of the study hall. They turned round and found themselves facing Mastif, still wearing his insulating gutta-percha diving suit. He was equipped with a glass balloon filed with a green-tinted gas and a large metal key. Without appearing to notice anyone, he stopped at the end of the hall in front of an apparatus whose organs he set about examining.

"That's really Mastif, isn't it?" asked Marcel "The man we glimpsed a little while ago?"

"Yes," Blas replied. "What we call an outcast."

"An outcast?"

"Don't interpret the term in its old sense. Here, we call an outcast someone who, although naturally well endowed, refuses to exercise his brain, out of ill will or idleness. Mastif, who you see there, has remained rebellious to science, letters

and philosophy. His peers aren't very numerous; one can barely count two million of them in the whole world. All of them,
like him, are occupied in the surveillance and maintenance of
apparatus. That penalty, if it is one, in very minimal. Outcasts
have the same nourishment as other people. Their labor isn't
fatiguing, and they have leisure. In any case, they can be reha-
bilitated simply by completing their studies."

"I was already feeling sorry for the poor fellow!"

"He has nothing of which to complain. In truth, idle as he
is, he's chosen the least difficult and least burdensome task.
The scientists who are responsible for the production of nourishment and its distribution, for the esthetics and hygiene of
habitations and the mental progress of humankind, truly have
far more worries than Mastif, who is perhaps, after all, merely
impotent or ill. In our worldwide society, the more merit and
intelligence one has, the harder one works, and the more
pleasure and honor one has in exercising one's faculties for
the general wellbeing."

"But what about placements, pensions and sinecures?"

"There are none any more. Commerce and administration have been subjected to a logical organization with which
no one seeks to compete, and in which all necessary objects
are distributed in accordance with need."

Marcel was very surprised. "What, then," he asked, "is
the recompense for the ambitious, for successful people in the
society of the year 3000?"

"Ambition no longer exists. It has given way to the competition to do good. Our successful people, as you call them,
have no other recompense than the intimate satisfaction of
their conscience and the pleasure of being useful to the weak
and the less well endowed. However, as paltry sentiments
sometimes die with difficulty in the human heart, our successful people can also savor the triumph of what you called glory,
which we call vanity or vainglory; they're surrounded by the
esteem, respect and amity of all the people in the world."

Marcel was thoughtful. Blas continued, with animation:
"Our outcasts do, in sum, what they want. They've chosen for

themselves the part that suits them best. Too bad for them if it's the worst. In any case, progress in morality, science and education is reducing their number year by year. We can foresee the moment when no more of them will exist among human beings."

"In the meantime, you can count, you say, on about two million. Are those outcasts distributed here and there, all over the globe?

"In truth, they're divided into two categories. Mastif belongs to the first. Those of the second are scarcely more unfortunate. At the North and South Poles, they occupy the two industrial cities that furnish us with the electrical force necessary to the functioning of all the machines in the world..."

A sudden idea occurred to Blas. "Look," he proposed, "Since we have a few hours of leisure, and you appear to be particularly interested in the situation of our outcasts, would you like us to go visit Artika, the city of the North Pole? I have a cousin who, alas, has been an inveterate idler all his life. He can serve as our guide."

VII. Artika

Marcel and Blas left the study room. After following the circular gallery for some time they went over a footbridge to a comfortable elevator. A few minutes later, they disembarked on the highest terrace of the school. It was a vast oval surface surrounded by balustrades in the Italian style, decorated at intervals by large pots in which flowers were growing.

At one of the extremities was a sort of hangar, from which half a dozen steel and crystal hulls were projecting, surmounted by large wings, vertically raised. One might have thought that they were strange ships with metallic sails.

"These," said Blas, "are aeroscaphs, aerial ships that we use as a means of transport."

Marcel was alarmed by the mere thought of that audacious navigation. "You know," he said, "I've never been up in a balloon, or any apparatus of a similar sort. Are you sure that we're not running any danger?"

"Not the slightest. Aeroscaphs are in current use among us. There is no public or private establishment that doesn't possess several of them. You can judge for yourself the facility with which they're governed. A starter wheel and a simple lever command the entire mechanism. After two or three trials you'll be able to handle one as well as I can."

Blas and Marcel had already taken their places aboard a light aerial skiff when they perceived one of their comrades on the far extremity of the terrace, who was walking nonchalantly, contemplating the immense perspective that was unfurling at his feet.

"Look," said Blas, "here comes Serge, one of the witnesses of your mysterious arrival, if you remember—one of those who were introduced to you by Monsieur Futural and me."

"Shall we take him with us?" Marcel suggested.

"As you wish. I'm certain that Serge would find it a veritable pleasure to come with us. Nothing whets the appetite and is more hygienic than an excursion through the pure oxygen layers of the high atmosphere."[24]

While Marcel and Blas were reaching that agreement, Serge had drawn closer, and after having bowed courteously he said: "I see you're about to depart for a little aerial excursion."

"Yes," Blas replied. "I'm taking our new comrade to visit the city of Artika, which he's manifested a desire to see. It's up to you, my dear friend, if you'd like to join the party."

"I accept gladly. Let's take our places, and forward ho!"

---

[24] This is odd, as oxygen is heavier than nitrogen, and requires constant regeneration by photosynthesis. The meteorological management systems of the year 3000 must be far more complex and ambitious that the description so far given.

The three young men crossed a metal footbridge and found themselves inside the hull, which was about ten meters long.

The carcass of the aeroscaph was formed by sold metal circles, which served as an armature for thick sheets of crystal. To the right and the left, above and below, nothing arrested the gaze of the travelers. They were able to contemplate at their ease the earth or the clouds, the region that they were quitting or the one toward which they were steering.

After having shut the door of glass and metal through which they had entered, Serge installed himself at the starter wheel. Blas sat next to the lever that served as a tiller.

"All set?" Serge asked Marcel, who was sitting at the back of the apparatus, not without a certain anxiety.

"Yes," he replied, tremulously.

"Let's go, then," ordered Blas.

At that signal, Serge pun the wheel he was holding through two rotations. There was an audible release. The aeroscaph slid slowly over an inclined plane and fell into the void...

Marcel uttered a cry of fright. "We're doomed!" he cried, pale with terror.

It seemed to him now that the aeroscaph was motionless. Under the impulsion of a powerful electrical motor, the wings were agitating so rapidly that their form was no longer perceptible.

"Have no fear," said Blas, smiling. "All's well. We're flying at the tidy speed of fifty kilometers a minute..."

Marcel, who had recovered promptly from his fright, looked in front of him.

The landscapes were succeeding one another with a vertiginous rapidity. Marcel scarcely had time to see them before they were effaced, giving way to others. He noticed, however, that in all the regions they traversed, the ground presented the same aspect of prosperity, luxury and beauty. One might have thought that it had been changed into an immense garden, designed by a landscaper of genius, and strewn with splendid edifices in which sandstone, porcelain and colored glass competed in splendor with gold, silver and marvelous blue, green and violet metals unknown to him.

"In spite of the rapidity with which the perspective is unfurling," said Marcel, "I can see at intervals exceedingly high towers that don't resemble other buildings. They must have been constructed with a particular purpose?"

"Those towers," Blas replied, are nothing but aerial stations. They're all constructed on the same model as the one from which we departed. They each have a hangar, which serves as a garage for the aeroscaphs, an inclined plane for departure and an arrival platform. Many of them are fitted with wireless telegraphy and telephony equipment, which have rendered communication between human beings very rapid, and thanks to which the diffusion of ideas and news has become instantaneous."

The aeroscaph had traversed successively the countries formerly known, as Belgium, Holland and Denmark. They had just passed the North Sea, a small gray pond that disappeared rapidly. The travelers were now soaring over the Dofrine Mountains in the heart of Scandinavia.

To Marcel's great astonishment, that chain of mountains, which the geographers of his time had represented to him as covered with wild forests of firs furrowed by sinister fjords and buried for half the year beneath ice and snow, appeared to have a vegetation as rich as the terrain they had just traversed. Everywhere, even on the same high summits, a large number of which had been utilized as aerial stations, beautiful trees and cheerful habitations rose up.

Thus, Marcel was able to convince himself of the exactitude of the information Blas had given him a few hours before. Yes, it was true that human genius had triumphed once and for all over the vicissitudes of the seasons; it had equalized all climates harmoniously, and all the productions of the earth.

Another subject of preoccupation soon came to absorb his thought.

"How is it," he asked Serge, that I can't perceive any other aeroscaph similar to ours? You told me yourself that this mode of locomotion was the most commonplace."

"I wasn't distorting the truth. At this moment, thousands of aeroscaphs are moving in the atmospheric layer we're traversing, but they're traveling, like us, with such velocity that they're almost invisible. With a little attention, however, you can perceive some of them. Over there, for example, do you see that blue flash?"

Marcel looked hard. "Yes," he said, after a moment's attention. "I can now distinguish sparks of a sort, doubtless produced by the rapid reflection of light from steel and crystal." After a momentary silence he added: "It's veritably amazing."

The aeroscaph was now soaring over the open sea. Marcel perceived that Blas, still sitting at the tiller of the machine, was slowing the progress of the apparatus. They had to be approaching an aerial station, because aeroscaphs became visible in all directions, doubtless having relented their own speeds. They were gliding through the air in hundreds, like swallows.

Abruptly, Marcel saw a Babelesque circular rampart surging forth at the limit of the horizon, the base of which lunged into the sea, whose summit, more than a hundred meters above the waves, was covered with towers and edifices of every kind.

"We're arriving," said Serge. "We're no more than sixty kilometers from the city of Artika. The titanic wall that you can see is called the Polar Rampart.

"A strange name!"

"Which says, however, exactly what it means. That wall, which leaves far behind it the Pyramids of Egypt, the sole monument of ancient ages with which it can be compared, cost humankind more than a century of labor; but it's thanks to that rampart that the suppression of manual labor throughout the world began, by virtue of the utilization of the enormous force of congelation of the polar ice. It was only two hundred years ago that our ancestors finally renounced the employment of that still-imperfect procedure. We only conserve the wall as a monument to history and science."

"We've also installed numerous aerial stations and telegraph stations on it," added Blas. "That's presently the sole practical utility of the Rampart."

As Blas concluded his remark, the aeroscaph vibrated with a trepidation. It had just slighted on the platform of one of Artika's aerial stations.

The three young men emerged from the aeroscaph and got into the elevator.

On the advice of Blas, who had visited Artika several times, they went into a vestry that was placed near the bottom of the tower. They put on gutta-percha diving suits, which would permit them to circulate freely in that inferno of electricity.

A few minutes later, all three of them were in a vast plaza, swarming with a crowd clad like them in insulting suits.

Marcel gazed through the crystal lenses of his mask. The city that extended before his eyes did not recall in any fashion the esthetic landscapes that he had previously contemplated. It was bizarre, baroque and ugly. However, everything there was admirably clean. The broad streets and the spacious monuments showed that much had been sacrificed to hygiene in that industrial city.

Marcel and his friends were already leaning on the balustrade of a moving sidewalk that was taking them rapidly in the direction of the Rue Marconi, where Blas' cousin lived. In front of them filed constructions of a strange architecture. There were high metal towers devoid of any ornamentation, the shiny summits of which were pointed like awls. A blue-tinted plume of electric light floated at their summits, like a flag of flame.

Further away, there were large spheres like the domes of churches, perched on glass pillars. Finally, there was a forest of metal masts, towers in the form of spirals. slowly rotating, and metal platforms, extended like hands above edifices.

One sensed that all of that apparatus was powerfully charged with electrical fluid. Some were pouring it to the reservoirs and others distributing it. A magnetic halo became visible around them in spite of the daylight. In addition, long zigzag sparks sprang forth, crackling. Marcel understood how useful the insulating suits they had put on were to him and his companions. Without that precaution it certainly would not have been possible to take ten steps in Artika without being electrocuted.

Another detail surprised Marcel. He had been habituated, until then, to finding silence reigning everywhere, scarcely troubled by the harmonic sound of musical instruments. Here he was deafened by a continuous din of hammers, so numerous that their profound rumor fused, and one could have believed that one was at the summit of a cliff battered by a storm, or under a bridge furrowed by a dozen trains.

Fortunately, the gutta-percha hood rendered those sounds less terrible.

"What you can hear," sad Blas, anticipating the question, "is the din of machine-tools, which, in this laborious city, occupy an area several kilometers square. It's in Artika, and its rival at the South Pole, Antartika, that everything needed in the rest of the world is fabricated. It's here that the materials are prepared and all the repairs carried out."

"I thought," Marcel objected, "that no one among you worked manually, even here."

"What I told you," Blas replied, "is exact. The outcasts who inhabit this city only have to supervise the automatic apparatus, which knead and mold the sandstone and the glass, smelting, forging and fashioning the metal."

"I didn't think," murmured Marcel, "that one could arrive at that point."

"That progress," Serge explained, "was accomplished quite naturally. In anterior times, the division of labor had been adopted. Every worker, always carrying out the same task, went more rapidly and became moiré skillful. His movement ended up becoming unconscious and reflexive. His

194

will no longer played any part in his labor. From there to replacing a worker with an automaton carrying out the same movements was only one step."

During that conversation the three excursionists, still borne without the slightest jolt by the moving sidewalk, had reached a quarter in which no gigantic or ungraceful machine could any longer be seen. The streets were bordered by beautiful habitations in white sandstone, of a simple and severe architecture.

"We've just traversed," said Blas, "the quarter where the outcasts work. This one is where they live. At this time of day, my cousin Julius will certainly be at home.

A moment later, the three young men called a halt and penetrated into a vestibule, the porcelain walls of which were decorated with subjects borrowed from the history of science.

At regular intervals, names were inscribed on indicative plaques, and under each of those plaques was a telephonic apparatus. Blas stopped at the inscription bearing the name of his cousin Julius and hailed him.

"Julius! Julius! It's me, your cousin Blas. I've come to see you, with two friends."

"I'll be with you in a moment," replied a distant but distinct voice.

A minute later, Julius opened the door of the elevator situated at the back of the vestibule, in person, and shook Blas' hand. The introductions were quickly made. "I have to go back to work in an hour," said Julius. "Until then, I'm all yours.

They took another moving sidewalk. On the way, Marcel asked Julius: "Can you, who are better placed than anyone else to do so, explain to me how Artika's machines can capture force and re-emit it.

"With pleasure. I won't go into detail regarding the complicated machinery of which we make use here; I'll content myself with giving you the general principle. You doubtless know already, in your time, that the globe engenders, by virtue of its perpetual movement of rotation, a considerable electrical force. That electricity, of which the most intense center of production is on the equator, accumulates at the two poles. It's that inexhaustible force that our scientists have found a means of capturing, and which, from Artika and its rival at the South Pole, Antartika, are distributed to the rest of the world, according to the needs of humankind. The powerful accumulators that we supervise take possession of the fluid, which is found simultaneously in the atmosphere, the sea and the soil. It's thanks to the infinite calorific energy at our disposal that the Poles no longer freeze."

"I understand now," exclaimed Marcel, "how the temperature can be so perfectly equalized. The electricity of the equator being incessantly absorbed by your polar factories, typhoons, tornadoes and tempests of every sort are suppressed forever."

Serge added: "And besides, the poles only sending them water at normal temperature, Greenland, Iceland and Siberia now enjoy a temperate climate."

In the course of its progress the moving sidewalk passed an arched arcade, as high and broad as the façade of a cathedral.

"Let's get down," said Julius. "We've arrived at one of our numerous galleries of accumulators. If that interests you, you can cast an eye over it."

He opened an ebony door.

As far as the eye could see, lined up before them on porcelain supports were huge glass vats, in the acidified water of which metallic plates were soaking. Wires connected up the electrodes of every vat and came to end in a central cable are thick as a wooden beam, disposed at the summit of the arched vault.

Here and there, electricians were standing, their eyes fixed on the electrometers, all dressed in the insulating armor of gutta-percha. There was something fantastic about seeing all those men circulating in the midst of that crystal décor.

Julius opened a door. They found themselves under an immense cupola, where semi-darkness reigned.

"It's here," said Julius, "that we utilize the radiant fluid discovered a thousand years ago by the scientist Crookes."

In the penumbra, in fact, Marcel could make out series of gigantic glass ampoules, in the center of which, helices were rotting soundlessly, with a furious rapidity.

As they emerged from the radiogenic factory and traversed another gallery of accumulators, they perceived two men who were carrying the inanimate body of one of their comrades away on a stretcher, with a thousand precautions.

Marcel felt a shiver.

"What's happened?" he asked Julius.

The other murmured, sadly: "Alas, as you can see, there has been an accident. As sometimes happens, unfortunately, one of our comrades has been electrocuted. Doubtless he committed the imprudence of removing his mask, getting too close to a condenser, or putting on a suit of armor that had some imperceptible flaw."

"Do accidents happen often?"

"Only rarely. However, I have seen some terrible things. Sometimes, the electric fluid only leaves, after its passage, a carbonized cadaver with a blackened face, hideous to see. But its effects aren't always fatal. Often, those who are struck only feel a forceful shock, which leaves them absolutely unharmed. Sometimes, too, they're entirely deprived of their beard, hair and eyebrows. Others, finally, remain paralyzed or attained by nervous maladies. Artika, in any case, has hospitals for those victims of the work, installed in accordance with the latest scientific discoveries. When a worker hasn't been killed instantly, it's very rare that we don't save him."

The time had come when Julius had to return to work. He accompanied his guests as far as the moving sidewalk and bid them adieu..

When he had disappeared, Marcel could not help asking Blas: "How can your cousin support his lot? Does he think himself unfortunate?"

"No. The outcasts' hours of labor are very short. They're comfortably nourished and lodged, and they enjoy great liberty. Their lot would certainly have been envied by many of the rich and fortunate of your distant epoch."

The travelers were outside the aerial station again. The day was coming to an end.[25] The grimacing silhouettes of machines were glowing in the dusk.

Marcel and his friends hastened to change their costume and regain the upper platform, where their aeroscaph was.

Blas was careful to illuminate the machine's electric headlight, and they set forth.

Very pensive in his corner, Marcel watched the cloud of luminous mist that floated like a gigantic plume over the cupolas and towers of the city of Artika pale on the horizon.

The beacon lights of aeroscaphs shone in the sky in all directions around the travelers, like a rutilant rain of shooting stars.

VIII. A Laboratory Accident

The room to which Marcel Vernoy, put to sleep by Dr. Belzevor's marvelous liquid, had been transported was on the second floor of the right wing of the Château de Montbarzy. Very simply furnished, with an impeccable sobriety of ornamentation, it was known, because of the color of its decoration, as "the Blue Room."

Everything there was blue, from the carpet and the wallpaper to the azure-lacquered "modern style" furniture. Even the panes of the window, which overlooked the forest, were the same blue color that Dr. Belzevor, rightly or wrongly, considered to be more appropriate than any other to evocations of the ideal.

---

[25] This appears to be an error; technological climate control could not affect the Earth's axial tilt, and the North Pole would still have days and nights six months long. There would be no dusk during the month of July, when the sun would to be in the sky continuously.

The domestics had deposited Marcel on the bed fully dressed, had lit a night-light that was burning in a crystal chalice in the ceiling, and then had retired.

A few moments later, Dr. Belzevor came into the Blue Room. He was accompanied by Monsieur and Madame Vernoy, still both under the effect of the surprise occasioned by the almost instantaneous fashion in which Marcel had fallen into the strange slumber that, according to the scientist, would bring about the young man's mental cure.

"Will he sleep for long?" Monsieur Vernoy asked.

"Only a few hours," replied Dr. Belzevor, "until first light. But the visions of future time will succeed one another so rapidly in his brain that he'll believe that he has lived through several days. One of the most characteristic properties of belzevorine is to modify the sensations of space and time completely. It's only been a few moments that he has seemed to be asleep, but his soul has already traveled incalculable distances."

"You told me, Doctor," said Madame Vernoy anxiously, "that my son wouldn't be exposed to any danger in the course of this experiment."

"I told you that, Madame, and I repeat it to you. Be fully reassured in that regard." Leaning over the young man, the doctor added: "In any case, look at your son. Look at the half-smile floating over his lips. He's very happy at the moment. Believe me, if he were suffering, his face wouldn't offer that expression of serene placidity."

"You'll permit us, won't you, Doctor," said Monsieur Vernoy, "to remain with Marcel while the marvelous cure is operated"

"Certainly," replied Monsieur Belzevor. "Sit down, pick up a book—whatever you wish. As for me, I'm obliged to leave you. I'm in the middle of a very important experiment; I have to go back to my laboratory. I'll come back to witness Marcel's awakening."

The doctor had taken a step to leave the Blue Room. "But now I think of it," he said, as if changing his mind, "once

I'm at work, I forget everything. The hours go by without my perceiving them, so to speak. I might not be back at the exact moment. In that case, this is what you have to do. This little flask contains a few drops of the substance that must be used to wake Marcel. If I'm not back by five o'clock in the morning, you can wake him up yourselves."

"What is it necessary to do for that?"

"It's not very complicated. Pour the contents of the flask on to a piece of cloth and moisten the sleeper's forehead and temples. He'll open his eyes and wake up immediately. I've left instructions for a carriage to be ready to take the three of you back to the village of Montbarzy. *Au revoir*, I must hurry back to my laboratory."

Monsieur Vernoy took possession of the little crystal flask and put it down on a corner of the mantelpiece, Then he sat down by Marcel's bed, beside Madame Vernoy.

The father and mother began a conversation in low voices, darting a glance from time to time at the schoolboy, whose respiration remained regular and his face smiling. They were now completely reassured, and waited impatiently for the hour of awakening.

No sound could be heard in the château. Everything seemed to be asleep. Only the murmur of the wind in the treetops troubled the silence of the night.

A cool breeze came in through the partly-open window, perfumed by the aroma of wild flowers. The cloudless sky was strewn with thousands of bright stars. It was one of those beautiful summer nights, warm and transparent, in which everything in nature breathes calm and serenity.

Monsieur and Madame Vernoy felt the charm of that unique evening. Gradually, they had stopped talking, abandoning themselves to a reverie full of hope, of which the possible cure of their son was the object...

Suddenly, a detonation, as violent as a cannon shot, caused the walls and the windows to tremble, with a muffled disturbance. At the same time, there was a bright flash of light, illuminating the forest and the château for a few seconds.

Frightened. Monsieur and Madame Vernoy ran to the window.

"My God!" exclaimed Monsieur Vernoy. "There's been an accident!"

In fact, the other wing of the château, where the laboratory was, seemed to be ablaze.

"Let's go to help the doctor!" cried Madame Vernoy.

They both ran out.

Before leaving the room, however, they were able to observe that, in spite of the frightful noise of the explosion, Marcel was still asleep, in an even and peaceful slumber. The belzevorine had rendered him insensible to everything except the ecstatic contemplation that was putting a smile of delight on his lips.

When Monsieur and Madame Vernoy arrived in the vicinity of the laboratory they found all the staff of the château on their feet. Men and women alike, all the servants were actively occupied in fighting the fire that, alimented by carboys of alcohol and ether, was launching forth torrents of blue and white flames.

Dr. Belzevor, unconscious, his hair and eyebrows burned, had been pulled out of the flames at the start. In a neighboring room, first aid was being lavished upon him; his bloodied face and hands, cruelly lacerated by shards of glass, were being bandaged.

Panic and fear reigned among the domestics.

Fortunately, the Château de Montbarzy possessed a fire-pump. It was put into action next to the pond. After an hour of toil, they were finally able to put the fire out.

The château was preserved, but of the laboratory, the library and the study, nothing remained but a mass of muddy ash, broken glassware and half-incinerated volumes.

"Let's hope," said Monsieur Vernoy, "that the doctor's life is saved, and that the damage is purely material."

The physician, whom a servant had gone at a gallop to fetch from the nearest town, was awaited anxiously. He arrived as the last buckets of water were being thrown over the rubble. He declared that Monsieur Belzevor's wounds were very serious and very numerous, but that his life was not in danger, at least for the moment. Then he proceeded with the extraction of the fragments of glass and splinters of wood. After that, he prepared an initial dressing, wrote a prescription, and left, promising to return the next day.

Monsieur Vernoy wanted to stay with Dr. Belzevor. As for Madame Vernoy, she returned to her son, whom she was in haste to see emerge from the strange sleep in which he was plunged.

While his wounds were being dressed, Monsieur Belzevor recovered consciousness; he smiled weakly on perceiving Monsieur Vernoy. Until the physician's departure, he remained silent, but when the latter had withdrawn he pronounced, in a voice as faint as a whisper: "The fire?"

"Don't worry," said the archivist. "We've put it out. It's all over now."

"My laboratory?"

"It's very badly damaged, but this isn't the time to think about that. It's necessary to think about taking care of yourself..."

The wounded man had a nervous spasm. "Not worry about my laboratory!" he muttered. "It's easy for you to talk. That's the only thing that matters to me. My discoveries are my life!"

The eyes of the injured man were shining feverishly. An artificial energy sustained him momentarily. "I want to know the extent of the disaster, now!" he cried.

"But you can't move..."

"That doesn't matter! Have someone carry me to my laboratory! Call the servants!"

Deaf to Monsieur Vernoy's observations, Dr. Belzevor was obstinate in his caprice, and they were obliged to obey him. With a thousand precautions, he was placed on a chair garnished with cushions and transported to the ruins of the laboratory.

Like a mortally wounded general being carried by his soldiers toward the enemy while a breath of life still remained to him. Dr. Belzevor wanted to struggle until the last moment.

Monsieur Vernoy followed him, full of admiration and anxiety.

By the light of torches, the laboratory, still reeking of acrid vapors, offered a spectacle of desolation. Nothing remained intact there.

"How did the accident happen?" Monsieur Vernoy could not help asking.

"Oh," murmured the doctor, "by an unpardonable imprudence on my part—an imprudence that the least of laboratory assistants wouldn't have committed. I forgot to put the stopper back in a carboy of ether. The lamp was beside it. You can see the result."

After that explanation, Dr. Belzevor fell silent. On observing the total and irremediable annihilation of the result of ten years of toil and experimentation, however, tears of rage of discouragement trickled over his contracted face.

The cupboard containing the special elixirs that Dr. Belzevor had prepared had been pulverized. The tearful gaze of the unfortunate scientist searched in vain for some flask, some notebook of formulae that might have escaped the disaster.

Suddenly, he uttered a cry of joy. He had just perceived, lying on the ground, unstoppered but still half full, a small bottle of belzevorine.

He ordered that it be picked up and given to him; and his gaze remained, with a fixity full of dementia, on that tiny debris of an entire laborious existence.

The doctor was carried to his bedroom, but he had no intention of being separated from the flask found in the rubble. He wanted it to be placed beside his bed, alongside the potions and remedies that a domestic had just brought, and he did not cease to contemplate it with an ecstatic gaze.

The doctor seemed calmer; Monsieur Vernoy thought that he could quit him for a few moments in order to go to the

Blue Room to make sure that Marcel's slumber was still proceeding without a hitch.

Scarcely had Monsieur Vernoy left, however, than the condition of the injured man worsened. As the physician had predicted, a crisis occurred. Monsieur Belzevor became delirious.

At the risk of disturbing his dressings, he sat up in bed and pronounced inconsequential words and halting phrases, while gesticulating.

The domestic that had replaced Monsieur Vernoy knew that at each crisis, as he had been instructed, it was necessary to administer a sedative potion to his master. He had been told that the sedative in question was in the largest bottle.

The servant, well-intentioned but ignorant, did indeed look to see which was the largest bottle…and made the invalid drink all that remained of the belzevorine.

The elixir's effect was instantaneous. The injured man immediately calmed down; his fever disappeared, and he did not take long to fall into a profound sleep.

He too was now *en route* for the realms of the future.

IX. The Hall of Athletes and the Hall of the Muses

The aeroscaph that was carrying Blas, Serge and Marcel came to alight gently on the platform of the school's aerial station.

The three friends were delighted with their excursion, and did not feel the slightest fatigue. Marcel observed privately, with admiration, that in the thirtieth century a journey from Paris to the Pole was executed much more comfortably, and much more rapidly, than an excursion from Paris to Saint-Cloud in olden times.

The aeroscaph, as fast as lightning, comfortable and easy to handle, left far behind the steamers and the railways of times past, so slow, and of a mechanism that was both so rudimentary and so complicated.

Marcel was increasingly getting a liking for the society and the conversation of his new comrades. When he compared, by means of memory, Blas and Serge with the schoolboys of the twentieth century, the latter seemed pitiful in every respect. Those noisy, idle pupils, full of faults and occupied with futilities, appeared to him to be feeble and ridiculous individuals. He wondered, with surprise, how he had once been able to take pleasure in their conversation and interest himself in petty individuals of such limited intelligence and such defective education.

In reasoning thus, Marcel was committing the sin of vanity; he was taking no account of the fact that he had recently been no different from those he was now treating with so much disdain. The fact is that the frequentation of Blas and Serge, opening up new perfections on all questions, had caused him to measure the abyss of his own ignorance. Their mildness and their exquisite politeness had forced him to blush at his egotism, his sulking and his anger.

In spite of the efforts that he made to maintain himself at the same conversational level as his comrades of the year 3000, he sensed continually how inferior he was to them, and the fraternal indulgence with which they treated him added further to his humiliation.

What surprised him most about Blas and Serge was that they were entirely exempt from vanity. They did not seek, on any occasion, to put themselves forward, to shine. When they were wrong they admitted it, smiling, without showing any ill humor.

Marcel was far from being so perfect. Of a slightly susceptible character, he sometimes found himself abominably vexed when Blas or Serge, with a simple remark, devoid or irony of bitterness, caused him to observe his lack of logic or his stupidity. In fact, they took infinite precautions to avoid wounding him.

Thus, little by little, Marcel was touched to the depths of his heart by the amicable indulgence that his new friends testified to him. The sincere amity that he did not take long to feel for them had nothing in common with the affection he had experienced for his former comrades; it partook simultaneously of charm, respect and sympathy.

As Marcel, in the company of Blas and Serge, quit the elevator and set foot in the circular gallery of the school, the three young men encountered two of their comrades, Fritz and Lucius.

Serge saluted them from a distance. Fritz and Lucius, on recognizing Marcel, whom they had seen arrive in such a marvelous fashion, hastened toward him.

They asked him courteously whether he was experiencing much difficulty in forsaking his habits and tastes, and how he appreciated the system of education in vigor in the thirtieth century.

"You seem to be exactly similar to us, now," said Fritz. "No one would suspect, on seeing and hearing you, that you've arrived from the epoch of locomotives."

"It isn't too obvious, then," replied Marcel, flattered, "that I'm a barbarian?"

Everyone protested.

"Certainly," said Blas, "you still lack a little muscle and brain. In your epoch, people didn't know how to exercise their organs appropriately. With the rational methods of training that we possess, though, you'll quickly catch us up..."

Marcel had once been a fervent lover of croquet, tennis and football. The word *muscle* awoke an entire series of ideas in him. "I'm curious," he said, "to know what physical exercises you indulge in for preference, and in what fashion you perform gymnastics."

"We'll satisfy your curiosity shortly," said Serge. "We'll take you to the Hall of Athletes. But you're forgetting that we haven't eaten..."

"Nor have we," said Lucius. "We'll dine together, if you like."

Still following the circular gallery, now inundated with light by electric lamps encased in the capitals, the five young men headed for the room in which Marcel had taken the morning meal.

From the same urns and the same diamond ewers, they savored the same azure jam and drank the same reparative elixir.

After the meal, which was expedited in a matter of minutes, they went down a onyx stairway that gave access to the central garden via gentle flights of steps.

One might have thought that the foliage was illuminated by thousands of glow-worms, so cleverly had the light been managed and graduated. In the clumps of bushes and the arbors there was a sort of phosphorescent penumbra, which was not at all offensive or brutal to the eyesight.

In the pathways, young men were strolling in groups, nobly draped in their bright chlamydes. They were walking slowly.

Marcel overheard a few snatches of conversation in passing. Like Plato's disciples in the gardens of the Academy, the young strollers were discussing animatedly the highest problems of art, philosophy and morality.

"People work hard here, night and day," Marcel observed.

"The comrades you've just encountered," Serge replied, "Aren't working at the moment. They're simply relaxing, by means of cheerful conversations about subjects that interest them.

Meanwhile, they arrived on a part of the garden that was much more brightly illuminated. Columns of porphyry bore powerful lamps at their summit. Their radiance intersected to form a veritable luminous veil composed of a succession of bright bands in various colors. It was like walking under the vault of a cathedral made of rainbows. Those lights, although bright, had nothing reminiscent of the raw and ferocious glare that characterized the electric arcs and incandescent filaments of the twentieth century, the cause of so many opthalmias.

At the extremity of that avenue of radiance, a monumental fountain poured forth luminous waves that changed their form continually.

"That fountain," said Blas, "is due to the collaboration of celebrated scientists and artists. It's so skillfully contrived that it sometimes represents a flower bed from which cascades of corollas are falling, and sometimes a mythological scene. Chimeras vomit flames, and then give way to a swarm of winged spirits that soar toward the sky with fiery wings..."

Marcel remained in front of the luminous fountain for some time, in admiration. His friends were obliged to extract him from his contemplation.

"You're forgetting," Blas said to him, mildly, "that we were going to the Hall of Athletes, The evening's advancing, and we won't have enough time to see everything..."

Regretfully, Marcel turned his back on the marvels of the enchanted garden. Still accompanied by his friends, he went into the Hall of Athletes.

It was an enormous circular hall, with an arena in the center sprinkled with mica dust. All around the arena, which was surmounted by an enormously high dome, rooms opened that were each devoted to a different exercise.

In the central arena, a troop of young men clad in simple leotards were   performing leaps. A graduated mat permitted them to compare the heights attained. Marcel's eyes widened in surprise when he saw that the young men were jumping to heights of seven or eight meters, almost without effort.

"How are they able to jump like that?" he asked Blas. "I confess that I don't understand."

"A few of my comrades," Blas replied, "have very elastic muscles. They can't jump as well without the special shoes that they're wearing. As you can see, the shoes have double soles and are fitted with powerful springs. A light impulsion is sufficient for the jumper to rebound like a veritable rubber ball. It's by virtue of those shoes that we're able, whenever we please, to leap to the top of a tower in a single bound, or cross a wide stream. Thanks to them, the weight of the human body is considerably diminished."

Marcel gave himself the pleasure of putting on a pair of those shoes and executing a series of leaps that would have rendered the most agile acrobats and best trained gymnasts of his time jealous. One detail was, however, humiliating; in spite of all his efforts, he did not succeed in jumping half as high as Blas, Serge or any of those who surrounded him.

"I'm truly too inferior," he said, trying to conceal his discontentment.

"That's not surprising," replied Serge. "Look at our muscles and compare them with yours."

"In fact," Marcel observed, examining his companions' formidable biceps, "you all have a musculature that would make Milo of Crotona envious." And he considered his thin arms and beanpole legs, those of an anemic Parisian. "I performed honorably in all the contests at school," he remarked, with chagrin, "but compared with you, I perceive that I'm a very paltry fellow."

"It's necessary not to be afflicted by that," said Blas. "In your time, the art of making muscles grow artificially and conserving their solidity by means of appropriate exercises was unknown "

"What! You can make muscles grow artificially! I confess that I don't understand..."

"And yet, thinking about it, it's a discovery that goes back to the twentieth century. An American doctor, by electrifying the arm of a young woman afflicted by rheumatism, perceived that by the end of the experiment, the biceps had almost doubled in volume. Since that epoch, the primitive discovery has been greatly improved. Nowadays, everyone has biceps as large as he pleases."

"Why is it so important to you to have such vigorous muscles?" Marcel asked.

"Our brains being considerably hypertrophied, if we weren't extremely well-muscled, the equilibrium would be broken. We'd still be as intelligent as we are but condemned to neurasthenia and neurosis; we'd always be ill. Whereas, as you've been able to see, we're as healthy in body as we are in mind."

At that moment Marcel heard a noise above his head. He looked up.

Through a wide open panel in the glazed dome he saw a singular being penetrate it, with heavy wing-beats: a sort of human bat, who came to alight gently in the arena. Marcel immediately demanded explanation.

"You're simply seeing an aerial cyclist," Serge told him, "returning from a nocturnal excursion over the gardens."

"I would have thought," sad Marcel, "that with aeroscaphs as improved as those you have, such an apparatus would be unnecessary."

"So we only conserve them as instruments of sport. The aerial cycle is a rather complicated machine. It has something of the balloon, the kite and the parachute about it. It can only carry one person, who puts the propeller in motion with the aid of pedals. A sail-parachute ensures the direction of the apparatus and permits the avoidance of accidents. The aerocycle is especially employed in excursions of short duration, or for brief pleasure-trips. You'll see us, for example, leaving the school on our aerocycles on certain days to go and collect botanical specimens."

"And accidents never happen with such fragile machines?"

"Never. The worst that can happen is that a clumsy individual who can't steer his aerocycle, or an unfortunate whose apparatus has broken down, floats gently to the ground, borne without a shock by the sail-parachute. It's necessary to be exceedingly unlucky, in such as case, to collide with the spire of an edifice or to touch an electricity tower. So far as I know, that has never occurred."

While this conversation was taking place, more aerocyclists were entering and exiting.

Marcel was very interested in the manner in which they took off. They were all wearing spring shoes, and with an energetic thrust of the heels they rose into the air with their apparatus; then they started the propeller in motion and did not take long to disappear.

With a great deal of pleasure, Marcel visited the halls of trapezes, fixed bars, parallel bars and dumb-bells. He paused for a few moments on the edge of the swimming pool. Afterwards, Blas showed him a dynamometric machine that measured human strength exactly, in kilograms, and permitted the pupils to render an exact account, day by day, of their progress in gymnastics.

As they were about to leave the room that contained the dynamometer they encountered Monsieur Futural, who was heading for the Hall of Athletes, accompanied by his wife.

Monsieur Futural approached Marcel and asked him benevolently whether he was content.

"I have nothing but praise for my comrades," he replied. "They're been charming." He added, smiling: "Oh course, I'm very vexed to have observed my muscular inferiority."

"Don't worry about that," replied Monsieur Futural. "With us, you'll quickly be able to put on muscle. Vigor, like intelligence, depends greatly on hygiene."

"Since you don't seem to be taking pleasure in these corporeal exercises," Madame Futural put in, "perhaps you'd be more interested in artistic recreations."

"Certainly," her husband approved. He turned toward Blas and added: "Take Marcel, I beg you, to the Hall of the Muses. It will be an excellent way for him, and for you, to conclude the evening."

Monsieur Futural had spoken more in the tone of a friend giving advice than that of a master intimating an order. And after a slight salute to the young men surrounding Marcel, he went into the Hall of Athletes.

After having taken their leave to Serge, Fritz and Lucius, therefore, Marcel and Blas headed for the Hall of the Muses.

It was an elegant construction in green and white porcelain, situated in the center of a clump of oleanders and rhododendrons. The walls were decorated with bas-reliefs, the subjects of which had been taken from the history of art and letters. Homer could be seen there reciting his Iliad, surrounded by attentive heroes; Shakespeare was holding the horses of noblemen outside the door of the Globe Theater; Victor Hugo was contemplating the sea pensively from the island of Guernsey; and the musician Arachnus was composing his universally renowned cantata *Redemptive Science*.

A large number of other bas-reliefs, taken from the history of painting, sculpture and illustrious musicians, decorated the polychromatic façade.

Without wasting any time asking Blas for explanations, Marcel followed his guide into the vestibule of the Hall of the Muses. In the first room they went into, four young men were just finishing the execution of a quartet.

Marcel, who had often attended great Sunday concerts in the company of his father, remarked that they played with purity of taste accuracy and exquisite sentiment.

"Those are great artistes!" he could not help exclaiming.

"You're exaggerating. They're simply students distracting themselves after the day's studies by making a little music. You can see, however, that they're not bad."

Marcel would have liked to listen to another piece, but Blas remarked that it was getting late, and they went into the next room, where a young man was modeling a bust of one of his comrades. Marcel was able to observe that over the centuries the chisels and various other instruments of sculpture had only been slightly modified. He said so to Blas.

"However," the latter replied, "We have made progress; we now make clever use of machinery to complete the process." And he pointed to an assemblage of sharp rods in a corner, connected by screws that permitted their separation to be modified.

"We also posses sculpting machines," he added, "the mechanical chisels of which, armed with diamond tips, carve statues in the hardest granite. Needless to say, those machines haven't replaced artists. They merely facilitated the reproduction of masterpieces."

When they went into the next room, Marcel experienced a profound emotion. As he went in, a loud voice was declaiming two lines from Corneille:

The obscure clarity that falls from the stars
With the tide, enables us to see thirty sails...[26]

Until then, Marcel had only heard neo-Latin. The sounds of his mother tongue, purely emitted, struck his ear delightfully.

"I thought," he said to Blas, "that our French language was no longer spoken."

"It's no longer in current usage, that's true, but we have to know it in order to read the texts of the masterpieces of classic literature. Since that appears to be agreeable to you, you have only to come here every evening. As you can see, this room is devoted to declamation, reading and diction. It's one of the most popular."

Numerous rooms still remained to be visited, but Blas contented himself with showing his friend the room reserved for lovers of painting.

Marcel perceived that the material methods of pictorial art had been completely renewed. The majority of artists were painting with colors mixed with molten wax, and there was an electric heater above their palette.

"That method," sad Blas, "is renewed from the remotest antiquity. The frescoes of Pompeii and Herculaneum were executed in this fashion, for the most part. It's more solid than painting with oils, which can sometimes be blackened and deteriorate in less than a century.

In that room there were also young men painting on porcelain with the aid of fine powders of metallic oxides. In front of each of them was a sort of electric stove. When the

---

[26] The lines are from act IV of Pierre Corneille's *Le Cid* (1636).

painting was complete it was sufficient to turn a switch and the colors were vitrified in an even and perfect fashion.

"All this interests me enormously," said Marcel, "but I confess that I'm a little tired. I've seen so many previously unsuspected marvels today, and learned so many things that I didn't know, that my ideas are beginning to become confused in my head."

"A few hours of sleep will put you right," replied Blas. "I'll accompany you back to your room. Tomorrow morning, at the usual time of awakening, I'll come to find you."

Once he was alone in the luxurious room where he had woken up that morning, Marcel felt a sadness invade him. He thought about his parents, whom he might never see again, and who had doubtless wept over his disappearance. He reproached himself bitterly for not having followed their advice and avoided more carefully causing them chagrin when he was with them.

He went to bed with a heavy heart, but he was so fatigued that he had scarcely introduced himself into the silky glass fiber blankets that his head tilted and his eyes closed...and he fell asleep.

X. Paris in the Thirtieth Century

As on the previous day, Marcel was extracted from the slumber into which he was plunged by the sounds of a seductive and mysterious music. He woke up smiling.

This time he did not experience any astonishment. He felt that he would have no difficulty getting used to the new existence that had been made for him. There was, however, a shadow over his satisfaction, for he wondered with anxiety whether he would ever see his parents again, and the world of the twentieth century, so imperfect and so barbaric, but to which his heart was still connected by so many bonds.

But what could he do about it? It was impossible for him to return to the past.

Marcel thought that the best thing for him to do was to resign himself; and he hoped that he might perhaps be able, once again, to traverse the ocean of elapsed ages in the same inexplicable fashion that he had crossed it the first time.

He leapt out of bed, therefore, put on his glass fiber chlamys, and set about his electrical ablutions.

He had only just finished when Blas came in, greeting him with a cordial bonjour.

"Well," he asked, "did you have a good night? Are your muscles and your brain suitably rested?"

"I feel admirably well, thank you, and I'm ready to accompany you wherever you care to take me.

"The essential thing for you, I think, before studying anything else, is to familiarize yourself with the way in which the mechanism of instruction functions. In consequence, we'll go this morning to visit one of the most celebrated professors of anthropology. Afterwards, I'll take you to the palace where all the professors' lessons and courses are automatically centralized, in order to be distributed thereafter throughout the world."

"What mans of locomotion will we employ?"

"We can simply go on foot, if you wish. I think, in any case, you'll derive a good deal of pleasure from seeing what has become, over the centuries, of the old Parisian city, which your memories must retrace for you as a disorderly accumulation of buildings and factories. You'll see that we've improved the landscape greatly."

Blas and Marcel set forth. At one of the extremities of the oval formed by the circular gallery, they went through a large sandstone portico, which had no gate and no concierge to forbid access, and found themselves in the grounds of the school.

In front of them was a large avenue bordered by flowering tulip-trees and eucalypti. Marcel uttered an exclamation of amazement on seeing profiled, at the end of the avenue in question, the Gothic towers of Notre Dame.

He saluted the old cathedral with as much pleasure and emotion as he would have done for a childhood friend encountered in a foreign country.

"Everything hasn't disappeared from the world forever!" he exclaimed. Instinctively, he tried to get his bearings. He looked round. Apart from the basilica, however, he did not recognize anything.

"At which point in old Paris is your school constructed, then?" he asked.

"It covers almost entirely a hill that as once called the Butte Montmartre. The tower that serves as an aerial station for our aeroscaphs is built on the site of the church of Sacré-Coeur. We'll follow this avenue, which will take us, via a very gentle slope, all the way to the Seine, to the foot of the cathedral, the sight of which produced such an impression on you."

"And that's all that remains of Paris?" asked Marcel, who felt sadness invading him.

"No," replied Blas. "Not far from here, a large arch ornamented with sculptures subsists, which our historians say was constructed by a celebrated general of the nineteenth century, a certain Napoléon. I believe, if I'm not mistaken, that that was the name of the conqueror in question."

Marcel remained silent. Too many thoughts were overwhelming him.

He felt the vertigo of the centuries invading him.

Without saying a word, he continued to follow the avenue that led to Notre Dame, in company with Blas.'

At intervals, large roundabouts ornamented with spurting fountains and statues in marble, stucco or glass paste broke the uniformity of the perspective.

To the right and the left they perceived edifices of sandstone and porcelain protruding from the midst of the foliage, which scarcely differed from those of the school in greater elegance and sumptuousness. Finally, they arrived opposite the cathedral. Marcel perceived that the sculptures were admirably conserved and were shining in the sunlight as if they were varnished.

"Don't be astonished," said Blas, "if these ornaments, sculpted in a very soft and friable stone, are in such a perfect state of conservation. It has already been hundreds of years that the precaution has been taken of coating the whole exterior of that historic monument with a thin layer of molten glass, which sheltered it permanently from destruction. It's a method of conservation currently employed in our museums.

Another fact that astonished Marcel greatly was the beauty and limpidity of the waters of the Seine. The muddy, black and fetid river that he had known was now crystal clear.

Between the monumental quays, decorated with burnished gold lamp-posts, the bed of the river, paved with brightly-colored ceramics, could be discerned clearly, and the bridges, each with a single arch, were incomparably bold and elegant.

Marcel and Blas followed the course of the Seine for a while. Here and there they encountered passers-by who responded to their salute with cordial politeness.

"How is it," Marcel asked, "that we haven't yet encountered any poorly-dressed surly or deformed individuals?"

At that question, Blas manifested a certain astonishment. "You still believe, then, that in any human society there must be poor people, cripples and malcontents? You won't see anyone hunchbacked or lame here, because those disgraced by nature no longer exist in our midst. The progress of hygiene and medicine suppressed those infirmities a long time ago, which were easy to cure."

"Very good. But what about the malcontents and the poor?"

"Those people are no longer here for the same reason as the infirm. No one can be discontented with his lot, since everyone does what he wishes within the measure of his faculties, and he has the same rights and the same duties as his fellows. Fortunately, natural forces, aided by the labor of machines, produce enough to satisfy all needs. Our thirtieth-century society could become ten times as numerous without poverty, or even the need to economize, being felt among us."

Marcel and Blas, turning their backs to the river, had continued their route in the direction of the place where the Canal Saint-Martin is today.

"It seems to me," said Marcel," "That we haven't followed a direct route, that we've made several detours..."

"I perceived your emotion at the sight of the church of Notre-Dame; I didn't want to deprive you of the pleasure of contemplating it at close range. In any case, there's no need to hurry. A walk in the shade of these large trees, through parks dotted with flowers and enclosing beautiful buildings, is a veritable enchantment."

They had been walking for about an hour when Marcel uttered an exclamation of surprise. Between the trees, a large expanse of blue water had just appeared. Small boats of a shiny metal were bobbing, moored to the porphyry quays by silver chains.

"I confess," said Marcel, "that I'm utterly bewildered. What is this lake, or this sea? I would never have suspected that such major changes could have been produced in the geographical constitution of France."

"This change owes nothing to the action of geological forces; it's the work of human labor. It's the former Paris seaport. It was hollowed out seven or eight centuries ago. As long as the struggles of industrial competition lasted, it made the city the world's foremost commercial center. Now that we produce almost all the substances necessary to life locally, by chemical means, and indispensable transportation is operated by means of aeroscaphs, we have only conserved this vast basin and the channel that aliments it, because of their utility from the viewpoint of hygiene and esthetics. Those boats that you see are yachts, in which a few lovers of nautical sports devote themselves to the art, as old as the world, of guiding vessels in spite of wayward winds and furious waves."

"One more question," said Marcel, having ceased to reflect a great deal by virtue of what he had just seen. "What system of sanitation do you use? You've doubtless renounced the employment of sewers?"

"It's more than five hundred years since electric furnaces were introduced everywhere to burn detritus; you can visit, if you wish, the superb subterranean canal that once carried the water of the sewers from Paris to the sea, fertilizing the entire countryside on the way. The progress of hygiene and agriculture have renounced that. Now, it only serves to lodge electrical machinery."

Blas and Marcel went into a large garden, at the center of which rose two or three porcelain towers ornamented by balconies with colonnettes and topped with silver domes.

"This is the home of Monsieur Talab, the celebrated professor of anthropology," said Blas. "I'll see whether we're not disturbing him too much, and if he's able to receive us..."

Blas went into the vestibule and approached a telephonic plate, which a sandstone statue presented with a smile.

"Dear and venerated master," he said, "The young stranger from the twentieth century who has arrived among us, of whose advent Monsieur Futural has notified you, would like to be introduced to you. May we be received in your study?"

The response was immediate; a voice full of affability, which seemed to emerge from the mouth of the stature, articulated clearly: "You can come up; you aren't disturbing me at all."

Marcel and Blas went over the footbridge of the elevator, which deposited them on a square landing ornamented with alabaster vases full of flowers. They moved aside a curtain and found themselves in a spacious room surrounded by glass panels.

Monsieur Talab was a tall man with a face surrounded by a black beard sculpted in the Assyrian mode. He welcomed his visitors with a heartiness that was not exempt from a certain curiosity in Marcel's regard.

"I see," he said, "that you've already adopted our costume and our usages. I greatly regret not having seen you dressed as you were three days ago. But at least, thanks to you, I shall be able to clarify a few archeological problems that have been embarrassing me somewhat. First of all, why, in your time, did people have the habit of coating the undergarments that you called shirts with a broth of starch that, in drying out under the action of fire, caused them to become stiff and scratchy, and must certainly have transformed them into veritable instruments of torture? I have here the starched collar of an elegant man of the twentieth century, and I wonder how anyone could support such a harness for long. That custom must have a utility, some reason for being?"

"In truth, Monsieur," replied Marcel, blushing slightly, "I confess that in wearing starched shirts, we never had a practical objective in mind. It was the fashion; people thought it looked good, that's all."

"A strange aberration!" muttered the professor. "Those sharp collars must have sawn the neck and ears of those who wore them. But I thank you for your explanation. I had always thought that starched cloth possessed special properties, medical or otherwise. I'm glad to be undeceived."

He indicated a glass panel to Marcel. "Look, here's one of your contemporaries, whose complete harness we've been able to reconstitute exactly, He's even coiffed in a cylindrical hat ornamented with fur, which I believe was called a 'top hat' in that epoch."

Marcel turned round and saw, with stupor, a wax mannequin with glass eyes facing him, clad in a black evening suit almost exactly similar to those that men's clothiers exhibit in their shop windows. The archeologist had not omitted any detail. The hands were gloved, the moustaches turned up and curled with tongs; there was even a diamond stud glinting in the fissure of the waistcoat.

Marcel felt slightly humiliated in seeing that the wax individual excited the professor's zestful jeers. "Truly," said the latter, "I don't know how men were once able to deck themselves out in a livery so morose and so ridiculous. I'm not surprised that your epoch was an industrial one; one might think it the stump of a smoke-blackened factory chimney."

The professor asked Marcel a host of other questions. In order not to forget anything he heard, he placed an audiophonic recorder next to the young man. All his responses were faithfully inscribed on the plaque of the apparatus.

"Messieurs," the professor said finally, "in spite of the interest of your conversation, I'm obliged to take my leave of you. The hour for my lecture has arrived."

Blas and Marcel bowed respectfully and got ready to withdraw, while the professor, without paying any further heed to them, installed himself at his work table placing a large vibrant plaque. In a clear and crisp voice, he began his lecture.

"I explained to you in a previous lesson, Messieurs, that one of the causes that held back the progress of the human family for a long time was the great importance attached to an unoxidizable metal, nowadays very common, which is none other than gold.

"In ancient societies, the man who, by whatever means, succeeded in taking possession of a certain quantity of it found himself dispensed, by virtue of that fact, from any work and any initiative.

"Gold was the pretext for countless crimes and wars. By producing gold at a minimal price, chemistry changed the face of things..."

Marcel and Blas left on tiptoe.

When the elevator had deposited them in the professor's vestibule, Blas said to Marcel; "As you've just seen, nowadays, a professor gives his lectures at a long distance from his audience. That doesn't offer any inconvenience, because of the improved means that we have of transmitting the human voice. Monsieur Talab has pupils who live thousands of leagues from here; they've no less attentive and punctual for that."

"Explain that to me."

"Every professor, like the one we've just quit, pronounces his lectures in front of the plaque of a powerful transmitting apparatus. All his lectures are collected at the Central Palace

221

of Studies, from which they are then retransmitted all over the world, in such a way that at the same time, countless students scattered all over the face of the globe can receive the same lessons, as clearly as if they were only a few feet away from the professor."

"If possible," said Marcel, "I'd like to visit that Central Palace of Studies."

"Nothing is easier. We'll go there now."

Soon, the two friends penetrated into a vast agglomeration of buildings composed of numerous exceedingly high towers. The summits of those towers were reserved for wireless telephony apparatus, and put the Central Palace in communication with all the schools in the world. The interior offered a series of halls filed with receivers and transmitters, supervised by two or three men clad, like the inhabitants of Artika or Mastif in insulating gutta-percha garments.

Blas and Marcel only visited a one or two rooms.

"There's no need for us to see the others," said Blas. "They're all disposed in the same fashion. Instead, if you like, we'll hurry back to the school, and in order to get there more rapidly we'll make use of a mode of locomotion that is certainly unknown to you, for you're from the epoch of the Métropolitain."

"What is that mode of locomotion?"

"The pneumatic carriage."

An elevator took the two young men down to a subterranean hall, where a large number of cylindrical tunnels ended, and which was filled with a perpetual whistling sound.

Soon, that whistle intensified, and he faded...and a sort of projectile appeared, without the slightest sound, at the extremity of one of the tunnels.

"Here's the carriage," said Blas. He hastened to open a door accommodated in the wall of the projectile, and they both went into it.

An obliging traveler, who was already therein, closed the door behind them.

The interior of the carriage, illuminated by little electric lamps, contained half a dozen people sitting on comfortable banquettes. About ten places remained free.

Almost immediately, the whistling recommenced, and Marcel felt that they were carried away at a prodigious speed between the walls of an enormous tube.

He began to understand. The carriage in which they were traveling had been constructed on the same model as the pneumatic apparatus that, in his day, had served for the rapid transmission of dispatches over short distances. Messages were placed inside a hollow piston; the cylindrical container was then disposed in a tube of which it had the exact dimensions. With the aid of a pump, a void was created at one end of the tube, and the pressure of the air was sufficient to impel the piston rapidly to the far extremity.

A few minutes later, Marcel and Blas emerged from the pneumatic carriage and set foot within the grounds of the school.

XI. A Future Sorbonne

While Marcel and Blas took a few moments' rest, the latter gave his friend supplementary information regarding the professariat of the thirtieth century.

"Nowadays," he said, "The professors occupy very enviable situations. They're on the same footing as the administrators of the State who are responsible for the division of natural wealth, and for the wellbeing of all. They have the same rank as the artists, poets and philosophers who determine esthetic changes in the landscape, education and the interior decoration of edifices. They're honored and respected by their fellow citizens because they work hard and have a great deal of responsibility."

"Can you tell me, my dear Blas, what it's necessary to do to become a professor?"

"It's not only necessary to give proof, in very severe examinations, of memory and intelligence, and to show that one knows ideas and facts in an impeccable fashion, but also to be the author of an important discovery or original theory within the series of knowledge that one aspires to profess. Needless to say, nowadays, intrigue, favor and protections count for nothing. Our examiners are absolutely impartial. They don't even know the people they're called upon to judge."

"I have difficulty believing that no illicit favor ever occurs..."

"I can assure you that that never happens. The ignorant candidate and the venal examiner who protected him would be prey to such scorn, overwhelmed by such an insulting pity, that no one would ever dare to take the risk. In any case, the knowledge demanded of the candidates is so complex that fraud would be immediately detected." After a moment's silence, Blas added: "Then again what interest would there be in protecting incapable candidates? Places and distinctions don't bring, among us, any surplus of comfort or opulence. Thy only constrain people to greater endeavor; so the idle and those poorly endowed from the intellectual viewpoint are careful to avoid the redoubtable proofs of the professariat. They content themselves with rendering services to society within the measure of their faculties or their energy,"

"How do you choose the administrators and the artists that you mentioned just now?"

"We employ the same system as for the professors. We appoint as an administrator someone who publishes a plan for the division of wealth more equitable than those of his predecessors. It's the same with artists. Those who find new means of simplifying or magnifying the conception of beauty are immediately admitted to give their advice to the Great Council on which the embellishment of habitations and landscapes depend."

"Good...but what becomes, then, of political animosities and differences of opinion?"

"It's a long time since we renounced those vain quarrels, Present day society is no longer anything but one vast family, paternally administered by the most intelligent and the most honest."

"Are professors very numerous? Given the progress you've made in science, their number must be considerable."

"On the contrary; men distinguished enough to become professors are restricted in number. All the science of the past is taught to us by phonographs. The professors speak to all the students in the world, thanks to the apparatus you saw a short while ago...

"So, now we'll visit the lecture rooms. You'll hear repeated by our speaking machines the lessons that the professors proclaim from the depths of their study to the rest of the world. The only difference from what happened in olden days is that the courses you'll hear are no longer simple exercises in memory and application. Every lecture by our masters initiates us, if not to an entirely new discovery, at least to an improvement on previously adopted theories."

"I can't see very clearly," Marcel said, "with such a system, what might become of cities once celebrated for their universities, such as Florence, Heidelberg, Oxford, Madrid and Philadelphia."

"All those cities only exist any longer as names and memories. It's a long time since the development of means of communication and the rapid diffusion of ideas have entirely ruined the faulty system of centralization employed in your time. There are now only three great agglomerations of human beings: the Old Continent, America and the Oceanian Provinces. The world only forms, so to speak, a single vast city, or, if you prefer, a single country."

"I confess that I don't understand that very well."

Blas explained: "I mean that, as you've been able to see by means of our stroll through Paris this morning, uncomfortable and insalubrious agglomerations have disappeared entirely...and that's understandable. Why did the people of old build cities and seek to be as close to one another as possible? It was in order to help one another more easily, to exchange more rapidly ideas and inventions useful to the community.

225

Now, cities have become unnecessary. The wireless telephone permits me to debate freely with my comrades in Patagonia or Australia, and the aeroscaph gives me the facility of visiting them in a matter of hours. Presently, the solitary individual lost in the steepest valley in the Alps or the Himalayas enjoys the same advantages, the same facilities of existence, and the same refinements of civilization as the opulent citizen of the richest capitals of old. Cities, in the sense that you understand them, have ceased to exist because they became unnecessary..."

While talking, Marcel and Blas arrived opposite a majestic row of porticos that gave access to the lecture rooms. They went silently into an amphitheater already full of attentive students, in which each one had a stall of white porcelain and a tablet furnished with a phonograph destined to replace the rudimentary notebooks of olden times.

The hall, with entirely bare walls, was only decorated with a few paintings on porcelain.

"This is where the courses in history are taught," said Blas, in a low voice. "You'll notice that the frescos that ornament this hall never represent individual actions. They are all consecrated to collective manifestations of human will. There, for example, is the combat of the Spartans in the pass of Thermopylae...Christians precipitating *en masse* to the tortures of the circus...the French nobility generously renouncing their feudal privileges on the celebrated night of the fourth of August...the Peace Congress of the year 2400 decreeing the definitive suppression of permanent armies."

To Marcel's great surprise, the course in history was silent. No voice of any professor could be heard. On the screen disposed at the back of the room, however, facing the hemicycle, cinematographic images were succeeding one another slowly, dressed with the appearances and colors of life.

Marcel thought that he was witnessing a veritable battle. In front of him, a circle of hills extended, occupied by the two belligerent armies. In the foreground, under the direction of engineers and officers, artillerymen were installing a battery.

226

The cannons and the ammunition trucks were arriving at top speed, arranging themselves in a line. In the meantime, soldiers, with pick-axes and spades in hand, were constructing earthworks in all haste, which they fortified with faggots of wood and felled trees.

Soon, the battery was in place, and commenced firing. A fine white mist rose over the battlefield, and companies and regiments were seen dissolving under the artillery fire. The fugitives gained the shelter of a wood or a village, and then re-formed slowly, Cavaliers, swords in hand, arrived in a whirlwind of dust and came to break themselves against the massive square of the infantry, presenting the sharp points of bayonets everywhere. Soldiers were seen slipping from their saddles, and horses collapsing, dying, under their riders. The dull rumble of canons dominated the incessant whistle of bullets.

The battery in the foreground was assailed by projectiles. Minute by minute, an artilleryman or an officer fell, the mud reddened by bloody foam. A shell hit one of the ammunition trucks, which exploded; the majority of its servants were killed; of eight artillery pieces only two continued firing, at long intervals. The strident voices of clarions were heard. A company tried to storm the position with bayonets.

The last artillerymen were devastated by repetitive fire, and infantrymen with ferocious eyes, uttering howls of victory, took up positions in the ruins of the battery, amid the groups of powder-blackened and bloodstained cadavers...

Marcel followed the spectacle, his throat taut with emotion. "It's frightful," he murmured, in a low voice.

"That, however," Blas replied, "is how people made war in your epoch. Arbitration ended up replacing wars until, by the force of events, it became unnecessary itself..."

Meanwhile, the picture had changed.

Scrupulous statistics now offered a synoptic list, in capital letters, of the number of wounded and dead in the battle that they had just witnessed. Then, by way of conclusion, the voice of a phonograph explained the real causes of the war, and enunciated and commented on the text of commercial treaties imposed by the victorious nation on the defeated nation. But Marcel was no longer paying attention to the figures; he had been too profoundly moved by the spectacle of the battle. The cries and gasps of the wounded were still ringing in his ears.

"Let's go out, I beg you," he said to Blas. "I can see that you understand the study of history in a far superior fashion."

"Let's go to the literature course, then," Blas proposed. "The cadence of beautiful verses and the harmony of noble thoughts will exercise a benevolent influence on you. That will make you feel better."

Marcel took great pleasure in the literature course. During the short time that he stayed there, he noticed that the pupils of the year 3000 were not content to study masterpieces in Greek, Latin and French, but that they also paid considerable attention to the philosophy and poetry of the Hindus, the Chinese, the Assyrians, the Egyptians and the Incas. He heard a fragment of one of the heroic epics of Valmiki and a harmonious song by Li Tai-Po.

From the course in literature they passed on to that in mathematics, and then to philosophy. In the former Marcel admired the astonishing calculating machines that, while sparing the minds of the pupils any unnecessary complication, permitted them to make rapid progress and to deploy their ingenuity without fatigue. In the latter he saw a "machine for logical thinking" much more perfect than those at the disposal of the pupils in the study halls.

"The simplicity of the manipulation of this kind of apparatus," said Blas, "will astonish you, but at present, the explanation might perhaps be a little too arduous for you. We'll pass on to the course in geography, which might interest you more."

The geography hall had almost the same disposition as that of history. The professor's lectern was replaced by a screen facing a hemicycle, on the steps of which the students were seated.

"At the moment," Blas murmured, "They're following a course in historic geography, Look..."

Marcel perceived in front of him the somber vaults of a tropical forest where negroes and wild animals were wandering. Gradually, the forest brightened. Vast clearances allowed the perception of flourishing plantations of rice, tea, cacao and rubber. The plantations gave way themselves to a city of whitewashed houses, where two railways came to terminate. The negroes were replaced by soldiers and colonists in pith helmets and twill garments.

Until then, Marcel had not felt out of his depth; he had understood that he was watching the evolution of a colony; he had seen the "before, during and after." But the picture did not take long to become unfamiliar to him.

The air filled up with aeroscaphs and balloons. Locomotives without wheels, gliding along a single rail, replaced those he knew, and gradually, the city itself disappeared, giving way to a landscape of efflorescences, beautiful trees and porcelain edifices very similar to those he had seen since his arrival in the world of the thirtieth century.

In the meantime, the sonorous voice of the phonograph explained succinctly the geological riches of the soil in that part of the world, its vegetal productions, and the various human races that had succeeded one another there.

"You see," said Blas, "that we have been able to render geography as interesting as all the rest. It's no longer, as in your time, an indigestible mass of incomprehensible words, proper names and dates. The pupil who had once studied a region by our cinematographic method never forgets what he has learned."

"I can see," Marcel said, "that the cinematograph plays a large role in that kind of study."

"We don't only make use of cinematography for historical geography. We also employ the telephoto, which is for vision what the telephone is for hearing. Thus, look, I can read on the schedule attached beside the screen that the pupils are shortly going to study the city of Artika. You'll see it as clearly, and in more detail, without moving from the spot, than during the very brief excursion we made there yesterday."

A few moments later, in fact, Marcel saw emerging, as if from a fog, the metallic spires and domes of the somber polar city.

He left the geography course absolutely wonderstruck.

"I'm showing you all this," said Blas, "somewhat at the gallop. It's necessary, to begin with, that you have a general idea of our system of education, in order to delve more deeply afterwards. Here's the amphitheater of anatomy and physiology..."

"You still devote yourselves to dissection?"

"Not at all. The repulsive need for dissection was abandoned a long time ago. Thanks to the ancient Roentgen rays, we know the organs of the human body far better than our predecessors, without being obliged to undertake the macabre labor of the ancient physiologists. Look, in any case. You'll be able to study the skeleton of one of our comrades."

Marcel raised his eyes. An obliging student had placed himself in front of a Roentgen ray apparatus, and his skeleton, considerably enlarged, was projected on a dark plate. Marcel noticed that not only was the bone structure designed with all its reliefs, but also with its veritable colors. The bones appeared pink under the blue-tinted periosteum, with the nacreous ligaments of the articulations.

"I see," he said to Blas, "that you've improved the Roentgen rays considerably. In my time they only gave the relief, sometimes only the silhouette, and that was still found utterly astonishing."

"What do you expect," replied Blas. "You understand that in a thousand years, progress has marched on. Thanks to the apparatus you see, not only is dissection no longer in usage, but physicians have no more need to feel the pulse of patients, ask them to stick out their tongue and question them about their appetite. They content themselves with examining each of the organs attentively; then they write their prescriptions in the full knowledge of the cause and without fear of error. I'll also mention that maladies have become extremely rare in the human race, and that the number of physicians is diminishing every year. Everyone looks after himself. One could count the specialists who still devote themselves to medicine. Hygiene has killed malady, and medicine itself."

From physiology, Marcel and Blas passed on to chemistry.

Marcel was astonished. "But I don't see any retorts, round flasks, Bunsen burners, test tubes, or any of the objects that were seen in laboratories in my time..."

Blas could not repress a smile. "Excuse me," he said, "and pardon my stupidity. I forgot that in your epoch, people still admitted a hundred simple substances."

"And now?"

"We've reduced them to one alone, and we transform one substance into another without the slightest difficulty."

"What! You've actually realized the dream of the alchemists?"

"You could have perceived that already. I've already told you, I think, that we employ gold and precious stones for the most common usages, and only value them for their splendor and their inalterability. Matter, multiple in its transformations, is one in its essence."

Before the eyes of the fearful Marcel, a block of iron, submitted in certain conditions to the influence of an electric current, became, successively, a block of copper, a block of gold, a lump of carbon, and finally a bubble of hydrogen, which the demonstrator allowed to evaporate.

Marcel left the course in unitary chemistry to go to the hall of interplanetary communications, which Blas had saved, as they say for a final treat. That hall was situated at the top of a tower and equipped with telephotic and telephonic mirrors of infinite power.

"What news is there?" he asked a student who was coming out of the hall. "Is the communication from Mars legible this morning?"

"Quite legible. The inhabitants of Mars are now responding to fourteen of our luminous signals. Within a month, perhaps we'll be in possession of a common alphabet."

"You can see from here," Blas said to Marcel, "the results of that interplanetary understanding. The inhabitants of the two worlds will exchange their inventions, their masterpieces, their progress of every kind. Our power and our well-being might be multiplied tenfold..."

"There's already question," added the student that Blas had questioned, "of setting up a committee of Interastral Relations."

"That's marvelous!" Marcel exclaimed. "And how have you arrived at establishing communications with the planet Mars?"

"Thanks to geometry," replied Blas. "In one of the vastest plains in the world, in Siberia, we built luminous walls more than a hundred leagues long, presenting in relief the essential figures of geometry. Years of waiting went by. Finally, the Martians responded with similar signals, and after long groping on either side, we've finally arrived at admitting a common alphabet. That was the most difficult part. Now, the inhabitants of the two worlds will be able to march in the same path of fraternal progress."

XII. In the Family

After the midday meal, which was rapidly expedited, Blas took Marcel to the infant classes, which the latter had expressed a desire to see.

In the different rooms they traversed, the strictest precepts of hygiene were applied. The children, installed on sandstone chairs, were maintained with a cleanliness and care that excluded any deleterious miasma, any negligence and any disorder, so they were fresh and rosy.

Marcel was both delighted and surprised not to observe among them any of the rickety bodies or pale and chlorotic faces with dead eyes and weary already-geriatric gestures that populated the elementary schools of Paris in his own day. All the children he saw had clear complexions, lively eyes and plump hands. The smiles of contentment that illuminated their faces showed that, in making them study, a means had been found of avoiding any constraint of difficulty on their part.

That happy and smiling infancy was truly a joy to behold.

"What do you do, then," Marcel asked, "to have little schoolchildren as docile and as happy at the same time? In order to obtain that result you must employ complicated and expert methods?"

"Our method is perhaps expert, but not complicated. The pedagogues of the year 3000 never make use of force, or even constraint, with the youngest children. They content themselves with observing the pupils entrusted to them carefully. A child always has a liking or an aptitude for something; it's those tastes and aptitudes that they try to discover. That's the whole problem. If a child likes drawing, he's enabled to draw; if he has a good memory and likes learning by heart, he's provided with moral maxims, interesting stories and harmonious verses. If, on the other hand, he gives evidence of reflection and logical thinking, his young imagination is steered toward mathematics or philosophy."

"Pardon me," said Marcel, "but with that system you must form little specialists whose knowledge will necessarily remain incomplete."

"That's a great error," Blas replied. "Human intelligence forms as a whole. From the moment that one has a liking for one of its manifestations, one arrives, by the force of circumstance, in interesting oneself in the universality of the others. Thus, the child who begins by drawing doesn't take long to perceive that, in order to draw correctly, it's necessary to know anatomy, perspective and mathematics. When he's in possession of that knowledge, he notices many other lacunae. He perceives that he knows almost nothing, and his ardor for work is augmented. And he arrives inevitably at studying philosophy and history, which furnish him with subjects and general ideas, so that, gradually, whatever the art or science was with which he began, he eventually climbs the entire ladder of human knowledge.

"I'll add that studies thus organized are far better than those accomplished by force. The pupil, only ever having worked on what interests him, never forgets anything. One avoids, as far as possible, fatiguing his memory, leaving the field free for his reason, his imagination, his logic and his initiative. It's sufficient for a study not to please the child for it to be abandoned immediately. So, thanks to that method, the ignorant no longer exist among us, while good pupils—those who were called swots in your day—are numerous."

"There must be a good deal of indiscipline, disorder and idleness in your schools."

"That's an error. Children never disobey, precisely because no one ever seeks to impose any constraint on them. We always make appeal to their reasoning and their curiosity. No one ever seeks to intimidate them. A child is the most logical being there is. Far more than an adult, he is avid for explanations and knowledge. It's sufficient to speak to him gently, to provoke his questions and to put the answers within the range of his young intelligence. Thus, the pupils in our schools, from the most tender age, give proof of an exemplary attention and docility. They wait for recreation time without impatience, and one has to use subterfuges to make them accept the days of leave necessary to their health, so much attraction do they feel to study.

"In sum," Blas concluded, "pedagogues, nowadays, are little more than attentive psychologists. They cultivate in perfection the art of interesting themselves in young intelligences, and that's the sole reason for their success."

"I admire that system of education greatly," said Marcel. "But permit me to raise an objection. It must happen frequently that you run into ingrate natures, encounter primitive intelligences that aren't interested in anything at all."

"That does sometimes happen, but the result is not what you might imagine. It merely requires a little more trouble and a little more attention, that's all. No child exists who isn't interested in anything. As he's never constrained, he lets his veritable penchants show right away. We favor them, and it's through that breach, however narrow it might be, made in his ignorance, that the army of other knowledge doesn't take long to penetrate. Thus, we've had backward children—this is the case that presents itself most frequently—who initially show a taste for gymnastics and violent exercises, fond of wrestling, for example, or excursions by aerocycle and aeroscaph."

"And what happens then?"

"It's by dint of conducting aeroscaphs and aerocycles that they become passionate about mechanics. Every sportsman likes to know the organs of the apparatus of which he makes use. In order to understand mechanics it's indispensable to know physics and chemistry. You can see the logical sequence. Our initial idlers become, in the end, as knowledgeable as their comrades."

"Permit me to ask one question," said Marcel, "a very important question. What, in your era, is the role of the family in the education of a child?"

After a moment of reflection, Blas replied: "Affection between parents and children is profound. Children never cease, in our society, to cherish and respect their parents. They consult them about everything, and never have the slightest disagreement with them. But in other respects, the role of the family is not at all what it once was. In barbaric epochs, parents kept close watch on their children, not losing sight of them for a minute, with the objective of protecting them against the dangers they might run outside. Today, there is no longer any reason for such a close surveillance. As much from the moral as the material viewpoint, the child enjoys an absolute security. Outside, he isn't exposed to any danger or any bad example. He only sees around him spectacles of beauty and goodness. From the most tender age, he is habituated to loving all those who surround him, and not being afraid of anyone or anything. The people of the thirtieth century respect

235

all old people as if they were their parents, and cherish all children as if they were their own."

"When I was younger," Marcel murmured, "I wasn't permitted to cross the street, because of the vehicles or the crowd. I can see that all that has changed."

"I think," said Blas, "that you understand sufficiently now the fashion in which our elementary schools function. If you wish, we can employ the rest of the afternoon visiting my parents. I haven't seen them for three days. I never let such a long time pass without going to embrace them. The delay is partly your fault. I'll introduce you and you can take charge of excusing me."

"Do your parents live far away?"

"No, they live on the shore of the ocean, a quarter of an hour away by aeroscaph. The place where they reside is part of the ancient French département of Landes. My father is an architect. He's the author of several ameliorations in the internal design and external decoration of edifices, which were universally adopted a few years ago."

Marcel was eager to meet Blas' parents. The two friends ran to the aerial station and leapt into a aeroscaph.

This time, they went at a lower speed than during their journey to Artika, but Marcel still judged it vertiginous.

A few minutes later, they were within sight of the sea. A vast forest of pines, pomegranates and palm trees, dotted with white towers of sandstone and porcelain, extended beneath them when Blas exclaimed, joyfully: "Halt! We've arrived!"

They both disembarked on to the terrace of the house in which Blas' father lived. The elevator deposited them at the door of a drawing room ornamented with large vases of flowers and white statues. Blas' mother and sister did not take long to appear. Both were very beautiful, and Blas' mother appeared so young that she might have been mistaken for her daughter's older sister.

Like Madame Futural, the two women wore no jewelry or feathery hats. They were simply dressed in glass fiber tunics with broad pleats, of an admirable richness and good taste.

They gave the young refugee from times past a very cordial welcome. They even went to fetch cups and urns of red jasper, which they placed on a chrysoprase side-table, and invited Marcel to refresh himself. He excused himself; he was neither hungry nor thirsty, having eaten copiously in company with his comrade in the school refectory.

Blas' sister was named Hyla. She was presently finishing her studies, after which she had decided to take up a position as a teacher of elementary classes. She adored children, and, while awaiting the moment of her marriage, would be glad to spend a few years in their company.

Like all young women, Hyla was very curious. She bombarded Marcel with questions. After a few minutes of conversation, he did not take long to perceive, to his great confusion, that the young woman was much more learned than he was. Without any pedantry, she discussed, playfully, a host of questions that had been the exclusive province of the most rebarbative scholars in his day.

"You're not unknown to me," she said. "We've already been informed of all the details of your arrival, and up to date with the excursions you've made in our world."

"Really?" said Marcel, nonplussed.

"Do you want proof?" said Hyla smiling. And she pressed the button of a phonograph.

"You'll see," she said, "that your arrival has been reported in our newspapers."

The apparatus began, in a monotonous and, so to speak, impersonal voice: "By virtue of a combination of circumstances that our scientists are in the process of studying, and which the will clarify in a few days, an inhabitant of the distant and still-barbaric epoch of the twentieth century has made an appearance among us.

"He is young and appears to be mild in character. He only possesses the singularly limited education that was provided in his time, but he seems avid to learn...."

The rest of the article contained the most scrupulous details of Marcel's person and the actions. Another article took account of the most plausible hypotheses that scholars had advanced in his regard. Without committing any indiscretion, the author of the second article studied the tastes, aptitudes and faculties of the young stranger in depth.

Marcel had never been passed through such a clear and exact analytical sieve.

"There are still journalists among you, then?" he asked.

"With an astonishment full of politeness, Hyla replied: "But everyone is a journalist nowadays. It's sufficient for that to have something interesting to say. The scholar who has made an interesting discovery, the poet who has completed a fine work, and anyone who had witnessed an interesting event, hastens to telephone their discovery, work of art or item of information to one of the regional receivers, who transmits it to the rest of the world."

"In that case," said Marcel, "you must be exposed to hearing many items of padding, many poor works, many idle and futile reports and many challenged discoveries."

"Why?" said Hyla, whose beautiful eyes expressed a naïve astonishment. "When one has nothing of interest to say, one says nothing. In our day, journalism is not a salaried profession, and no one has any interest in spoiling phonographic plates needlessly."

"Once," said Marcel, in a low voice "there were many people who wrote in order to say nothing, and who were well paid for it."

Hyla emitted a frank burst of laughter. "I've read that," she said, "but I thought it was greatly exaggerated. I'm glad that you've confirmed the item of information."

The conversation was at that point when Blas' father came into the drawing room. He was a man in the prime of life. From the outset of the conversation he gave evidence of a perfect affability and courtesy toward his guest.

"Your intelligence and your polite manner," he said to Marcel, "make me doubt that we have made much progress in a thousand years. I see that after ten centuries of endeavor and ordeals, humankind is not as greatly improved as we had the conceit to believe."

"You'll permit me to doubt that," replied Marcel, politely.

"You know, Father," said Blas, "that a maxim already current in the twentieth century says that a host is responsible for the wellbeing of his guest during the time that the latter spends under his roof. What distractions can we offer our friend?"

"I confess to you," Marcel said, "That I'd take great pleasure in visiting your habitation in all its details; and if it isn't indiscreet, I'd like to take account of the arrangement of your domestic life."

"You're not committing any indiscretion," replied Blas' father. "We live in broad daylight. Only vanity, vice and ambition have any need to dissimulate. Since those faults no longer have any reason to exist, the house of any citizen is wide open to all the others."

"First of all," Blas commenced. "You must have noticed that in our society we don't have any species of domestic staff. Electricity has become, for us, the most obedient, the most exact and the least onerous of servants. It's sufficient for us to unleash the current of an electric oscillator to clean our apartments, our beds and the few utensils of which we make use in the most antiseptic fashion."

"But what about the cooking?"

"Backward human being!" said Blas, smiling. "You must have perceived, however, that humankind is presently content with a single aliment, whose chemical preparation is very simple. Cooks, scullions, roasters of meat and makers of sauces, wine-waiters and arbiters of taste of every sort have become legendary beings, who are only seen in the theater. In all the world there is only one cook, an inoffensive maniac who, once or twice a year invites a few of his archeologist colleagues to historical repast prepared with great difficulty, thanks to hothouses and zoological gardens."

Marcel, in confusion, dared not ask any more questions.

Accompanied by Blas and his father, he visited all the rooms in the habitation one by one. It stood in the center of a large park, whose last trees bathed their roots in the sea. They began with the park and its hothouses. Then they visited the basements, which contained, along with the electric accumulators, the machines that powered the elevator and the wireless telegraph and telephone, as well as the oscillators.

The bedrooms, although more luxurious, were very similar to the one in which Marcel had slept during the previous two nights. There were the same ceramic walls, the same glass dome and the same bed in the form of a conch.

There were several drawing rooms, heated or cooled at will by calorific plates, and decorated with statues and clumps of plants.

Marcel did not see any paintings, books or trinkets. He made that observation.

"The objects of which you speak," Blas replied, "are only found in our museums. We've suppressed everything futile, cumbersome or ugly, as much for reasons of hygiene as esthetics. We detest complications, and we have a horror of microbes."

Afterwards, Marcel went into the library, where phonograph cylinders were accumulated by in thousands. Then he was taken to the museum—for every house had one of its own in the thirtieth century.

There, he saw with pleasure volumes carefully arranged, statuettes and utensils of all kinds, not to mention numerous photographic and cinematographic albums.

"You've seen everything," said Blas, finally. "It only remains for us to visit the terrace where we disembarked. There's a splendid view over the sea from there."

"I've had an excellent idea," said Hyla to her brother. "In the twentieth century, little was known about the oceanic depths. I'm sure that your friend would be delighted to make a submarine excursion."

Marcel welcomed that proposition enthusiastically; and they immediately set about making preparations for the projected excursion.

XIII. Gardens Under the Sea

After having traversed the park, the entire family headed for the shore. The blue waves of the ocean came to caress the roots of pine trees and eucalypti weakly. From time to time, flowers were detached from the tall trees and fell gently into the water.

Following his friends, Marcel penetrated into a small building located at the extremity of a kind of peninsula that was almost entirely covered by vegetation.

"You see here," said Blas' father, the graving-dock where we keep the submarine that we employ in our excursions.

Marcel looked. A long crystal spindle was extended on ebonite rollers. Through the transparent walls the propulsive engines were visible, disposed at the rear and made of a metal as pale as silver.

Blas' father opened a hatch circled by the same pale metal, the closure of which could be rendered hermetic by a rubber ring.

Everyone sat down on banquettes disposed in the interior. Blas bolted the door and secured the rubber strip while his father set in motion an apparatus for the continuous production of respirable air. The submarine, sliding along its rollers, soon plunged gently into the sea. The propeller began to spin, and they did not take long to draw away from the shore.

Thanks to the transparency of the walls Marcel admired the submarine landscapes that filed before him.

Inside the submersible there was a delightful sensation of freshness and silence.

"This," said the architect, "is my preferred work space. When I have some serious task to execute, or when I want to reflect without being disturbed, I retire within these crystal walls. I've spent the finest afternoons of labor here, in the cool and the silence of the submarine depths."

To Marcel's great surprise, the bed of the sea did not resemble any image that had been made of it in olden days. He saw before him clumps of white and pink coral, beds of large blue and green flowers, arbors of lianas, and giant seaweeds spreading out thousands of lacy and vibrant sheets; but the idea of disorder seemed to have been banished from the entire region, The clumps of coral and the forests of algae were interrupted by avenues and clearings carpeted with fine sand.

"Oh!" exclaimed Marcel. "I didn't think submarine nature was so rich, fecund and harmonious One might think that the perspectives we're traversing had been disposed by gardeners of genius, but their beauty owes nothing to human labor, does it?"

"You're mistaken," Blas replied. "This superb flora is due to skillful horticulturalists. In a little while you'll see the golden helmets of their diving suits shining. This requires a few explanations, however. The great depths of the ocean were an inaccessible domain, closed to human kind for a long time, until the invention of submarines, and progress in chemistry, which finally permitted the manufacture of respirable air at will, gave us the means of exploring those mysterious depths."

"In the twentieth century," Marcel put in, "people were already beginning to construct diving suits and submersible vessels."

"Yes," Blas replied, "but in your epoch, the submarines only descended to feeble depths and were only used to place torpedoes loaded with explosives beneath enemy ships. In the following centuries, however, it was understood that better use could be made of them. Societies were formed for the exploitation of the riches of the ocean. The carcasses of sunken ships were fished up, mines were exploited, and the inexhaustible forests of algae and lichens were utilized as fodder. Chemical factories manufactured, on a large scale, iodine, chlorine and all the other substances that the waters and the sea-bed contain. The wellbeing of humankind was considerably increased thereby. Pisciculture, aided by scientific methods, took on an enormous extent. Dearth and famine were banished from the world forever. Science also obtained great profit from those explorations. Natural history and geology were completed. It was possible to explain the evolution of our planet with the aid of broader and more accurate theories."

"And now?" asked Marcel.

"Nowadays, the relatively recent discovery—since it only goes back a hundred and fifty years—of a substance unique in chemistry, has simplified the production of wealth further. The exploitation of submarine mines and fields of algae has been abandoned as too tiresome and too complicated. Except for the neighborhood of the coasts, the ocean depths have returned to their solitude. For humans they're no longer anything but a vast promenade, a goal of excursions and a subject of study."

"Those promenades can't be free of danger," Marcel objected. "How, for instance, do you defend yourselves against sharks, giant cephalopods, narwhals, and whales, not to mention poisonous or electric fish such as electric eels and Moray eels."

"For a long time," replied Blas' father, "those species have only existed as museum exhibits. All harmful animals have disappeared from the ocean, as they have been exterminated on the land surface."

"However, Father," Blas corrected, "one can't say that those dangers have entirely disappeared. Last year, a crab of such enormous dimensions and strength that one of its claws could crush a man's thigh was discovered in a cavern in the Indian Ocean, An encounter with such an animal would certainly be dangerous." Addressing Marcel, he added: "But I hasten to assure you that that's very exceptional." Then, pointing at a wooden cane terminated by a metal tip suspended in a corner of the vessel, he said: "In addition, we have the electric lance. If we have a whim to put on a diving suit and take a walk in the shade of these fine arbors of algae with crimson

243

and gold foliage, we'll take that lance with us. Whatever the size of any animal that decided to attack us, it would be sufficient to touch it with the tip for it to be killed by the electric current."

"That reassures me," Marcel replied, smiling. "However, I confess that I regret the sharks slightly, and all the monsters that served in my day as a pretext for such dramatic stories."

Meanwhile, the submarine had surpassed the zone of the cultivated depths. Now the landscape was harsher and wilder. The forests of algae became inextricable. Shoals of fish. the color of nacre, frightened by the passage of the vessel, rose up from blonde meadows of wrack, like flocks of skylarks rising from a field of wheat at the approach of a hunter.

Blas, who was holding the wheel of the tiller, had slowed their speed. The crystal hull passed slowly underneath vaults of lianas florid with brilliant corollas, which resembled human eyes opening among green tresses. Jellyfish swung their bells, ornamented with all the colors of the prism. Marcel saw large turtles lying idly on the sand.

They continued to advance. The landscape was abruptly modified. They passed over a bare plain strewn with ruddy blocks, alternating with black needles of basalt. In the center was the debris of a vaulted construction, the round domes of which, almost at ground level, were reminiscent of bunkers.

"What are those ruins?" Marcel asked.

"Similar ones are encountered quite frequently in the submarine solitudes," Blas replied. "That's all that remains of the mining exploitations of the societies of old. Those barracks served to lodge the personnel. Abandoned now, they've become a favorite abode of fish and crustaceans.

They had soon surpassed the ruins. Again they were moving under the bleak vaults of the submarine forest.

"I believe," said Blas, "that we'd do well to accelerate our speed somewhat. The lianas and weed are much less dense hereabouts. We can go forward without any risk." While speaking, he had given the wheel a turn.

The submarine moved on with such rapidity that the landscapes seemed to be fleeing abruptly to the right and left. Marcel hardly had time to glimpse them before they were replaced.

Suddenly, the passengers felt a slight shock.

"Clumsy fellow!" cried Blas' father. "The crystal keel touched the bottom!"

He had scarcely finished speaking when there was a muffled detonation.

Some distance behind the submarine, a flash of white light had sprung forth, and the vessel spun, caught by a terrible eddy. Under the impulsion of a formidable shock, the submarine had capsized. The passengers had tumbled, bumping into one another, uttering cries of fright.

Blas had released the wheel and fallen backwards. He and his father were the first to recover their composure. Although bruised, they succeeded in getting to the helm. By leaning on the direction levers with all their force, they were able to restore the submarine's equilibrium.

They examined the engines, which had not suffered any damage.

"It's fortunate," the architect declared, gravely, "that that accident, whose cause I can't explain as yet, didn't occur in the vicinity of a rock. The pressure produced by the explosion was so violent that our crystal hull would have been shattered into a thousand fragments."

Hyla and her mother only had slight bruises. They were quickly reassured. As for Marcel, he had gone as pale as a corpse. His fear had been so great that he remained in his corner, incapable of saying a word.

Blas approached him and tried to comfort him. "It's nothing," he said. "The danger's over now. We'll return to the house at low speed, taking all sorts of precautions." He added, sharply: "But you're wounded! You're bleeding!"

He had taken Marcel's hand, which did indeed have a slight scratch, which the young man had sustained in falling against the latch of the metal door.

"Don't worry," he replied to his friend, with an effort. "It's not serious. I was more frightened than hurt. But please, tell me how that terrible explosion was produced, which nearly cost us our lives."

"I confess that I have no idea."

The father reflected. "I believe," he said, after a few moments of silence, "that there's only one plausible means of explaining that accident. You know that one of the most frequently employed engines of war in olden days were torpedoes. Some were constructed that were so advanced that, in order to activate their detonator, it only required a slight impact, a mere brush, sometimes even a ray of light. I believed that we just touched one such engine with our keel, abandoned centuries ago."

"How is it," Blas asked, "that after so much time, the powders and fulminates have been able to conserve their explosive power?"

"That's not surprising. Sheltered from contact with the air, powders aren't modified significantly. And the sea, by depositing around the torpedo a thick layer of calcareous incrustations, must have contributed to their conservation."

"We were lucky not to have been annihilated."

"That has two causes," the architect replied. "Firstly, the extreme speed with which we were traveling. In the short interval before the detonation was produced, we had already had time to gain a little ground. If we'd been traveling more slowly, our doom would have been certain."

"And the second reason?"

"Well, I believe—but I'm giving you this explanation for what it might be worth—that the thick layer of petrifaction that covered the detonator must have delayed its effect, perhaps by a few tenths of a second. That small space of time undoubtedly permitted us to get out of the danger zone."

During this conversation the submarine, this time steered by Blas' father, was moving cautiously between the cliffs of a kind of ravine covered with quivering foliage, between which myriads of fish were playing.

Ten minutes later they were back on the edge of the magnificent submarine arbors that Marcel had admired at the beginning of the voyage. He felt completely reassured.

"Now," said Blas, "all peril has disappeared. In any case, if we've sustained any damage, the horticulturalist divers who are numerous in this region will come to our aid."

"To what class of society do those divers belong?" Marcel asked. "Are they outcasts as in the city of Artika?"

"No, they're men like any others, whom their work or their personal tastes bring to submarine culture."

A few moments later, the submersible arrived opposite its graving-dock.

After disembarking, the travelers headed for the house. In spite of the marvelous spectacles that he had contemplated in the course of his excursion, it was not without a veritable sentiment of pleasure that Marcel found himself back on solid ground.

The wound on his hand was no longer bleeding, but it was causing him some pain. Hyla and Blas poured a few drops of a strongly-perfumed balm on the cut, applied a drop of collodion, and told the young man that in a matter of hours it would no longer be visible.

The submarine excursion had awakened a host of ideas in Marcel's mind. He could not get used to the thought that blue whales, sperm whales, sharks and even sea-lions had disappeared. He could not help questioning Blas, whose complaisance in answering him remained indefatigable.

"Why, then," he asked him, "haven't I perceived any animals during the journeys we've made together on land?"

"For the excellent reason," said Blas, "that except for those we conserve in our zoological gardens, the majority of the wild and domestic animals of your era have disappeared."

"Really?" exclaimed Marcel. "I would never have believed that!"

Blas went on: "The disappearance of living species took place in a gradual and, so to speak, methodical fashion. After the extinction of prehistoric races annihilated by geological

upheavals and abrupt shifts in temperature, the carnivores became extinct in their turn, incessantly hunted by humans and
driven from solitude to solitude by the ever-increasing expansion of cultivated and inhabited land. Already, in your epoch,
there were no more wolves in the Auvergne, and the Emperor
of Russia was the only person still to possess aurochs, in a
park surrounded by a solid wall. As the intertropical forests
were felled, lions, tigers and snakes became rarer."

"In fact, in the twentieth century, the English and French
governments were already paying bounties for the destruction
of wild beasts and poisonous reptiles. Attempts were even
made to transplant mongooses, diehard enemies of snakes,
into many colonies. I can understand the destruction of harmful animals easily enough, but what became of the others?"

"Domestic animals were only tolerated because of the
services they rendered to humans. The extension of railways
and the progress of automobilism, and then aerial and submarine navigation, suppressed all beasts of traction, from the
elephant to the donkey. Horses became so rare that they were
only seen in museums. The animals that were only reared because their flesh was edible, such as pigs, cattle and sheep,
were dethroned in their turn by the chemical fabrication of
nutritive substances. Game disappeared when humans renounced the barbaric pleasure of hunting, and no one any
longer took the trouble to preserve it at great expense."

"What about the birds? And the insects?" asked Marcel,
with a hint of sadness. "Did they also disappear before the
omnipotence of your civilization?"

"Yes, the birds were gradually destroyed. The powerful
electric currents that we employ for long distance communication by wireless telephony or telegraphy were mortal to them.
Those that didn't break their skulls against the glass of our
electric globes, the blinding light of which hypnotized them,
were killed or paralyzed by the currents. Like all the other
animals they were relegated to scientific collections. As for
insects, parasites or vehicles of microbes, we ended up getting
rid of those too. Electric plowing, by destroying their larvae

and eggs, once made a considerable contribution to that; powerful insecticides did the rest. Flies, mosquitoes, woodlice and fleas are only a memory.

"I know full well," Blas continued, "that the world must seem to you to be a trifle depoeticized, thus deprived of creatures like the dog and the horse, which had animated it at the beginning of its evolution, but when you've been living among us a little longer, you'll see that in our society, poetry still subsists. It's different; it has been subject to the law of progress, but it remains. Our birds are our aeroscaphs!"

However, it was getting late. After taking his leave of Blas' family, Marcel climbed back into the aeroscaph in the company of his friend, and they set a course for the distant towers of the school, to the enclosure of which they had to return before nine o'clock.

XIV. The Palace of Art and History

Marcel now knew the majority of the usages and customs of the society of the year 3000. Nothing astonished him any longer. He no longer experienced the wonder and the amazement of the first day.

As the species of vertigo that the novelty of objects and the bizarrerie of his situation had produced in him dissipated, however, and he put more order into his ideas, the memory of the old world haunted him. The image of his saddened parents cast a kind of melancholy veil between his gaze and the marvels that surrounded him.

The world of the thirtieth century was splendid, admirable, almost perfect; but when Marcel looked into himself he could not help admitting that he would gladly separate himself from all that magnificence in order to rejoin Monsieur and Madame Vernoy, to see them again and embrace them.

What caused him the most chagrin was not so much being separated from his parents as thinking that they were doubtless mourning his death, or at least his disappearance.

I've never been anything for them, he reflected, *but a cause of cares and anxieties. I haven't procured them the satisfactions that they had a right to expect of me...*

And Marcel reproached himself bitterly for his bad conduct, his sullenness and his idleness. Oh, if it had only been possible for him, at that moment, to retrace the course of the centuries, to rediscover the smoke-blackened landscapes, and the men bizarrely clad in dark suits and cardboard hats, of the old Paris of his childhood, how he would have worked, how happy he would have been, and what satisfaction he would have given to his dear parents!

Fundamentally, his new friends, Blas, Serge and Lucius, were so perfect, so impeccable in their thoughts and their conduct, that Marcel, involuntarily, experienced far more admiration for them than real camaraderie.

Since getting up, Marcel had been rolling those ideas around his head, and in spite of the desire he had to show a good face to Blas, who had come to wake him up, he felt his heart gripped by an implacable sadness.

Entirely given over to his thoughts, he listened distractedly to the explanations that his friend furnished of the manufacture of glass and porcelain in electric furnaces.

Blas eventually noticed that Marcel was not involved in the conversation.

"You're distracted, it seems to me," he said. "You appear quite melancholy. Perhaps you regret the cherished individuals you left in the past. It is, I fear, materially impossible for me to procure you a means of rejoining them. Since you're among us, resign yourself to your fate, and make a virtue of the necessity."

Blas reflected momentarily, and then went on: "I anticipated that we would start serious work today, but, given the sadness that is overwhelming you, I believe that it's preferable, in the interests of your mental health, to grant ourselves—both of us—one more day of leave. I'll do everything possible to offer you interesting distractions. Perhaps you'll forget, in the end, the old world that holds you so forcefully by the heart."

Marcel affirmed that he was ready to set to work, and that another day of leave was unnecessary, but Blas replied: "Don't worry, we won't be wasting our time. It's a most instructive spectacle that I'm going to show you. It's indispensable that you have, at least in its broad outlines, and idea of the events that have taken place between the twentieth and thirtieth centuries. For that, we'll go together to the Palace of Art and History, the sumptuous crimson and gold edifice that you can see from here."

Marcel accepted Blas' proposal with enthusiasm, and the two friends went down to the subterranean station of the pneumatic line. They climbed into a carriage, and got down again at the Palace of Art and History, the vast buildings of which occupied the entire surface of the ancient hill of Ménilmontant.

Its architecture was exceptionally majestic. The arcades and cupolas, in a severe style, were a crimson porcelain on which massive golden ornaments stood out.

Marcel noticed that the exterior was not decorated by any statue, and that the very trees that surrounded the palace offered something grave and serious, in complete rapport with the majesty of history. Only laurels, oaks and palm trees grew around the palace. No flower cast a cheerful note into the severity of that somber verdure.

"You see," observed Blas, "that nothing has been neglected here to prepare the mind of a visitor for the meditations that the history of humankind ought to suggest to him."

Marcel and Blas went through a vestibule decorated with noble panoplies of weapons of all times and all nations.

The stone axes of prehistoric man lay next to the arrows and javelins of Oceanian savages, the gilded armor of knights and the rapid fire rifles of modern times. One panel was entirely devoted to artillery; it presented in all parts the meaning maws of machine-guns and automatic cannons, mingled with the bombards and culverins of the late Middle Ages.

Marcel perceived another host of engines that were unfamiliar to him, and which stood out by virtue of their extreme simplicity. They were aerial and submarine torpedoes, electric mortars, liquefied gas shells and other devices invented after the twentieth century.

All those panoplies decorated the pedestals of smiling goddesses crowned with olive branches.

"Here," said Blas, "there is not only the museum of history and war, but also the temple of peace and art."

Marcel and Blas went through a lateral portico and into a gallery of mediocre dimensions, on to which opened, to the right and the left, rooms that contained the marvels of the painting, sculpture and furniture of times past.

"You'll find there," said Blas, "the principal masterpieces of the ancient Louvre, the British Museum and the Uffizi Museum of Florence."

Marcel went into one of the rooms. He took pleasure in seeing, in rooms ornamented with furniture of the same era as the canvases, the taste and care with which the paintings had been disposed.

"In my time," he told Blas, "we had less respect for masterpieces. The paintings were piled up at random, tightly packed together, in galleries exposed to sunlight, which caused them to deteriorate. In that mass of canvases, it was impossible to find at first glance the one for which one was searching. A walk in a museum was a veritable torture for the eyes and the brain.

Marcel would have liked to pause again in the rooms of paintings, but Blas dragged him away.

"Many of these masterpieces," he said, "are from your century. Later, you can study them at your leisure. For the moment, we don't have time to waste, We're going to go at this pace to the great central hall of historic cinematography."

Marcel and Blas arrived in an immense circular gallery with a ceiling in a cupola, and a mosaic pavement. All around the hall, broad arcades opened. There were a dozen of them, which served as frames for unpolished glass screens.

"Each of these arcades," Blas explained, "represents for us an interval of a hundred years. Here, we're surrounded by all the centuries that have passed since the invention of cinematography, and we can evoke at will the events that have taken place in the last thousand years. It's sufficient to spend a few hours here to take account of the evolution of the human race during that long span of years. Unfortunately, I can only show you the events that have occurred over ten centuries. Before then, cinematography, and even photography, had not been invented, and all we possess of those abolished epochs are statues, drawings—which constitute meager documents— or the accounts of historians, inexact, partial and deceitful."

"In that case," exclaimed Marcel, enthusiastically, "I can contemplate with my own eyes all the memorable events that filled the ten centuries to have elapsed between my epoch and yours!"

"All those you wish. Here, stop facing the arcade of the twentieth century. I'll activate the mechanism of the cinematograph, and you'll see filing before your eyes all the scenes of that historical panorama."

Marcel had approached the indicated arcade.

"Would you like to see a battle?" Blas proposed.

"Thank you, but I was too disturbed by the one that I saw in the history course. If it's all the same to you, let's begin with something more peaceful."

"As you wish," replied Blas, starting the apparatus.

Immediately, the mat pallor of the screen brightened. A landscape suddenly appeared. The sky and the sea had their natural color, and an immense crowd was gesticulating enthusiastically.

In the foreground there was a seaport, from which departed the metallic arches of a gigantic steel bridge, boldly launched across the waves. The causeway was majestic in its width. Five rows of electric locomotives, decked with ribbons and flowers, were getting ready to depart.

Suddenly, the immense crowd massed on the shore uttered a formidable acclamation. Flags were hoisted. The smoke of artillery salvos rose up. At the same instant, the five locomotives moved off. The port and the crowd were seen to decrease in the distance. And there was no more, after that, than a scene of sky, sea and metal.

Soon, another city was designed at the opposite end of the bridge.

The arrival of the locomotives was greeted with the same enthusiasm by another crowd, massed like the first on the quays and jetties of a port.

"What am I seeing?" Marcel asked. "What is that bridge, the most immense that had ever been constructed, and between the arches of which steamships loaded with people are gliding like mere boats?"

"The bridge that you have just seen connected Dover and Calais, France and England. It's the Channel Bridge, which appeared to your contemporaries, for a long time, impossible to construct. The sea, since then, no longer separates the two peoples."

"An extraordinary spectacle!" murmured Marcel, who could not believe his eyes.

"Now," said Blas, "we're going to jump forward two hundred years. You're going to witness the great electric catastrophe to which the American city of Chicago fell victim in the year 2197. That city, completely industrial and commercial, had become the head of more than three hundred railway lines. It was entirely composed of buildings of between thirty and forty stories, all constructed of steel, aluminum and incombustible wood. Everything there was done by electricity, from the slaughter of livestock—for canned meats were the city's principal commerce—to the automatic distribution of letters and aliments. Unfortunately, the engineers of those days did not know yet how to manage appropriately the mysterious and terrible power known as electricity, and they abused it in all sorts of ways.

"The city of Chicago was furrowed by networks and bundles of cables of all dimensions, intersecting in all directions, under the ground as well as above the summits of the

254

buildings. The city was, so to speak, saturated by electric fluid. A great storm, which occurred in the month of July, led to the catastrophe, which had been foreseen by a number of scientists. The insulation separating the various wires from one another melted; the millions of currents that were circulating in all directions were combined, and became one single mighty current. A kind of electrical aurora borealis, which illuminated the region with its sinister light for hundreds of leagues around, enveloped the city. Under the action of that inconceivable current, stone was charred and reduced to dust; metals burned and melted.

"The inhabitants, almost all electrocuted before the commencement of the conflagration, perished instantaneously in hundreds of thousands. Only a small number of them, protected by the vicinity of the great Lake Michigan, were able to escape death miraculously. Of the splendid city, the pride of North America, which, by virtue of the number of its palaces, its theaters, its railways stations and its factories, was considered as the Queen of the New World, nothing remained but a vast circle, several leagues in extent, covered with ash and scoria, in which ingots of molten metal were mingled with vitrified sand and profoundly calcined earth..."

While Blas was speaking, Marcel, trembling with fear, had followed all the phases of the cataclysm. He had seen the white aureole of electric fluid envelop the city like a shroud; then he had seen the gigantic forty-story buildings annihilated like wisps of straw in a furnace, launching jets of colored flame.

The destructive power of the fluid having done its work it had slowly been reabsorbed in the sky, the earth and the water. The banks of Lake Michigan now appeared to Marcel's eyes, as bare beneath their mantle of ash, and as sinister and desolate, as the edges of the Dead Sea

After allowing his friend to recover slightly from his emotion, Blas continued, in a seemingly impassive tone.

"That lesson was not lost on humankind. The Chicago catastrophe had an immense repercussion all over the world.

For a long time, the dread of the electric fluid preoccupied everyone. Scientists set to work studying electricity with a new ardor. They discovered other laws, and they provided means of preventing the repetition of similar cataclysms. Now, we have almost entirely suppressed wires and conductors of all sorts; our transmitters and our receivers are stalled at such a height in the atmosphere or such a great depth underground, that the region in between, the inhabited terrestrial surface, is henceforth shielded from any catastrophe."

Marcel listened, marveling.

Blas, however, had activated the trigger mechanism again.

"In spite of your horror of blood and carnage," he said, "it's indispensable that you should again witness the spectacle of a war. Reassure yourself, however; it is the last that human-kind sustained. Europe, Africa and Asia, organized in a con-federation, fought America, allied with the Oceanian States. Never had such a massacre bloodied the world! But look, ra-ther...

On the screen facing him, Marcel saw horrible scenes appear.

He thought he was in the midst of a nightmare.

Flotillas of balloons and aeroscaphs were pouring tor-rents of shells over cities and over armies. Torpedoes charged with asphyxiating and poisonous gases were felling entire bat-talions. Giant machine-guns were launching cannonballs and shells instead of bullets, covering several square leagues of ground with projectiles, razing crops, destroying forests and cities.

Set ablaze by powerful ardent mirrors, exterminated by torpedoes, fleets at sea burned and disappeared. Elsewhere, Marcel saw colossal automobile steel towers advancing slowly on their squat wheels, sowing death in all directions

Those cinematographic views were assembled and grouped with so much artistry that they succeeded one another without any confusion.

After the aerial war and the terrestrial war, Marcel witnessed submarine battles. He saw regiments of men in diving suits armed with electric rifles and broad-bladed daggers rushing upon one another, lying in wait for one another in the corners of forests of algae, and killing one another ferociously, in the vast prairies of fucus and wrack. Submarines passed by like huge blue-tinted fish, seeking to transpierce one another with their spurs, spitting torpedoes in all directions, and exterminating defenseless battalions of divers with their pneumatic artillery.

Marcel felt cold sweat beading on his forehead. He was prey to an inexpressible horror.

The cinematograph now represented views of landscapes devastated by the war. There were plains devoid of trees, without a single blade of grass, where bands of men, mutilated and in rags, dragged themselves along painfully.

Blas, who had perceived Marcel's terror and consternation, flicked a switch on the apparatus.

"Enough horrors," he said. "Enough carnage. Now you're going to witness more consoling scenes."

Still under the influence of the anguish that was gripping him, Marcel gazed.

In a vast arena that descended from the summit of a mountain covered with olive trees and oleanders all the way to the sea, a multitude of men clad in white and crowned with flowers were gathered. There were representatives of all nations and all races.

Perhaps for the first time since the origin of the world, the Celts, the Anglo-Saxons, the Latins, the Negros, the Chinese and the Oceanians were fraternizing sincerely. The universal pact was solemnly pronounced by the delegates of all the peoples.

Marcel saw entire trains departing of cannons, swords and rifles, the metal of which was surrendered to industrialists, about to be transformed into agricultural implements, automobiles and tools of every sort.

There was a general celebration throughout the world. The weapons, of which the soldiers of all nations hastened to rid themselves, formed gigantic heaps in public squares. Everywhere, people rejoiced. Setting off marvelous firework displays. The tables of Pantagruelesque banquets were extended over several kilometers. Diplomats were embraced and congratulated by women and children. A surge of fraternity caused the hearts of all humankind to beat in unison.

Marcel thought he ought to ask Blas for some information about the political state of peoples in that epoch. He learned to his surprise that only two great republics existed in the world at that time: the United States of the Old Continent, which comprised Europe, Asia and Africa, with their fringes; and the United States of the New World, formed of Australia, North and South America and their fringes.

It was those two demimondial republics that, by means of the solemn peace pact, had just sworn an indissoluble alliance between them.

"My God," cried Marcel, "how glad I am to have witnessed the proclamation of peace between men! I didn't think that would ever happen..."

"You'll see now," Blas continued, "what immense progress the state of peace permitted to be realized. Here's one, among many others. But for that, let's skip a number of years. We're in the year 2450...."

On the screen, a maritime scene now appeared, shaded by beautiful trees and animated by a host of busy people. A large number of parallel jetties advanced from the shore far out to sea. At intervals, they were covered by constructions.

"What's that?" asked Marcel

"That's the system of 'wharfs' equipped with turbines by means if which people were able to utilize the force produced by the flux and reflux of the tide. Those turbines powered dynamoelectric machines that furnished the power necessary for lighting, heating, transport and machinery of every sort. It's since the installation of those wharfs that people began to abandon the exploitation of coal mines and oil wells, and that difficult and dangerous labor ceased to be carried out by humans..."

When Marcel had contemplated the Atlantic wharfs sufficiently, Blas showed him a bird's eyes view of one of the capitals of the year 2500, the city of Afrika on the shore of Lake Chad. Marcel saw before him an accumulation of palaces and gardens, ornamented with exotic trees, and he learned with surprise that the city of Afrika, founded only a few years before by a group of engineers and industrialists, was renowned for the number of its scientists and artists.

"In that epoch," Blas explained, "Africa was more knowledgeable, more civilized and better cultivated than the Europe of your epoch. One did not encounter desolate regions there like the steppes of Poland or Russia..."

"What are you going to show me now?" asked Marcel, avidly.

"This," said Blas, modifying the scene abruptly. "A submarine view of the subatlantic railway. Thanks to it, one can go from Paris to New York in a day. That was already good for the epoch—which is to say, for the year 2700."

Marcel saw the subatlantic trains, like long metal snakes, traveling like flashes of lightning through the ocean depths, with their headlights illuminating the abysms of the ocean in the distance.

Seized by a fever of curiosity, he did not pause for long on each scene, and the obliging Blas made new ones pass before his eyes continually.

"What am I looking at now?" Marcel demanded, suddenly. "I can only see a severe monument of bronze and granite ornamented by urns and bas-reliefs."

"What you see is a tomb. It was constructed in 2817 in honor of several of the inhabitants of the planet Mars who had attempted to reach us and who were victims of their scientific audacity. The centrifugal nacelle that carried them deposited them, horribly wounded, on our soil. They died. That tomb, which can be seen on the shore of the China Sea, immortalizes their courage. It's since their arrival among us that the initiative of scientists has borne them particularly toward interplanetary communication, which has finally yielded the marvelous result that you were able to observe yesterday."

Marcel remained silent, lost in his thoughts.

"I'm a little tired," he declared, finally. "So many vertiginous visions have just passed before my eyes that my brain hurts and my ideas are vague."

"Just look at this, though," said Blas.

Marcel saw, in the midst of a blue sky, high above the region of the clouds, a city that seemed to be floating in mid air.

"You doubtless want to show me the effect of a mirage," said Marcel.

"Not at all, Meteorville, the city of aluminum and pegamoid, which you see before your eyes, really existed until the year 2910. It was inhabited primarily by scientists and invalids, who went there to observe atmospheric phenomena and to breathe the vivifying air of high altitudes. Flotillas of aeroscaphs put the city is communication with the regions beneath."

"How is it that at the present time you no longer posses a similar city?" Marcel objected.

"What would be the point?" replied Blas. "The latest endeavors of our hygienists have had the effect of rendering the atmosphere of the lowest regions as healthy, as pure and as devoid of microbes as that of high altitudes. Then again, when it pleases us to study or travel though the upper layers of the atmosphere, are our aeroscaphs not to hand?"

XV. Psychophotography

Marcel's visit to the Palace of Art and History had caused him a real cerebral fatigue. The extraordinary efforts of attention and imagination that he had been obliged to make had exhausted him.

"That's enough for the first time," said Blas. You've just had an excellent history lesson. In a few days we'll return to the Palace, and you can complete your documentation at your leisure. Today, you've only glimpsed the broad outlines, the principal events of that history of ten centuries. It will be necessary for us to study it in detail. The subject is interesting enough not to become tedious for you."

"This morning's trip," Marcel replied, "our rapid excursion through the ages, has been a veritable revelation for me. It's only now that I can take account entirely of the vices, faults and imperfections of the men of my time, how ignorant and coarse they were, and how little they understood their veritable interests! They spent their lives tearing one another apart, instead of uniting against their enemies and combining the power of their intellect in order to render themselves masters of natural forces and trying to subjugate them."

"We've realized some progress," relied Blas, modestly, "at least from the point of view of mutual understanding and concord, but with respect to the sciences we've accomplished hardly anything."

"You're difficult to please," Marcel protested. "I confess that, speaking for myself, I find your society admirably well-organized, and my mind takes fright at the thought of what humankind might become after another forward step of ten centuries, in the year 4000."

"That will certainly be a splendid epoch," Blas replied. "We can already foresee that by the year 4000 humans will have discovered the means of prolonging their existence almost indefinitely, that they will have tamed the occult forces of nature definitively, and will doubtless have realized the dream of traveling through the celestial spaces and going from one planet to another at will."

"One question…in your opinion, will the outcasts still exist in that blissful epoch? For, after all, however perfect the future world might be, you'll always need fitters, mechanics and handymen."

"I don't think so. On the contrary, I'm convinced that in the year 4000 there will no longer be any outcasts. You can see that our society has already reduced, in considerable proportions, the number of manual workers. The inhabitants of the two polar cities only form a tiny part of the population. Machines construct other machines themselves. In ten centuries, that tendency will be further accentuated. By then, science will have simplified and improved everything. I'm sure that then, our aeroscaphs and submarines will be considered crude, cumbersome and primitive machines. They will have gone to museums to join the steamboats with paddles or propellers and balloons of varnished silk inflated by hydrogen or lighting gas that were employed in your time."

"Undoubtedly, but it seems to me that, having arrived at that degree of perfection, having nothing more to desire, sated with comfort and happiness, art and science, humans, no longer having to struggle, will suffer ennui. Won't spleen be the end result of this exaggerated progress?"

"You have a strange and misanthropic way of seeing, Marcel. Your fashion of appreciating future things is utterly illogical. The more intelligent and robust a man is, the more reasons he has for interesting himself in what surrounds him. By increasing the duration of his life and the volume of his brain, the human being will only augment the number of bonds that attach him to existence. Science and art are infinite realms; the further one advances in their mysterious pathways, the greater the perspective becomes. Human curiosity will be eternal, like the universe and the human soul itself. Humans will never be perfect from the moral point of view, but the higher they rise, the more they will attempt to approach that perfection. You ought to understand that, in those conditions, spleen, discouragement and ennui will no longer have any place in future societies.

Blas' words opened for Marcel such dazzling horizons of wellbeing, beauty and fraternity, that it was as if he were overwhelmed by the weight of his thoughts. Blas too seemed lost in his dreams. It was silently that the two friends took their places again in the pneumatic carriage and returned to the school for the midday meal.

An electric massage followed by a walk in the magnificent arbors of the central garden dissipated, as if by enchantment, the headache from which Marcel was suffering. He found himself as keen and well-disposed in imagination and intelligence as he had been that morning.

For some time, Blas and Marcel strolled beneath the shady vaults of the circular gallery, inhaling with delight the warm breeze charged with the embalmed odor of the gardens.

"You talked this morning," Marcel said, "about the considerable progress that humankind still has to realize from the moral viewpoint. It seems to me that in that regard, you're not backward."

"Evidently, what we've done is enormous. A long time ago we recognized that in protecting the weak, humankind was not only augmenting its moral potency but its material strength. But what we've realized in very little by comparison with what remains for us to do."

"I find your morality sufficiently perfected already, my dear Blas, and I'd be curious to know by what means you've been able to obtain such fine results."

"Firstly, by the diffusion of ideas, the progress of education and, above all, the facility of communications. When people knew one another better, they lost the prejudices and hatreds that separated them from one another. The nations of times past only detested one another because they didn't know one another. It's also necessary to add that we've been powerfully aided by certain discoveries, among which I'll cite, in first place, psychophotography."

"I don't even know the name of that science. If it wouldn't be tedious for you, I'd be grateful if you could give me a few explanations."

"Of course, my dear Marcel. Psychophotography, born of the radiographic photography of the brain, is the science that treats the means of photographing thoughts, sensations, and, in sum, all cerebral impressions."

"Ah!" exclaimed Marcel. "I'd be glad to observe experiments in psychophotography. That would interest me, if possible, even more than the views of historic cinematography that you enabled me to admire this morning."

"I'll take you there. I had, in any case, planned to show you those experiments one day. That's the employment of our afternoon determined."

Following Blas, Marcel went into a dimly lit corridor. They went into a room completely plunged in darkness.

When Marcel's eyes had habituated to the darkness somewhat, he distinguished half a dozen students, silent and attentive in the gloom, who did not even turn their heads at the approach of the newcomers.

Soon, in the depths of the darkness, ampoules were illuminated by a pale green light, similar to that of glow-worms or burning phosphorus.

On a platform at the black of the room Marcel perceived screens, flasks and mirrors, the employment of which was not evident to him.

"Now pay attention," murmured Blas. "As usual, we'll begin with the simplest experiments. Watch the luminous traces that appear on the screen."

On a large plate of sensitized glass, Marcel saw stripes and patches appear against a dark background.

Blas explained: "We've succeeded in preparing plates of such sensitivity that they're even impressed by the fluid emitted by the active brain. Those large white patches have been produced by the fluid emanated by an angry man; the small ones are due to the fluid of a brain attained by a fever. We've succeeded by this means in photographing, as you can see, hatred, pride, idleness, and even ambition. But these are only elementary experiments. By photographing certain nervous centers, we succeed in obtaining images that represent, cerebrally, the person placed before the apparatus, even including his thoughts. We witness the formation of a reasoned argument in the bosom of the cerebral circumvolutions. Thanks to psychophotography, the human brain is like an open book, which we can decipher fluently."

"I'm no longer astonished by the progress you've accomplished in morality. No vice or fault would be able to resist the marvelous clairvoyance of that apparatus, which allows you to fathom the utmost depths of consciences."

"It's certain," Blas replied, smiling, "that with the progress of psychophotography, lying and hypocrisy are no longer secure. A man with evil designs against his fellows would soon be unmasked. He could no longer harm anyone; he would simply be covered in ridicule. What point in there in lying, then? What is the point of trying to hide one's faults? On the contrary, anyone among us who has evil penchants informs everyone of it, in order that the means of correcting him can be procured. Personally, I don't let a week go by without coming to examine my brain in confrontation with the psychophotographic apparatus, in order to see whether, unknown to myself, some unfortunate tendency might be developing within me..."

Marcel listened, amazed and alarmed.

"Psychophotography is also a great help to us in the examinations that serve as a sanction for studies," Blas added. "That way, no cheating is possible, and the timid but laborious pupil no longer has to fear seeing himself put off until the next session because emotion has paralyzed his means of expression. Evidently, psychophotography only constitutes a part of the evidence; it simply serves as a check on the opinions of the examiners, who have already interrogated the candidate at length."

Blas fell silent abruptly. A sensitized plate, much larger than its predecessors, had suddenly brightened.

Against a pale background of a phosphorescent glow, landscapes, faces, numbers and even musical notes were designed, fading out to give way to others, and then reappearing, only to fade again.

"The images you can see," Blas murmured in Marcel's ear, "are those that are forming in the brain of the student placed in front of the apparatus at the moment. Just now he was thinking about a landscape; it was at the very moment that his attention was concentrated on the object in question that the landscape appeared clearly on the plate. He thought about one of his friends, and that memory evoked the image of the absent friend."

"Permit me an objection," said Marcel. "It seems to me that what you're photographing are images produced on the retina, not the brain itself."

"That's a great error, but quite understandable. A few words will dissipate it. It's the cerebral centers, not the nervous extremities, that are the seat of sensations. A man whose eyes have been put out can evoke in the imagination the landscapes he once saw. Wasn't Beethoven entirely deaf when he composed his best symphonies? I could multiply examples, but I think you've understood."

"Perfectly," Marcel replied, "except that, I confess that I too would be glad to make a trial of the psychophotographic apparatus and take account of its magical effects by means of personal experience..."

"Nothing is simpler. Place yourself before the apparatus; concentrate your will forcefully; focus your thought on an object or a person that is well engraved in your memory, and you'll see their image appear on the sensitized plate."

Slightly emotional, Marcel got up and went to sit facing the psychophotographic apparatus.

He closed his eyes.

And with all his might he concentrated his will-power on the person of Doctor Belzevor.

When he looked a few seconds later, the doctor was before him, coiffed in a brightly colored felt hat, impeccably dressed as an elegant man of the twentieth century.

His face was illuminated by a sarcastic smile...

Fearfully, Marcel thought that everything was sinking around him.

His ideas became blurred; his brain exploded

He extended his arms abruptly, in a convulsive start, and uttered a terrible scream.

XVI. The Return

When Marcel Vernoy opened his eyes and looked around, he perceived his parents, anxiously watching out for the moment of his awakening.

With an instinctive movement, Marcel leapt out of bed.

His legs buckled.

His father and mother leapt forward in order to sustain him, and he threw himself into their arms, weeping.

He was incapable of pronouncing a word, he was so emotional.

After those expansions, which Monsieur and Madame Vernoy did not trouble with any question, Marcel sat down, exhausted, on one of the blue velvet armchairs and passed his hand over his forehead with a gesture of profound lassitude.

"Excuse me," he stammered. "It seems to me that I'm emerging from a hallucination. I don't know yet whether I'm really awake. I don't even know what world I'm in, or what the date is. I fear that dementia might be taking possession of me."

"My dear child," replied Monsieur Vernoy, emotionally, "calm down, I implore you. Rest, reflect... You went to sleep yesterday evening under the influence of an elixir that Doctor Belzevor made you drink, and which, according to him, ought to have transported you in thought into the bosom of the human society of the future..."

"Then everything I've seen was only a beautiful dream!" exclaimed Marcel, with a bitter disenchantment. "Humankind perfected, fraternal, rid of its paltriness, its ignorance and its brutality, only exists in Doctor Belzevor's flasks! Like the gold and crimson clouds of the sunset, which the darkness swallows, the progress and the ideal by which I found myself summoned for a few hours have vanished like a nocturnal phantasm in the first rays of sunlight.

"Oh, certainly," he added, in a voice vibrant with sincerity, "I swear to you that the admirable spectacles I've witnessed, and the moral lessons in which I've participated, have already borne their fruit. You're going to find me regenerated and transformed, very different from the ambitious, egotistical and idle schoolboy who made you despair. Now, I shall love work, struggle and abnegation, for the sensual pleasure they contain.

"Henceforth, in my own eyes, I want to be proud of myself. I shall no longer have the cowardice of choosing as the aim of my life the conquest of a sinecure, in which I can stagnate in idleness and mediocrity. I'm ready to endure poverty, privation and the scorn of the crowd in order to follow through the ideas of beauty and truth that are germinating within me. I want to be one of the anonymous workers of that progress, that good will and that future fraternity, the splendors of which I alone, of the men of my time, have been able to contemplate.

"Oh, that dear Doctor Belzevor, how much gratitude I owe him! In revealing to me, by the sovereign mastery of his science, the magnificent humankind of the future, he has regenerated me. Henceforth, I shall advance, in the social struggle, protected by my convictions as if by a diamond suit of armor. But I'd like, this very minute, to go and see Doctor Belzevor, to throw myself at his knees and assure him of my infinite gratitude!"

Monsieur and Madame Vernoy looked at one another sadly.

With a gesture of tenderness and melancholy, they invited Marcel to sit down again.

"My dear child," said Monsieur Vernoy, gravely, "I have some very sad news to give you. While you were asleep, watched over by your mother and me, under the azure wallpaper of this room, while your mind, temporarily freed from the tyranny of time and space, was flying toward future worlds, Doctor Belzevor, your benefactor and ours, has been the victim of a terrible accident."

"What's happened to him" asked Marcel, with an indescribable emotion.

"His laboratory caught fire, alas."

"The doctor isn't dead, though?"

"He's very seriously injured. His life is in danger, and his condition is aggravated terribly by the despair caused by the irreparable loss of his notes, his formulae and his elixirs. His laboratory is no longer anything but a heap of rubble."

"I want to see Doctor Belzevor!" Marcel exclaimed. "I won't have any tranquility until I'm sure that his life isn't in danger."

"My child," replied Monsieur Vernoy, sadly. "You'll only see a wounded man, shrouded in dressings and bandages and plunged in a profound slumber. In consequence of a servant's error, the doctor has taken a large dose of the contents of the last bottle of the same elixir that permitted you to visit the realms of the future. He's drunk all the belzevorine that remained after the catastrophe that destroyed the laboratory."

"With what result?" asked Marcel, fearfully.

"With the result that Doctor Belzevor must be traveling at this moment, in thought, in the regions that you've just quit."

After that conversation, Marcel remained plunged in a bleak silence, which his parents dared not disturb.

His overtaxed brain could not succeed in recovering its equilibrium.

Chagrin, amazement and wonder nailed him to the spot, and he was making vain efforts to coordinate logically the ideas that were pressing upon him.

After having ascertained that Monsieur Belzevor's condition was stable, Marcel and his parents returned to the village of Montbarzy in one of the château's carriages.

That short journey, under the profound shadow of the oaks, was silent.

"Permit me, Father," Marcel had said, "to collect myself, to rest and put my impressions in order. I'm succumbing under the weight of too many ideas and too many sensations..."

Marcel recovered, slowly. Little by little, he regained the complete equilibrium of his faculties. He was, however, completely transformed. Judging by his seriousness, his patience and his mildness, one might have thought that he had acquired the experience and the wisdom of an old man.

A capricious and sulky schoolboy had gone into the Château de Montbarzy a few days before; he had emerged as a man.

Marcel had recounted to his parents all the phases of his vision of the year 3000, and they had listened to his story with admiration. They dared not call into doubt what their son said. His dream appeared to them as a mysterious problem, which they did not want to solve. Modestly, with a little respectful anxiety, they contented themselves with applauding the astonishing transformation that had taken place in their son. A sentiment of deference and terror was involuntarily mingled with their affection.

Twice a day, Marcel and his parents went to the Château de Montbarzy to see Doctor Belzevor.

To their great astonishment, the condition of the injured man was unmodified. His wounds, it is true, slowly scarred over, but he did not wake up from the placid and smiling slumber into which the absorption of belzevorine had plunged him.

The domestics and the physicians were chagrined, not knowing what to do. In order to awaken the doctor they had employed the most energetic revulsives, in vain. Acids, electricity and the tips of hot needles had not returned his sensibility. The ecstatic smile that seemed to be fixed on his lips remained immutable.

Fearing to compromise themselves, the local physicians ceased their futile attempts. After having conferred, they declared unanimously that Dr. Belzevor was plunged in a catalepsy of a particular kind, not previously catalogued, and that it was indispensable to submit his case to expert specialists.

The end of the vacation arrived without the doctor having woken up. His wounds were completely scarred over, his pulse was perfectly regular, and his physiognomy was still smiling.

Monsieur Belzevor's colleagues in the Académie des Sciences were informed of the strange case. They all knew the doctor and thought highly of him. They sent a delegation to the Château de Montbarzy. A scrupulous investigation was decided.

The savant academicians were unanimous in concluding that, in order to awaken their colleague, it would have been necessary to make him absorb a little of the special elixir that counterbalanced or annulled the effects of belzevorine after the dose had been taken. Unfortunately, the elixir and the antidote had been annihilated along with the laboratory.

The delegates of the Académie des Sciences searched the ruins, and studied the slightest fragments of paper that had escaped the conflagration, without obtaining any result. Dr. Belzevor's methods were so original, and so personal, that there was no chance of recovering by analogy the principle of his discoveries.

The delegates of the Académie found themselves in a great embarrassment, all the more so because Monsieur Belzevor had no family, no relatives that could make a decision in his regard.

After a series of discussions, it was agreed that the competent tribunals would be asked to appoint a judiciary counsel to supervise the administration of Dr. Belzevor's property temporarily, and that he would be transported to a sanitarium near Paris, where his colleagues and friends could visit him frequently, and where no effort would be spared to obtain his cure.

The strange circumstances of Dr. Belzevor's malady had excited public opinion. Periodicals and newspapers published his biography and listed his discoveries. His photograph took its place among those of celebrated individuals. The doctor had never enjoyed such renown before he went to sleep.

Gradually, the fuss died down. Dr, Belzevor still did not wake up.

With the aid of esophageal probes, the physicians at the sanitarium where he was being cared for enabled him to absorb meat extract, beef tea and albumin. The cataleptic condition was unmodified.

His face was still smiling, his pulse regular, and his limbs relaxed. The specialists were bewildered, and ventured a thousand audacious hypotheses, with no result.

Marcel had resumed the course of his studies. He now provoked the admiration of his professors and his comrades, as much by his ardor for work as his mildness, his cheerfulness, his kindness and his politeness. He was loved by everyone, and no jealous person or enemy could be found to denigrate him.

Monsieur and Madame Vernoy, at the peak of happiness, only pronounced the name of Dr. Belzevor with gratitude.

Every week, Marcel and his parents went piously to visit their friend, the prolongation of whose cataleptic slumber Monsieur and Madame Vernoy did not see without sadness. Marcel, on the contrary, did not seem at all worried by his benefactor's malady.

One day, Monsieur Vernoy addressed a few slight reproaches to him on that subject. "Your attitude toward Monsieur Belzevor," he told him, "chagrins me all the more as I have no reproach to address to you in other regards. Have you a desiccated heart? Do you lack gratitude? One might think that you were almost rejoicing to see the man of genius who saved you remaining in a slumber that isolates him from the rest of humankind, and makes him an unconscious and vegetal being."

"Pardon me, Father," Marcel replied, gravely. "I'm as sensible as you are to what you describe as Doctor Belzevor's misfortune. If I thought he were prey to any suffering, however minimal, you would see me utterly afflicted. But I confess to you frankly that if I'm not more emotional, it's because I believe the doctor to be completely happy."

"Why is that?" asked Monsieur Vernoy, surprised.

"Has not Dr. Belzevor absorbed the miraculous elixir that permits the mysterious river of Future Ages to be surpassed on the wing of unknown forces? At the present moment, Doctor Belzevor is doubtless strolling, as I have strolled myself, in magical palaces and enchanted parks. He is the respected guest of scientists who will be born ten centuries from now. Clad in gilded armor, he is exploring the submarine depths. He is flying through the air in crystal aeroscaphs. He is enjoying the beauty and the wisdom of a more perfect world. My dear Father, Doctor Belzevor certainly has nothing of which to complain. Let him sleep for a long time yet. He is so happy in his beautiful dream!"

Pierre Grasset: *The Discovery of the Earth in 2009*
(1909)

Lying back in the cushions of his aeroplane, his eyes half-closed and veiled by a kind of vertigo, whipped by the wind of his course, Henri Dumont could hardly see the extended, sparkling white wings of his flying machine and the silhouette of his chauffeur, sitting beside him at the helm; the entire world was nothing but blue, a uniform blue, bright and fresh, in the midst of which he was floating, his body and mind delectably light.

The soft and monotonous song of the motor, the incessantly even and excessively bright color of the sky, and the regular flow of the air over his cheeks, caused him to lie back further and would soon have sent him to asleep; he decided to wake himself up, and with a nervous movement of his body he sat up, opened his eyes and grasped reality again.

"I'll take the helm," he said.

He gets up, and while the standing chauffeur kept one hand on the steering wheel, he takes his place. Without any interruption to its progress, the nacelle oscillates, pitching like a frail boat in the ocean of the sky, ready to capsize.

Dumont reviews the controls of the engine with a glance; in his memory he operates them all: there is the one of the right helix, the one of the left helix, and the governor of altitude...

Well awake now, having become the mind of the great soaring bird, leaning forward, his eyes scanning more rapidly, he senses the living vehicle vibrate beneath him at the order of his fingers, hesitate, and finally fly like an arrow when the bowstring is released with a click. The mechanisms, the helices and the white wings are an extension of himself; it is his beating heart that is sending his blood into the supple machine, and it is really his weak muscles and his tensed muscles with which he his cutting through the sky, cleaving and possessing it.

A small helicopter, all its helices vibrating, overtook him effortlessly. Dumont then caught up with an aerobus, which was purring heavily on the spot, like a maladroit bumble-bee, He brushed it with the tip of his wing, with a precise flight that nevertheless trembled slightly in the wake of the huge machine. With the solemn racket of an official vehicle a Cook Agency flying wagon went past and fled, carrying away its lined-up Englishmen.

Helicopters were multiplying now and populating the joyful sky; no longer able to pierce the air in a straight line, they were making abrupt detours, readjusting their course, and swerving again with the harmonious movements of supple fish in a Hokusai print. It was evident by the light sureness of their evolutions that they had no consciousness of being heavy bodies—or, rather, that they had only kept, of the ancient notion of weight, that which is necessary to experience the voluptuous sensation of vanquishing it continuously.

Gliders slid between them, wings open. They were becoming rare in the year 2009, for machines with helices, easier to control, defying the wind more easily, were beginning to replace them. A few sportsmen continued to maneuver them even so, because they loved their grace and the skill that they had had the opportunity to develop.

That very day, in fact, the aero-club had organized an aeroplane race. That contest between the sailing ships of the air, in an era of helicopters would doubtless by comparable to the regattas of past centuries, which played on the sea with sailing boats in spite of the definitive triumph of steamboats.

Dumont had to speed up.

He could already perceive a black mass on the horizon, motionless in the air, which began to quiver and flicker, became a flying ant-hill, and appeared to run toward him, growing strangely, soon showing that it was formed of a multitude of vehicles pressed tightly together. The black mass elongated and split, and Dumont, who was heading toward it at top speed, was able to distinguish the vehicles clearly, arranged in two parallel long black serpents to either side of a blue ribbon of sky, an immense fictitious floor on which the race was about to be disputed.

He was obliged to slow down; the air thickened around him in every direction, and he had difficulty maintaining level flight in that buzzing hive. They were aggregated so closely, one was so far from the habitual sensations of free space, that one might have thought that one had descended to earth in the midst of a stifling crowd. Impatiently, he let himself fall to a lower altitude, disengaged from that swarm of huge importunate flies, found the sky again underneath, passed under a roof of quivering helices and rose up again into the highway of light that was the racecourse.

A cable retained at its extremities by two strong helicopters traversed the broad blue road. Dumont came to hook himself on to it alongside his competitors, switched off his engine and waited; he was to the last to depart.

One by one, the gliders hanging above the abyss released their mooring at a given signal; the long hulls were seen to fall, their great awkward wings inert, into the gulf of the sky, but soon, supported by the air, they were redressed, acquired a soul, rose up and fled, soaring like giant seagulls or fantastic dragonflies.

There was a disturbance, and anxious cries; one of the gliders, number 5, was carried away by the wind; it was soon no more, above the heads looking up into the dazzling sky, than a small dot which changed course abruptly, heading southwards.

"That's Henri Dumont..."

"Dumont of the Aero-Club?"

He race is over; the ribbon trembles and breaks; all the vehicles scatter like a swarm of bees whose hive has been tipped over.

Soon, the movement is organized in the direction of Paris, and, at low speed, aviators cluster, overtake one another, salute one another with their hats and amiable words; chauffeurs link their flight and then separate again. "Pay attention, you!" Meanwhile, slightly apart, and even between the strollers, a few lunatics traveling at high speed go whistling past and disappear.

A long time before that, the Earth was immense. The sea was something imprecise and terrible, on which people embarked, uncertain of the return, resolved to risk death in the tempest, to land after a long voyage in a promised land.

Journeys over land took as long as journeys over the sea. Old engravings show the arrival of diligences in the main square of towns. The innkeeper, his bonnet in his hand, welcomes the travelers who emerge from their box marveling at having escaped thieves and precipices, finally able to breathe freely. The houses do not look like the houses of today, the people and the costumes are new; it is another air, another world.

Railways striped the old world with their shining double lines; trains emerged from stations whistling, in the midst of signals of all colors; they pulled the towns toward one another and began to mingle countries. Ships brought winter visitors from Paris to Egypt, who had departed for Nice in previous years.

The locomotives, weary of marching along tightropes, emerged from the rails to speed along the roads; automobiles, gliding, raring and bellowing, hurled clouds of dust in the faces of those who still made use of horses, or even their feet, to travel.

Auto routes and railways did not waste their time, like the roads of old, running over plains, scaling hills and making detours in order to go through mountains by choosing passes; they bestrode valleys on gigantic bridges and excavated long tunnels through the mountains.

That trellis of routes brought al the continents of the earth closer together, filled in vales, flattened mountains; in tightening its mesh, it reduced and leveled the earth.

Heavy boats, strengthened by powerful engines, removed the frisson of danger from the longest crossings. The Mediterranean ceased to be the marvelous country of Ulysses; the great chocolatiers of the nineteenth century no longer encountered in their cruises either Circe or the Cyclops. The Mediterranean, which Herodotus called a sea, became a lake; the Ocean opened up and then closed again, vanquished in its turn. The dragnets of Oceanographers did not catch sirens, and submarines, having explored the forests of the sea-bed, emptied them of all their mystery; and thus the abysses were filled in

Already, people were striving to extract themselves from the small, flat earth in order to find space to cross, air to breathe. They took old balloons from which the impatient had long hung down enclosed in little baskets, and were then confided to the winds; those old balloons were stretched and elongated, their nacelles fitted with helices, which, until that day, had only beaten water but learned quickly to support themselves on air.

Aeroplanes bounded and fell back, breaking a wing. Then, one day, those dragonflies with open wings, immobilized in level flight, glided gently between two layers of air. The motors had become more powerful, the useless wings were broken; helices purred all around the nacelle and the helicopter entered into the air, and rose above it, corskscrewing its mass with its spinning helices.

Were they not the autos of old, increasingly bold, that had taken off like that? The racing autos with trenchant prows had been seen elongating into speedy beasts, bounding to the right and left when they were given the signal to depart, and it was necessary to hold the steering wheel with a firm hand in order to oblige them to follow the thread of the road. Finally victorious, they had reared up with a vigorous thrust of the back, and set a course for the sky, breaking in their passage the roof of leafy branches of the plane-trees of the highway.

It is said that Pythagoras was the first to teach that the Earth is round. Before him, the earth was flat; it stretched for-ever and ever, promising terrestrial paradises to discover, and, in the end, was confounded with the sky. Can you see that demiurge seizing the earth in his two giant hands, lifting that disk laden with men and women, howling with hatred or amour, and twisting that plate with a magnificent effort, bend-ing it and fashioning it into a ball? And then, much later, Gali-leo took that little ball and hurled it, with all his strength, into the fantastic system of worlds. Meanwhile the inhabitants of the Earth did not perceive it, and, having heard what those two madmen said, unfolded the world in their imagination, spread it out again and fixed it at the center of the world. Bent over it, without raising their eyes toward the heavens, they applied themselves to knowing at and loving it, all the way to its smallest corners.

But when there were no more lands left to discover, when the auto races had made a tour of the world, when the ice of the Poles and the populations of Africa could be visited by Cook's tours, when India and Japan were no longer any-thing but picturesque museums appended to the lines of circu-lar voyages, it was necessary to agree that Pythagoras and Galileo were right, the Earth is round, and it is tiny.

The face of the Earth appeared utterly contracted, as withered and wrinkled as the face of an old woman, with toothless jaws, hollow cheeks and gummy eyes, irremediably sad.

People straightened up then; a fine effort of escape enfevered them. Paris, first, constructed iron towers above its roofs, whose upper platforms were points of departure for the sky; the little flying machines pushed back with their feet in order to launch themselves upwards.

From the street one saw, on looking up, frameworks of iron, spring up more numerously every day, forming the uprights of an immense loom, between which innumerable shuttles flew: helicopters, weaving interminably a pattern that was continually unraveled. And those who were still walking on the pavement sensed that they were one stage below normal life; between the walls of the houses they thought they were at the bottom of a ditch, in the bed of a river emptied of its water.

When one descended from an aerial vehicle, one stifled in houses attached to the ground; the rooms were too narrow, with windows opening too low; the lungs were habituated to more air and the eyes to more space. Then some people wanted to detach their houses from the old earth and suspend them above the city.

Driven by a new need, architecture, which had become slightly dormant, woke up. Two centuries before, in the nineteenth, the Gallery of Machines and the Eiffel Tower had shown what can be constructed with iron, making use of the old technical discoveries of the Roman vault and the Gothic arch, and there had been a giant step between the Greek temple and the Gallery of Machines of 1889. In the twenty-first century, an even greater one was made.

A feverish activity, similar to that which had invented cathedrals, planted in Paris the foundations of an aerial city. Monstrous arches bestrode the old houses; further arches were grafted on to those; to the deafening din of iron being riveted, a metallic brushwood gripped the suddenly-obscured city, a brushwood whose highest branches sprang forth disengaged and free into the open sky, swollen at the tips, blossoming and finally sustaining in the air. Like huge fruits, houses with large windows; little flying autos were thus able to hook on to the balconies of vestibules in order to repose.

Those thirsty for air even wanted every room of their houses to have windows in its four walls open to the air; the house was obliged to explode like a ripe pomegranate, to fragment into a cluster in which each seed was a room; vertiginous, long and supple footbridges, like bridges of tremulous lianas above rapids, where launched from one room to another, reuniting the grapes of the cluster.

Municipal regulations prescribed an order of alignment for those aerial fruits. The Town Hall and the ministries consented to abandon darkened Paris in order to rise up to new Paris.

The beautiful fantastic city, of which Scheherazade had not dreamed, launched its blue streets following the three dimensions of space, horizontal streets like the good horse-roads of our ancestors, but superimposed at different heights, cut by vertical and oblique streets. Maps of the city, difficult to draw, had to become numerous, in accordance with different imaginary cross-sections of that monstrous vibrant hive.

The principal street was vertical; the horizontal streets, which extended from it like the spokes of a wheel from a central hub, poured forth a multitude of helicopters; those changed direction, rose and descended in the large well of light, rapid bizarre elevators sliding without shocks along invisible cords in a cage of air.

At the top, the vertical avenue was terminated by a triumphant crown, for such arches in the Roman mode had no longer been fashioned at ground level for a long time, but immense crowns hung outside the city like round portals to the sky. Men erected them as a homage to their own genius; it was their cry of victory, finer than the meager olive branch that the Ancients planted on top of their houses when they had terminated the paltry construction. The sheaf of gliders and helicopters rising up the avenue passed through the eye of the needle and then dissipated and spread out into the plains of the sky.

Gradually, old Paris was submerged, inundated by the foundations of the new city. The poor stone houses were abandoned to workers; then only the wretchedly poor accepted to live in them; and it was there, in a perpetual demi-obscurity, that a crawling population began to swarm like vermin, progressively buried far from life, like Pompeii beneath its ash or the city of Ys under the waters.

In the evening, the living city lit up, and the abundantly windowed houses were suspended like enormous lanterns between the black void below—old, dead Paris—and the black void above, the sky punctured in streaks by the headlights of flying autos.

In 2009 there was a centenarian old woman still alive in Paris who had spent her early childhood in houses on the ground. Paralyzed and confined to a chair, she surrounded herself with screens in order not to see, through the large glass windows of the room, the bizarre vehicles passing in all directions. She could thus forget that she was not reposing on the ground; but sometimes, raising her head, she saw above the screens, running over the wall, the fleeting and disorderly shadows coming from the street; then she thought that she felt the house oscillating in the wind and its framework creaking, and she closed her eyes because she had vertigo.

At the start of the race, when Henri Dumont realized that he was being carried away by the wind, he tried to struggle against it with forceful thrusts of the helices, but he then perceived that one of his wings was hanging, broken at the root; it was necessary to land as soon as possible.

The glider was making desperate efforts not to capsize, and it fluttered like a huge butterfly. An abrupt gust of wind tried to tear the aeronaut from his seat and project him into the abyss. Dumont only just had time to cling on to the steering wheel like the pilot of a doomed ship clinging on to the tiller; and, without even trying to steer his fall, hunched up, with his head sunk between his shoulders, he awaited the impact that was about to crush him on the hard ground.

The captive apparatus, shaken by the victorious wind, spun like a dead leaf, and then fell vertically; the man was conscious of no longer being anything but a thrown pebble that nothing can arrest, and he closed his eyes in the vertiginous rush of the air through which he was lunging, making a hole, like a lead bullet through water. Suddenly, he felt himself borne up softly, carried by a supple cushion of air; the wounded seagull, rediscovering some strength, soared on one wing. But again the aeroplane spun in the ocean of the sky, like a thin sheet of paper spiraling madly as it falls. And finally, he landed on his clumsy wing, which folded up and broke—and Dumont, bewildered to be still breathing and able to move his intact limbs, stood up and detached himself from the poor injured plaything.

What a strange country! A village with very low roofs, as they were made a century before: not a single aerial house, not a single helicopter in the sky. Oh, he had really fallen on to the vulgar ground, resistant to the feet. It was no longer the sky, in the impalpable matter of which one swims in all directions, with no other limit than one's whim. He had descended to the base earth beneath the free sky, the earth as flat as the bosom of an old woman, the little earth whose horizon one could touch with an extended hand. Lifting his head toward the space that he could no longer attain in his broken glider, his breast unquiet and lacking air, his leaden feet riveted to the ground, he had the impression of being at the bottom of a well.

Henri Dumont was, in fact, a true Parisian scarcely living anywhere but the Paris of aerial houses. His excursions in gliders or helicopters brought him back every evening to dine in the city, and if he changed his roof on certain fixed dates of the year, he chose for holiday destinations the towns that had replaced such destinations as the Nice and Trouville of the nineteenth century; he found the houses, the people and the habits of Paris there. One could therefore say that he had hardly ever emerged from the great aerial city.

He had landed in a village set close to a wood not far from Versailles. Civilization, which flows very rapidly, had doubtless passed over this village with a flap of its wings, disdaining to pause so close to Paris, for it appeared to be lagging a century behind the rest of the world. The great lines of flying machines were several kilometers away, and in order to go to the nearest station there was only one service per day of an old auto furnished with a petrol engine!

The auto had just left; Dumont was therefore obliged to wait until the following day. A hotel by the roadside opened its door at ground level; that house, similar to its neighbors, seemed small and dark to the man fallen from the sky, more like a rabbit warren than a habitation for humans, but it was necessary to settle for it.

Throughout the long and sad night, he could not sleep. He was troubled, disorientated, even anguished. How could he not have been? Until that day he had only lived in the sky. He knew all the winds, the great fixed currents and those that changed in accordance with the seasons; he knew their names, their direction, their strength, their manias and their caprices, and even their colored form. He had read the poems of contemporary authors who chose their metaphors and images from the things of the air. He had traveled in all its regions and knew them well, a region being a certain atmosphere, bright or transparent or heavy and misty, with, underneath, very low and almost futile, a mosaic or an Oriental carpet whose arabesques and colors hardly changed. And now, an accident had nailed him to it, paralyzed, in a corner of that extended carpet, that smooth mosaic, devoid of beauty.

Morning illuminated Dumont's room with its paltry light. He went out, exhausted by a feverish insomnia, and began to revive as soon as he had swallowed large draughts of the matinal freshness.

Not far away, a poplar raised up its petty height in the sunlight like a silvery flower that would like to be plucked. Dumont directed his stroll toward it, for no reason, simply in order to kill time; but the tree seemed to recoil as the man marched toward it. Then he became interested in the pursuit.

The landscape changed its form; the poplar disappeared behind a fold in the terrain and reappeared even larger; the aeronaut had not reached it. He persisted, stubbornly, heading toward the tree, which grew. Now he experienced difficulty lifting his heavy feet, as if he were emerging from a plowed field. Was it by virtue of a mischievous game that the little earth was growing under his feet?

That day, he allowed the auto that was due to take him back to Paris to depart. The next day, and the days that followed, accepting with delight to be dominated by a mysterious force that retained him in the lost village, he did not leave. He was astonished to sense born and growing within him a strange, perhaps unhealthy, amour for the paths and roads of the earth: the morning road that comes toward you and greets you; the road of the day that invites you to stroll and continues to flow when one stops, weary, on its edge; the long evening road whose terminus flees endlessly. He loved the grassy clay on which the foot slips, the round pebbles that roll and the sharp ones that claw the sole; the dry earth of the path across the plain, the moist earth of the path through the woods, the white dust of the highway, the russet cushion of dead leaves.

Every path that one discovers is different; and even a single path, the shortest and the narrowest, changes its face so often with the hours of the day that a lifetime would not be long enough to travel it from one end to the other.

As his eyes became accustomed to the terrestrial scale, they remembered having had a similar focus in Dumont's ancestors. Dazzled, he witnessed a renaissance of the world. The smooth mosaic, the extended Oriental carpet, that he had once perceived from his glider was agitated by a secret, violent and patient life that changed it completely. For him alone, valleys stretched and hollowed out, and hills swelled up and sprang forth. The Earth was a withered fruit that a miracle had caused to ripen again; it became immense and mysterious.

One evening, a cool wood opened before and closed again on the man fallen from the sky. The sun had scarcely disappeared, but two stars were already twinkling in the bright sky; watching them brighten while the sky darkened, he did not experience any desire to detach himself from the earth that retained him amorously. Hugging him against it like a prodigal son or a lover returning to all its paths of the plain and mountains, he was not far from believing that the sky is only a round and hard vault to which the stars are nailed.

The wood had closed upon him. In the silence, the colors faded away in somber spectra, while the odors of moist plants rise in shriller and more forceful scales.

At a bend in a path, a forgotten shred of light hung between the trees. He stopped in order to gaze at it. He thought he saw it move. He saw the whiteness move, and perceived distinctly a rustle of foliage. Emotion suspended his respiration in his breast. A faun and a nymph came forth and fled between the trees.

Transported by enthusiasm, Dumont launched himself in their pursuit. He could not see them any longer, but he heard the rustle of dead leaves under their feet and the whiplash of branches violently bent in passing; sometimes the branches broke. Then he no longer heard anything.

A long avenue opened up, the trees of which combined their beautiful foliage in a vault. That silent gallery appeared to end at a high portal, gaping under the pale nocturnal light. He crossed its threshold.

A pool of water was lying ideally flat and smooth, and it reflected, while enlivening it, a luminosity of limbo, which filled pure space all the way to the delicate stars. Dumont had just entered the park of Versailles.

Alone in the midst of the magnificent deployment of pathways, fountains and statues, he was gripped by such an emotion that he thought he might sink into the sand, and he leaned on a marble pedestal. He shivered with anxiety, awaiting I know not what supernatural punishment. At the same time, he was uplifted and swelled with pride at sensing himself at the center of such a beautiful landscape. The park was as pathetic as a corpse with open eyes; however, it was not dead, for a living odor of trees, grass and moist earth rose therefrom. And Dumont thought: *I cannot know whether I am dreaming.*

Then he perceived the faun, sitting on the rim of a fountain. The nymph had disappeared. The face of the faun expressed a discreet satisfaction that was not lacking in elegance.

Dumont saluted it, with the casual lightness and easy familiarity that one has in dreams toward the noblest individuals.

At that moment, a helicopter landed at the end of the avenue, as brutal as a bird of prey; then it rose up, quivering, bearing into the night the man who was maneuvering it.

"Those who come from the sky," exclaimed the faun, "are not worthy to enter here!"

The faun was cultured, for it continued to speak with a certain pedantry. I imagine that the King's gardeners, in the days when they had mapped out the park of Versailles, would not have been frightened by it. It had doubtless remained in the wood that had been transformed into a garden. And while the trees submitted joyfully to human intelligence and allowed themselves to be disposed and sculpted in accordance with the rules of art, he too had been modified and his mind had learned to organize his thoughts.

"Those who come from the sky," he repeated, "are not worthy to enter here; they cannot enter here. Those whose eyes are not habituated to terrestrial equilibria; those who can cross the park of Versailles by taking off in their flying machines, with a single stride of their seven league boots, cannot penetrate its beauty. If they have not descended the staircase whose steps have been carved with genius for human feet, if they have not gone astray in the boscage, this garden is enchanted for them; they cannot see it."

The faun laughed, and he added: "In any case, they no more possess the heavens than they do the Earth. They believed that they were detaching themselves from the earth, but they have not emerged from the atmospheric peel that surrounds it. In traveling through that transparent bark made of winds, mists and clouds they have only discovered new terrestrial regions. When a man flies, in his lightest helicopter, it is still the earth to which he remains fixed, as his seat.

"Once, Icarus burned his wings in the sun and fell. Humans have believed that they were Icarus resuscitated, but in spite of themselves, the force of the earth inclines them toward her and forbids them to leap any higher than the limit of her respirable air, holding them, as it were, by a thread. The jump a little higher, for a little longer, than the little girl dancing on a rope, but like her, they fall back after every bound. Little Icaruses, your wings of wax are melting again!

"Who among you would have the courage to leap outside the earth. to hurl himself, infinitely small, into the system of worlds? Which of you, in good health, would dare to anticipate the death that is the only thing, thus far, that can cause someone to vanish before our eyes and forever from the earth that gave us birth?"

He had become agitated; he calmed down.

"It is necessary to love the earth, from which one cannot escape," he said, by way of conclusion. "It is necessary to love that which one cannot prevent. That is the secret of joy and power."

Dumont, however, was pensive. A strange desire was forming within him: that of discovering the Earth, Why had he not gone, at once, to explore the old Paris that must be buried beneath a forest of iron, in the midst of the foundations of aerial Paris? Perhaps one could, with the methods of the archeologists of the nineteenth and twentieth century who had discovered Greek and Roman status under the ground, recover in the year 2009, between the mesh of an iron felt, the little church of Notre-Dame and the Palais de l'Élysée.

The faun stood up and drew away, not without having saluted the pious human. Dumont saw then that it was holding a book; with its hairy hand it caressed the spine and the boards bound in leather stamped with gold. By the uncertain light of the stars, the title was decipherable; it was a volume of the works of Racine, doubtless forgotten there, which the faun had picked up.

Pierre Billaume and Pierre Hégine: *Journey to the Isles of Atlantis*
(1914)

The centuries led then to the inevitable day, the disastrous night, when, in an earthquake, amid floods, all our warriors were dragged into the abyss, and the isle of Atlantis was covered again forever by the waves... That, Socrates, is the story that old Critias heard Solon tell.

Plato, Timaeus.

Part One

I. The Tempest

"Captain," I cried, "are we doomed?"

"Go to the devil!" replied the mariner, coldly.

"Alas," I said, "we're going."

The ocean swelled and seethed, seemingly wanting to mingle with the sky, to renew the ancient confusion of chaos. To the obscurity of the night was added the opacity of the atmosphere charged with compact mists. The heaviness of the air scarcely permitted respiration. When the wind chased away the fog, flashes of lightning showed my bewildered eyes livid clouds like immense rocks suspended above the waves.

Our wretched ship was spinning in the eddies. It descended into the hollows of colossal waves, and then, lifted in to their crests, seemed to quit the sea momentarily. It creaked and groaned beneath the thunderous breakers. The squall whinnied horribly in the rigging. Surges of sea-water swept the entire deck. Sometimes the bow plunged into the water, sometimes the stern. Then the vessel almost lay on its side. I heard the howls of those close by who disappeared. The mariners ran around; the captain shouted into his loud-hailer; and the rest of us, desperate travelers, hung on to ropes with both hands, to the rails, and to all the asperities of the deck.

It was the third and most terrible night of the tempest, the mighty breath of which had been driving us for sixty hours. Until that moment I had conserved hope, but it finally appeared to me that black destiny was about to be accomplished and that we were going to sink.

Stoical people, it is said, support such proofs proudly. They gaze with a cold eye at the horrible death that besieges them and scorn the elements that are engulfing them as they perish. Resigned men, whose soul remains serene in the midst of calamities, I am not one of you and I have never been able to remain fearless in such circumstances.

Alas, I said, weeping, *I have merited this great misfortune. Why did I abandon firm ground? At this moment I could be sleeping in a dry bed and having sweet dreams after an agreeable meal. What obliged me to venture on to these fragile planks? My debts, only my debts! The most insufficient of all pretexts! A fine motive to go and drown in a savage sea! I must be stupid! And you, my creditors, by whose fault I am perishing, all my blood is on your miserly heads. Did you desire my death? At any rate, you'll have caused it. I'd still be at home if you hadn't harassed me so much. Your debtor is going to die, and your debts with him.*

I was lamenting thus when the main mast collapsed, with the noise that poplars make when uprooted by a tempest. As it fell, it broke a part of the planking to which several men were clinging. Some fell into the sea, and the least crippled dragged themselves, moaning, under the tangled ropes and the debris of yardarms. The ship lurched.

"Use the axes!" cried the captain. "Clear the deck!"

In a matter of seconds, the mariners finished severing the cables that retained the mast and shoving it overboard. The vessel straightened again.

Lying face down in the middle of the deck, I clung with all my might to a small capstan whose situation and solidity seemed favorable. I was resuming the course of my interior laments when I perceived a wounded mariner who was crawling toward me slowly.

He made one last effort, and succeeded in reaching my capstan, which he seized in such a way that we were face to face, our arms intersecting.

"I have a broken leg," he said, calmly. "It's the work of that villain of a mast that has just fallen. I'll stay here now. We won't come back from this."

"Do you think so?" I said, fearfully. My eyes saw the victory of the tempest and my reason believed in the final disaster, but my heart conserved an insensate hope.

"I'm sure of it," the sailor replied. "Before the day's end, we'll be sailing underwater."

My fate appeared to me to be more frightful than I could say. I'm astonished now by my terror then, and reproach myself for my cowardice in that situation. Thanatos is not a cheerful divinity, but one owes it to him to put on a brave face, as to a patient creditor. The fear that one conceives of him doesn't help to escape him, and only aggravates the horror of him. Why, in danger, do we forget such accurate maxims?

"Where are we?" I said.

"I have no idea, Monsieur. Not on our route, at any rate. We don't have the Antilles before us, you can be sure of that. From three days we've been running northwards at a crazy speed, and we won't find any land or ships there."

It's cruel, I thought, *to die like this at twenty-eight. Those who die in their beds, late in life, surrounded by their friends, of some petty malady don't know what death is. For them, it's a gentle, gradual termination of existence, and enviable, by comparison with this long, terrible agony, from which one suffers all the more because one is in good health.*

I remembered my flask then, large and marvelously stout, and full of liquid consolation, the delicious soul of good wine known as cognac. When I leave home, I don't leave it in the house and I don't forget to fill it up. It cheers me up in ordinary times, comforts me in peril, and this time, like the others, makes my heart the heart of a lion. Holding on to my support with one hand, and the flask in the other, I took four large swigs, and invited my companion to savor the noble elixir.

"The sharks won't have it," I said, when the flask was empty.

"Yes, Monsieur," said the man, "they will."

On reflection, I was convinced of my error, and the conversation continued, punctuated by gusts of wind and claps of thunder.

A wave as high as a bell-tower loomed up, all white, to starboard; then, with thunderous crash, collapsed over the ship. I pressed the capstan to my heart. For a minute, I remained submerged without letting go. My body floated in the water like a flag in a storm wind. An instant later, I found myself out of the water, but when I opened my eyes, I no longer saw my comrade, the mariner with the broken leg.

The situation was worse. The vessel was no longer bounding lightly from one wave to another. The water had broken the awning and invaded the depths of the hold. The engines were drowned and the rudder had been carried away.

A calm followed, however. The waves and the wind diminished. Rain began to fall, dense and mingled with hail.

It was the end of the tempest. Salvation became possible. Of the ship, nothing remained but the hull, razed but it was unbreached. In good weather, we might remain on the surface, on the wreck, for a long time, and eventually find aid.

Everyone breathed again. The captain went back and forth, shouting: "The hardest part is over. There's hope."

In spite of the wind having dropped, the ship, borne by some current, was still advancing rapidly. The deplorable vessel was never as fast when it possessed propellers and a boiler.

I was unworried by that at first, thinking that the more headway we made, the more chance there was of encountering a ship or a shore, but our velocity became so precipitate, so frenetic, that a sinister thought seized me: "Where are we going like this?"

From time to time the crew fired rockets. Their lines of flame rose up vertically to a great height and fell back in a curve, to burst into multicolored sparks.

The moon rose over the calmed sea. The ocean appeared to us bright and green-tinted, and the sky half black and half dark blue, speckled with stars.

Suddenly, a great solitary rock loomed up head of us. The water was seething at its base. Tall and narrow, it resembled those raised stones that one finds in Brittany. We were heading straight toward it. We no longer had a tiller and we judged ourselves doomed. Several people uttered loud cries. Women wept and hid their faces. But we left it to starboard and passed ten meters away from it.

And the fantastic navigation continued. The clouds hid the moon and all the stars. The night seemed never-ending.

It was then that a horrible shock ripped the ship, with a muffled detonation. We had run on to reefs. All the timbers creaked, and I sensed them dislocating beneath me. The vessel stopped, described a semicircle, and set off again slowly, like mortally wounded beast still trying to flee.

We were sinking.

A voice dominated the lugubrious clamors: "Launch the lifeboat!"

Everyone ran. I quit my capstan in order to race to the lifeboat; but a further impact threw me on to the deck so brutally that I lost consciousness.

II. Land

When I recovered consciousness, beautiful sunlight was warming me gently.

Motionless, I stared at first at the infinite profundity of the blue sky. I had no consciousness of the place or the situation I was in. I only seemed to be escaping from one of those painful dreams, the memory of which dissipates at the moment of awakening, but the confused horror of which still stirs us momentarily.

On looking down, my eyes perceived the sea and the deck of the ship. The masts, severed at the base, a few battered cadavers forgotten by the waves, and the solitude in which I found myself, represented all the circumstances of the previous night to me.

Surprised to be still alive, and wondering by what means the vessel was still afloat, I got to my feet, painfully. My knees were wounded, and it was that injury, combined with exhaustion, that had made me fall into the weakness from which I was emerging. I leaned over the edge and perceived that the keel was wedged between reefs at water level, some of which, protruding further, were sustaining it in places.

The sea was absolutely calm. There was no wind. Albatrosses with huge sparkling wings were circling and calling, descending in spirals, seizing invisible fish from the waves, which they carried away high into the sky in perpendicular flight.

I discerned a long, thin, cloudy streak limiting the sea on the edge of the horizon, the blue silhouette of a coast, the sight of which rendered me more madly joyful than the Hebrews before Canaan or Xenophon's Greeks perceiving the Black Sea at Trebizond

Then I glimpsed the difficulty of reaching that shore. All the means employed by shipwreck victims whose memoirs I had read returned to mind. I suspect the majority of those honest men of never having been in maritime peril except in the imagination, without leaving home. Their inventions are inapplicable, and, although full of charm and whimsy, they appeared to me at that difficult moment as pure mockery and extravagant lucubration.

Those fellows always assure us that they found on their apprehended wreck an infinite number of objects of dire necessity. This one was furnished with barrels, tools and nails; that one inherited some large sheet of fabric with which he made a sail for his raft. I can only speak from memory of those who collected various food provisions, not only salted and smoked meat and fish, but also livestock and fat poultry. Were they sailing on Noah's Ark? And what of the one that lived on his hunting, with the aid of a complete artillery that he contrived to discover on his vessel, with a profusion of powder and bullets of every caliber? Those people are joking, I tell you, and their words make me angry.

I went around the deck three times, and only found shards with which the most industrious man would not have been able to do anything. Everyone knows, besides, that mariners at the height of a tempest, throw overboard everything that might weigh down a ship, with the exception of people. One traveler of times past, if the tale is true, profited from such an occasion to send his wife to the fish, attesting to all the gods that no object weighed upon him more.

The ship, therefore, with its denuded deck and its hold in which the waves were splashing, did not offer me any resource. There was only rope aplenty, with which I might have been able to lash the planks of the vessel together to form a raft. I tried for some time to detach a few of them. My fingernails were bloody and my fingers bristling with splinters, but I did not get any further benefit from the labor.

Sitting on the deck, I gazed at the coast, my last and only hope. *Oh, the beautiful shore!* I thought. *The admirable, sublime, delightful shore! Why is it so far away from me? Why am I so far away from it? The land is surely deserted: not a single sail, not the smallest boat.*

I sobbed, discouraged.

"Great gods!" I cried. "How hungry I am! How thirsty I am! How unhappy I am! Why didn't I die just now? Unconscious as I was, I'd have passed away without perceiving it. Or rather, why didn't I die a long time ago, on the solid earth of my homeland? Why was I even born, if it was to run to such a destiny and perish in such a frightful manner?"

And, turning my eyes toward the cadavers, I continued: "That's what I shall soon be. I'll be worse, alas! I'm going to die of starvation, and my body will be as dry as a smoked herring. O insupportable thought!"

Looking at the sea again, I saw a long object floating a short distance away, like the spine of a sleeping sperm whale. I recognized the lifeboat on which the crew had embarked, leaving me to die on the vessel in perdition. I had cursed those mariners furiously, so impatient to save their own lives that they had neglected mine. My sentiment changed when I had observed that the boat, overturned, was displaying its keel I desisted from all complaint against the disappeared and begged the Lord very devoutly to have mercy on their poor souls. Then, seizing a long piece of rope, I knotted one end around the capstan that had served me so fortunately the previous night. Holding the other end, I leapt into the sea.

After a hundred brasses I reached the boat and attached my cable to the hook of the tiller. I swam back to my wreck, from which I began to haul, so much and so well that I drew the launch slowly toward me. I succeeded, with difficulty, in making it assume a position more appropriate to the usage I wanted to make of it. It only remained to rid its vast hull of the water that half-filled it. The operation might seem easy, but remember that I was disinherited of all useful objects, such as jugs, buckets or saucepans. But the Creator has been kind enough to put into my mind a faculty that informs me, in moments of peril, of the necessary expedient.

The tempest had left me my hat. It was a complicated item of headgear. Folded three times with the aid of clasps, it acquired a vast capacity on being spread out like an accordion. This distended, it resembled the canvas buckets that masons use. With its office, and a lot of patience, I slowly dried out the lifeboat. Then I found myself in possession of a buoyant hull, still furnished with a few oars.

I set forth. The tranquility of the ocean permitted me to advance and steer quite easily. The crossing was fortunate and short. On the way, I perceived the cadavers of my traveling companions. The overloaded boat had doubtless capsized, causing them to drink more sea-water than one can swallow without dying. Perhaps it was God himself, irritated, who ordered that chastisement, and then wanted the vessel to return to the abandoned man, thus offering to the impious a marvelous and very edifying miracle, for which I shall be grateful to him for as long as I live, and even thereafter, if I can.

The coastline increased gradually, and toward the end of the day, my boat ran on to the sand. I leapt ashore and stated running like a madman. That was the greatest happiness of my life.

I found myself confronted by a steep cliff. Landslides would enable me to scale it, but my exhaustion made me dread false steps, and I postponed the ascent until the following day. The dusk might also have deceived me and caused me to fall into one of the cavities that it was filling with shadow.

I was hungry. Here again I knew the exaggerations of the stories of so-called castaways. On the deserted shores where they run aground they always find trees laden with fruits, under which game of all kinds is waiting to be cooked. I only had rock-pools. I fished in them for crabs, which I ate raw. A waterfall was running between the rocks, hollowing out the sand of the beach as it fell. For the first time, I took pleasure in drinking water.

Finally, the obscurity becoming total, I lay down on a mound sheltered from the waves and went to sleep, lulled by the song of the sea.

III. The Old Man

Dawn woke me up. I began the day with the necessary reflections. Was the land deserted? Was I going to subsist there like a petty Robinson Crusoe? *That would, however*, I said to myself, *be preferable to the company of cannibals.*

Would I have traversed so many dangers only to end up on this shore roasted over a little fire under the greedy eyes of black men?

The dangers run, my wretched situation and fear for the future changed my soul, and, from its previous irreligious state, made it devout, sanctified by dread, ready to repent if time gave it a chance to do so.

Aloud, I implored the Eternal and the benevolent principles. Don't mock, I beg you, incredulous individuals who live tranquil lives by your firesides, for there is no merit in being impious in security. A stormy sea would extinguish your blasphemies, and you would fall to your knees, saying in a pitiful voice: "Celestial Father, if I escape this, I shall bring to your chapel the most beautiful candle that has ever been seen." The example is frequent, and I have seen many atheists, in dangerous circumstances, summoning to their aid by means of invocations and supplications, all sorts of gods and goddesses, and saints of both sexes.

In my homeland there are many strong minds who do not admit either God or the Devil. They rejoice in mocking the passage of priests and processions. They laugh publicly, to excess, at our pious superstitions, but those people don't undertake journeys on a Friday. If in counting guests, they find thirteen, the go pale in mid-meal, lose their thirst and their appetite, and get up, sure of being in evident peril of death all year long. They secretly conserve against their heart a scapular full of medallions or punctured coins, by the virtue and singular benediction of which they seek to escape the accidents and calamities of existence.

Without wishing to displease those bizarre souls, I confess to having found relief and consolation in my ordeals in supplications to hypothetical divinities.

I scaled rocks heaped up into steps and reached the top of the cliff. I finally discovered the country. It resembled in every respect the most beautiful part of Normandy, which is near Aubec and is called Vallée d'Auge. Apple-trees with twisted trunks projected their shadow on to the grass of meadows.

Fields of barley and wheat extended all the way to the horizon, designed by rounded hills. A multitude of streams ran between the trees. In the distance, smoke denounced thatched cottages buried in the verdure. The wind brought me the thousand perfumes of trees and fallow fields. Wheat with heavy ears undulated and rustled.

Joyfully, I headed toward the habitations I perceived, not doubting that I had landed on the territory of some great and hospitable nation. I stopped continually, charmed by the song of warblers, a curious admirer of butterflies, flying flowers dancing in the sunlight. Everything seemed new and astonishing to me, full of a pure beauty. Having escaped the maritime desert, the terrors of shipwreck and death, I savored the emotion of a man who, after a long winter, travels through verdant woods and florid plains, weeping tenderly at the contemplation of a nature entirely similar to that of my homeland.

I arrived on the bank of a stream whose rapid current was stirring the pebbles of its bed, ornamented with large bright water-lilies, where blue irises grew in abundance.

The stream reflected my frightful image. I knew than what a sad figure I cut. The beautiful princess Nausicaa, kind to castaways, would not have listened to such a miry Ulysses. My muddy hair fell over my face. My scrawny nudity was veiled here and there by damp rags; I gave the impression of a drunkard still covered in the filth of the sewer in which he has slept.

I washed myself and gave my rags a more decent arrangement. Kneeling on the bank still looking into my mirror, I suddenly saw the reflection of another man. I turned round. Too emotional to say a word, I considered the individual: tall, old, clad in a fashion very similar to our peasants. He was gazing at me sadly.

In the end, I said, in French: "I'm an unfortunate whom the tempest has cast up on the shore. Help me. Tell me what land this is."

He expressed by means of signs that he did not understand. I spoke to him in English. He shook his head.

He spoke, and I understood. He was speaking in a sublime language believed to be dead for two thousand years, a language with harmonious syllables that can only be compared to ours. The old man was speaking ancient Greek.

But I can hear the clamors of collegiate pedants and other scholarly rodents of stupid books in which they think all knowledge is contained. Listen to them crying in their jargon: "No people uses that dialect today. Even if it had been conserved, it would have been subjected, by virtue of changing mores, over the succession of the centuries, to such profound alterations and such numerous admixtures, that it would have become unrecognizable." Don't agitate so in your pulpits, O ignorant quibblers, for it isn't the first time that your reasoning has proved false. I'm not relating hearsay. What I'm reporting, I haven't read in your compilations. And as I'm not advancing anything that isn't the fruit of experience acquired through terrible dangers, I shall find your insolent contradiction difficult to tolerate.

But you will find the means of educating yourselves in the seven folio volumes that I shall soon publish. Therein are inscribed all the definitive explanations, all the necessary information, sustained and justified by a marvelous abundance of evidence. Read that great work and then come, if you wish, to treat me as a liar, a crackpot and a faker. But in truth, I have no fear.

The man said to me: "You are in one of the isles of Atlantis, a vast, populous and fertile land. But it would have been better for you to perish last night in the tempest than to land on our shores. The law orders the death of all strangers. Those who are collected are executed as traitors. Weep then, young man, for I don't believe that you'll live for another three days."

"What!" I cried. "Are you so barbaric? Have the Hellenes, from whom you seem to be descended and whose language you speak, given you such lessons in hospitality? In every other land, people care for, nourish and comfort castaways. You massacre them! Execrable fury!"

The old man seemed troubled. "Listen," he said. "I won't betray you. Come and live in my house. You know our language and, passing for a native, you'll doubtless escape. Remember never to tell anyone your adventure; you'd cause our doom."

I embraced his knees, weeping. He lifted me up. We crossed the stream on an old stone bridge covered in moss and wild vines. Then we followed a path through a wood of crimson beeches.

"What is the reason," I asked, "for that frightful law directed against innocent travelers?"

"Know, my friend," he said, "that it is not as unreasonable as it seems. We owe to it the liberty and security in which we live. Four hundred years ago, our forefathers learned from voyagers, who were welcomed then, that the peoples of distant lands had put armies on the sea, which traveled the world burning cities, ravaging territories and annihilating nations. Our only chance of salvation was to remain unknown. The various kings and republics of our islands agreed to kill all those who disembarked on their shores if they were not born in the archipelago. Our forefathers all swore to observe the treaty. Many unfortunates have been sacrificed thus. For you, I am violating the oath of my ancestors. But you will never return to your homeland, and your existence will not be divulged by my fault."

We arrived at the old man's dwelling, a cabin of planks backed up against large trees and surrounded by an extensive garden in which a multitude of edible plants were growing. My host invited me in, gave me a stool, and disappeared.

A moment later he returned, carrying dishes and bottles. He sat down facing me and said: "Drink and eat, my son, without any more ceremony than in your father's house."

It was a memorable meal. Never had wine seemed so good to me. The fresh cheese and vegetables cooked in milk appeased my formidable hunger delightfully.

The old man dressed me in his best clothes. The charitable man was named Agathos, which means "good," a name thrice merited.

He took me into his garden. "You see here my means of subsistence," he said. "You can work here if you wish, to keep ennui at bay."

I accepted, saying that I like gardening more than any other occupation, being agreeable, poetic and conducive to meditation.

Agathos smiled. "The cultivation of salad vegetables," he said, "requires little labor here. My industry is different. On these plants I raise innumerable insects of the same family. They are ladybirds.[27] The people of the town make delectable preserves with them. They also extract a famous alcoholic beverage from them. You can't imagine the care and the science that livestock demands. Those tiny beings are susceptible. They dread heat and cold. Rain drowns them, wind carries them away. They have mortal enemies in birds and snails. This year has been disastrous for them. I lost a great many last month, a little more than four hundred thousand, as many by virtue of an epidemic as because of an invasion of frogs.

"However," he added, "I lead a happy and worthy life in these travails. I owe nothing to anyone, and no one owes me anything. I'm neither rich nor poor. May I end my days thus."

IV. In which the traveler reports some of Agathos's stories

Several days went by. I reposed in the calm of that new life. I did my best to help the old man. My curiosity grew with the sentiment of my security and I interrogated Agathos inces-

---

[27] Most coccinellids [ladybirds] are predators eating other insects, but there are a few herbivorous species, and other kinds of beetles of similar appearance were sometimes added to the category at the time when the story was written.

santly regarding the inhabitants and the customs of his homeland.

One morning I saw that he was very sad, and when I
questioned him affectionately, he took me into the country
without saying a word, to an elevated place from which one
could see the plain and the ocean.

He sat down on a stone and said to me, in a plaintive
voice: "Today is the twenty-fifth anniversary of a great battle
that we lost in these fields during the war against the Barbarians."[28]

"Good father," I said to him, "tell me about that war."

"Oh, my child," he sighed, "don't ask me that. My heart
bleeds when I think about it. You see me very close to weeping."

"At least," I said, "tell me who these Barbarians are."

"Know first," said the old man, "that our island is not
alone in the midst of the waves. At the time when the sea
swallowed up our ancestors and their territory at a stroke,
when the ocean established its bed over populous lands and
powerful cities, only the high plateaux and mountains emerged
above the plains of the sea, like pyramids erected in commem-
oration of the past—pyramids beneath which the old
Atlantidean continent reposes like an incorruptible cadaver.

"All those eminences were populated by inhabitants
spared by the cataclysm. One of them, although vast and well
protected, nevertheless remained deserted. That is the one we
call the land of the Mainomenes,[29] because it is now the refuge
of a savage, dishonest, quarrelsome nation, an enemy of ours
all all times.

"In ancient days, the absence of living beings on that
land gave rise to the idea of a mysterious curse, and it was

---

[28] If this is construed as a disguised reference to the battle of
Sedan, it might imply that this part of the story was written in
1895, long before its publication.
[29] Mainomenes signifies "madmen," as in the epithet Dionysos
Mainomenos.

believed that the gods forbade its habitation. Legend relates that after many centuries, a large ship ran aground on its shore. No one knows where it came from. It carried for its personnel a troop of faithless men from different lands: thieves, traitors, murderers, forgers, soldiers charged with crimes, prostitutes and licentious or violent women. Under the leadership of a chosen chief, they had taken to the sea in search of a refuge where the vengeance of people could not attain them. The winds, to our misfortune, brought them to our vicinity. They pullulated like rats and lice, for countless generations. From the outset they committed frightful depredations did not belie in any way the ferocity of their origin. That is why they were given the name of Mainomenes, which means 'furious,' people avid for massacre.

"In the long series of ages we have been continually at war with them. They were always vanquished, except for the last time when we suffered an incomprehensible disaster.

"Since that day, their pride has increased immeasurably. They are only occupied in insult and provocation. They affirm that their illustrious race ought to absorb or destroy all the others, in order finally to reign over the entire world. Oh, my son, what a desolating spectacle a world invaded by such pirates would offer!

"At this moment they have a worthy sovereign, King Katagelaste.[30] If such a man, by some impossibility, were born in our country, he would be imprisoned with his brethren, poor devils deprived of sense with crippled brains, or, by virtue of his extravagances, would make idlers and little children laugh in public squares. Caparisoned by an ancient suit of armor too large for him, he drags a long and ridiculous sword around, noisily, so rusty that he would never be able to draw it from its

---

[30] This Greek term, which refers to someone who mocks, survives in the modern designation of the psychological condition of katagelasticism, in which people enjoy laughing at others and seek opportunities to do so, as by contriving practical jokes. Wilhelm II succeeded to the German throne in 1888.

sheath. His words are menacing. To say everything in brief, even his own people find him exaggerated. He had militarized the nation. In the streets of his great city the citizens go abroad in ranks, at the same pace, scullions and little girls marching like soldiers on parade."

"That," I said, "is risible. And the gods are jesting stupidly in opposing such savages to the sons of this Hellene nation, the noblest there ever was. By the way, a doubt crosses my mind in saying that, and I wonder whether any race has been combined with yours, and whether your isle of Atlantis is only inhabited by the descendants of the ancient Atlantideans?"

"Very nearly," said Agathos. "People of other birth, in small number, have insinuated themselves among us, but they have not corrupted the race, for they only marry one another. They came, a long time ago, from a distant Oriental lands. They worship a certain Jehovah and scorn the meat of pigs.

"With that exception, our population is homogenous. The eleven other nations of the archipelago cannot say as much. Also know that our land alone has the right to the name of Atlantis, and retains priority over all the others for the ancient beauty of its civilization and the splendor of its past.

"However, a few imbeciles among us take it into their heads to imitate the mores of another nation, a nation still in its infancy, which inhabits a large and marvelously fertile island to the West. That people has no history; it is a son without a father, free of the weight of tradition but a slave to its labor. It only esteems industry, commerce and speculation—in a word, everything that tends to earn money. People out there only dream about factories, machines, financial conspiracies and other objects worthy of a people who are still savage. Art is unknown there. From that land, a poisonous wind blows in our direction, which corrupts feeble brains. Even their language, still barbaric, dares to mingle its rugged and dissonant words with our soft speech."

Thus the old man educated me, gradually. He often spoke to me about the nearby city, Thalantide, a rich, busy commercial port, the capital of the province.

I knew that the nation was nominally governed by a king, elected by a few nobles. He only reigned for seven years, and resided in the principal city, Atlantopolis the Great.[31]

V. Erythronos

A certain Erythronos exercised the same industry as Agathos in the valley, but his inefficiency prevented him from obtaining good results. His ladybirds were small and tawdry in appearance. He had difficulty selling them, at a low price, for they could only be made into insipid sauces and poor quality conserves. Hateful, jealous and ferocious by nature, that unfortunate competitor had become the old man's mortal enemy. The latter had often said to me:

"When you see a man coming with green-tinted skin and a beard the color of terracotta, draw away rapidly and threaten him with your staff. He's capable of any villainy. One night, he set fire to my house. Not long ago he spread floods of vinegar over my insects. He's plotting my ruin and desires my death."

One day, Agathos had gone to the city on business, and as I was awaiting his return, I saw Erythronos arriving, followed by four soldiers and an officer. The latter said to me in an insolent one:

"Is this the dwelling of Agathos?"

"That's correct," I said. "I'm his nephew, come to help him because of his great age."

"Good," said the man. "We're agents of the Treasury. Your uncle and you are criminals, thieves from the State. This honest citizen has denounced you as offenders, avoiding tax by means of deceitful declarations and inaccurate accounts of your ladybirds."

At that moment, Agathos appeared. As he arrived, he only saw Erythronos, who had prudently remained in the rear.

---

[31] In the early days of the Third Republic, its presidents were elected for seven years.

306

Taking him by the shoulders he began shaking him roughly, calling him a brigand and an arsonist, and repeating that he would break his bones.

The man with the green face howled: "Murder!"

The guards ran and seized Agathos. The officer repeated to him what he had just said to me and drew a long scroll out of his pocket.

"You have declared," he said, "That you possess thirty million insects. It's manifestly the case that you have more. The theft is evident, and you'll be punished

"Please believe that I'm telling the truth," said Agathos, "or count them yourself."

"The man's mocking us," said the Treasury official. "He's a dangerous malefactor. Put him in chains immediately, for fear that he'll do harm." After a moment, he continued: "I estimate that you possess triple. At three drachms fine for each undeclared ladybird, you'll have to pay a rather large sum. We would have stopped there, but for your rebellion just now and the blows with which you assailed this worthy man. You'll regret that excess of violence in prison."

Erythronos advanced and, pointing his finger at me, said to the officer: "I affirm that Agathos has no relatives, His only brother, who is dead, had no children. This one is therefore lying, and is not his nephew."

Agathos tried to speak. He was gagged.

The man of law frowned. "Who are you? Don't hope to deceive me."

"This madman," I cried, "doesn't know what he's talking about. Agathos is my uncle; I know that better than anyone."

"Don't you think," said Erythronos, "that this young man speaks with a strange accent? I believe he's a stranger. He arrived the day after the violent tempest that caused a large ship from the East to sink near here, the debris of which is still littering the shore."

I understood that Erythronos knew our secret, and felt doomed. I was troubled in thinking that the old man would die too, and could not help weeping. That was taken for a confession. I was put in chains. The soldiers took us to Thalantide. Our enemy went with us, rubbing his hands.

As soon as we had entered the outlying districts of the city crowds formed to look at us. People murmured: "It's the murderers of poor Chrysippos" or "There go the bandits of the Torcos Woods who rob travelers and rape and murder young girls."

People shouted as we passed by and ran behind us throwing stones at us. One of them hit the vile ape Erythronos, and punctured his right eye. The wretch ran away, screaming. The populace mistook him for a captive and pursued him. The guards could not prevent him from being torn to pieces.

We finally arrived at the prison, a somber and noxious building. There I was locked up on my own in a narrow cell as dark as a cellar. In fury, I started circling in my ditch like a mouse in a tin can.

VI. The Cell

I had not been in my cell for long when the door opened. An individual entered, followed by a torch-bearer. The jailers went to fetch an armchair. The visitor sat down. He was clad entirely in black and wore large spectacles.

The guards arranged themselves against the wall. One of them advanced and said to me: "Stand up and reply to the examining magistrate.

"Where do you come from?" the magistrate demanded.

"I come from a land where strangers are given a better welcome than they are here," I said. "What do you have against me? What have I done? Why have you arrested me?"

"I'm here to apply the law, not to debate it," said the magistrate. "Do you admit that you were born outside the Archipelago?"

"I can't deny it," I said, shrugging my shoulders, "but in truth, it's much against my will that I visited your accursed island. Is it criminal to be shipwrecked on your coat?"

"Silence! You admit that you're a foreigner. You shall die. Condemned men of your sort benefit from a special grace. They're allowed to choose the death that they prefer; in accordance with their sentiment, they're drowned or hanged. Hurry up and decide. It's necessary that it's done tomorrow, at sunrise."

"I don't want either water or a rope," I cried. "Murder me as you will."

With that, the magistrate wrote a few words in a notebook. Then he got up, wished me good night, and went out with the guards.

I had exhausted all despair. The announcement of that imminent death scarcely moved me to begin with. I thought, dolorously, about the excellent Agathos, certainly condemned as I was. Soon, the horror of my situation appeared to me in its entirety. The dangers I had traversed had made me cherish existence more, and, seeing myself in that catastrophic extremity, I let myself fall into a mortal anguish.

Night fell; my prison became even darker. Between the bars of the narrow ventilation shaft, a beautiful star appeared. I thought that it was mine, which was gazing at me and had come to console me in my final hours. I showed my fist to the pitiless star. Then, throwing myself on the floor, I wept for a long time. In the end, I lay down on my bed and tried to go to sleep.

The door opened again. My cell was illuminated. A young woman came in, followed by three jailers. She dismissed them with a gesture. The men bowed and went out, after having stuck the resinous branches in rings attached to the wall.

I thought I was dreaming. She sat down on the stool and said to me, in a soft voice: "I knew that a stranger was here. One can't let such an opportunity for learning go to waste. Permit me to question you for a moment."

She explained to me at length that she was a woman of letters. She had, she said, acquired a great notoriety with a recent work entitled *Thisbe; or, The Amorous Ass*.

She asked me countless questions that were quite bizarre.

"That's enough!" I cried. "I'm dying tomorrow morning. Leave me in peace until the time I must perish. I don't want this night to serve for your amusement. Your curiosity is exasperating me. Have you no pity?"

Desolate, she persisted. "At least do me the favor of answering one last question," she said. And she added, in a learned tone: "How many ways of making love to the people of your homeland count?"

I replied gravely that we knew of an infinite number. That caused her to marvel.

"By Zeus," she said, "we only know twelve, and even some of those are very uncomfortable and reserved to voluptuous acrobats."

I smiled scornfully. "Truly," I said, "That's a very savage people."

She stood up, and murmured, with simplicity: "My confusion is great, my dear seigneur, in being ignorant of so many beautiful things. I have a marvelous thirst to learn better ways."

At this point I have to draw a thick curtain over my cell; prudish hypocrites demand it; but the reader will divine the lesson that my pupil received. What doubtless astonished her, and by which I was very surprised, is that the beautiful child knew more about it than I did.

VII. The High Priest

I awoke suddenly, struck by rough hands. When they opened, my eyes contemplated the faces of jailers. Memory returned to me. I thought I saw the phantom of Death: a skeleton with transparent bones, crouching in a corner, he was modestly drawing the flaps of his shroud over his knees and silently sharpening a rusty scythe. His hollow orbits were staring at me.

I sat up on my bed and, addressing the judges who had come to preside over my decease, I cried: "Seigneurs, yesterday you gave me a choice between hanging and drowning. Neither of them pleases me, but, in truth, I can only accept being hanged. I've always held water in scorn and hatred, and I don't want to belie the sentiment of my entire life in my final hour."

The magistrates shook their heads benevolently.

"Good," said one. We'll grant you that. Moreover, the reason is excellent. It's regrettable to kill a man of such judgment. But we're not here for nothing, and I beg you not to see us as anything but the instruments of the law, intermediaries between it and the gallows."

A bizarre individual advanced toward me, lowering his eyes. The men of law immediately stood aside and looked up in the air, as if they were studying the trajectories of flies.

The odd fellow was clad in a long orange robe. In his complexion and his bearing he resembled the sellers of elixirs in our public squares, individuals with a talent that is sometimes very estimable, and whose eloquence has give birth to that of our political orators. But he spoke with unction, and I realized that he was a priest.

"Dear son," he said, "rejoice in what is happening to you. Think of the calamities of existence. Contemplate from now on the blissful realm of souls where you will soon be. Would you dare to complain about no longer suffering? You will not have had the time, at the end of your rope, to count to twelve, and already your body will be calm, almost cold, insensible, careless of the wind, the rain, the sun and the snow. O bliss! You will have every right to dwell in a beautiful star, where all the dead lead a joyful live eternally. You will see the gods in their glory and speak to them in familiar terms, for they are not as proud as you might think. You will dwell in the company of all the virtuous people of previous centuries. As for them, they have become honest up there, I assure you. Oh, my child, bless this execution that is taking you so soon to the agreeable cities of death, and thank the divinities who are welcoming you still young, while they often wait to deliver mortals for a long and disastrous series of days."

"Oh, my father," I said, "for I understand that I am your son, my heart is magnanimous, be sure of it. Very close to enjoying that felicity, I suffer in leaving a pious person like you in mortal ambushes, despairs and miseries. I propose a treaty to you by which you would know the bounty of my soul. I permit you to be hanged in my place, and cede that step to you as the more worthy. Do not let any shame hold you back. As for me, I prefer to live and suffer still, and to merit by my virtues to come an eminent place in the star of the dead."

"Alas, my child, I would like that. It has, moreover been predicted for me that I shall end my days between heaven and earth; but, I believe that it will only be as late as possible, and it is a matter here of a substitution inoperable in fact, fraudulent in law and most horribly heretical."

"Hey," said a guard, "the sun's rising. Hurry up."

"It's done," relied the priest. "My pious duty is accomplished. This young man, thanks to my cares, will be able to die in a befitting manner. I wish you all as much."

Who will believe me? At that horrible moment, I was only thinking about the night's adventure. Was it a dream? At the moment of the final departure, an uncertainty is more unnerving than ever.

As I rose to my feet, however, I put my hands on the bed for support, and pricked the right one with a golden pin. Furthermore, I saw several blonde hairs on the sheet, which I would have collected piously in order to keep them if I had not been assured of perishing immediately.

I heard noises in the corridor. Four men with shaven heads came in, clad in orange surplices, and arranged themselves to the right and left of the door. A fifth, of a more consequential appearance, speared then and announced in a grave voice: "The Very Venerable High Priest Katodipsa is here."[32]

---

[32] The Greek prefix *kato* means lower; *dipsa* refers to drunkenness.

The guards and the men of law remained in a silent immobility, and my preacher knelt down and waited, his head bowed.

Then a marvelous old man penetrated into my prison, entirely clad in crimson silk. He was supporting himself with one hand on a scepter and the other on the shoulder of a young priest. His creased forehead was supporting a miter sparkling with rubies, amethysts and emeralds. A long white beard, long curly hair, a slender and straight nose, very bright eyes and narrow, pale lips: such were the features of his fine face, in which gravity, nobility, determination and power were legible. Everyone bowed.

"Where is the governor?" he said.

One of the two magistrates advanced and said: "Here I am."

"A grave event," said the High Priest, "troubled my repose last night. Listen. The twelfth hour had just elapsed. While asleep, I heard a noise similar to that of big waves battering cliffs. The eyes of my soul were filled with a blue light and my god appeared in front of me. While dazzled and prostrate, I was worshiping him and singing his praises, and this is what my ears heard: 'I want you, O my priest, at the hour when I shall make the sun rise tomorrow, to go to the prison. You will find a man there whom I have sent to Atlantis, and whom the judges want to put to death. Tell them to do no such thing, under pain of perishing soon themselves, with their wives and children. Let that man be sacred to all men, for I have destined him to accomplish secret designs.'

"I woke up with a start and said to myself: *These are crazy figments of imagination.* But then, being outside slumber, I heard a terrible voice shouting: 'Obey!' Then there was a great clap of thunder, which you might have heard as well as me.

"So here I am, before you, in order to acquit my divine mission. The law gives me the right to liberate prisoners. But I have said enough, and I beg you to incline, like me, before the will of the god."

In fact, everyone looked at one another, going pale, frightened by the miracle. It seemed to me that things were looking up.

I was handed over to the High Priest. He testified to me all the respect due to a messenger from Heaven. I climbed up with him into his large carriage, drawn by four horses.

When we were some distance from the prison, he put his miter on his knees and, holding his sides, burst into powerful and prolonged laughter. Then patting me amicably in the midriff, he said: "You see, my child, we should never speak ill of the gods; they sometimes come in handy."

VIII. Helena

I had not finished rendering thanks to the pontiff when we arrived at his dwelling. It was a very fine palace dominating the city, from which one could see the sea. An ancient park surrounded it. An avenue of centenarian elms led to the central building.

The carriage stopped in front of the perron. A young woman was leaning over the balustrade whom I recognized very well. It was the visitor of the previous night. I understood that she was the operator of my salvation. *It's true, then,* I thought, *that a good deed never goes to waste.*

She came all the way to the vehicle and, as soon as the High Priest had set foot on the ground she kissed him three times, very religiously. Then she said to me: "Yesterday evening, while going about my meager affairs the city, I heard the sound of a mob and I perceived a multitude of people in agitation. I saw you; I was told about your adventure, and I wanted to save you. I wouldn't have been able to do it without the great generosity and omnipotent amity of the good father."

I thanked her, and was careful to speak to her as if I had never seen her before. She smiled.

She was obviously the mistress of the High Priest. The servants of the gods have delicate tastes. The ecclesiastics of the majority of religions are supposed to abstain from the joys of the flesh, but when, in exceptional circumstances, they infringe that commandment, it is always for an object that compensates them in advance for the tribulations of Hell. They do not damn themselves on credit.

My benefactress, in a Catholic country, would have been judged worthy of the bed of a cardinal-archbishop, not to say a pope; she was blonde, with blue eyes surmounted by horizontal eyebrows very far apart. The nose and mouth were small and the teeth regular and shiny. She walked with a harmonious sway of the hips. Under her blue tunic it was easy to divine firm, beautiful breasts. Precise and charming memories came back to me in a host.

"By all the sacred tribe of the gods," said the High Priest, "Let's go! Can't you see, Helena, that this child is dying of thirst and hunger? We're keeping him standing here as if he desired nothing else. Let's go restore ourselves.

He had spoken, and we turned out backs on the house. Katodipsa directed us through the park. We arrived in an agreeable arbor, a huge tunnel clad in clusters of grapes. We sat down. I don't know exactly how it happened, but numerous servants immediately surged forth, laden with a quantity of delectable things. Some were carrying holy and dusty bottles respectfully, others supporting silver trays on which roasted fowl were fuming. Glasses of large capacity were placed in front of us, which were filled immediately.

"That," I said, after having drunk, "is a very delicious wine, such as I've never drunk before."

"It's the product of the vines of the Great Temple," replied the pontiff. "The King himself only tastes it once a year, for I offer him a bottle for his New Year celebration. But our sovereign is of low birth; he has neither science not finesse, and wouldn't be able to appreciate the merits of such a noble vintage. However, he's so miserly that he accepts my little present with joy, and so vulgar that he hides it in order to drink it all himself. Now try a little of this white, my son, and tell me what you think."

He poured me a full glass, as vast as a helmet in the time of Homer.

"Oh!" I exclaimed. "This is a glorious liquid! I sense my soul being enriched, lightened and swelling as I drink it. That is certainly the emperor of all beverages. You must certainly possess an opulent collection of excellent spirits in this land, for my travels have assured me that, wherever one finds good wine, one is sure of seeing incomparable men, of high mind, great heart and profound sensitivity. Where the vine only produces insipid juice, I've only known ordinary souls. Stop in a city where the juice is adulterated, rancid in its nature, criminally diluted with water and poisons, and believe me, you'll only encounter men of unhealthy, perverted understanding, as vicious and counterfeit as the liquid they drink Now go among beer drinkers, go to Germany—although that land is fortunately unknown to you—and consider the people. Nothing human about them; they're bears, masses of hairy flesh, slow of movement and incapable of thought, sentiment of imagination. In truth, what was the Creator thinking the day when he placed men on those deadly terrains where he had forgotten to plant vines?"

"My child," said my savior, "Don't talk to me about the Creator. I've never seen him, or any other god, so I scarcely believe in the celestial powers. Talk to me instead about Creation, which I adore devoutly. Admire with me the amiable richness of its gifts in all of nature, and how lightly we dispose of them for the short time that we live. Consider a little the beauty of women, the sweetness of good wines and the great, sublime and inestimable imbecility of people. The last point ought to be the dearest to us; it is the basis of our felicity and the keystone of our powerful political edifice. Everywhere that the vulgar are left for a while to turn away from its laws, the result is always a universal calamity. Every time revolutions have been seen fomenting in the populace, massacres, terrors and superhuman horrors have arrived at the same time, the lamentations of those living well, the suffering of the religious and the upheaval of kingdoms.

"Our country has suffered from that, but we've put in good order. We've said to the people: 'You are the master, the king; we obey, love and adore you. We'll build temples to you. We are all brothers, all free and all equal. Leave it to us to make the laws that you want, employ your money and render you the worship that is due to you. We are your servants.' After which the people allow themselves to be led with the best will in the world. We extract more taxes from them than ever. They're submissive to frightful military charges. When they're dissatisfied, the national militia, which they revere, gives them a few blows with a stick. But they're happy, because we call them sovereign, and they applaud when shrewd governors come to them and say: 'We've consented to carry on our shoulders the ingrate burden of political affairs, for love of you!' O marvelous principle of creation! The unshakable foundation of the order of the world. Worthy and idle popular stupidity, without which we, the great, would be nothing!"

Thus the conversation roamed, at hazard, over a thousand various subjects. The High Priest, a jovial and sage seigneur, burst out laughing continually, and my dear Helena gently leaned her feet on mine.

The devout old man emptied his glass three more times. Suddenly, he leaned forward, folded his arms on the table, and on that pillow, went to sleep, snoring.

Helena withdrew her sandals from above mine. She went very pink, looked me in the eyes and said to me, smiling: "He's profoundly asleep, and for a long time. That's his custom, after breakfast. The temple bells don't wake him up."

The invitation troubled me. I don't like putting horns on people when they're not away traveling. But a refusal would have covered me with shame, and I served the lady with the master's beard.

After an hour and a half, the sleeper awoke. He considered us with an anxious eye. Motionless in my armchair, holding my half-full glass, I pretended to be studying the transparent color of its contents. Helena, on the lawn, was modestly picking red sunflowers.

"By all the gods!" exclaimed the High Priest. "I've just had a very strange dream: I dreamed that you cuckolded me!"

We all laughed heartily. Katodipsa poured himself a drink. Then we clinked glasses, for people clink glasses in Atlantis exactly as we do.

"But it's necessary to take stock," said the pontiff. "What do you want to do now."

"Live," I replied. "The manner is of scant importance. I've nearly perished twice this week, I don't want to risk it a third time. It might be without recourse. So I only ask to live in peace, health, leisure and security."

"I understand," said the priest. "With regard to your life, no one will touch it, since I'm protecting you, and I'll give you a good safe conduct, which will render you sacred for everyone."

"But the young man is devoid of resources," said Helena.

"That," sighed Katodipsa, "is the delicate question. I don't want to do things by halves. The child pleases me. But you know how my finances stand, my dear Helena. I spend my income before I receive it, not by virtue of lightness of mind but prudent reflection. For if I were to die tomorrow leaving my coffers full of coins and my heirs a culpable joy, would people say that I was a man of common sense and good order? Quite the contrary, I apply myself to enjoying everything enormously, at great expense, affirming and demonstrating that the present moment is the unique reality. In brief, I rarely have a hundred drachmas in my house. I don't know what I can do, except wait until I receive some money."

"Do better," said Helena. "Tomorrow is the great festival of the god Demos. All the hypocrites in the Archipelago are meeting up on that day in the Great Temple. When you're in the pulpit, tell some fine tale to your congregation. Describe your dream to them. Astonish them with admiration for the envoy of the gods. Then order a great collection in support, promising the Elysian Fields to those who give a great deal and perpetual suffering in Hades to all the rest."

The excellent man clapped his hands. "Helena, my love," he said, kiss me. What a glorious idea! I'll do it. The collectors can travel the city to the sound of trumpets. I can hear—hear, I tell you—the sound of the money raining down on the bronze platters. Oh, my friend how rich you'll be!"

"Good father," I exclaimed, "how can I ever thank you? To save an unknown man, isn't that already too much? And now you're welcoming me, comforting me and enriching me! Divine man!"

"Let's leave it there," he said. "The prayers of this dear child can't remain sterile. I promised to save you; I won't let you die of hunger and poverty."

Helena had left us. She came back with a sheet of parchment. The priest took black-tipped stick out of his pocket, which he used as a pencil. He covered the page with tightly-packed characters, reread it, signed it and handed it to me.

At the top, imprinted in the paper, the sacerdotal arms and motto were inscribed. A worthy preamble flowed on the power of the gods, a good part of which they transmitted to their priests. After that he had written that a man had come on their behalf of the island, and that everyone should treat that emissary well. Those who had no regard for his mission and did not respect him were warned of a thousand torments in this world and the other.

"That," Katodipsa told me, "is a weapon more powerful than all the swords on earth. The believers will adore you; the miscreants will fear you. Now you're a divine, sacred individual. As for the rest, don't worry about it. Come and find me tomorrow evening; we'll count the money collected. In the meantime, here's some small change to keep you going between now and then. There you go!"

So saying, he embraced me affectionately, recommended me not to lose the safe-conduct, and accompanied me as far as the road.

I was surprised not to have seen Helena at the moment of my departure, but as I drew away, thinking about that, I put my hand in my pocket and found a note. The ardent young woman had written very sweet things therein. She told me, in addition, to come during the night to a place in the city where she had her private abode.

IX. Thalantide

It was midday, I had just quit the High Priest. From the top of the hill I could see the broad green triangle of the ocean. The sky seemed to be steeped in white cloud in the vague distance of the horizon. I saw ships dancing in the port. My gaze plunged into the multicolored streets. The houses of Thalantide, in fact, are built with materials of all hues, or painted in red, violet, green or orange. The action of the air, the rain, and also decrepitude, corrected the crudity of those tints and modified the appearance of the old dwellings harmoniously. Time slid its varnish slowly over the walls, and nuanced them with the warm colorations with which its coats the paintings of old masters delightfully.

Canals divided the city into a multitude of artificial islands linked by bridges. The hovels and cabins of the poor people were huddled together to the west over a considerable area. Near the sea and on the hills rose the rich residences. Between the high city and the low city there had to exist, as there does everywhere, a perpetual and felonious war.

There is no spectacle more superb or more gripping than that of a maritime city seen from above, like Antwerp contemplated from the belfry or Marseille from Notre-Dame de la Garde. Ports are the workshops in while human accomplish their most extraordinary labor. They advance their tentacles of cement into the sea and dare to hold the waves prisoner; and twice a day, profiting from the amorous assaults that the male ocean delivers to the female land, fragile vessels laden with men and riches sail without dread toward the high seas, mocking the most ferocious power of nature.

As I wanted to visit Thalantide, I considered attentively the bird's-eye map deployed before my eyes. I did not know where to go first, and devoted myself to learned reflections.

The voyager with a profound mind, I said to myself, *seeks to know the soul of cities. For cities have subtle individual souls. There are stupid ones and spiritual ones, vulgar ones and proud ones. Shall I go to see those palaces and temples with domes the color of gold? No. I shall only comprehend the monuments, the debris of the past, when the complexion of the people who built them has been revealed to me. This city is, above all, maritime; it's to the quays that it's necessary to go first.*

Satisfied with that reasoning, I went down the avenue slowly.

At that moment I was perfectly happy. I had escaped death and anxieties. To that sentiment of liberty and security was added the consciousness of my future glory. Was I not an emulator of Christopher Columbus and Marco Polo? Would history not inscribe my name in a good place, among those of the greatest voyagers and the most astonishing navigators? I hoped firmly to see my homeland again. What consideration my fellow citizens would have for me then!

Alas, my naïve soul forgot envy. It scarcely supposed that few people, on my return, would want to believe me, or that my creditors, indifferent to the grandeur of the fatherland, would pursue me with their inconsiderate rage. That is the destiny of great men. Columbus died in disgrace; I shall render my soul in the hospital. I am proud of that, but not satisfied. Let's pass on.

I followed long roads, quite different from ours, traced in circular, spiral or elliptical curves. In consequence, the facades are convex or concave. The windows are ordinarily round. The dwellings of prosperous people comprise several buildings parallel to the street, separated by courtyards. Each of them dominates by one floor the one in front of it. The flat roofs support gardens with trees, vegetables, flowers and cheerful arbors covered with God's good vines. You can have no idea of the agreeable aspect of those houses, painted in pastel colors, only showing the summits of their five or six buildings, cliffs surmounted and crowned by fruits and foliage.

Colonnettes of stone or sculpted wood sustain open galleries forming projections. Capitals receive the overlap of their arcades. On the entire edifice one senses a concern for and sentiment of proportion. Every dimension is regulated for the harmony of the ensemble, and the architect does not seem, as in some countries, to have composed his plans in order to excite stupefaction or hilarity.

The curvature of the avenues seemed to me at first to be inconvenient for vehicles, dangerous for pedestrians and likely to prolong everyone's journeys considerably. But I saw neither vehicles not riders. Special roads, in straight lines, serve chariots and carriages. An admirable disposition! Remember that more people die in Paris in a single year under the hooves of horses than in a murderous battle.

The canals that I had seen from afar, infinitely subdivided, pass through the dependences of the majority of habitations. Butchers, bakers, merchants of wine, milk, vegetables, etc., bring in their goods on barges. That gave me a good opinion of the people.

These people, I thought, *are philosophers. They willingly reduce the intensity and convenience of transportation in order to increase their tranquility. The odious din of our cities is unknown to them. Their children play outside in all security. These sages esteem and respect life.*

Then I heard a monstrous clamor. I wondered where the racket was coming from, but could not see anything. Continuing my route, I perceived at a street corner a crowd of some three hundred people. Everyone was crying: "To death! Drown him! Flay him! Burn him! Break his bones! Death! Death!"

I drew nearer. A man of about thirty was lying in the gutter. His face was bloody, his clothes torn, his body riddled with wounds. Struck by all the hands that could reach him, he raised himself up at intervals, moaning, as if to beg for mercy.

The blows only rained down harder. The women, pitiless creatures, elbowed their neighbors aside in order to get to the unfortunate fellow, to scratch his face with their fingernails or stab him with needles.

The spectacle made me feel ill. I asked someone: "What has he done?"

"Oh, the wretch!" was the reply. "Oh, the wretch! He's a filthy informer. He revealed to a husband the profligacy of his wife. The husband murdered his spouse. He's now in prison, waiting to be hanged. As for him, we're going to kill him. Look at the traitor's face!"

"In truth," I said, "that's a lot of bruises for something so trivial."

A pretty young woman arrived, armed with a hatchet for splitting wood. She cleaved a passage all the way to the poor devil and raised her arm. I turned away in order not to see. As I went, I heard the last cry of the victim. The crowd fell silent, without dispersing yet. I hastened my pace, sickened.

That's atrocious, I thought. *What savagery! But is it necessary to feel sorry for informers? If only they were treated in that fashion at home. That species of sneaks would be near extinction. That death is a good example.*

As the same instant I was jostled by a troop of people who were running and gesticulating, shouting: "Stop! Stop! It isn't him!"

"Alas," I murmured, "the justice of the crowd is no better than our great legal justice. Poor young man!"

And I continued to follow the streets.

I finally arrived in the port, similar to all others. The ships, small, with sails and oars, resembled those of the Greeks and the Romans.

Then I perceived numerous taverns.

Truly, I said to myself, *I'm stupid. I reflected maturely as to where I would find the reflection of the soul of this people. The soul of a people is in the tavern. That's certain. It's the popular microcosm. Between tables stained by lees, the spirit of the mass in concentrated and concretized. The will, the de-*

sires, the vices and the virtues of the plebeian is formed there, develops there, is exited there and blossoms there. That is where mobs are born, elections are trafficked and upheavals of humankind are prepared. In truth, it must be said that all elective power emanates from the tavern. Every democratic constitution leads to the reign of the wine-merchant. How many men, back home, having commenced their harangue standing on a barrel, have ended it on the tribune as dictators?

Having said that, I went in and sat down.

X. The Tavern

"Hey!" I shouted. "Bring me wine."

My bizarre accent impressed the noisy clientele of the tavern, but I was still wearing my peasant garments, and my appearance reassured everyone.

At the table where I had sat down, several sailors were chatting and drinking. The one nearest to me, a man with a white beard, greeted me politely.

"You're an old mariner," I said to him, "And must have seen many lands."

"That's true. In the forty years I've been a navigator, I've learn to know the coasts of the Archipelago. I've never surpassed the line of the king's triremes that forbids access to unknown seas, though, as a few others have done. My longest voyage was one that I made for twelve entire months along the wretched littoral of the isle of the Mainomenes. A sad escapade. I lived miserably on bitter beverages and old potatoes. Nowhere have I seen people so heretical or so unpleasant. Nature is ingrate there, the soil miserly and the air so corrupt that I caught an afflicting malady that I can't decently name."

At that moment several other drinkers started shouting so loudly that I could no longer hear anything else. I listened to what they were saying, therefore, and tried to grasp its meaning.

"They're mocking us," howled a tall, thin fellow with a squint, whose voice dominated the racket. "What! Work like that for six drachmas a day! Can you live on that? Add it up. To slake your thirst you shell out a good four drachmas. That's a necessary expense, without which you can't work. Our profession gives us a perpetual thirst. Is it with two drachmas, then, that you can feed yourself, clothe yourself and lodge your family? I'm not talking about the small expenses of existence. Oh, indigent worker, perhaps one day you'll know you strength and remember your rights. Get up and fight if you don't want to perish from hunger."

"He's right," said the others.

"Look as well," the orator went on, "at the unjust manner in which we're paid. Poor caulkers of ships like you and me barely scrape a living. Slaves are less unfortunate. We're clad in dismal rags, poorly nourished, ill-considered, scarcely drunk once a week. In truth, it would be better to die than endure so much misery. Now look at those fat master pilots. They're paid three times as much as us. Do they have larger stomachs, more delicate throats, costlier needs or greater desires than ours? Certainly not, that's impossible. There's only one price for bread and wine. We're exactly similar men, equal by nature. Why are wages so different? Don't tell me, as our adversaries do, that a master pilot knows more than us, that his job is more difficult, that it takes him years to learn it. So what? If there are men more knowledgeable, more skillful and more intelligent than us, it's the fault of the gods, not ours."

"If you owned ships," shouted my neighbor, the sailor, "you wouldn't think like that."

"Son of a bitch," said the caulker, "Who's paid you to contradict me all the time? It's traitors like you who are preventing us attaining our goal, which is to live well and work less."

"Don't you see," the mariner replied, laughing, "that on the day when your fellows are paid like pilots, no one will take the time any longer to serve an apprenticeship, or the trouble to study the sea and the currents. Caulkers would take the helm and run the ships on to the rocks of Sikus and the sands of Colocusthe. By Poseidon, I wouldn't embark that morning!"

"Look at that old man in infancy! He's lost his teeth and still wants to bite me! Don't bore us with your nonsense. You're not of our epoch, you're reasoning in the fashion of our grandfathers."

"And you," said the old man, standing up, "are talking like a man who wants to become a senator like the filthy Ictis, who got himself elected by spouting the same stupidities."

The audience smiled. The caulker went pale, and drank in order to give himself countenance. He went on, forcefully:

"You now, however, you old viper, that the welfare of my comrades is my sole ambition. And why, if you please, shouldn't I be a senator? If that came about, believe that your affairs would go better. Earn twice as much, three hours' work a day at the most, the founding of national free taverns where everyone could drink as much as they liked, and a thousand other admirable and necessary advantages: those, my friends, are the reforms of which I dream, reforms indispensable to the grandeur of the people, the felicity of the proletariat, the sublime and irrevocable Progress of laborious humanity. In the Senate, my voice would dominate all the others, for they'd tremble at the thought that democracy entire is standing behind me. And know well, old octopus, that I'd have the eyes put out of criminals of your species, paid by our masters to abuse us!"

The assembly applauded, and showed its esteem for the orator by means of cries of joy. The refractory sailor, threatened and told to get out, made his escape as best he could.

Then an individual sitting next to the caulker climbed on to a table and shouted: "Companions, have no doubt about it, Espinosos is a dozen times right. He alone is capable of rendering us justice. You know now what great projects he's meditating. Permit him to accomplish them. Elect him in place of that renegade Ictis, who has us massacred by the hoplites when we dare to complain. That's all he does for us. Punish him! We have three months to prepare for the triumph of the shipworkers. Down with Ictis! Long live Espinosos!"

And the drinkers took up the refrain in chorus: "Long live Espinosos!"

XI. The Great Archinatos

There is, I said to myself as I went out, *some appearance of truth in the proverb that the voice of the People is the voice of God, for that voice is identical everywhere.*

Continuing my peregrination through the city, I observed several strange things. The most marvelous appeared to me to be the abundance of gold and its vulgar employment. Vagabonds cooked their pittance in it; vessels were fashioned in it, pots of every species and household utensils for the usage of poor folk. I saw children playing quoits with ingots of the precious metal. Five or six saucepans from a hostelry frequented by the lower orders would easily have paid my debts in France.

As gazed open-mouthed at a butcher's table whose top was a long, broad a thick plate of gold, I saw a handsome priest in a long orange robe coming toward me. I accosted him and, showing him the cause of my astonishment, I said to him: "I come, Sire Priest, from a land where that substance is rare and venerated, an instrument of good fortune and limitless power. In my homeland it procures everything, honest and dishonest; and virtue in our countries is estimated in accordance with the quantity of gold that it requires to yield it. If you desire the amour of a virgin, if you covet an honorific title, if you want to be assured of the devotion of your friends, you take out your purse, and if it is well-garnished with gold coins, you will be contented in all your enterprises."

"I don't know what your nation is," said the ecclesiastic, "but I recognize you as the envoy of the gods, the protégé of the High Priest—in sum, the man with whom the entire city is occupied this morning. Suffer that I adore you."

"No, no," I said, "I won't suffer it. Merely reply to my previous question."

"Well," he said, "in our islands, for a long time, gold was as sovereign as in your homeland. Silver money has replaced the old, but mores are still the same."

"Undoubtedly," I said, "this land abounds in newly discovered mines, or your rivers carry flakes, like the rivers of Chalcidice, where your forefathers the Greeks went to collect them?"

"No, gold is naturally rare in the Archipelago, but one of our ancient scholars rendered it common by means of a memorable discovery."

"What!" I cried. "You manufacture gold?"

"It's true, and if you have the time to listen to me, you'll know how it was done for the first time."

I accepted, and he commenced:

"Eight centuries ago, the value of everything was, as you say, estimated as a certain quantity of the metal in question. Only noble lords, rich merchants, the heads of the Church and prostitutes of great renown possessed it. At that time, there lived an old and savant priest named Archinatos. His long, strange life was spent in arid secret studies. Nasty rumors ran around on his account. He was reputed to be affiliated to the subterranean powers, and, although his activities were unknown, everyone repeated that they were impious.

"A high-ceilinged room, tiled and vaulted, served as his laboratory. On the floor and on shelves fixed to the walls, singular jars and bottles were arranged. By night, passers-by heard inexplicable noises and saw the high windows illuminated by rapid flashes of white light, as if lightning were enclosed behind the panes.

"The master had a disciple, who left us the story that I'm about to tell you, and also the formula by means of which we make gold.

"One evening, old Archinatos is poring over his furnace, surveying his crucibles. He is troubled. His hands are trembling. He is murmuring anxious phrases and stirring the ardent embers. Red liquid is boiling in retorts, and the alembic is making a terrible noise.

"The terrified pupil looks at the quivering Archinatos. He has never seen such emotion. He senses that the old man, reaching the conclusion of his labors, is attempting a final and decisive gamble tonight.

"With long forceps, Archinatos the Great grasps two bronze receptacles on the fire. Drop by drop, he pours their fuming liquid into an iron vase, which then rings like a bell, reddens and swells, its coiled tubes agitating and whistling. The priest, upright, his arms folded, considers the experiment. The noise ceases, and everything resumes its habitual form and color.

"Archinatos, fainting, lifts the lid. He looks. He waits. Finally, he plunges his hand into the cooled apparatus and pulls out the residue that he finds there: a few green crystals with red reflections. He contemplates them dubiously. Their weight, light at first, seems to be increasing by the second. Soon, his hand can no longer support them, and falls alongside his body. But the hot stones remain encrusted there. He can no longer move his fingers, and the paralysis rises all the way to the shoulder. Approaching the light of the furnace, he sees and understands: his entire arm has been transmuted into gold.

"He falls. The disciple runs forward.

"'Don't come near me!' cries the master. 'I'm going to die. Soon after, cut off this hand and enclose what it is holding in a steel container. It's the only metal refractory to my discovery.'

"The disciple, beside himself, contemplates the old man. A superhuman joy illuminates the wrinkled face of Archinatos. 'My son,' he says, 'may you find such a beautiful death, later. I've discovered today what I've been seeking for sixty years. I possess the secret for which my master and his ancient precursors pursued for five centuries. Fortunate is the man who, like me, attains the distant goal that he has proposed for himself and dies immediately, heaped with a divine satisfaction. Adieu, my son.' He falls silent, and at the same instant, renders his soul to the gods.

"Thus died Archinatos the Great."

Moved by that story, I took my leave of the priest, who wanted, in quitting me, to kiss the hem of my robe three times.

At nightfall, I remembered that Helena was waiting for me, and went to join her at her house. The dear child was putting the last touches to a novel that she had just written in three days, with the aid of her secretary: a very fine work, too! But the false virtue of our country would assuredly have found it too licentious.

"I shall not relate the welcome that she gave me, nor our pastimes until morning. That which only interests me I shall pass over in silence. The labors of which I could speak, in any case, are not susceptible of veritable novelty, and are carried out in very nearly the same forms in all the countries of the world, as Strabo proves in the ninth volume of his *Geography*.[33]

XII. The Festival of the god Demos

The following morning, quite early, I resumed my exploration of Thalantide. The aspect of the city had changed. Only people in their Sunday clothes were to be seen. The shops were shut; the streets were overflowing with drunkards.

Remembering that the day was consecrated to the god Demos, I decided to witness his celebration and went to the temple.

A considerable crowd had gathered all around it. It was a monument of bad taste but rich and immense. The high columns sustaining a roof resembled the Ionic columns of ancient

---

[33] Book IX of Strabo's *Geographica* is the second of three volumes describing the Greece of his era (the first century B.C.), commencing with Attica. It includes a brief account of the prostitutes of the temple of Aphrodite in Corinth, which was greatly exaggerated by subsequent fabulists.

Greece, but they were swollen like barrels and sculpted in marble veined with red and white. One might have mistaken it for a colossal pork-butcher's shop. The capitals, bases and moldings were all gilded. Allegorical figures were accumulated in the frontons symbolizing, I believe, the popular virtues, without exception. Distributed everywhere one saw statues of benefactors of the people, in numbers so great that I envied the nation, heir to so many benefits.

I climbed the steps and went into the sanctuary. It was full of a silent audience. Incense and candles were burning everywhere. The priests were putting the final touches to the preparations for the solemnity.

In the background I perceived the formidable idol. The god, seated on a sculpted throne, was twenty meters in height. He was fashioned in bronze and clad in scarlet veils. The head, very small in proportion to the enormity of the body, was crowned with branches. His prodigious limbs, swollen by tormented muscles, supported terrible large extremities. One of the hands of Demos held a hammer and the other a symbolic two-edged sword. His enamel eyes shone in the gloom, reflecting the illuminations of the altar.

Whenever a servant, while decorating it, brushed the statue lightly, it resonated for a long time, like those Oriental bronzes that the wind causes to vibrate. Then the faithful prostrated themselves, affirming that the god was speaking, and each of them attributed a meaning to his mysterious words. For that day, the divinity was to designate a viceroy personally, and many men had come to beg him to select them.

A stand had been erected facing Demos. On the highest level, in a pulpit sparkling with gems, my friend the High Priest was enthroned. He was wearing his two-stage miter, the miter he wore on important days. Motionless and draped in his embroidered mantle, he resembled a simulacrum of the god, seated facing the other and presiding over his worship. On the inferior steps, the members of the clergy were huddled in hierarchical order.

Suddenly, trumpets sounded, the members of the congregation fell to their knees and Katodipsa stood up, leaning on his crosier.

"Very dear brethren," he said, in a grave tone, "We are united before our master, the very good, very strong and very just Lord. He is our common father. Nothing of him is sweeter that the fraternity in which we live, and which assembles us at his feet. Our quarrels irritate and afflict him, as the father of a family is irritated and afflicted by hostility that rises between his grandchildren."

At that moment, the priest who was swinging the censer let go of it, by mistake. Demos received it full in the face; he did not blink, but he rendered a horrible sound a dozen times louder than the great bell of Notre Dame de Paris. The fearful faithful did not know how to interpret the event, and believed that the divinity was very annoyed. The poor fool of an ecclesiastic stood there stupidly, still holding the remnant of the cord of the perfume-burner in his maladroit hands.

"A miracle!" cried Katodipsa. "A miracle a thousand times miraculous! Understand that parable! Heaven inspires me at this moment, my brethren, and I understand all that it wants to say. The incense is the nation inflamed with amour for its god. It will break everything, the chains, bonds and obstacles by which its enemies would like to retain it; it will break them, I tell you, and hurl itself into the lap of the invincible and all-loving power. That signifies both that our prayers have been heard and that the delectable odor of our piety is so agreeable to the sublime Demos that he is drawing it to him, in order better to respire, to scent, to possess the incense of our common devotion.

"Sing, my brethren, sing the praises of Demos. Your holy orisons will rise up to him. He is the inexhaustible source of all wealth. Adore him, and he will heap you with the greatest goods of the earth. Flattering words are his preferred nourishment. Do not be miserly with them and you will receive solid benefits in exchange.

"And you, O Demos Esomantos, enlighten us now as of old. Remember that on this day every years you designate a new governor for the region of Thalantide. Speak, and we will bow down. You see us all, Lord, awaiting young divine word."

The High Priest fell silent. Then commenced the accomplishment of the strangest rite of the ceremony. Subaltern priests moved around the temple giving each adult male a little square of papyrus. Each received it on his knees, with so much demonstration of respect that I thought at first that it was a host of the Catholic species. I realized my mistake on seeing that the majority were writing their name on it. I did as everyone else was doing and wrote mine.

The citizens arranged themselves in two files and the long procession advanced toward that statue. As they passed before it, the people gave their leaf to a priest. That one transmitted it to others installed on the steps of a large ladder stood up against the statue. The most highly perched collected the pieces in a basket and then threw them through an opening into the empty head of the motionless divinity. The procession went on for a long time. Eventually, everyone having accomplished his office, a lid was put on the head of Demos, and the crowd remained expectant in silent trepidation.

Katodipsa rose to his feet for the second time. He descended the steps of the platform slowly, set down his crosier and knelt down, lowering his forehead to the ground. The entire audience prostrated itself at the same time.

The man placed on the highest step of the ladder seized the bronze head of the simulacrum in his hands. It was certainly articulated, since the operator was able to shake it rudely three times and make it oscillate in all directions.

The assembly was breathless. One might have thought that its members were a thousand gamblers, trembling and full of hope, at the decisive moment when the sparkling wheel of the lottery rotates. All of them, pale, with open mouths and clenched fists, were staring at the idol with shining eyes.

The officiator introduced his fingers into the divine throat. He pulled out a white square, which he folded as he turned round. He sealed it and handed it to the priest on the second rung. That one passed it to the man on the third, and so on, all the way to the bottom.

Having finally received it, the High Priest stood up again and returned majestically to his throne. He broke the seal, and said in a loud voice: "The god has chosen Agurthes!"

Then, all the men uttered a long despairing cry, as if they had received a mortal and painful wound. One might have thought that a single voice was raising that frightful clamor toward the vaults, the frightful voice of a monster whose throat had be cut, the plaintive voice of vanquished ambitions frustrated of their hopes.

I saw an old man clad in a scarlet toga advance toward the altar. More than a hundred people threw themselves at his feet, crying:

"Agurthes, I am your slave!"

"Agurthes, give me you orders, whatever they might be!"

"My wife is beautiful, O Agurthes!"

And he could not rid himself of all those people, who seized him by the robe or stopped him by prostrating themselves before him. He succeeded nevertheless in arriving before the statue, and cried: "O Demos, your servant Agurthes thanks you! You have chosen me to conduct your people for another year. I will always direct them in the right path, be sure of it. No wrong or injury will be done to them during my government. May the birds of the sky come to eat my eyes if I do not keep my word."

"This Agurthes," a neighbor who realized that I was uninformed told me, "has been administering us or forty years. He possesses the favor of Demos. He's a good lord, but too expensive. He maintains in the city, at our expense, a hundred and ninety-seven courtesans of the greatest beauty and high reputation. I won't mention those of lesser importance, all young and pretty, of whom he possesses a marvelous collection. So he's a great inventor of new taxes. He works all night to spend them, and by day, with his head in his hands, he thinks of ways to draw into his municipal coffers the drachmas in our wallets. Believe that he does it successfully. We pay taxes on our slippers, or dogs, our carriages and our wives."

"This election of a governor," I said, "differs from the fashion of appointing the Senate. Why, in the former case, is it the god who chooses, and in the latter the citizens?"

"Good peasant," said the man, "it comes to the same thing. In any case, don't ask me to explain the constitution. First of all, it's dangerous, and then, neither I nor anyone else has ever been able to understand it."

"Very well," I said. "But with regard to Agurthes, I believe I know the name. Isn't he a great general, an illustrious captain in the last war?"

"You're joking," said the citizen. "When the Mainomenes attacked us, that great general was in command of the army and the fleet of Thalantide. One morning, he took to the sea with sixty triremes of war full of good mariners and veteran soldiers, fooled by a hundred and thirty galleys less strong but new and fast. He encountered the Mainomenes manning thirty-five ships from the times of the Kephalides. The enemy turned away and tried to flee. The pursuit commenced. Agurthes did it so well that he ran his ships aground on the great sandbanks off Colocuathe. The enemy stopped and peppered out ships with fire-arrows. Our admiral, gripped by colic, jumped into the sea, climbed on to a galley less exposed than the rest and fled under full sail, followed as best they could by the vessels still afloat. The majority of our big ships were burned to the waterline and their crews almost all perished during and after the action, for the Mainomenes massacred the prisoners.

"Agurthes, returned to port, raged and wailed that the gods had done him a bad turn. 'No matter,' he said, 'my fleet is lost but I still have my army.' He shut himself in the city with all his troops—to wit, a hundred and twenty thousand men, as many foot-soldiers as cavalry. He forbade them, on pain of death, to cross the walls.

"Fifty thousand barbarians disembarked and besieged us. An enterprise so presumptuous ought to have cost them dear, but our chief prudently refused to engage them in battle, saying that it would be an irreparable misfortune to lose it. 'The sage tactic,' he pronounced, 'is to wait. The enemy will become weary.' But we had no food. All the animals in the city were eaten, including the rats in the sewers and the shrew-mice in the burrows. When Agurthes found his own table devoid of meat, he capitulated, on condition that no harm was done to him and that his property would be respected."

Katodipsa stood up thereafter and commenced his speech in my favor, First of all he related the miraculous dream by means of which the gods had enlightened him. He added a host of details and terrifying presages. He made the most flattering portrait of me.

"Give," he said, as he concluded, "give with full hands, my brethren, to the envoy of the celestial powers. Your offering will be returned to you a hundredfold. Your affairs will prosper throughout your life. After your death, you will participate in divine enjoyments."

And collectors went through the crowd, and people put their hands in their pockets. One threw a drachma, another a handful of silver coins. Observed by my neighbors, I generously contributed the remainder of my money.

The religious festival was over. The temple emptied out. I took advantage of that to explore it at leisure. I did not see anything remarkable there except for the images of the three principal monsters once cast down by the terrible Demos. One was named Basileia and wore a closed crown. The second was named Treskheia and displayed a bloody wound in the breast. The third, Paradosis, although riddled with wounds, appeared to be still breathing.

An initiate came to tell me in a low voice: "Those demons aren't dead; I think we'll see them again someday." He told me that the paintings represented Royalty, Religion and Tradition.

Outside, the city presented the most singular aspect. Country folk had invaded Thalantide. Drunken musicians were playing barbaric tunes. Men and women were dancing in the intersections, while little children threw fireworks at their feet. The tavern-keepers had installed tables and benches in front of their establishments, with the results that in many of the streets the pedestrians had to turn around or sit down and drink with everyone else.

One that occasion, the local people abandoned all modesty. Many hands wandered under skirts without anyone getting annoyed; and toward evening, I perceived couples, of whom nothing could be seen but the backs, lying on the ground in the most crowded places.

XIII. The Necessity of Departure

On the evening of the same day when Demos was fêted I was in the house of the beautiful Helena again, engaged in my amours. I had no suspicion that I would soon be quitting her; but for a long time, a malign divinity had been taking pleasure in breaking my sweetest bonds by means of ridiculous accidents.

In one another's arms, on thick cushions covered with painted silk, we were enjoying ourselves with those delicate marvels that nature gives to gods and humans in order to enable them to kill time, to perpetuate their race and to amuse themselves between meals. Prudes cannot abide anyone talking about the marvels in question. They are an object of horror to them. The ancients, however, divinized them; and no worship was ever rendered more wholeheartedly, nor more sincerely served. But hypocritical old men, who claim to govern our century, prefer to frankness a niggardly appearance of virtue.

At the precise moment when voluptuous pleasure was extracting ineffable groans from us, the bedroom door opened and Katodipsa appeared. Helena immediately fainted, with a

337

consummate science, but I remained, stark naked, white, immobile and annihilated.

"Please don't disturb yourselves," said the High Priest, sitting down. "Continue; I'll be patient."

"Alas," I cried, "I'm a wretch. Now I've betrayed my benefactor."

"Not at all, my son, not at all. May it please Heaven that no worse treason is ever done to me. These adventures are familiar to me, and I'm not one of those poor fellows who place their honor in that exposed location where you are presently sowing such a fine crop of horns for me. You could have testified in another manner the gratitude that you promised me, but, in truth, I can't hold it against you. Am I not the cause of this? What do you think I thought when Helena tormented me like a remedy in order to obtain your mercy. Do you take me for a fool? The dear child desired you. I don't regret having saved you. My age doesn't permit me to give her sufficiently frequent proof of my affection. I'm an old charger fatigued by a thousand expeditions, and henceforth, a languid trot at long intervals is all that I can manage. I am, therefore, obliged to tolerate her occasional amusements. I think the dose is sufficient now; my sweet Helena must be sated for a while, so you can leave."

"Well," I said, "Since it's thus, listen. A wise man like you must know that such a woman isn't so easily sated. On the contrary, for the appetite increases in eating, if one can believe the doctors of my homeland. If I go, do you think she'll leave it there? Not at all. She'll need four lovers to replace me, so you'll be cuckolded fourfold instead of one. You won't gain anything. Add that perhaps her gallants might not be good fellows like me. They might rob you, mock you, and publish your misfortune in the city. Abandon your plan. Take me as a substitute. No one will know and everything will be for the best."

"Young man," said Katodispa, smiling, "Your reasoning is faulty. Helena has already had a great many servants. I've prevented her from getting strongly attached to any of them by making them disappear, one after another, by persuasion, brib-ery or suppression. Don't force me to have you killed."

"I'll go, then," I cried, "but don't revoke your benefits and leave me your safe conduct."

"Certainly," said the pontiff. "I'll conserve my protection for you, and know that, in addition, I've received fourteen silver talents for you. The collection was copious and worthy of us. Agurthes alone has given three thousand drachmas. I've sent a small sum on your behalf to old Agathos, whom you mentioned to me. You can take all the cash you can carry. The rest will be given to you by a money-changer in Atlantopolis on presentation of this letter.

"These are my decisions: I'll grant you tonight to say your adieux to Helena. At first light a servant will come to find you on my behalf. He'll give you two bags, one full of money and the other of food supplies. The slave will explain to you the route to follow to reach the capital and will accom-pany you as far as the gate of Thalantide. You'll march with-out looking back and without taking a single step that would bring you closer to our city. Otherwise you'll perish. Go on foot; it's the only way of not being remarked while traveling. Only make use of the safe conduct in case of extreme danger. If, in spite of its office, you find yourself in peril, have me notified, and I'll help you."

He fell silent, embraced me paternally and left the room. Helena immediately emerged from her faint. Although uncon-scious, she had heard the entire conversation. At first she sobbed like a little fountain. That did not last long, and she fell into accord with me when I showed her the necessity of taking full advantage of our last night.

The first indecisive light of morning had scarcely filtered through the curtains when someone knocked on the door. I got dressed, and kissed dear Helena a hundred times; she was in tears because I would never see her again. She had wept with the same abundance on the departure of my thirty-three prede-cessors, her lovers. I learned five days later from a traveler that a one-eyed judge and a market porter had shared my succession and fulfilled my prophecy.

I went out and found the slave. He was carrying the agreed two bags. We traversed the sleeping city silently, the roofs and highest walls of which were gilded by the rising sun. We went up the hill as far as the fortified gate from which the road to Atlantopolis departed. I looked at the sea and the city one last time through the white mists of dawn.

Then the servant said: "You must go straight ahead until dusk, through two large towns and seven villages. You must not stop anywhere, except in bare country, to stop and eat. You must not speak to anyone and must respond evasively to any questions. My master will know everything you've said and done. If you don't slow down you'll arrive around nightfall in a small town, Arkaios-Prourion. You can stay there for a while if you wish. From there, continue your journey as you wish, but don't think of returning to Thalantide."

He gave me my light baggage, which I hooked over my shoulders by means of leather thongs. Then he bid me adieu and remained on the road to watch me depart.

I cut a branch from a bush, carved it rapidly, and made a staff adapted to my stature. Finally, I started walking, singing in order not to weep.

XIV. The Beginning of the Journey

I walked all day, sad and anxious, paying no attention either to the countryside or the towns. I pressed my pace, even running at times, because I was in such a hurry to reach Arkaios-Prourion. I resembled a gnat fallen into a spider's web, to whom the hope has been left of getting out of it, on condition of making haste. Katodipsa's voice, still resonating in my ears, frightened my heart and gave me legs. I thought about Lot fleeing Sodom consumed by the fire of Heaven, dreading to turn round, like me. I knew that the High Priest was powerful enough to make of me, not a statue of salt, but a cadaver bleeding in the dust, floating in a stream or hanging from some thick branch. In all passers-by I found a suspicious manner, and every peasant seemed to me to be an attentive spy or a disguised executioner charged with putting me to death.

Toward midday I sat down under an elm distant from any habitation. I opened the bag of food and lightened it as much as I could. I did not delay long and resumed my course precipitately.

Short before nightfall I reached the end of that stage of my journey. Delighted to find myself in a place where I would be more at liberty, I stopped and considered the locale at length. It was a sizeable town on the bank of a river. A military acropolis bearing a crown of fractured ramparts surmounted by old towers rose up in an amphitheater on the sides of a hill. That ancient ruin, dominating the houses from a great height, seemed still to be protecting them, reminding them by its wounds of the history of ancient sieges and great battles.

In the distance, eyesight perceived nothing but hills covered with vines or forests. The river ran from valley to valley, describing a thousand harmonious curves in which the sky and the clouds were reflected.

I followed an avenue shaded by tall trees, traversed a populous outlying district and passed over a humpbacked stone bridge. There, fishermen were casting their lines and children were leaning over, contemplating a pinnace that was going upstream with a slow majesty.

Further away, on the quay, stood the statue of a man, standing up and leaning on a pile of books. He was looking at the most distant horizon, like the bronze portrait of Admiral Ruyter in Flessingue in Holland. Without the volumes depicted on the monument, I would have thought that he was a great man of war, so bellicose did the individual seem. Perhaps, instead, he was some roaring prophet, once celebrated, born in the vicinity.

As I was standing still, in profound reflection, a man approached and spoke to me.

I am the ordinary prey of the tiresome. An excessive politeness prevents me from driving them away, even when they are annoying me excessively. I could hardly take a step without being embarrassed by some tedious old man or a dogged talker. This ne, although still young, was the most enraged I had encountered

"You see there," he cried, "the state of Chrenes, the great Chrenes. You certainly know him. Doubtless you've read his works? An admirable man, Chrenes; I would say very admirable, more admirable than any other."

"No," I replied, "no, I don't know this Chrenes at all. I've never read his works. But I believe that he's admirable, since you say so."

"Is it possible?" said the loquacious fellow, more surprised than if he had seen a donkey on a roof, "to be unaware of such an individual!"

"I'm traveling for my education," I murmured, "and I'd be annoyed only to see things already known to me. I consider as a benefit an encounter with any new object. In addition, I'm not a scholar..."

"Poor man!" cried the city-dweller. "Know that Chrenes was a great writer of past centuries. He composed, it's said, many excellent works. I can't talk about them, never having read any. As for that effigy, I can tell you that it's fine bronze and dates from three hundred years ago. The sculptor was a skillful artisan, as you can clearly see by the beauty of the work. It isn't maintained and cleaned as it ought to be, but the money is lacking for that."

"What are you complaining about?" I said. "In my homeland there are public gardens in which statues are put in such great quantities that they're almost touching, but in the trees and the nearby lawns, a quantity of pigeons, turtle-doves, large sparrows, magpies, blackbirds, ducks and other fowls are nourished, whose role is to idle continually on the simulacra of stone or bronze, so the poor great men are encrusted like the ladder of a hen-house. That makes us think that there's no honor without admixture. And our people, philosophical and fond of allegory, see in that ordure the image of that which pretentious historians spread over the most illustrious and most respectable memories."

"Good, good," said the bore, annoyed at being interrupted. "Let's pass on. I want to show you the old castle. Don't fear importuning me. You want, I believe, to educate yourself. I'll take charge of that. You'll know everything I know, unless I run out of saliva. In any case, we'll have a drink, if you like."

"Let's go right away," I begged.

"No," he said, "I'll take you to the castle. Afterwards we'll visit the rest of the town at leisure."

My tyrant seized me by the arm and drew me through rising streets, pronouncing words without number and without consequence, to which I was no longer listening. He talked about himself, his wife, his children, his neighbors, his lawsuit, the temperature, the fish in the river and the burden of taxes. He greeted all the passers-by, and to those who stopped he said, pointing to me: "This is a seigneur I'm showing around for his education. He didn't even know the name of Chrenes."

I became enraged, and would have preferred to hide on a clump of nettles. When we met young women he smiled with a malicious expression, then named their lovers for me and related their adventures. There was no end to it.

We arrived at the ruins via a step stairway. A long oval enclosure, interrupted by crumbling towers, sustained a terrace planted with trees, where one could still see the vestiges of razed constructions.

"Nothing known," he cried then, "can give you an idea of the antiquity of these walls. I don't know it myself. You see, in that building, the window with iron bars? It's that of an ancient cell. There, the unfortunate King Theodoros was imprisoned, the next to the last of the Argide dynasty. That prince remained there for forty years while his servants reigned in his name. Death terminated his captivity. That dates back thirty centuries at least.

"Under our feet are subterranean tunnels of infinite length. No one knows where they end. Weapons have been found there, sarcophagi and objects of great curiosity.

"Contemplate now that immense landscape. But for those hills one could see Thalantide. It wouldn't need much to be able to perceive the sea."

He named each of the hamlets, streams and accidents of the terrain for me. He discoursed about every house. My ears were buzzing, my head resonating; my eyelids closed. I was drunk, furious, terrorized.

I wanted to finish with it. When he turned his back to me I fled at a fast run. I heard him calling me, and then pursuing me. Bounding like a tiger, leaping down steps and over ditches, I tried to outdistance him. Futile fatigue! Finally, I turned the corner of a street, threw myself into the kitchen of an inn and knocked over two cooking-pots and an old woman as I went in.

I dined in that house and went to bed soon afterwards. My slumber was troubled by terrible dreams, in which Katodipsa always played a role.

I got up late, asked for directions, and departed immediately. I had become joyful again, having completely forgotten Helena and lost all anxiety on the subject of the High Priest, whom I had obeyed exactly. After leaving the town I found myself in dense woods populated by multicolored birds.

XV. Constantin

As I was walking through the forest, following a path bordered by twisted mossy trunks, I perceived a young man walking in front of me, who seemed to be drunk or mad, or under the empire of a profound sadness. I followed him at the same time as my route, only being careful not to attract his attention by the sound of my footsteps.

Gesticulating and shouting very loudly in a strange language, first he sat down at the foot of a large oak. Then he held his head in his hands, without moving any longer. Suddenly, he got up abruptly and tried to climb the tree. He succeeded, and sat in the fork at the birth of a rather large branch. Finally, he took a rope out of his pocket and began to knot it around the tree. I understood then that he wanted to hang himself.

I ran forward and, with my eyes raised toward the serene and despairing man, I begged him to come down. He did not want to hear of it, and from the height of the foliage he affirmed that he found himself in such an extremity and frightful calamity that it only remained for him to die.

To that, I replied in my bad Greek: "I'm a fellow of good breeding, and I wouldn't want to cross the designs of anyone, but at least come down for a moment and have a drink with me, for in the article of death as in that of marriage, it gives mental strength and courage, without which one can't pass lightly from liberty to slavery or from life to death."

So saying, I agitated two large bottles that I had just taken out of my bag. At that sight, the sad companion could not help smiling joyfully. Leaving the knotted rope up there, he slid down the trunk and presented himself to me very politely. I stopped him from talking before having sat down, and ventured the opinion that he should drink abundantly by way of a preamble. That he did, with a good enough grace.

In the meantime, I observed him, His aspect commanded sympathy, by which I mean that he had the external complexion of people who know how to live: a red nose, shining eyes, and strong, sensual lips. He might have been twenty-five years old.

When he lowered the bottle in order to draw breath, I asked him mildly the reasons for his sadness. "Doubtless," I hazarded, "you're in love?"

"Ah!" he said. "I see that you take me for an idiot. Do I look so stupid that I could be suspected of killing myself for a woman? I beg you to believe that it's nothing of the sort. If I want to perish, it's only because all means of living well have been taken away from me, and if I remained in this existence I'd see myself constrained for a long time, by virtue of the profound distress into which I've fallen, only to dine rarely and refresh myself with water. Isn't the rope preferable?"

"So it's poverty that is driving you to suicide?" I said. "But you're young; you could find employment; you'd still be able to drink and eat discreetly. Before hanging yourself, try to find a way of earning a living."

"Worthy man," he said, "I can see that you're not from here. On our island, no employment or labor can be exercised without one having passed examinations to that effect. The woodcutters you see in these woods have diplomas, and all emerge from a school that they entered at the age of seven, only to leave at that of twenty-three. Pastry-cooks, charcoal-burners, ditch-diggers, masons, soldiers, mariners, judges and thieves—everyone, in sum—are in the same position, quali-fied, decorated, hierarchized and examined in natural and tran-scendental sciences."

"Why, then," I said, "haven't you done as they have, and how is it that your parents haven't directed you since child-hood into a certain path?"

But he replied: "Exactly. I've always shown a very marked taste for drawing. I studied or long years in the hope of one day passing the professorial examination thus finding a living. Very recently, I quit my birthplace at the other extremi-ty of the kingdom in order to come here to present myself to the judges. During my journey, however, the program had been changed and the subject of drawing replaced by a test in swimming. It's in that exercise that I've been refused, so shamefully that I've been forbidden to present myself again. I only have half a drachma left my mother and father are dead, no resource remains to me except death."

"Friend," I said, "I like you. If you want to come with me, believe that you'll be well treated. You've divined that I'm a foreigner. Without a guide I'll have great difficulty in seeing and studying the country as I intend. For the rest, I pos-sess sufficient resources—which leads me to think that in helping one another, we can be fortunate.

The poor fellow accepted without hesitation, said adieu to his rope, and followed me. As soon as we set forth he gave me the most ample details regarding himself and told me that his name was Constantin. A little later, I told him my whole story.

XVI. The Death of the Giants

Three days later we were traversing a profound forest of enormous trees. Constantin took me by the arm and led me to the edge of the road. There I saw a colossal rock covered with moss, on which one could still read, in ancient characters: *Here the last giants died.*

My guide said to me then: "These immense woods where we are cover the territory of an ancient nation. This was once the Republic of the Giants and Dwarfs. The former were the descendants of the Cyclopean race; the others were innumerable pygmies, industrious and skillful in the labors of the earth. They harvested wheat with axes and had their little carriages pulled by dogs. The Cyclops were good, brave and formidable in battle. They governed and protected the weak race of little people. When avid or bellicose neighbors invaded their land, those Titans marched to encounter them, and always came back victorious. Many of them perished in those wars, but they did not complain, deeming that their role was to risk themselves. And from their colossal dwellings, built on places dominating towns and villages, they considered the prosperity of other people with a satisfied eye.

"However, the dwarfs hated them. They accused them of pride. They complained of subsidizing their needs, for the giants didn't work with their hands except in combats. Revolts burst forth. Every time, the rebels were punished. A mortal discontentment agitated the population of homunculi from then on. The fire brooded secretly for a century. Then a horrible conspiracy was formed.

"One night, in all the parts of the country, the gigantic warriors were surprised and massacred in their sleep. Some perished stifled in their beds; other were burned alive in their fortresses; many had their heads cut off by the axes of their servants. A few escaped and retired to this place. Astonished by the ingratitude of their vassals and inconsolable at the death of their brothers, they resolved to die. They heaped up hundreds of tree trunks at this spot and mounted the pyre together. Their ashes formed this column, under which their great bones sleep. Thus ended that illustrious race.

"Immediately afterwards, our forefathers invaded these provinces and reduced the dwarfs to slavery. The insensates gradually disappeared, and only a few of them can still be found, hiding in the woods, where they live on roots and wild plants. It's in memory of those things that we call this country the forest of the Cyclops.

"In their time, the last of them had as habitual enemies wandering troops of centaurs. They were an adventurous and piratical people. They owed their origin, according to legend, to the amour that Zeus once experienced for a mare. That nation was annihilated too; but when I walk in this woodland, I seem to witness the marvelous battles that those heroes fought here."

And Constantin remained pensive, thinking about the heroic centuries. For myself, silent, I thought I could hear the hooves of centaurs striking the ground, and the foreheads of Titans brushing the crowns of the trees.

XVII. The King of Brigands

On the evening of the following day we found ourselves in a savage and mountainous place. Huge rocks were piled up confusedly. Ancient oaks of a frightful size plunged their roots between the joints. Their thick, dark foliage, their twisted and wrinkled trunks and branches, the ravaged aspect of the place and a thin cascade reflecting the scarlet clouds of the sunset, all composed a terrifying and sublime ensemble. The breeze mingled its long moans with the monotonous sob of springs.

We had gone astray. Anxious and harassed, we sat down. We took some food out of our bag and began to restore ourselves.

My companion said: "We should have followed the road. I have no idea where we are. I no longer hope to encounter a house and dread having to pass the night in this sinister gorge. The air is already cold, and we'll catch some nasty chill here, if not a rheumatism of all the limbs."

I was in a bad mood and made no reply. I only like sleeping on grass in the middle of the day after a good meal. I tried to swallow my anger and I ate as best I could. It happened that our dinner was paltry and we had hardly anything left to drink.

My fury burst forth. "Are you stupid, Constantin?" I said. "I've entrusted you with the care of directing me and provisioning us, and you've bought me into this lost corner without the consolation of any decent nourishment!"

Then we heard strange whistling, three times, followed by rustling and the sound of footfalls. Emerging from obscure thickets and intervals between the rocks, numerous men appeared and surrounded us at a distance. Then, forming a circle of which we were the center, they drew closer to us. They were armed with sabers, épées and long iron-tipped staffs.

I rose to my feet, shivering. The adventure seemed to me, with reason, to be disastrous. Then again, there are times when I am very brave, and others when I become cowardly; I was in the latter disposition. Take note, please, that it cannot be otherwise for a poor traveler, fatigued, lost in the mountains at dusk, who has not had supper.

Constantin continued eating and hastened to swallow the morsels, as if he were afraid that they might be stolen from him. With his mouth full, he said: "They're brigands. We couldn't have a worse encounter."

One of the individuals advanced, and, taking off his hat and bowing very deeply, he spoke to me as follows:

"Have no fear, Seigneur, and, above all, refrain from fleeing. You're in our domain, and the custom of visitors is to leave us, in memory of their coming, something from their baggage. Don't go against that custom. Consent with a good grace. No one wants to harm you, but we'll be constrained to do so if you resist."

"Messieurs," I said, bowing in my turn, "take whatever you please, but by all the gods, don't despoil me entirely, or I'll die of famine."

The bandits began to inspect our luggage, and laid bare my fortune. The sight of so much money rejoiced them to the point that several made as if to dance. I was very sad. I thought that after having robbed me, those people would doubtless kill me, for the pleasure of it, as assassins do here.

They found the fortunate safe conduct from the High Priest of Thalantide. The chief read it by torchlight. Immediately, he cried: "Stop! Stop!" Then, turning toward me, he said in a respectful voice: "Deign to pardon me, illustrious Seigneur. If I had known that the protection of the gods and priests extended over you, believe that I would have respected you more. We only hate governors, senators, men of law, usurers, tax collectors and all other oppressors and starvers of poor people. Know too that the noble Katodipsa is secretly our friend. We would not, for any profit, offend him or cause him any prejudice." He added: "I beg you to accept our hospitality. You can't remain in this place tonight. And then, the King, our master, will be glad to see a foreigner of your sort. If you'll permit, we'll take you to him."

I would have been delighted to refuse. I could not, and I accepted, thanking him. My valise was repacked before my eyes, without anything lacking. Finally, escorted by the brigands and led by their commandant, we followed a rising path through the woods.

We marched thus for about an hour, astonished by the affair and increasingly reassured. We arrived in a clearing in which a large tent was erected. Our guide went into it alone. He reappeared shortly afterwards, and invited us to enter.

In the depths of the tent, which was illuminated by countless torches, the king was seated on a throne with three steps. He was surrounded by motionless guards.

He spoke to me mildly and with consideration.

"Truly," he said, when he knew where I had come from, "I would not have believed that the inhabitants of your country were made thus. I've been told that they had black skin and ordinarily walked on all fours."

Then he took us to dinner gallantly, and we went with him into another tent, marvelously fitted out as a banqueting hall.

An iron table occupied the center, laden with dishes with enormous sides and bottles as tall as columns. The principal brigand captains, with their wives, were awaiting the arrival of the king. I had never seen a more beautiful assembly, nor guests of better quality. They were all princes of old stock, and represented the purest residuum of the ancient nobility. In fact the other patricians of Atlantis, ruined by political vicissitudes, had lost their rank and corrupted the illustriousness of their race by rich misalliances with low-born foreigners.

The king placed me to his right. He was very eager to hear my story. I related it in its entirety, without any falsehood. Then the sovereign talked to me about himself and his subjects.

"I ought," he said, "to reign over a part of this kingdom, because, for fourteen centuries the eldest sons of my family were the suzerains of half this island. A hundred and thirty years ago, a revolution took away their crown and united their realm with that of the Kephalides. My great-grandfather, vanquished by the mob, retired to these mountains. A number of his great lords remained faithful to him, and followed him, with a few vassals. You see their descendants here. But they were unable to subsist for long in that manner; they were forced to become brigands. I do not think that any shame is attached to that profession. It demands bravery, prudence and tact. The public powers fear us and respect us. They have informed me several times that if I abandoned my legitimate pretentions to the throne of which I am the heir, I could live in perfect accord with them, but that is an extremity to which I have never been able to resolve myself."

While talking, the King drank nobly, as did all his audience. He was the most magnificent sovereign that I have seen in my life. He was called "the Lion," the twenty-fourth of that name, and his reign had lasted nearly twenty years.

"In my homeland," I said, "your colleagues are rather badly treated. It's necessary to confess that among us, that profession has degenerated and is only any longer exercised by a vulgar rabble. Not long ago, however, we saw noble and important thieves, whom the State revered and supported with its coin. They did not hide at crossroads or in the shadow of forests; they had palaces in our cities. The government collected a commission on their enterprises and the poor people were duped without recourse. It is very difficult, in our countries, to distinguish robbers from politicians.

The Lion said: "But what difference do you make between brigands like us and the individuals who preside over the responsibilities and sovereignties of the Republic?" Seeing me hesitate, he continued: "There is none. Both live on rapine. Theirs, they say, are legitimate and necessary; they call them taxes. They want to make people believe that they employ that money for the good of the nation. By the thrice sacred shadow of my father, I could say the same. The money that I steal, I spend. Thus I bring a marvelous aid to local commerce. But for me, how many treasures would be buried at present in coffers, in cellars or even in the hands of the Treasury? I disperse the spending power. I'm a source of wealth for everyone and the evident cause of the prosperity of the State. Thanks to me, money circulates and is multiplied, all without costing me anything.

"Consider now the governors of Atlantis. The new Constitution only leaves them in power for a short time. Their avidity increases while they await their turn; when it arrives, they know that it will soon pass. Thus, they fill their pockets rapidly, pressure the people, put employments and distinctions up for auction, exaggerate tolls and taxes. They accumulate, but they do not spend. They lend at interest and live like misers. The money that they extract from the people, the people never see again. They pass laws by which people are bound to furnish them with everything gratuitously. They travel and eat without expense. I don't know whether they pay their courtesans, but I know that they often contaminate them."

The good king was indignant. His magnanimous heart was overflowing; but he continued to drink copiously.

The conversation and the repast had not concluded when daylight arrived. Shortly afterwards, Constantin and I were each taken to a tent where we found a good bed and several pleasurable things, but I dare not say exactly how far the magnificence of royal hospitality went.

XVIII. The Toll-Collectors

Toward mid-day we presented ourselves to the King in order to take our leave. We praised him and thanked him greatly. I assured him that I would conserve a very high opinion of his person and his power. The potentate made me a thousand amities and gave me magnificent presents, including his portrait, the work of an eminent artist who had been his guest.

An officer conducted us to a carriage, and, arguing the length and difficulty of the route begged us to borrow it. I accepted, having a desire to reach Atlantopolis soon.

We quit the mountains and the brigands thus. I retain a pleasant and perpetual memory of that night spent under the tent. Why did I have to quit that oasis? How many misfortunes I would have avoided by staying with the good sovereign! He understood existence in the best fashion, and if he recovers his hereditary scepter some day, I am sure that he will conduct himself as an honest prince, worthy of eternal human remembrance.

As for me, continuing my voyage, I saw nothing that merits being reported for two days. On the third morning after my departure the postillion informed me that we were approaching the capital.

The road was flat and bordered with meager stands of trees. The country never wearied of being beautiful, but frightful houses, all alike and increasingly numerous made it ugly. They were trivial and pretentious dwellings with red roofs, walls of plaster and brick, with gates painted a horrible green. In the midst of their little gardens devoid of shade they rose up like mushrooms over the damp dust.

Throughout the region nature had been marvelously corrected. The dammed streams ran in straight lines. Of ancient forests, felled not long ago, nothing remained but sparse and paltry trees, like the last hairs on a bald head. And the sewers of the great city, which, by virtue of a marvelous invention, discharged in the midst of the fields, transformed them into nauseating marshes.

I fell asleep contemplating those effects of human ingenuity. Suddenly, savage cries resounded, the vehicle nearly tipped over, and I woke up.

A troop of badly-dressed men, armed for war, surrounded my carriage. Several had thrown themselves ahead of the horses. They were all shouting at the driver in injurious, menacing terms borrowed from the language of the gutter. Without any warning, one of the wretches flung open the door against which I was leaning. I fell out, face down on to the ground. I did not have the leisure to get up again, for while I was lying n the mud they struck me on the back and shoulders with sticks, so forcefully that it is a marvel that I recovered. They searched me. Angered by not finding anything precious on me, they climbed into the vehicle.

Constantin had disappeared and the coachman, for fear of blows, fled across the plowed fields.

Sitting on the road and recovering my senses somewhat, I considered with astonishment the bizarre behavior of my aggressors. They split the floor of the vehicle with axes and made holes in the walls with the aid of large drills. One might have thought that they were looking for treasure. After that they returned to me. I showed them the safe conduct that had won me the esteem and protection of the brigands. They paid no heed to it, saying that they did not know that High Priest and were absolutely scornful of his protégés. They added that they were acting on behalf of the law.

Suspecting that I was hiding something, they undressed me brutally and tore my clothes to shreds in order to make sure that the linings did not conceal anything.

Finally, the captain of the pirates approached me and said: "In the name of the King, know that you have satisfied the inspection, I permit you to continue your journey." And when I asked politely who he and his men were, he replied: "We're the royal and sworn toll-collectors. We make sure that no one transports merchandise from one city to another without paying the duty. You can see how vigilant we are."

And they went away, after having covered me with insults and sneers.

I therefore remained in the middle of the causeway, as naked as my hand, bleeding from the nose and bruised all over by blows. I had never found myself in such a calamitous posture, except when I was shipwrecked.

I was slightly reassured on seeing Constantin emerge from the ditch. He had hidden in the mud, preferring discomfort to the woes that awaited him at my side. He had saved the small valise in which I kept my money.

We left our broken-down vehicle and our battered horses. Fortunately, we found a hostelry where I was given garments, and we forgot the morning's misfortunes in feasting.

XIX. Atlantopolis, the Admirable City

In the middle of the afternoon we resumed our route. The land was covered with black and low houses and the roads encumbered by carts and pedestrians.

Finally, we arrived on a hill from which we perceived the city, as vast as a sea.

Beneath our feet a great circular plaza extended. Avenues terminated there coming from all directions. In the center stood a stone pyramid, a hundred and twenty meters high and wide, the summit of which surpassed the hill from which we were gazing. Its base was surrounded by a colonnade in a severe style. A door opened in the middle of each face. We approached, and when I asked my guide what that monument was, he replied that it had been erected to the glory of the great emperor Phoberos, conqueror of the entire archipelago.

We went in and climbed a step spiral stairway. Loopholes combated the obscurity weakly. At the summit we found a terrace.

Then Constantine said to me: "Look carefully, with the eyes of the body and those of the soul; look hard at Atlantopolis the Great, the sovereign city of this realm. Do you see that immense plain covered with houses, palaces, temples and tombs? Do you see the shining river that divides it into two unequal parts? In these illustrious streets a powerful and pensive people agitates and toils. All nations contemplate it and fall silent when it speaks. It is the forger of new instruments, the creator of ideas, the light in the midst of darkness. O stranger, if you could perceive the invisible radiance that emanates from this city and comes from far away to illuminate souls as you perceive that of the sun, your eyes would close, wounded by its glare."

"I don't know," I said. "But there's something terrible and delightful in the aspect of this populous city. The smoke that conquers the sky, the high dwellings, the innumerable monuments, the transparent water spanned by all those bridges and the rhythmic noise that I can hear now all move me and charm me. It's the only capital that appears simultaneously so incomparably beautiful and powerful. And you tell me that it's a forge, where thought creates thought; I believe you, Constantin. Look, night is arriving now, and one might think that a population of stars was coming to inhabit this earth. A fog of flame is rising over Atlantopolis and surrounding it with a golden aureole.

"Can you hear the voice of the bells?" said Constantin. "If you knew what they're saying! For centuries, they've been ringing in their old towers, and often, on hearing them, men have drawn their swords. The ancient walls that you are con-templating have sent the echo of revolutions all the way to the limits of our world. Then distant princes trembled in their palaces and peoples rose up everywhere, repeating the symbolic words proffered by the admirable city.

"Men with empty heads and envious hearts have thrown mud at it. They have said: 'That nation is vain, noisy and superficial. Atlantopolis is a prostitute. It welcomes all worshipers.' No, it is a great furnace in which everything fuses and burns relentlessly, and from which a metal precious to prosperity emerges every day. The eternal and fecund battles between contrary principles rages here."

"Let's go down," I said, "let's go down. I want to live in this city, in order that I might comprehend what it cries to the universe."

Part Two

I. A Walk in the City

Entering into Atlantopolis and exploring it at hazard, several spectacles astonished me to begin with. That of the streets astonished me above all. What is most remarkable in cities is not what one perceives immediately, and I confess that the perfection of the monuments made less impression on me than the strangeness of the crowd. That crowd is formed of people in haste who jostle one another, incapable of slowing their pace, and who stop rather than go gently. When they stop thus, they remain motionless for some time, open-mouthed, contemplating minor accidents or unimportant objects.

Two contrary currents of carriages of all forms race along the avenues, which it seems chimerical to want to cross. The pedestrian population accumulates on the sidewalks. When a gap appears between two vehicles, the pedestrians advance; horses rear up, people are knocked down, others are constrained to retreat, but some succeed in reaching the middle of the causeway, where they form a troop. Those have still to confront a second row of carriages, and thus find themselves prisoners between the two files. Soon taking advantage of a new interval, they attempt the crossing again.

You would have difficulty finding people in the city who do not bear the scars of injuries received in similar circumstances. However, the citizens have acquired a marvelous skill and suppleness in such exercises. You see them running, crawling, walking backwards, and sliding under the breasts of horses, but there is no security for them.

Their destiny is no better if they hire carriages. The velocity of the latter is so precipitate, and surpasses natural possibility to such an extent, that they are often seen colliding, overturning, or even, as if crazed, deviating from their legitimate route, smashing into shops, going over the parapets of bridges, or hurling themselves headlong into trees, heaps of paving-stones and objects of great resistance of every species.

A rapid movement animates everyone and everything. People run, animals gallop, and one cannot consider that confusion without a kind of bewilderment. The traveler thinks he is seeing a people combated by cavaliers, or a chariot race in an excessively crowded location.

At intervals, in the middle of streets, I saw individuals clad in dirty uniforms. At first I took them for men condemned to death who were being punished for their crimes by obliging them to be crushed to death. Nothing of the sort; they are low-ranking officers charged with supervising the traffic. They do not have the mission of moderating its speed or repressing misdemeanors. They only make sure that every vehicle carries a certain plaque of engraved iron, which is delivered by the Treasury and is a kind of tax receipt.

The window displays of shops merit an eternal contemplation. Objects of every sort are presented there tastefully and favorably illuminated. Everything that there is of the most delicate in every industry, displayed in an appropriate décor, gives everyone a hunger to acquire it. Here, in lace and embroidery, are delightful products of the provinces; there, glasses and vases of thin colored crystal, decomposing the light, are tinted with all the hues of the rainbow. Carpets are piled one atop another in calculated disorder, in which their tones are juxtaposed harmoniously. Woolen and silk fabrics, sculpted jewels and gems, bronze statues, the most beautiful inventions of luxury, are all found along the streets in astonishing boutiques that one might mistake for museums.

Several merchants, under signs in foreign languages, offered the public objects of barbaric taste. One tailor, whose sign bore a name from overseas, made a profession of selling people garments that were much too large. That inept fashion succeeded, however and one saw many elegant individuals in the city decked out in tunics in the form of sacks.

My greatest joy was looking at the women. Nowhere else in earth is it possible to see so many beautiful women. Atlantopolidiennes have a particular and sometimes paradoxical style of dress. That style modifies their appearance to the point that one thinks at first that their anatomy differs from the ordinary anatomy of their sex, but if one sees them naked, one perceives that they have the same forms as their sisters of other nations.

They walk with very small steps, as if their legs were incapable of extended movements, and there too it is necessary not to trust the appearance. They stand on tiptoe, very straight, raising their head, advancing their bosom and dissimulating the abdomen. In consequence, the rump, enclosed in clinging fabrics, makes a forceful projection in rear, and inspires concupiscence. Their hair, when I arrived, was, for the most part of the same gilded shade. I discovered later that the shade changed every year and that, by virtue of an astonishing marvel of art or nature, the color of the skin varied as well. Thus, when the hair turns red and resembles fire, the face becomes as white as chalk, so that the entire head, seen face on, is reminiscent of a freshly plastered all crowned with new bricks. The mutations are no less astonishing when the women become brunette or blonde. For the citizens, it is a precious distraction to observe those phenomena. But does one not see similar changes elsewhere? The ermine exchanges its coat the color of earth for a coat the color of snow, and several other animals are known for transformations of the same genre.

One might think sometimes that a painter had retouched the faces of those ladies, underlining their eyes with a brown streak, designing the curve of the eyebrows, exaggerating the redness of the lips and hiding the imperfections of the epidermis with a varnish.

When I arrived, I spent a long time examining women's hats. They were then as large as bucklers and entirely covered with flowers, butterflies, impaled animals, tissues and feathers. They fixed all that on their heads by means of long needles whose head was ornamented and whose tip menaced passers-by. Later, a change occurred; hats were no broader than necessary, but augmented in height, in sum taking the form of bonnets; but those bonnets descended so low that only the chins of elegant women could still be seen, and some of them were constrained, in order to be able to steer, to have eye-holes pierced in them.

When I arrived they were dresses made with little fabric, very tight at the base; their gait was embarrassed by them, and they only advanced at a child-like pace. That gait appeared to me to be contrary to several natural laws.

Constantin was kind enough to enlighten me in that regard.

"It is because," he said, "by virtue of an inconceivable relaxation of mores, violence against women has become frequent these days. You can well imagine that the narrowness of those skirts can, on occasion, collaborate in saving modesty."

"Oh," I said, "is there any need for that? Do you know the story of the false virgin who told her mother that a boy had ravaged her by force? The mother didn't say a word and carried on sewing. A moment later she asked her daughter to thread a needle for her 'because,' she said, 'I can hardly see.' The child could not do it, and cried: 'Maman, how do you expect me to succeed; you use the needle incessantly.' 'Well, little wretch,' said the angry old woman, let that be a lesson to you!'"

"Oho!" said Constantin. "Do you doubt the virtue of our women? Learn to see nothing in their manners but a laudable desire for beauty, a determination to please for which it is necessary to thank them; and know above all, Monsieur fabulist, that they are the most honest women on earth. They are virtuous, which is nothing, but they are virtuous without being ridiculous, which is divine. Our capital owes them its most vivid splendor. The least of them appears a princess. Many queens, coming here on solemn visits, have appeared by comparison with them to be provincial ladies dressed for the theater. And a number of kings, lords and foreign pontiffs passing through Atlantopolis have been glad to choose a wife here, in which they are acting sagely, for our daughters are less loqua-cious and quarrelsome than others. But that doesn't take very much."

"That's fine," I said, "and cuckolds must be rare here?"

"I don't make that claim," said my guide. "The number of cuckolds is infinite, but the majority are thus with their full consent. One cannot reckon as a crime on the part of ladies an action tolerated or commanded by their husbands, in contem-plation of the poverty of their household.

II. In which the author takes lodgings and visits several principal monuments

The employment of the first day was the search for an abode. I found one that suited me in a quiet quarter near the river. The house was old, agreeable and pleased me. It also pleased Constantin, who liked the town houses of Atlantopolis, so nobly built two hundred years before.

From my apartment I had a view, in one direction, over the quays planted with trees, and especially the west of the city, all the way to the surrounding hills. To the east, my win-dows opened over a rather deserted back street. I did not per-ceive anything singular in that direction, or any horizon, but the solitude of the passage was not without utility for me, in the excursions I undertook subsequently.

I had the necessary furniture brought, and I spent a great deal of money, but I had so much and it had cost me little that it was a joy to disburse it. For one thing, I did not perceive that it was running out; and for another, spending it did not remind me of any labor accomplished in order to acquire it.

When I had the furniture necessary for every man of property—which is to say, a bed, a table and several bottle-racks, I considered myself installed. The desire gripped me to resume my walks and, in particular, to see the monuments whose distant aspect had charmed me in the preceding days.

"It will require many days to visit them all," Constantin told me. "Each of them offers a great deal to look at and think about. A few will be sufficient for today."

First he took me to a temple, the principal sanctuary of the old religion, a religion persecuted and turned to mockery. The plan of the edifice is rectangular. The façade presents two high towers of several stages, pierced with narrow openings and flanked by coupled columns. Arcades connect the towers. All of it is sculpted with the figures of humans and animals. The complication is extreme and the organization grandiose. At first, one can only make out the general lines, in which the vertical are dominant, extending very high and strongly expressing the idea of infinity. Those verticals seen from below, seem bound to join up in the clouds, like the ridges of a narrow pyramid of which one can see the base, while its summit is in the heavens.

In the interior, a forest of pillars bears vaults so high that one can scarcely distinguish them. To the right and the left, arched galleries reign along the walls.

"This temple," Constantin told me, "will soon be demolished. People remain in accord with regard to its beauty, but they claim that it serves no purpose. The true motive is that it recalls the centuries of error, the centuries when people did not think as they do now. The monument causes chagrin to the powerful men of today because it is a doctrine of stone built to inform men of the contrary of what our governors preach. Who will defend it? The people prefer stupid novelties to the masterpieces of old. They are influenced by the foreign, brutalized by politicians, and in any case, even if they wanted to prevent the scandal, they couldn't. For the beautiful, in our democratic state, is nothing to the people except a label.

"For myself," Constantin continued, "there's nothing I admire as much. Contemplate this mass of stone carefully. Wouldn't one think that it is praying? It is thinking, thinking the thought that its pious architect imprisoned within it. It is thinking about ancient days, the noble sanctuary, set on the edge of the river the color of steel, before this square where its

363

dormant parvis is buried, with its old enclosure, and the three temples built by the Argides. I cannot get used to the idea that it will die, and that its old bones will be dispersed in all directions. On that day, a great soul will leave us; and our grandchildren, going past this place, will no longer hear the sound of bells but that of factories. Instead of towers, columns of smoke will rise up. I fear that Fatality will then stimulate in our Oriental plains some people marked to destroy ours; or people who deny their traditions are unworthy to live."

And Constantin wept.

Then we saw a marvelously grandiose palace, which dated back four centuries. Its architecture recalled ancient Greek architecture, differing from it in the extent and the height of its buildings, and a host of details; but the inspiration was the same. It was the former dwelling of kings. Presently, feeble-minded sons of families, incapable of earning a living are maintained there. Well-lodged and well-nourished, they thus have a place in society. They are said to be in charge of caring for works of art belonging to the State. We went in to see the paintings contained therein, but we were thrown out because the place can only be visited for one hour a week.

From there I was taken to an equally beautiful edifice. King Helios the Victorious had had it constructed to house soldiers crippled in battles or rendered infirm after long service. But I was told that those veterans had been shamefully expelled from their refuge and that a troop of pen-pushers had replaced them, so the admirable monument was full of bureaucrats, unpleasant people sullen of face and ferocious in character.

In the courtyards, surrounded by sculpted porticoes, trophies recalled military glories. The galleries were full of arms and standards captured from enemies in battles, but the parquets were all stained with ink and the wind was agitating scribbled pieces of paper in the gardens instead of dead leaves.

A temple covered by a cupola sheltered a colossal tomb. Constantin bared his head as he went in. I did likewise, impressed by the majesty of the place and the gravity of my guide. The latter knelt down and said to me in a low voice: "Here reposes the Emperor Phoberos, the last of the demigods."

III. The Choice of a Historian

We visited the principal edifices in that fashion. There were large ones and modest ones, but all of them, venerable witnesses, recalled an epoch of the history of the city. Revolutions had marked their traces on the degraded walls. Here and there I was shown paving stones once red with blood, where illustrious men had fallen for their cause.

I saw the sepulchers of sovereigns, empty for the most part. In days of trouble the populace broke their stones and the royal ashes were thrown to the winds. I also saw the temples, the triumphant monuments erected in memory of victories, the palaces where the dynasties had lived. However, I wearied of admiring so many things, the beauty of which could often surpass explanation, but only awoke in my heart the emotion of memory.

I expressed to Constantin my desire to know the annals of the nation. He replied that he was not capable of reciting them to me in their entirety, but he had several historians among his friends, acquaintances of his years of study. I asked him to take me to one, and he set out in quest.

Shortly afterwards, as I was leaving the table, a dirty, bearded man with a hint of madness in his eyes appeared. He assured me that he was a doctor and professor of the historical sciences and that he wanted to render me service if I paid him well. I explained my desire; he replied, learnedly: "I hope that you're a partisan of the new method?"

"Monsieur," I said to him, "I know neither the new nor the old, and I don't care about that. Simply tell me your history, beginning at the beginning."

"I'm your man," he replies, "but wait for me for a moment."

He takes his hat and leaves, in such haste that he pays no attention to the offer I make him of refreshment. After a long hour, I am deafened by an unaccustomed racket coming from the street. I get up and lean out of the window, and perceive an accumulation of carriages on the quay, caused by an overloaded cart awkwardly skewed across the causeway. The passersby are aiding the coachman, pushing the wheels and pulling the horses by the bridle. The rig advances slightly, and stops at my door. The carter gets down from his seat. I look at him in astonishment; it is my historian.

He comes into my house. Now he is in my room, out of breath.

"Sire," he said to me, "we can begin."

He hands me a volume. I leaf through it uncomprehendingly. It's a list, a list twelve hundred pages long.

"That," the doctor explains, "is history such as it is conceived. It is all in this book, in its entirety. You have there the complete enumeration of all the memoirs of all times, copies of authentic decrees, accounts of food production and finances under every reign, the correspondence of kings, princes, ecclesiastics, millers, butchers and blacksmiths. The catalogue is in your hands. The numbers in the catalogue correspond to the documents that it is necessary to study, one by one. I have brought in my cart those which relate to the commencement of the first part—for we divide our history into a hundred and forty-three epochs, each subdivided into sixty periods, which amount to seven hundred and eighty-nine divisions, which, in their turn..."

"Enough!" I said. "Enough! Do I look like a fool? Are you drunk? Go away, historian of misfortune, go away with your cart, your catalogue, your epochs, your periods and your divisions. I shall not be your pupil."

The man thought I was mad, all the more easily because he was himself. He withdrew, calling me incorrigible. I summoned Constantin and told him my story.

"I was sure of it," he said. "These people are all the same, and I consider them enraged. That one wants to crush

366

you with the weight of a hundred thousand volumes. You'll see a whole barrel-full of them. This one, a skeptical philosopher, will tell you right away that history is a chimera, that other individuals of whom it speaks doubtless never existed and that the events it relates are even more dubious. Some flatterer of the present government will sustain falsely that history commences with the last revolution, the others being nothing but mustard. We have twenty-five historical sects, all enemies of one another. They are only in accord in declaring the nullity of all the others. I don't share their opinion, and if you believe me, you'll send me to the bookshop to look for the *Annals* of Eudoxus. It's an excellent book, although it dates back half a century.[34] There's a prejudice in the long story that is sometimes annoying, but a breath of life animates that history. Reading it, you believe you're living in the midst of the events and people it depicts. That's a rare merit in works of that sort.

"Run," I said, "run and fetch me that book. You ought to have told me about it to begin with. If you happen to encounter a historian on the way, don't send him to me, I beg you, for I wouldn't be able to stand the sight of him."

Constantin soon brought me the twelve volumes of the *Annals of Atlantis* by Eudoxus. It is a book written in good, clear and passionate Greek. As soon as I started reading I was seized by interest and emotion. In less than a week I had finished the study. Today, I repent of not having spent more time on it. Many events and names have slipped my mind. I shall, however, attempt to indicate to the reader the principal features of the history of Atlantis.

---

[34] The author might have Jules Michelet's *Histoire de France*, dating from the early 1860s, in mind as a model for this history of the isles of Atlantis..

IV. In which is found a brief history of Atlantis, according to Eudoxus

When Atlantis sank entirely beneath the waves, the people who inhabited it had attained a civilization and a singular power long before. That island, as extensive as North America, to the east of which it was located, was originally colonized by the Greeks and was absolutely subject to their domination. The invaders mingled with the autochthons, who were Gaels. A new race was born, worthy of those which emerged from it, vigorous, literate and warlike.

Of the epoch anterior to the cataclysm, history knows almost nothing, and allows legend to speak. The latter tells a thousand fine tales, names heroes similar to Achilles and describes wars in which the gods fought. It adds that after a time of felicity exactly similar to our Golden Age, the nations began to be corrupted, and obliged Zeus to annihilate them. Plato himself tells us what happened that night when the order of the elements was subverted and Atlantis was erased from the earth. Plato, understandably, did not know that a number of lesser isles remained, either by chance or because the divinities, as they usually do on the occasion of deluges, having considered the virtue of certain men, had saved them deliberately.

The difficulties of the new life and the loss of all wealth, particularly the destruction of ancient writings and monuments, reduced the survivors to savagery.

Kingdoms were founded; the earliest was that of Atlantopolis, where the despicable dynasty of the Argides reigned to begin with, somnolent princes incapable of command, who allowed their servants to share in their power.

After eight centuries a man of great genius undertook to restore the traditions. That was the Emperor Megalopodas. He united the various islands under his laws. The hordes of the Mainomenes, newly formed, were already ravaging the Archipelago. Megalopodas made war on them victoriously and reduced them to slavery. He created the government and was able to administer it. Letters and arts were reborn and he spared no effort to encourage them.

After his reign of sixty years, everything fell back into chaos. The tribal chiefs cut up the imperial robe into the mantles of kings and took hereditary command of minuscule states. One of those chiefs, by the name of Kephalos, had himself elected the sovereign of the entire region of Atlantopolis. A courageous prince, he set out to pacify the land, so he perished in battle.

His descendants, the illustrious race of Kephalides, gradually augmented the dependencies of their crown. For fourteen centuries they labored on the establishment of the royal power and the preeminence of their fatherland. It was then that the valor and strength of the people of Atlantopolis was felt. Weak in origin but of a character superior to all others, it ended up subjugating and absorbing the populations of the entire island, forming them into an invincible nation superior to all its neighbors.

Many interruptions, from century to century, halted its progress, but, the sun seems brighter after the darkness of an eclipse, every time the periods of malediction came to an end, the kingdom of Atlantis emerged more powerful and more glorious. For there are peoples marked in advance to reign, which misfortunes can afflict, but cannot annihilate. As the flame of a torch vacillates at first, having difficulty igniting the resin, and is enveloped by smoke, just as one thinks it extinct, it is reborn, rises up in triumph and illuminates the spectators; and, just as the light pales under the wind that torments it and seems vanquished by darkness, in the same way, the predestined people whose mission is to enlighten, sometimes seems to fail and go out. Then the rapacious tribes approach, growling; for they do not know that there are fires that do not go out, the fuel of which is inexhaustible, which remain to enlighten the word, and which it is necessary to reignite if they come to perish.

Six hundred years after Kephalos, his descendant Eudoxus destroyed forever the power of the dissident princes. The territories of Atlantis then began to fuse, and continued so well that in the end, they no longer formed anything but a well ordered whole, each part of which was distinguished by particular qualities. In the other islands, on the contrary, that unity was only superficial, and several races opposed throughout the ages continued to make war under the same flag.

A mild religion had been established a long time ago. The belief in a forgiving God had replaced the ancient myths. Memories of the gods, demigods and heroes were mingled with the new rite. Zeus, Poseidon and all their associates had conserved their emblems and specialties. Each believer worshiped one or other in particular but all of them placed above the Great God, the living God. That worship, abolished since, has been replaced by bizarre superstitions that conceal political deceptions ineptly. It is not for me to judge that persecuted church, but I can see that it was the operator of national grandeur; it made the scepter of kings a sacred scepter, whose force was irresistible. It wanted the crown to be regarded as a divine charge, and its enemies as sacrilegious. Without that power, which was regarded as the power of God himself, nothing great could be accomplished, and the thousand anarchic cantons of Atlantis tore one another apart again, or carried the yoke.

The clergy, meanwhile, often struggled against the prince, sometimes resisting him and sometimes striking him with anathema. There were continual wars. Finally, the alliance collapsed forever.

The kingdom increased from century to century and was elevated above all the states of the Archipelago. Closer to us, King Helios the Victorious brought the illustriousness of his fatherland to its peak. Helios was great, invincible in battle; he crushed three coalitions fomented by the Mainomenes, which invaded his realm. He was surrounded all his life by the greatest geniuses that had been seen in the arts, letters, sciences and warfare. He shone at the center of all that glory, and his radiance caused a thousand immortal flowers to bloom. He gave his name to his century and I swear to you that the century in question can be inscribed in history alongside those of Pericles and the Medicis.

The successors of Helios were incapable. Vanquished, inert, abandoning the country to the intrigue of ministers, the last four Kephalides were unable to conserve the glorious heritage of the Victorious, and allowed the decisive causes of catastrophe to accumulate.

When the unfortunate Adunatos the Second was elevated to the throne, the hurricane was ripe. The finances dilapidated, the armies deflected from their duty, the people crushed by taxes, poverty and hatred, the preaching of philosophers and the insouciance of the nobility prepared a terrible funeral for the race of kings.

Rebellion was suddenly unleashed. Its first gesture was to cut off the head of the Kephalide. Then commenced the flow of the scarlet river into which Atlantis was to pour all its best blood. Insensate masters of the populace lowered the foreheads that surpassed the rest. The massacre lasted for three years. Then the people repented, and realized that they had decapitated the nation itself. The leaders of the revolt continued, however; they abolished the primordial institutions of the State, broke the traditions, ruined the ancestral monuments and drove the entire country into extreme peril. But the rage they had unleashed turned against them and they perished in their turn on the scaffold they had erected, a scaffold of which they were unworthy, since they had ennobled it with so many fine victims.

Foreigners had invaded Atlantis, it seemed bound to succumb, but the revolution had Phoberos at the head of its armies. That great warrior annihilated the Mainomenes, drove the other enemies into the sea, and returned to Atlantopolis to be crowned Emperor.

He departed again, and for ten years he went from one end of the Archipelago to the other. He conquered entirely and restored the empire of Megalopodas. Having grown old, betrayed by his own people, he fell in an epic battle in which the victors believed themselves vanquished for a long time.

At this point the illustrious pages of the history concluded. As much as those shone with glory, those that followed were tarnished and humiliated.

On the death of Phoberos a certain caste took possession of power; I am referring to the bourgeoisie. The bourgeoisie out there are cowardly, ferocious, uneducated merchants, stupid, proud and corrupted by all vices and mercantile habits. The old regimes had been able to scorn them and contain them, so they proclaimed themselves the grateful sons of the revolution. It was for them, alas, that the rabble of the streets had shed blood.

They put on the throne an elective phantom, a parade king, chosen from their ranks. That sad sovereign made a semblance of reigning for seven years, and was then replaced. That still endures, to the public shame, in spite of uprisings. The nobility was regretted thereafter by all people of benevolence and common sense, especially when they contemplated the ridiculous faces of their potentates.

Letters and sciences paled; decadence commenced. The masters of the nation only encouraged works that resembled them. And that country, which the entire Archipelago admired as we admire Greece, only offered an uncertain reflection of its grandeur.

In the domain of exterior power there were grave checks. Twenty-five years before my arrival the Atlantideans fought a war against the Mainomenes, and no war was ever as strange. Their generals had only studied strategy in the beds of prostitutes. Several turned traitor, the rest were vanquished, defeated by the barbarians. The latter, astonished by their victory, abused it like highway bandits, and tore away from the land the fertile Edeia peninsula.

Since then, in spite of the anger of the people, the leaders of Atlantis no longer dare contest with the Mainomenes. During my sojourn they abandoned under threat a colony that had cost them a great deal of money and soldiers.

That is what I read, with details in the *Annals* of Eudoxus. I owe contemporary notions to Constantin. I apologize for having narrated such great things briefly and having omitted many. My memory forbids me to extend myself further, and I have even passed over in silence a thousand events that I remember. I have suppressed the names of ministers, kings and captains sufficient for the illustriousness of twenty peoples, so fertile was Atlantis in heroes and geniuses of every species.

V. In which the traveler is taken to two theaters and describes the spectacles he saw there.

Fatigued by such long reading I wanted a little recreation. I appealed to Constantin.

"Inform me," I said, of some agreeable pastime. "I have a mind fully laden with heavy thoughts. I want to distract myself this evening."

"Truly," he said, "I have what you need. Let's go to the Theater Royal. I know that they're performing a very fine play there. The author is the celebrated Limnathson. As for the title, I don't remember it."

The play was being performed in the afternoon. We only just had time to get ready.

As we were about to leave, Constantin informed me that my attire was not suitable.

"Change your costume," he said "or you'll be mistaken for a pauper. The public with which we're going to mingle is composed of merchants and bourgeois of every species; those people only go to the theater in their Sunday garments. Do as they do or you won't be allowed in."

I obeyed. We finally set forth. The theater hall resembled ours. The elegance of the audience amused me greatly. The men were dressed, with few exceptions, like provincial undertakers, and the women draped in garish fabrics. It was the only place in Atlantis where I observed so much bad taste.

The action commenced on the stage. I can't recount it in detail. It was nothing but one long and flat obscenity. The first act passed entirely in a bed, in which a lover and a husband alternated with the same woman. The actress who had that role played it marvelously, to the extent, at moment, of showing herself almost naked. Then all the spectators stood up in order to get a better view. At every coarse word and every obscene situation, bravos burst forth, and the audience praised to the skies the genius of the author and the talent of the performers.

The second act cannot be recounted, firstly because it presents the densest intrigue I have ever seen in the theater, and secondly because it is too dirty. The husband searches his wife's dressing room, for evidence of her treason and proceeds from deduction to deduction and discovery to discovery to the knowledge that he is a cuckold. He vomits filthy imprecations and the curtain falls.

The end surpassed all the rest. The husband, dagger in hand, pursues his wife and her accomplice. He inflicts a slight wound on the former; by means of a marvelous artifice, real blood falls on to the stage. The audience howls with joy, applauds, and wants to see it again.

At the moment when the husband sets about cutting throats, he learns that the shady speculations in which his fortune is engaged had failed. He is ruined. He changes color. The knife falls from his hand. A contract intervenes. The lover will lend the husband money. The wife will remain the indivisible property of the two men. Everyone embraces.

"Let's get out," I said, "out of this evil place. Constantin, my friend, where have you brought me?"

"Is it possible," cried my servant, "That you are so severe? That is entirely in the taste of the day and infinitely distracting. The public has proved that to you. You can see that it has made that play a success worthy of the work and itself."

"It's necessary," I said, "to see a better work. Take me to another hall, if possible. But if I only see a play like that one, let's not talk about returning to the theater. I'd rather visit taverns with large lanterns, where comedies like that one are played for real."

"In that case," proposed Constantin, "let's go to the Old Theater this evening, on the other side of the river. The doors open in two hours."

"Good," I said, "But let's go to dinner first.

That was what we did. I was conducted to a distant quarter. The Old Theater stood next to a large garden. We went in. In the hall I counted forty spectators.

However, the actors performed an admirable tragedy admirably. It attained the grandeur of Euripides, with more purity, delicacy and harmony. The noblest sentiments that the human heart and soul can experience were depicted therein. In that play everything was noble and everything was divine.

I went away enchanted, but very surprised.

"Why," I asked, "is such a poor welcome given to that great poet? Nowhere have I seen or read anything comparable."

"Know," replied Constantin, "that the author in question has been dead for three hundred years. Since his death, a thousand memorable events have occurred: the overturning of established beliefs, new inventions in all the arts, and a marvelous flourishing of literary theories. We've made great discoveries. One, above all, has modified the theater and the whole art of writing. It's a method known as 'Naturalism,' I don't know why. It consists of only reproducing the most commonplace acts and the mot vulgar lives, but studying them precisely. The spectator and the reader want to encounter themselves on the stage and in the novel. They don't only want to see heroes, emperors or gods there. The thoughts of great souls bore them. The sublime seems ridiculous to them. The new authors follow the public taste, and they display in the theater, instead of characters of great breadth, all kinds of vicious and paltry individuals, who are found to be more alive and have more resemblance to those of the century. Then again, people don't want to go to sleep at the theater. Scabrous scenes and spicy words, and the pretty things that actresses show, all please the multitude more than the most sublime verses."

"I understand," I said. "Your people want to be amused. That's legitimate. But those who are taking charge of distancing them are serving them very coarse fare. Tell me, then, why it is that the Old Theater, putting on such a fine play, only has forty spectators?"

"By all the gods!" said my friend. "You think that's very few! What, there are forty people with good taste in the city, and you're protesting! How many do you have in your country? Forty people have disturbed themselves in order to hear beautiful verses, have appeared to understand them, to like them, and you're not content?"

Constantin fell silent. We walked silently for a while. Then we talked about the present literature of Atlantis. My companion claimed that there was decadence there, as well as in all the other nations of the archipelago. And, suddenly becoming animated, he cried: "All the evil stems from this: too many people know how to read. The vulgar are the sovereign judge of mental labors. Don't think, Monsieur, that they are a good judge."

VI. Of art in Atlantis, and painting in particular.

In the days that followed we visited the museums in which ancient works of art are preserved, and the exhibitions in which new ones are shown.

First we saw the palace of the kings, the galleries of which contain all the masterpieces that the painting and sculpture of the Archipelago have accomplished.

In the first rooms we found the debris of ancient statuary—debris that dated from before the cataclysm, and which recent excavations had returned to the light of day. It was exactly the art of Ancient Greece, I found metopes there similar to those of Selinunte and smiling Apollos like those of Orchomenos.

An abysm of five centuries separated those vestiges from the works that followed them in the museum. A few pallid frescoes announced the birth and presaged the glory of the School of Atlantis. Short individuals and animals copied from antique reliefs, moving in severe landscapes or in front of excessively small architectures, composed scenes full of expression and grandeur. The plasticity of the Greeks was no longer found there, but something unknown to the Greeks was manifest here for the first time: soul; a soul full of tenderness and austerity. It was that sentiment that was to dominate for a long time and form the basis of primitive tradition.

As we advanced further, following the order of the years, every century showed us its best effort, the modifications to which it had been subject, and the progress that it had accomplished.

We arrived at the hall where the paintings of the age of Helios the Victorious were. I perceived that that epoch had seen the Art of Atlantis in its finest flower. Every era almost always finds the genus that summarizes it. That one was entirely contained in the painter Ornithion. He is, in my opinion, the greatest man of the entire earth. He combines in his works the purity of antique forms with the sentiment of the primitives. He dominates nature; his humblest characters are as beautiful as gods; his great landscapes have the aspect of lost paradises.

In the last room, we contemplated the work of the previous century. Some of them were sublime. Three masters, in particular, struck me. The greatest genius of the three was only preoccupied with inventing human forms of an immortal beauty. His virgins and heroes descended directly from those of the Greeks, but he added to them something of the most tender and even of the voluptuous.

Stauros, the second, a soul slightly troubled by the superstitions of his time, left an oeuvre made with less amour and more passion, but he painted with a color so bright and so forceful that one was forced to deem it good.

The third, specializing in landscapes, had discovered a new nature, with trees with quivering foliage, blue horizons, gilded skies and nymphs dancing in the twilight.

When we had contemplated those marvels for a long time, transported with admiration, we quit the Palace of the Kings.

Then Constantin said to me: "You've just seen the painting of our old masters. Now let's go and admire that of the young ones. Know that many people say today that what we have just seen is very little by comparison with modern works.

We therefore went to a great market in which more than thirty thousand canvases were being exhibited at that moment. The market was being held in a vast edifice of an architecture in bad taste.

Constantin explained to me that all those paintings were not hung under the same label. Three enemy groups divided the enormous location between themselves. And it was fortunate, it seemed, if a painter of an adverse party ventured into the neighboring territory without having his throat cut.

First we passed under a placard which read: *Traditional Painters*.

"Good," I said, "let's be hopeful. These people want to show me that they have not forgotten the masterpieces that I've just seen. Let's go."

And I began examining the walls covered with paintings. At intervals, I only saw a few canvases of a certain merit. The others were as many insults to good taste. It all appeared to me to have a poverty to make one weep, and an insolent pretention. Constantin explained to me that a great many of those colorings were made by persons of quality, not painters at all, but who wanted people to believe that they were artists. Those amateurs, by virtue of their relations and protections, had taken possession of the exhibition, and disposed recompenses in accordance with their competence, which was null. I refused to give the name of works of art to what I saw there, and I passed on.

378

As I was about to enter the second section, I perceived an old man struggling in the hands of twenty young men, a very animated group. The old man was begging them to let him go, but one of them was holding him by his collar, another by the back of his coat; two or three were embracing his knees and several were prostrate at his feet. They were all howling: "A medal! I want a medal!"

"Look," said Constantin. "That poor fellow is one of the judges of the exhibition that you've just quit, one of those who award the prizes. Around him are the candidates; the most obsessive will carry off the plum."

We turned our back on that scene and passed under a second placard, on which was inscribed in letters a foot high: *Society of Modern Painters*.

"A bizarre title," I said to Constantin. "How the devil, living in modern times, could one not be a modern painter?"

"Understand more fully," said my friend. "The people here only title themselves modern in order to treat the others as fossils. They are informing you, by that epitaph, that you will find among them artists who study their century and who possess personal tendencies, whereas their neighbors only copy old paintings..."

"Not sufficiently," I said, "not sufficiently. There are several, from what I can see who have need of it."

We were in the second hall. It was impossible for me to differentiate the works I perceived from those I had seen shortly before. The work, in general, seemed to be just as stupid and of the same strength."

The true difference between the two sections consisted of the fact that only the first profited from the patronage of the government, which generally bought its vilest specimens.

We passed through that enclosure distractedly. Finally, we arrived at the limit of the third, where one read: *Painters of the Future*.

That engaging subscription gave me courage. I overcame the numbness that the sight of twenty thousand canvases had given me, and I threw myself among the "Painters of the Future."

There, my feeble understanding found itself immediately surpassed. I thought at first that the works had been hung backwards; nothing of the sort, but it would have been easier for me to read Hebrew in the text than to discover the slightest intention among those daubers. I dare not say, however, that they were devoid of merit. They reduced nature to a violet fog in which strange objects agitated confusedly. Squares, diamonds and all kinds of geometrical figures collided there. Underneath was written "Portrait" or "Study" or "Landscape," but as often as not, even the title signified nothing.

The public in that final hall was composed of two sorts of people. Those of one kind were exclaiming, while laughing: "What filth!" while the others were repeating, in chorus: "That's admirable." But none of them were looking at the paintings.

I emerged from there with my head spinning. I felt ill, and I said to Constantin: "Let's go have a drink."

We went into a beautiful tavern, where I recovered gradually.

"Oh, my friend," I sighed, "What does that nonsense signify? Those painters have the same effect on me as loquacious people; they have nothing interesting to say but talk incessantly. Let them put down their brushes for a moment and their ugly inventions, and go to the Palace of the Kings, where I found so few people, and try to understand the significance of masterpieces."

"Since when," said my guide, "Do the loquacious shut up? That's not common sense. And then, the true guilty party is the public. It has bad taste; it is given works devoid of taste; it likes the strange; here's the strange. Now, know that there are other painters, but they can't exhibit, because the three schools reject them. They're the masters of the situation; whoever isn't allied with them has to remain in obscurity. That's what happens to anyone who wants to take up the great tradition, because impostors claim to have sole custody of it. Those impostors are the leaders of the Traditionals. You've seen just now how they justify that title.

"I ought to mention one of those liars, the famous Sideros. Creation has made no man uglier or more pretentious. He's not the most stupid of painters, but as a courtier, he's worth his weight in gold. So he's more covered in ribbons and medals of honor than a standard of hoplite musicians. His works are inept, but people say: 'The King holds him in esteem; important men commission their portraits from him.' Alas, the important men of today are rich grocers, money merchants and interloper functionaries.

"The man is powerful. He has a school, only teaches fools, and keeps good minds away. He grows in dignity, tough. He's seated among the twelve State painters. His paintings are sold very dear. But when he dies, people will hide them in attics and the cellars of provincial museums. And later, exhuming the vile canvases gnawed by rats, our descendants will wonder whether they are really the works of the celebrated Sideros."

VII. In which the author makes the acquaintance of an illustrious person named Kacos the Prude.

In the center of Atlantopolis is a public garden where young city-dwellers are taken to play. I know no place more charming. I loved the organization of the trees and the avenues, the perspective of the lawns and the water features, the perfection of the marble statues and the grass speckled with bright flowers, where a population of little children frolicked.

It was the day after our escapade among the painters. Constantin had asked me to meet him under an old sycamore. Having arrived first, I was respiring voluptuously the odor of the flowering plants suspended over the edge of the lake, watching little boys and girls running and jumping. I imagined that I was back in my homeland, and felt glad to be alive.

After a few moments a perfectly ugly old man came to sit down next to me. I am not difficult in the matter of the beauty of men, but this one was frightful: a dirty beard, a tremulous nose pierced with holes, asymmetrical wrinkles in which dirt was hiding, a squint, a twisted mouth, sagging lips from which drool was trickling slowly; such as my neighbor. I moved to the extremity of the bench in order to avoid contact with him.

Visibly swollen with anger, his deplorable visage was crimson in places—to wit, the tip of the nose, one of his cheeks and two or three of the wrinkles in his forehead. The monster was muttering words that I could not hear, but whose tone was one of indignation. Soon, he took me as a witness, and, indicating with his finger a statue of a naked nymph four paces away from us, he cried in a furious voice: "Century without modesty! Lascivious people! Until when will you feast on such obscenities? What has become of you, chastity of our ancestors? A pure man dare not walk through the streets. If he raises his eyes, he sees at every instant images and actions that incite the body and soul to frightful carnal operations. When will these abominable representations, in which brazen workers paint and sculpt the shameful parts of man and woman, be reduced to dust and ashes?"

I considered the statue and saw nothing in it but the beautiful. The nymph was showing the tops of her thighs without thinking evil. That was what shocked the old man so much.

I have known people of the same stripe in other places. I know that it is necessary not to contradict them. I therefore left him free rein for his diverting speech.

"My entire life," he said, "is one long battle against im-modesty. My name is Kacos, and people recognize my virtues by nicknaming me 'the Prude.' I sit in the Senate, but that's not where I deliver my battles. From dawn onwards I roam the city. I introduce myself into houses that I suspect of being clandestine brothels. The valets, bought for a price of silver, hide me under a bed or behind a curtain. I can't describe what I see there or repeat what I hear there. What debauchery, sir, and what speech! But I'm its irritated judge, and not a day goes by when I don't signal those criminals to our idle police.

"Then I prowl the bookshops. I pass myself off as an old sadist, and insist on seeing indecent images. What a harvest I made just now! Just look at this morning's crop."

Then he took a large package out of his pocket, which he unwrapped. He showed me an infinity of prints of the most precise obscenity. He contemplated them at length and analyzed them in detail. All his pockets were bulging with analogous booty, which he scattered all over the bench. It was the richest collection of erotic images that one could see anywhere in the world.

When he had shown all of them to me, and he had carefully put his documents back in their place, he said: "The authors will be punished, be sure of it. I've already had more than a thousand hanged. But there are others, more difficult to attain, whose ruination I'm pursuing. I mean all those who, under the criminal cover of art, dare to exhibit paintings and sculptures in which people are represented stark naked.

"If the gods lend me life, such things will soon no longer be seen. I also want women to hide their cleavages under high necks, and that they no longer show their legs to all comers under the pretext that it's raining. All that corrupts and demoralizes youth. It's necessary that pregnant women remain at home, because of the association of ideas that the sight of them provokes. Enough obscenities, enough filth, enough..."

He interrupted himself suddenly. His eyes shone. Then he bent down, so far that his head and hands were touching the ground. And I saw then that he was studying from below, with an attentive emotion, a little girl who, in all innocence, was sprinkling the grass.

VIII. Of the extraordinary education that infants and the young receive in the schools of Atlantis.

Constantin joined me at that moment. I therefore quit the old man with the obscene soul. Beforehand, I spoke to him in these terms:

"Sir, I could not admire you more. Continue to fight for virtue. Forge laws against immorality for us; pray to the gods to revoke the deadly gifts that they have given us; ask them to take back from men and women those enraged organs always desirous of coming together. They can give us children by means of an invention more decent and less subject to the passions."

But he was scarcely listening to me and seemed to be occupied with something else.

We had agreed to visit schools that day. I was taken to one of those to which poor people send their children.

In a large dusty room I saw a young man surrounded by eighty children. The pupils were crammed on benches. The master, seated in a chair, was speaking in a harsh voice. When we came in he was teaching morality.

"Children," he said, "render thanks to the mild, great, providential Constitution. All the good things that you enjoy come from it, so you owe yourselves to it entirely. Think about its benefits. Not the least of them is this divine education, which it spreads over your heads.

"Oh, if you had lived in the ancient times, how you would bless that holy Constitution! Before it, darkness reigned over our isles. The people, less fortunate than beasts of burden, knew neither repose not pleasure. They were poor beings, prey to maladies and miseries that have now disappeared. Crowned brigands governed them cruelly. Commerce, industry and science did not exist. It was night, a night populated by nightmares.

"But giants with free hearts rose up. They constructed with their hands the noble edifice in which we live. Our nation now has a history. We are the people that has the most worthy government in the world."

He fell silent and made a sign to a child, who stood up and repeated the preacher's words rapidly, without a single omission. I congratulated the latter on his eloquence and the efficient training of his pupils.

Outside, Constantin said to me: "As you see, that instruction is dogmatic. It presents the new principles as revealed truths. It is as well; otherwise children, even at seven years old, would be unable to believe it."

"Where do masters like that come from?" I asked.

"They're formed in certain convents," said Constantin, where they learn exactly what they ought to teach. Their unique occupation is the exercise of their memory. They have to retain word for word, axioms of every sort. When their head is stuffed with all that nonsense, they consider themselves to be scholars and gladly take charge of demonstrating it to anyone. In their class they repeat with authority the speeches that they learned themselves. They whip the children until they know the official catechism by heart. I ought however, to say several things to their glory; they teach their pupils to read, to write and to count to a hundred; all things considered, they are excellent, if one compares them to their predecessors.

"Those schools are called popular schools, and are free. Now come and see those in which the pupils pay. The education is different there, lasts longer, and provides more knowledge.

We were then transported to a more considerable and better equipped edifice. We went from room to room and took account of what was happening there. All the sciences were studied—or, rather, skimmed. Instead of showing the child the common foundations of various kinds of knowledge, they were given a shadow of knowledge in each area.

That somewhat superficial instruction was regulated by programs, which divided up knowledge into an infinity of pigeon-holes with no links, a veritably scholarly mosaic rather than an educational enterprise.

Afterwards it was necessary to visit the great institutions where young people study from the age of eighteen to twenty-one. That instruction seemed to me to be remarkable in several ways, but incomplete and often doctrinaire. I perceived great lacunae therein. There was profound commentary on all the dialects of the Archipelago, but the national language did not have the place that it merited. Great professors, illustrious historians, expressed themselves in bad Greek worthy of water-carriers, cooks and other people of little consequence.

Quitting the scholars I wanted to see the artists; I was taken to the Institute of Arts. It is a well-constructed palace harmonious decorated with antique marbles and copies of masters. Wandering through the courtyards we saw guards in livery here and there, asleep on chairs. We woke one of them up and asked him to guide us.

First he took us into a glazed from where young men were painting.

"You see," said the warden, "that the studio is not very busy; that's because the professor never comes here."

We went into another similar room. There we saw no one, although there were easels in place and freshly-painted canvases. "If you don't see anyone working here," said our guide, it's because the master, Seigneur Sigeros, is going to come. He's a nasty fellow who gives bad advice."

Then we went into a third and last studio. More than a hundred painters were crowded into it, covering canvases of all dimensions with colors. Their works resembled one another, as if they had been copied from one another: the same jarring forms, the same crudity of tones, and the same vulgar aspect. The corrector, the illustrious Eutomon, came twice a week. He only occupied himself with a single canvas, and that correction was applied to all the others.

When I expressed astonishment at that poverty, Constantin said to me in a low voice: "Unfortunate young men are attracted here by the renown of the school and the recompenses it is awarded. Their reason is obliterated by falsified doctrines. The directors of this Institute claim to possess the veritable tradition. Entirely to the contrary, they are impoverished, corrupted and betrayed. They are the legislators of false art. But have no fear, their method will soon be scorned by everyone. Those of their pupils who open their eyes go away angrily, bemoaning their most precious years wasted in simulacra of study."

IX. The Glorious Forty

Three days later, Constantin came to find me at the hour when I awoke. His ordinary calm had deserted him.

"Monsieur," he said to me, beside himself, "I've learned that the Glorious Forty are holding a public session this evening."

"The Glorious Forty?" I said. "Doubtless you're talking about a troupe of actors or expert conjurers?"

"What are you saying!" cried Constantin, offended. "It's the assembly of the greatest geniuses of the time. All the excellent men of letters that Atlantis counts have the honor of figuring therein, and are not always admitted. The people venerate it considerably, calling its members the Sublime or the Eternals.

"Excuse me," I said. "If I've sinned against them, it's by virtue of ignorance. I'll go without fail to visit them this evening, if there's no difficulty in doing so."

"There's none for us," Constantin went on. "I've obtained tickets from one of my friends, a dancer who is now the mistress of one of the great men."

Well before the hour of the spectacle, Constantin took me to the palace of the Glorious Forty. The edifice had all the allure of a temple to Glory. Crowned by the most illustrious cupola of all, it's said, it directs a majestic façade toward the river. An innumerable crowd was gathered in the square and everyone was brandishing a piece of blue or pink cardboard. We plunged into the crowd, using our elbows to reach the front row. A triple rank of mounted hoplites was immobile at the foot of the steps.

While we waited for the doors to open, Constantin informed me.

"The Assembly of the Glorious Forty," he said, "was instituted three centuries ago by the greatest of our Ministers of State. In truth, he was also an execrable writer, the author of ridiculous tragedies. That's unimportant. He redeemed a thousand times over the wrong that he did to the Atlantidean language, heir to the Greek, in assembling by that foundation, under this sacred vault, all those men of science and inspiration, those workmen of God who toil every day on the purity, the nobility and the beauty of the language.

"And with what to those fine minds occupy themselves in their meetings?" I asked.

"You shall see," said Constantin, with a mysterious smile.

At that moment, a tumult rose up outside one of the doors, above which one read: *Entrance reserved for Members of the Assembly*. Guards were occupied in repelling a number of well-dressed individuals.

"It's nothing," my companion explained. "That slight scandal is produced frequently. Those are people who want desperately to be seated among the Eternals. They don't have the right, and are driven away."

In fact, the hoplites were driving them back with great blows of the wooden shafts of lances on their backs, while the intruders were protesting, not about the blows but because they had been refused entry. The people heaped them with insults, and a clamor rose up, after which a stout usher decked out in silver appeared at the top of the steps and shouted, in a grave voice: "Silence! Silence! Don't wake the Eternals!"

Then, like a sea appeased when the wind drops, the crowd became so calm and silent that one could hear the tock-tock of the large clock mounted in the fronton of the edifice. It was now marking the hour of the session. The door opened. We were the first admitted, thanks to the color of our tickets. A man in livery forced people to take of their shoes, and presented them with slippers.

These are very demanding lackeys, I thought.

We were conducted through long corridors and crossed the marble steps. Carpets stifled the noise of footsteps everywhere.

We went into boxes overlooking a hall. The spectacle I beheld astonished me greatly. On gilded armchairs turned toward a platform, the Eternals were sitting in a semicircle. The greater number remained motionless and silent; their heads, with eyes closed, sometimes tilted to the right, sometimes to the left, or even forwards or backwards. But by virtue of a slight sound escaping from their open mouths I knew that they were asleep like veritable Eternals, imitators and possessors of Olympian traditions and privileges. They wore a gracious uniform. The torso, naked to the waist, was striped by a crimson sash. On the flesh, to the right and left, blossomed green palms, skillfully tattooed. From the belt, a violet robe fell all the way to their feet, which were shod in cothurnes with golden soles. Military helmets gleamed on their heads, or were gallantly carried in the hands of the least bald. I learned subsequently that their costume was completed by a red cloak and a sword, which they left in the vestry.

My attention turned to those who were not asleep. I saw a devil of a man, rather old, with an anxious expression, plying a razor over a notebook. Soon I discerned, scattered in front of him, a certain number of hairs of different colors. He was striving, with a meticulous care and infinite study, to cut into them and divide them in the direction and totality of their length. From time to time, he set down his razor and sat up straight on his chair, mopped his forehead and shouted, in a desperate voice: "Cruel enigma! Cruel enigma!" and then resumed his scrupulous labor.

Not far from him I perceived an individual with a prominent hooked nose, before whom stood a small cage. On his left fist a strange bird was perched. Examining it attentively, I found a resemblance to an eagle—I mean an eagle barely emerged from the nest, still covered with a little down, as large as a long-eared owl at the most. Soon, I was convinced that the bird also had something of the parrot about it, for it began to recite verses in long tirades, of which I understood very little. I nevertheless admired the astonishing aptitude of the animal, and gladly pardoned its ridiculous appearance.

The man with the hooked nose opened the cage. Then an admirable and monstrous beast emerged. The head and neck resembled those of a cock; the rest belonged exactly to the nature of a duck.[35] Fluttering noisily, the bird came to perch on its master's hat. There, solidly planted on its webbed feet, it remained motionless for a few moments. Its neck undulated; the monster was about to utter its cry; I listened. But from the open beak of the fowl emerged a mighty: "Coin! Coin! Coin!"[36] Doubtless you are familiar with the thunderous voice of the ducks of out poultry-yards; it was that, but more nasal and more heroic, a frightful howl of which the cupola end back the echo for a long time. A few Eternals woke up.

Nudging Constantin with my elbow. I asked him: "Who is the man with the two birds?"

"Lower your voice," he said. "He's a great poet. I'll list his merits for you later. He invented the line with thirteen feet. He has brought to perfection another prosodic form known before him, the lame iamb. He's the most popular of all the Eternals. He married a distant princess, Cameliande, a poet of equal merit to her spouse. A son has been born to them, who adds to their glory. As soon as he quit his mother's womb he emitted harmonious sounds. Scarcely was he laid in the cradle, as the paternal lyre was within his reach on the night-table, he touched it and caused incomparable chords to resonate. He's now in his ninth year. He hasn't ceased to frequent the Muses.

---

[35] The French *canard* [duck] is also a slang term for a scurrilous rumor, especially one published by a newspaper.

[36] The noise ordinarily made by a duck, or a cock, is not conventionally represented in French by the onomatopoeia "Coin!" which is more often found in a popular exclamation akin to the English explanation; "Surprise!"

His poems already form forty-eight volumes, all equally sublime.

"The modesty in which that trinity of genius takes pleasure forces universal admiration. They are never heard to talk about themselves except to under-appreciate their value. Oh, such minds are thrice or four times great! Sometimes, at nightfall, at the foot of the southern mountains where the three poets reside, one sees them taking a leisurely stroll. The wife follows her husband and the son follows his mother. Their words unite in a sublime chorus, and the animals flock to hear them, as to the voice of Orpheus."

My gaze settled on a man with a scarlet face. Was he asleep or not? In truth, I couldn't say. His compatriots, I was told, didn't know either. He was a somnolent hero. May Heaven forgive me, but, contemplating that colorful face, I took it for that of a drunkard. That consideration, in any case, does not give me a poor opinion of people. I have a mortal hated of water drinkers, vegetarians and other hypocrites. Later, I discovered that his somnolent appearance had made our man suspected of profundity of mind. His sole text only had a dozen lines; by a fatal coincidence, its publisher was declared bankrupt just as the work was about to appear; heartless creditors had it pulped. No one had read it; but as the author was assumed to have eminent merits, justice constrained the Glorious Forty to open their doors to him.

He participated in an analogous society recruited from the princes of the Fine Arts. He knew nothing about music, sculpture, painting or architecture but he frequented the banquets of known artists assiduously—they hold banquets in Atlantis at least as much as they do here—with the result that when he placed his candidature before the august company there as no one among the elect who did not owe him some gratitude for taking him home on one of those days when the earth trembles and spins more forcibly and more rapidly than usual.

I saw other astonishing individuals. One Eternal seemed to be mortally bored, but, thinking that people were looking at him, struck majestic poses that made me think of our first emperor. Many were passing the time catching flies.

One of the men stood up and climbed the steps of the platform painfully. He sat down in front of a pulpit and agitated a bronze hand-bell three times. He spoke, and spoke, in a sad voice that was scarcely audible. In any case, I can say nothing about his speech; almost as soon as he stated speaking I fell asleep myself, involuntarily. I know that the entire audience did the same, not by chance but out of habit.

Shortly afterwards I found myself outside, dazed, like a man who has taken a narcotic and who is obliged to get up and walk. Having returned home, I went to bed and remained in a complete lethargy for three days and four nights.

X. The Voyager's Recriminations

Thus I explored the city, instructing myself more and more in the study of its institutions, its inhabitants and its government. I found few subjects of admiration. The preceding epochs had left noble debris, but the destructive generations had tried to annihilate it. A rabble of agitators sponged on the people, exciting them in the name of reason against everything reasonable. Hatred separated the nation's three castes.

The first comprised the bourgeois, the people enriched by trade, a vulgar race, avid for gain and animated by a monstrous pride.

Functionaries formed the second class; the least of them lived meagerly on tedious labor. In the evening one encountered them in the streets, covered in the dust of their offices, as thin as men who do not eat their fill, humbly saluting surly chiefs with the faces of pedants. But character varies with hierarchy; the important functionary is obese. Incapable of work, he unloads it on to his subordinates. He is idle and well-considered. The most cunning devote themselves to various speculations, sometimes serving the police by denouncing the secrets of people whose secrets their profession allows them to discover, sometimes closing their eyes to what they ought to see, and enriching themselves by extortion. Sometimes a highly-laced functionary lends his support to some politician, and his recompense is not long in coming.

The army participates in all the castes, some of its generals are functionaries like any other, or even politicians ready for treachery.

The third class, the people, insouciant, capable of anything, stupid or noble, turns to all winds and believes what it is told, provided that it is promised the impossible.

Not long ago a swarm of loquacious individuals born in the southern provinces descended upon Atlantopolis and started to preach to idlers. Their pronunciations, ringing but devoid of sense, captivated the people. They said that they wanted to change the order of things and give the populace the wealth of the rich. They were made senators, and became great men; they no longer cared about keeping their promises.

Other men from the same region then came to harangue the crowd, and showed themselves in speech to be more terrible than their predecessors. They affirmed the necessity of killing everyone, burning and destroying, wanting to edify a new city on the ruins of this one, in which everything would be communal. The indigent and the workers were in accord on that. The later preachers replaced in the Senate those whose promises had not been kept; but, seeing themselves honored, the newcomers turned their coats and no longer talked about pillage. And the poor people were astonished to see that things remained the same, the rich still being rich and the ragged still in rags.

Unfortunate individuals tried to put into action the principles of their teachers. They set fire to houses, cut bridges, and attacked rich businessmen, believing that they would bring about an era of fraternity by those means, but the poor fools saw themselves ignominiously slain by order of their elect.

Parliament was not occupied with the affairs of the nation; it played at overturning ministers. The latter, governors for a day, tried to content those who shouted loudest, but they fell nevertheless after a few hours, consoled by seeing their enemies tear one another apart in the hope of seizing power. Everything seemed to be dragged into that confusion. The state was regulated by contradictory laws. The directors, corrupt and incapable, resembled blind and one-armed pilots. They were, for the most part, drawn from the men I mentioned, impelled to important employments by their southern loquacity. The King of the Brigands had described them to me with exactitude.

Everything lacked nobility: the State, Art and Science were encumbered by charlatans. So, people of good sense desired a change of regime and wanted to restore the descendant of the Kephalides to the throne. A dubious descendant of Phoberos also accumulated some support. Dangerous theoreticians wanted to pass into government, and live as they pleased without paying taxes.

All reasonable minds, however, were in accord on two points. Firstly, it was necessary to expel the lees of parliamentarians, insupportable parrots who repeated meaningless words in their assemblies and pretended to fight. The second point consisted of the necessity of putting out the eyes, tearing out the beards, and cutting off the noses, tongues, ears and all the limbs of all the members of the sect of Devourers.

A religious society to begin with, which had become by virtue of the malignity of time a political association, the Devourers formed a deadly brotherhood. It was joined by all petty ambitious individuals despicable enough to share their views and stupid enough to submit to their savage rites.

They wanted the state to belong to them, in order to share its authority, thinking that the nation was a big farm on which they ought to live, milking the cows till they bled, drinking the wine without letting it age and selling the wheat to the highest bidder. They succeeded in all points. They exiled the competing religions and appropriated their wealth. They had laws passed that flattered the people while ruining them. Above all, they had recourse to underhanded means, spying on and deceiving everyone, so much and so well that they became the secret masters, the bad shepherds of the nation.

They held strange meetings in which they devoted themselves to ceremonies less spiritual than those of cannibals. They worshiped saucepans, geometrical figures and other appropriate objects. That would have been unimportant if they had not formed, on the other hand, the most evil congregation imaginable. Having become all-powerful, they carried out great ravages, sucking the country dry, spoiling everything and sticking their dirty claws everywhere.

One day, I said to Constantin: "Poor comrade, you deceived me the other day when we arrived in sight of the city. You promised me a thousand marvels and you painted me a picture of strength and labor. What have I seen? An unhappy people tormented by agitators, like a thoroughbred horse devoured by lice, a king who cannot command, ministers enslaved by a filthy sect, and insensate senators. What are your art, your literature and your present government worth, Constantin, if I compare them to what they were in the past?

"Master," sighed Constantin, "you possess good eyes and good ears, but you have only seen and heard those who show off and shout loudly. We know other people. But the gods do not give everyone the same gifts. One has talent, another has honors. Who has the better share?

"You talk about our art. It has never shone more brightly. However, you find nothing in our exhibitions of paintings but an infinity of execrable canvases. Know that the same exhibitions refuse remarkable works every year. I'll enable you to see them. But there is a sect of the genre of the Devourers everywhere. Here and there, the mediocre unite and triumph over people of value. Then too, the favor of the people goes first to false thoughts. Later, it will be revised, bear to the Pantheon those whom it scorns today and castigate the conspiracy of vainglorious incapables.

"Yes, yes, we posses great men today. No one sees them, no one knows them. They hide, for fear of ill-treatment. When they die, their work will impose itself, while the glories of the

395

present will vanish. I don't take back any of what I said the other day. Yes, a strong thought lives and works here. It concentrates and struggles quietly. It is awaiting its hour. The victory is certain. The pontiffs know it, so their hearts are anxious."

"But can I not see one of those men who bear the burden of thought for the whole society?" I said. "Show me their works; then I'll be able to believe you."

"I'd like to," said Constantin. "I'll take you to some of them shortly. Excuse me in advance; we're going to visit attics in the suburbs, but it's there that the light shines of which I speak, which illuminates the world. Cover your ears in order not to hear the false prophets. Close your eyes in order not to see their works. Seek to understand the new words murmured by men who are awake while others sleep all their lives."

XI. Sedition in the People

Having descended into the street we found a marvelous effervescence there. People were arguing irritably outside every door. Workers were arming themselves with sticks, swords and arbalests. People were occupied diligently in digging up paving stones and building high barricades at intervals. The closed shops, the rarity of carriages, the war cries and the weapons ready for use all presaged a riot.

We learned that the Parliament, on the advice of certain of its members sold to the Mainomenes, wanted to issue a decree that would disband the frontier troops. That law would deliver Atlantis to the foreigner.

A multitude of people invaded the boulevard where we were walking. That crowd of men of all ages, ragged children and furious women was crying with one voice: "Death to the Senate!" and then resumed in chorus a terrible song full of menace.

At the end of the avenue, the armor of hoplites suddenly gleamed, with their helmets charge with scarlet crests. They lowered their sarissas and launched themselves forward at a gallop. Already, people were fleeing. The horses, carried away, ran faster, trampling the women and children, caught up with the foremost, I saw lances raised, bending under the weight of little cadavers.

No one remained in the square but the dead or wounded, crushed or with heads split Blood was trickling slowly into the gutters. The cavaliers continued their charge and pursued the rioters.

Constantin and I, dragged away by the currents of the crowd, stopped several times by soldiers, renounced going home and spent the night outdoors.

The entire city was in uproar, but the constitutional troops had the advantage everywhere. The popular mob fled in all directions. Brief battles were engaged. Toward midnight, the Government forces were almost in control of the capital.

Then the military rebellion burst forth. A large number of soldiers refused to participate in the massacre and retired in silence to the west of the city.

Thyamis, a renowned general, a very popular man, came to join them and harangued them. He affirmed that the hour had come for the nation to be liberated; he exhorted them to destroy the Constitution and the Parliament in order to restore the Kephalides. The refractory troops applauded him. He put himself at their head and gave the signal for combat.

The battle changed face. The king's guards were cut to ribbons near the river. The cavaliers paid by the Parliament opposed a longer resistance, but finally surrendered. The rest of the army fraternized with Thyamis's infantry.

The latter marched on the king's palace when daylight returned. The entire people followed the victorious general. No one was found in the palace; the sovereign and his retinue had fled in order to take refuge in a citadel a few hours away from the city. Thyamis assembled his troops in order to go to lay siege to it. Beforehand, a few senators guilty of theft and treason were hanged, and three generals allied with the Mainomenes were thrown into the river with stones tied around their necks.

A statue of Thyamis was paraded through the streets triumphantly and worshiped like those of the gods. People were shouting his name everywhere, adding to it the titles of Savior and Liberator, and demanding in a loud voice that the rebel general assume the temporary government of the nation.

For myself, I don't know how to excuse myself for having shared in that infantile enthusiasm. At any rate, infected by the contagion, I did not want to stay out of such a fine row. I said to Constantin: "Let's take up arms and follow the combatants; let's go with them in pursuit of the king. He'll undoubtedly oppose other forces to those of the revolt. Let's do our duty."

"Oh!" he cried. "How imprudent you are! Thyamis is a hero today; how do you know that his corpse won't be lying in the gutter tomorrow? As for this great popular movement, one can't say anything about it; this is only the beginning. Revolutions are deceptive goddesses. At birth they give hope to everyone; every ambitious man thinks he can see his career commencing; every crackpot flatters himself that his political conception is going to be realized. Scaffolds are erected facing podiums, and the victorious party, sitting in power, finds nothing to serve as a scepter but an ax, and nothing for support but the executioner's assistants. The people, who love the horrible, applaud ever more loudly. That lasts until the revolution, like an excessively greedy beast, goes mad for having devoured everything, and is punctured bloodily, leaving in its place a government which resembles the one that was expelled closely enough to be mistaken for it."

"Are you a coward, then?" I said. "So I, a foreigner, want to fight, without having any interest in the affair, and you, a citizen of this land, you're thinking of remaining in peace? Your reasoning reeks of fear. It's indifferent to me, in sum, whether this finishes one way or the other, but it would be shameful, in my opinion, to remain stupidly tranquil when everybody is amusing themselves delivering and receiving blows."

"So be it," said my friend. "I'll fight, if that's what you want. I didn't know you were so bellicose. Let's go, then. Let's arm ourselves. Once isn't custom. May the god of battles protect us."

We enlisted as volunteers. We were given swords, a helmet and a breastplate. Shortly afterwards, we quit Atlantopolis with the army to go and lay siege to the fortress of Arachnion, to which the king had withdrawn.

XII. The Siege of Arachnion, the Royal Citadel

The following night, at the foot of the hill, Thyamis and his men were waiting, lying face down in the damp grass and brambles. Constantin was close beside me. The moon appeared intermittently and caused breastplates to glisten like pools of water. A river ran to the right; mist had risen from it like a sinuous gray wall, as high as the trees on the banks. Bats were circling above our heads. Black clouds seemed to be cemented with incandescent gold.

Facing us, the walls of Arachnion formed a somber mass holed by the sparkling eyes of windows. A high tower lifted its pointed roof, covered with slates, toward the sky.

A modulated whistle, an agreed signal, told us that it was time.

The grass stirred. Like a multitude of snakes clad in steel, all those men commenced crawling over the hillside. Some carried bows of yew-wood on their backs, capable of launching iron-tipped arrows three hundred paces; others were equipped with long double-edged swords or curved sabers from the Northern Isles, which shone in the grass like glow-worms. Some were dragging fire-hardened beams, immense stakes made for staying indoors. Some were carrying ladders destined for scaling, fitted with iron hooks.

All were climbing slowly, hanging on to tufts of grass, advancing each limb in turn, dragging themselves on hands and knees, and stopping continually.

A metallic friction followed by a mortal howl frightened us suddenly. A man had fallen into a pitfall trap, impaling himself on the iron spike contained therein. He could be heard coughing and gasping in his ditch.

Immediately, a torch thrown from a tower described a luminous parabola and landed in our midst. Our weapons reddened, and the castle's sentinels undoubtedly saw the hill glinting. Bells rang at full tilt, so that we felt our breastplates vibrate. The moon reappeared; helmets and spears shone on the walls.

Furious, Thyamis crushed the torch, still crackling, under his heel; then, raising his sword, he cried: "Attack! Kill! Kill!"

Everyone stood up and rushed the walls. Then we heard a splashing sound on the ground. It was raining stones and lead pellets. Several men fell.

"To the ladders!" howled Thyamis; and, hitching himself to one of them, he ran at the ditch. It was wide and full of water. On the other side, the base offered no point of support.

The leader retraced his steps. He disposed his archers in three ranks and ordered them to aim at the men they could see between the crenellations. The arrows sang, and screams resounded up above.

Releasing the arbalesters, Thyamis set himself at the head of the hoplites and the volunteers. He searched for the citadel's weak point—which is to say, the entrance. We had to follow a semicircle before discovering it; we finally found it.

Under the projectiles, with the aid of a beam, the assailants started battering the portcullis on the far side of the ditch. Twenty men to the right and twenty to the left, replaced continually, activated it incessantly. The enormous spike went back and forth with the regularity of a pendulum and the force of eighty arms.

The raised drawbridge protected the door itself, and its joists of hardened wood rang under the impacts of the battering ram like iron on an anvil. The noise reverberated under the vaults of the shaken fortress. And that went on, and on; and our warriors fell, pierced by crossbow bolts and crushed by the stones of catapults.

The drawbridge cracked first and was split with a noise like that made by a tree in its fall. The pointed bars of the iron portcullis appeared between the broken planks. A second beam was brought into play and the two of them alternated their blows. The door yielded and the two battering ramps sank into it, furnishing the jambs of a footbridge crossing the ditch, where wounded men were howling who could not be seen. Bucklers and branches were placed on top of it. The besiegers rushed across it and arms clashed. Constantin held me back by the arm. The others were engulfed beneath the vault, howling confusedly

But long pikes descended from the ceiling pierced with square openings, molten lead flowed, stone blocks crashed down; and another portcullis, suspended in the middle, fell upon the soldiers. It crushed several of them and separated the others into two groups.

Defenders filled the courtyard. They drove back the first arrivals with sword-thrusts. The stones and the fire were falling so densely outside that no one was able any longer to go into the passage or to emerge from it. Our men, therefore, were prisoners under that vault, in that inferno full of fire and smoke, cries, groans, gasps and the odor of burned flesh. The survivors crouched down, covering themselves with their bucklers. One might have thought that there were frightened tortoises. But floods of boiling water came though the trapdoors, to the extent that the passage became a river in which the wretches were howling, cooked in their carapaces.

Outside, Thyamis was stamping his feet, his eyes fixed on the furnace, understanding that no one would emerge from it. He had a third battering ram slid into the entrance in order to dismantle the last portcullis, without taking any account of the unfortunates that it crushed. The long beam went into the corridor through the debris and the cadavers, as if to mark out the blow that it was about to strike. Then, drawn backwards abruptly under the effort of the men harnessed to it, it was projected toward its target, crushing people and things like a pestle in a mortar. With a rhythmic movement, it struck and was retracted, to return again full of red human pulp. And the noise and the terror were augmented by the impacts of the battering ram, funeral creaks and a barbaric and bellicose old song that the peltasts of Phoberos had once brayed over a thousand battlefields.

Finally, like a dyke battered by a tempest, the portcullis broke, its chains snapped, and it shattered.

The general wanted to deliver the supreme assault; he cried: "Forward!" But among the hoplites and the volunteers, no one moved. No one wanted to perish under there, like the others, meeting an almost shameful death, like a blind man killed by wasps. For the sword, the arrows and the stones, pass, but the massacre under the vault by fire and boiling water was too much to ask. Rather end everything there, under the gaze of the stars and the moon than enter into that trap, like an oven, from which howls and flames were still emerging.

Thyamis planted himself in front of us and folded his arms. We stood before him, eyes lowered. He cried: "Cowards! Women!" Then he spat on the ground before him, not being able to reach all the faces. No one budged.

Then, striking the ground with heavy footfalls he went alone, sword in hand, amid the arrows, through the grass strewn with cadavers. He climbed up on to the footbridge and, turning round, he said in a scornful voice: "Go back to the city. Tell those who ask for Thyamis that you left him to take Arachnion alone."

Then he resumed his route, vacillating, over the unsteady beams.

All of us, gripped by remorse, launched ourselves after him and entered the passage with him. Thanks to the abrupt reversal and perhaps to the lassitude of the besieged, the chief and many of ours passed through unharmed.

We ran forward, swords raised, and conquered a part of the courtyard. It was square, limited to either side by the walls linking the towers. In the middle rose a building crenellated from stage to stage.

Constantin and I never quit one another. My servant was a terrible combatant. Seeing how he fenced I regretted having called him a coward. It was me, now, who held him back. But in his turn he made me ashamed, saying: "Master, since we're here, let's go as brave men. Strike, by Zeus, and strike harder than that!"

At the same time, he cleaved skulls and ran men through like leather bottles.

The king's archers on the towers and the walls were firing inside and out. Their arrows went astray in the uncertainty of the melee and struck at random. And under the vault, conquered henceforth, with bucklers over their heads, our friends passed at a run. In the first rank, Thyamis, his buckler aloft, was whirling his sword around his head, and breastplates burst, driving into flesh, and helmets were dented, oozing blood.

We followed him, like binders of sheaves behind the reaper. The enemy ranks buckled and broke, undulating in the shadow. But darts were planted on the backs of the victors, who fell face down, reddening the uneven and grassy pavement.

When dawn broke, the citadel was in our hands and its last defenders taken prisoner. But we did not find the king. He had fled through some subterranean tunnel. That unfortunate lord was obese and impotent, and we laughed wholeheartedly, in spite of our discomfiture, at the thought that he had disappeared through some kind of mouse-hole.

In a corner we found his young and royal daughter. Why had she not gone with him? I think it was because she had a lustful desire. If that was her hope, it was not disappointed. More than twenty men violated her one after another. It was her finest night. She still talks about it with delight and often says to her husband, with a sigh: "When shall we have another revolution?"

403

XIII. Mourning

Suddenly, I perceived Constantin's absence. I retraced my steps, calling to either side. No one replied; I searched for him among the wounded and the dead, and it was there that I found him.

He was still breathing. With an arrow in his breast and a wound on his temple, my unfortunate friend was barely alive any longer. I laid him down in the grass, undid his garments and supported his head.

"Thank you," he said, faintly. "Thank you, Master. I would have liked to have died later. You've been very good to me, and I thank you with all my heart. I love you more than anyone, and death seems more dolorous to me because I'm leaving you alone, surrounded by enemies, and, in spite of my desires, engaged in a dangerous enterprise."

"No," I cried, "you can't die. I wouldn't be able to live myself. You're my friend, my brother…you can't leave me…"

"Go on," he said. "I can feel my strength ebbing away. Believe me, I'm doomed. Swear to me to abandon the struggle and be careful of your life. Otherwise, I'll die desolate…and then, if you can, Master, my good Master, leave this country quickly, if you can, or something bad will happen to you."

He thanked me again, and rendered his soul while embracing me."

XIV. Constantin's Eulogy

I shall try to give the reader an idea of what my excellent friend was like. A wise man full of knowledge, he loved life devotedly, revered old wine and beautiful women, noble books, ancient monuments, cheerful table talk and, in general, everything joyful and sublime. His soul was well-equilibrated: no anger, except against hypocrites, anchorites contemptuous of all beauty, and falsifiers of every species. I have not known any man as sincere, as modest or as far from egotism.

He laughed easily, sometimes wept but never put bile into his words. He was a man full of common sense, amour, gaiety and enthusiasm. He took pleasure in a thousand things that the vulgar do not perceive. An insect, a flower or a clear sky delighted him like a child. He never listened to the reasoning of hairy philosophers or their theoretical demonstrations regarding good and evil. He was accustomed to say that all beauty comes from the gods, and he adored all beauties. I cannot conceive of a more solid doctrine. In consequence, he preferred a sublime error to a vulgar reality. Often, in his stories, in imitation of the ancient Hellenes, he replaced history by legend.

He did not live long, but worthily. A savant drinker, an expert gourmet, a great tucker-up of well-garnished skirts, he knew how to make life a harmonious poem. I never saw him drunk, or suffering from indigestion, or exhausted down by an excess of amour. I would swear that a thousand little Constantins are now running around the countryside; many poor simpletons are caressing today an offspring more intelligent than them, whom they owe to the liberality of my servant.

Alas, why did a man like that have to die at twenty-five, when so many pedants are alive, in Atlantis as elsewhere? He died in all simplicity, regretting life without fearing death. His last words were for me, words of fraternal amity and apprehension in my regard.

On speaking about him, after so many days, my tears are flowing, and I can scarcely go on. I think I can still see him, bloody in my arms, his head already cold, leaning against my breast...[37]

---

[37] This chapter makes little sense in the context of the story, where no groundwork has been laid for it in the construction of Constantin's character, but it might make perfect sense in the context of the publication, if one were to hypothesize that the reason that the author of Part One—who is clearly not the same person as the author of the patchwork constituting Part Two—was cruelly interrupted in its writing by death, and that

XV. In which the voyager receives hospitality
in a convent of a sect of the old religion.

I rendered Constantin funeral duties. Then, throwing away my arms, I turned on my heels and cursed the war.

I wandered through the countryside for a long time. Entirely given to my dolor, I marched straight ahead. Night surprised me in the solitude of a forest.

I soon found an isolated dwelling illuminated by the moon. It was vast, partly ruined, and ancient in appearance. Lights were shining in several windows. I knocked on the door. A long space of time went by. It was opened. I perceived an aged man entirely clad in white. He stood aside in order to let me enter.

"I request hospitality for the night," I said to him. "I'm far from the city and exhausted by fatigue."

The man bowed his head and replied: "Be welcome, brother, and remain with us for as long as you please."

He showed me into a vaulted room where a large number of old men were sitting, similarly clad in white. They stood up and bowed to me silently. One of them brought me a chair. They all remained silent, and I was troubled, considering those beings, doubting their reality.

---

the writer of Part Two undertook to finish it for him as best he could, perhaps rather belatedly, in order that it might be published. In that case, this eulogy would be tacitly addressed, not to Constantin, but to the author of Part One—perhaps Pierre Hégine, to whom there appears to be no further reference after the appearance of the book early in 1914 (it was reviewed in the 26 January issue of *Gil Blas* and various other newspapers between February and May; an extract—the chapter describing "the Glorious Forty"—was published in the March issue of *Les Marges*); Pierre Billaume's name does appear in some subsequent references traceable though Google Books and *gallica*, albeit fugitively.

The oldest advanced slowly toward me. He held out his hands as if to bless me.

"The Divine Spirit," he said, "has ordered thus: 'Welcome the man who knocks at your door as you would me, for it is me who sends him to you.'"

He had a bronze bowl brought, and a jug full of water, and he washed my feet, without my daring to forbid him to do so. Then I was presented with milk and a few fruits. When I was restored, I addressed myself to the old man who was presiding over the assembly

"Pardon me, Father," I said to him, "but in truth, I would like to know more about you. Your generous hospitality and your venerable appearance already fill me with respect and affection for you. I am a stranger and know very little about this country, but I bless the fate that sent me to you at the moment when I am mourning the dearest of my friends."

The watchers gazed at me without saying a word. The one to whom I had addressed myself waited for me to finish, and nodded his head.

"My son," he said, "here you are among the last believers in the Living God. I do not want to expose our dogma to you. Know that our religion was once that of the entire nation. The people and their masters now worship vulgar idols, simulacra of divinities that never were. Since you have come from the city you must have seen that in reality, the people there worship nothing but themselves. The god Ego is the only one they know. May the unique Creator absolve them. May he enlighten them one day. That is our daily prayer.

"The governors of this land, viewing us with anger, maltreated us at first, and ended up banishing us. We are permitted, in return for money, to remain in this refuge. We spend our lives here invoking our God and affirming ourselves in the expectation of an eternal life.

"You have just said, young man, that you are mourning a dear friend. Believe me, weep no more. It is an article of our faith that will counsel you. We know that the soul is immortal.

407

The brother you regret has been born to another life, an aerial, spiritual life full of new knowledge

"My religion, Father, has a resemblance with yours," I exclaimed, "but I confess to you that I doubt that eternity. I would like so much to believe in it!"

"Listen," said the priest. "In the neighboring sea, seven hours by sail from the eastern coast, there is an island where the dead live. Perhaps I ought not to reveal it to you, but as a foreigner, you are not bound by our rules. That island, we are not allowed to visit. You can. In fact, you should, in order to remove the doubt of which you speak from your soul.

"Remember, however, that I am delivering a secret to you. The mariners of that coast know full well that there is something supernatural about that island, but they do not know what. No one dares disembark there. Navigators avoid it like the deadliest reef. Go there without dread, however."

Thus the chief of the followers of the old religion spoke to me. Then he wished me good night and had me conducted to a bedroom.

I slept poorly. The old man's words were going through my head all night. Sometimes I was inclined to think that it was some devout and excessively fabulous invention. Sometimes I was ready to add faith to it.

In the morning, I went to say my adieux to my venerable host. I asked him what path I needed to take in order to arrive at the edge of the sea in a convenient place to embark for the Isle of the Dead. He gave me all the necessary directions, and I left.

Three days later I reached the shore of the ocean. The sight of it reminded me of my shipwreck. I thought more strongly than ever about means of returning to France, and the last words of the dying Constantin returned to my memory:

"Master, my good Master, leave this country quickly, if you can, or something bad will happen to you."

I promised myself to reflect seriously on that as soon as I had returned from the island where I was going.

Finding sailors who were repairing their nets on the strand, I asked them to take me in their boat to a place where I had to go. They agreed, and asked me where that place was. I named the Isle of the Dead. They refused fearfully. I convinced them by means of money.

We took to the sea, and three hours after midday, the mariners, going pale, showed me the goal of our voyage.

XVI. The Isle of the Dead

When we had approached and my gaze had scanned the shore both directions and the interior of the land, I felt disillusioned, for it was an island like any other, with hills and valleys, streams, rocks and woods.

The sailors who had brought me refused to set foot there, and I disembarked alone and advanced over the firm ground, following a small rivulet. The accidents of the terrain soon his the sea from me and I suddenly found myself in a place planted with green oaks and myrtle bushes,

A timidity for which I excuse myself prevented me from advancing then. I remained pensive, not daring to go on and not wanting to recoil. Sitting on a stone, I waited. I thought I could hear faint and sparse syllables, as if the wind were speaking softly in a human language.

After a few moments, an exceedingly old man emerged from the wood. He was leaning on an ash-wood staff. A mantle of red cloth covered him entirely. I did not think that he was a shade, as he had all the appearances of a terrestrial complexion.

Approaching him, I said: "Old man, tell me who you are, or, if it is the case, who you were, and whether I have a living man or a phantom before me."

"Young man," he said, "I am living the same life as you. I lost count of my years a long time ago. Know, however, that I am to a centenarian as a centenarian is to an infant. I am one of the servants of the dead, and one of the youngest. Do not believe that I am eternal, for my hour also will come. But no matter: what are you doing here?"

"Very venerable old man, I have come to visit the dead. I have been assured that they inhabit this island. If there are any here of my nation, whom I once knew, or of whom the glorious rumor has reached me, I shall ask you whether it would be permissible for me to see then, and converse with them. But above all, I would like it to be given to me to see again a former friend from Atlantis, who died four days ago."

"I know your language," said the old man, "and the land where you were born. You have chosen fortunately in coming to this isle. Here you will find the souls of the great and immortal Latin race. If your evil genius had pushed your boat toward the Northern isles, eternally covered with mist and snow, you would only have found barbaric shades, the spirits of scarcely human races: those of Africa and the Pole, and also Germany. They are, as you now, disinherited peoples whose vulgar breath resembles that which animates the elephant or the seal. As for the Atlantidean you seek, you cannot find him here. His dwelling is in another place, which I cannot indicate to you. Speak now; tell me who you want to see. Perhaps you would prefer to wander with me in the great forest, interrogating whoever might seem good to you?"

I acquiesced to that proposition and we penetrated into the undergrowth. The murmur hat I had heard previously became clearer. I suddenly perceived, in places, the transparent forms of defunct souls. One might have thought them reflections, or imprecise images. From time to time, I perceived several. That rarity surprised me, and I expressed my astonishment.

My guide said: "This place is the abode of the great souls. Here you will only find those who passed over the earth like incomparable torches whose light is still resplendent over the living."

He was still speaking when two bright shades loomed up before us. One was great and majestic and the other majestic and small. They said to me, in unison: "You, who come from

410

our homeland, tell us how people think there, and how they act there."

Then, fixing my gaze upon those phantoms with effaced features, I finally recognized Charlemagne and Napoléon, who were holding hands. I knelt down in the grass, and, stammering with emotion, I told them what I had seen and heard in my fatherland since my childhood.

When I had finished, the great Emperor of the Occident hid his face in his hands, while the other murmured: "The French have become women." Then those illustrious souls disappeared, and I stood up, crushed by sadness.

We resumed our march. My eyes were fixed on the ground and my tears were flowing. My guide touched me on the shoulder.

"Look," he said, "at that shade sitting by himself on the edge of that stream. Doubtless you've heard mention of him; he's the great Florentine Leonardo da Vinci."

We approached, and I said to him: "Spirit that I admire among all others, will you deign to speak to a living man strayed into the Isle of the Dead? For your words would be an inestimable aid to me for the rest of my life."

The shade smiled softly. "You want a counsel," he murmured. "Listen, then: the finest work that one can accomplish on earth is to make one's life a poem and ennoble one's immortal soul by the exercise of elevated thoughts and sublime passions."

He made me a sign of adieu and fell back into his meditation.

While I was walking, thinking about what old Leonardo had said, the servant of the dead showed me a phantom a few paces away from us and said: "Of all the dead on this island, this is one of the most illustrious; Virgil is the first to salute him. Plato speaks of him with respect. He has turned the soul of Saint Jerome to derision, who has gone way, chagrined, to hide no one knows where. It is François Rabelais."

I went pale and started to tremble then. I ran toward the adorable shade.

"Oh, Master, my venerated Master," I cried, "is it really true that I can see you, that I am speaking to you? I would like to stay here for eternity, on my knees, contemplating you and listening to you."

Master Francois started laughing and said: "Friend, the praise of the living rejoices the dead of past centuries, but believe me, return very quickly to the sunlight and hurry to drink to the better, for the days on which one can do so are counted. For myself, I would gladly give the glory that is heaped upon me and this flattering Elysian solitude in exchange for four old bottles of the Chinon wine that I loved so much. O sun of Touraine, the young women of my village, friend Estissac's dinners, among men of good taste and heart, and profound science! Who can ever return all that to me? What a life a man can lead! But he prefers to play the weeper and the miser, to flee what he loves and seek bother."

"No, Master," I said. "For myself, penetrated by your doctrine, believe that I lead a sweet life, in spite of snags, and that I have never secreted any excess of bile. I love all good and beautiful things, and simply turn away from the unpleasant. For the rest, I am pleased to laugh at human infirmities and blindness, commencing with my own."

"Yes," said Master François, "You're right. But that's not all. Life, in order to be beautiful, must also be noble. I confess to you that Panurge, and Brother Jean des Entommeures, remain my preferred children. But don't go believing that, in order to be one of mine, it's necessary to be a rogue, ribald, to live off women, and all the rest. I adopt for disciples all those who love life and who, knowing how to comprehend it, don't see it through the black-tinted spectacles of our old astrologers.

"But as for you, don't stay here. The society of phantoms is depressing for a living being, and you'll have plenty of time to frequent the dead. It's not the same for the living. Go back, my son, believe me, go back."

I obeyed the sublime shade and quit the forest where the dead were wandering. My companion, the old man, suddenly slipped away and I found myself beside the sea.

I no longer saw the boat or the sailors. A strange change had transformed the entire island. The place to which I had returned was certainly the one where I had disembarked, but the foliage, green when I arrived, was now red and withered, falling to the foot of the trees. My crossing had taken place on the first of June, and now the russet grass of the meadows was strewn with autumn crocuses. I thought I had been in the forest for an hour but I had stayed there for five months.

Epilogue

Shall I recount how I made a raft, on which I embarked stark naked, once my garments, cut into strips, served to hold a few planks together, and how the current, which I thought would carry me toward Atlantis, carried me, on the contrary, southwards into the open sea? That would be quite pointless.

My provisions ran out. I had no fresh water. I thought my fate was sealed and understood that I was going to die of thirst in the middle of the sea.

Destiny treated my better than that. It sent me a ship carrying the English flag. I succeeded in attracting the attention of the mariners. The sight of a naked man gesticulating with all his limbs on a tiny raft appeared to them to be worthy of examination. A boat came to collect me.

The commodore interrogated me. I began to tell my story, but I was immediately taken for a shipwreck victim driven mad by terror, and they deliberated as to whether to throw me back in the sea. Fortunately, they did nothing of the sort.

That ship took me to Canada, where I spent seven months in a lunatic asylum, after which it was judged that I was not furiously mad, but a mild and stubborn maniac. The French consul had me repatriated. For fear that a further navigation might exaggerate my delirium, I was put in a straitjacket.

Disembarking at Le Havre, I found neither relatives nor friends on the dock, but my creditors were waiting for me, more numerous than on my departure. I nearly lost my reason veritably then. Pursued by that mob, I was only just able to escape and hide.

But what joy! I found my sky again and my fatherland, whose institutions, mores and inhabitants are so superior to those of Atlantis.

As I have already said, few people will want to believe me. I am therefore publishing this book. Another, reserved for scholars, containing evidence and documents, will appear in a few years, if God will lend me the life and my contemporaries the money.